INFINIT

The Infiniti Trilogy

Three

ALSO BY RACHEL HETRICK

The Infiniti Trilogy

Curse of Infiniti
Defying Infiniti

INFINIT

The Infiniti Trilogy

Three

Rachel Hetrick

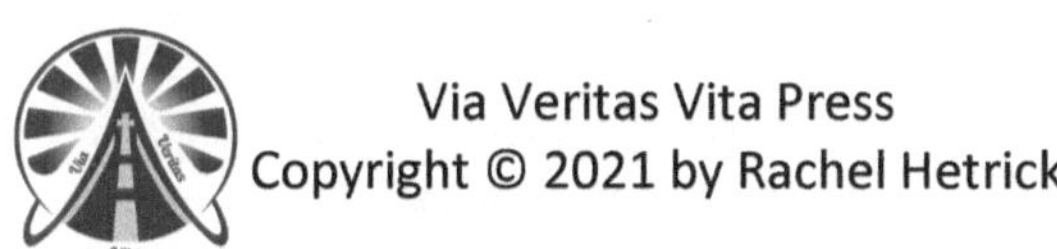

Via Veritas Vita Press

First printed in the United States of America in July 2021.

Cover Design by MiblArt
Editor: Enchanted Inc. Publishing

ISBN 978-1-953139-04-7 (paperback)
ISBN 978-1-953139-05-4 (ebook)

Published by Via Veritas Vita Press
Website: www.rachelhetrickwrites.com

First Edition
10 9 8 7 6 5 4 3 2 1

For YOU,
my wonderful reader,
who travelled with me to this final
book in my first ever trilogy!
YOU make my job as wonderful
as it is!

Thank you!

SIGN UP FOR MY AUTHOR NEWSLETTER

Enjoy interactive maps, short stories, and other exclusives from this series by subscribing to my newsletter and visiting my website at:

www.rachelhetrickwrites.com

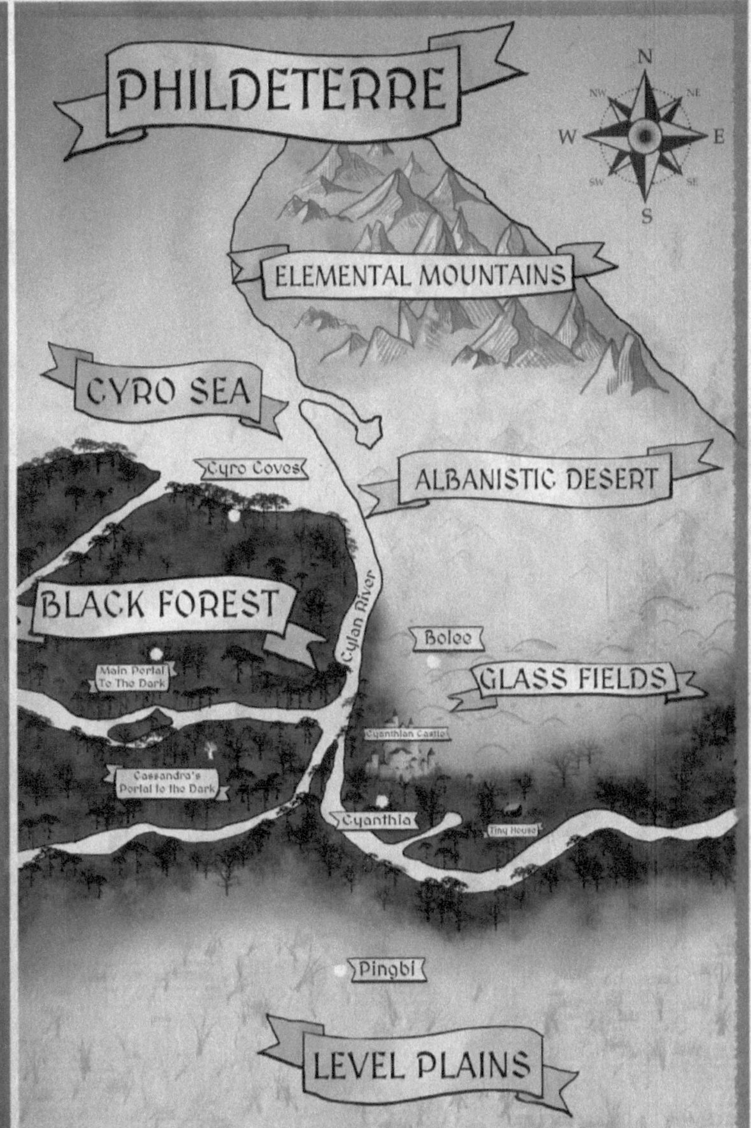

PHILDETERRE
N
NW
NE
W
E
SW
SE
S
ELEMENTAL MOUNTAINS
CYRO SEA
Cyro Coves
ALBANISTIC DESERT
BLACK FOREST
Cylan River
Bolee
GLASS FIELDS
Main Portal
To The Dark
Cyanthian Castle
Cassandra's
Portal to the Dark
Cyanthia
Tiny House
Pingbi
LEVEL PLAINS

Prologue

 he smoldering remains of a building crackled as Ellayne stepped into the center of the street. People scurried through the wreckage, passing water buckets back and forth to put out the last of the fires. Only a day ago, she had visited Pingbi, stumbling through a speech asking to make allies of the people there. The rural town had been humming with life, pausing to hear what the true queen had to say. Now she was back, and the consequence of the townspeople's decision was clear.

"It's because of their alliance with us, isn't it?" she asked, rubbing her hand up and down her arm to get rid of the goose bumps. "This is my fault."

The man standing next to her brushed his dark curls out of his face, placing his hands on his hips. "This was the king's way of showing his true colors," Kade said with a sigh. "It's not your fault."

"The kid is right," Armannii said, striding up to them. He'd been talking to one of the villagers to find out more information about the attack. "That guy over there said the king himself came to threaten them to renounce their alliance with you. When they refused—"

"He destroyed Pingbi," Ellayne said, rubbing the bridge of her nose with two fingers. "He said he was going to reveal his power to the world." She muttered the last part to herself.

"We need to prepare for an influx of people arriving in the Glass Fields," Armannii said, crossing his arms over his chest.

"Right," Ellayne said, nodding, though her thoughts were not completely on the conversation. "I'd like you and a few others to put more wards around Bolee. Just to be safe, you know? And it might be a good idea to warn our allies in the Black Forest. They're going to want to put up more protection against attacks as well."

Armannii and Kade exchanged a glance above her head, but she barely registered it as she watched a young woman being carried out of the smoldering remains of a house. It sent a shiver through Ellayne.

"I'll go discuss with the town leader to see how she wants to organize the people into groups." Armannii bobbed his head toward a woman patting a young man on the back. He waited for Ellayne's nod of approval before striding over to the pair.

"How are we going to accommodate everyone left from Pingbi when we've barely had time in the last week to rebuild Bolee?" Kade asked Ellayne.

"We're just going to have to make it work." She kept scanning the people around her. The town of Bolee where they were staying may have had a few buildings still standing, but not enough for all the refugees in front of her. "We'll find a way."

Kade placed a hand on her shoulder, pulling her from the devastating scene around them. "We have to. You're the only thing protecting them from that monster." He left her alone with her thoughts, probably wandering off to inspect what was left of his cartography shop.

Monster. Ellayne repeated the word in her head. Up until her brother, the king, cursed her when she was eighteen years old, she had never once thought of him as a monster. Even now, staring at the decimated town in front of her, a war erupted inside as she tried to tie him to the demon who'd caused the destruction. How many more lives would be lost in the battle between them?

Chapter One

he sun hadn't yet climbed above the horizon when Ellayne snuck out of the house. She shut the door with careful hands, lifting the doorknob to keep it from squeaking. Before she'd even left the bedroom, she'd tucked all of her blond hair into a low bun, hiding it underneath a ripped maroon cloak and hood. Though the three moons of Phildeterre still hung low in the sky, she wanted to avoid attention from any early birds roaming around the town.

Glass crunched under her boots, a sound which had become normal to her over the past two weeks. *Two weeks*, she thought, navigating around the back of the buildings. *It's only been two weeks.* Underneath her cloak, she wrapped her arms around her waist. Her fingers shook, but despite the chilly morning air, heat radiated through her hands—heat intertwined with the light magic inside her.

"Stop," a voice ordered. A figure stepped in front of her, blocking her path. "Show yourself."

Ellayne stood motionless. Raising her hands to her hood, she lowered it to reveal her face.

"Oh, Your Majesty, I'm sorry. I—"

"Sh." She held up a finger, shaking her head. "You were doing your job," she whispered as she passed the lookout. "Keep up the good work, and if anyone asks, I wasn't here."

"I understand, Your Majesty." The man, a vampire by the looks of his extended canines, saluted as she passed him.

With her hood back on, she continued her journey out of Bolee—a town nestled in the middle of a valley. The glass underfoot grew finer the farther out she climbed. When she reached the top of the hill, she turned and looked down at Bolee. Even at that height, the lightning post standing in the center of the town square towered above her.

From where she stood, shadowed rolling hills spread out in a seemingly endless horizon. The Glass Fields sparkled under the last of the moonlight. The glass, created by seasonal lightning storms, flickered like stars as she walked away from the town.

Her destination wasn't too far, and she reached it as the sky began to lighten to a soft pink. Hundreds of flowers encased in glass surrounded the gravestone—a gravestone Ellayne had visited every morning since she'd buried her father beneath it.

Aches in her knees from a battle two weeks earlier prevented her from kneeling in front of it, so she stayed standing instead. A wisp of hair escaped her bun, twisting around in the light breeze. She tucked it behind her ear with a trembling hand.

"I miss you." She knew full well he couldn't hear her. The words she spoke were for her own benefit because they were utterances she hid from everyone else. "I don't know how you did this. Making decisions, creating speeches, considering every possible outcome, risking people's lives—I can't do it. Not like you."

Just like every other time, silence wrapped around her as soon as she finished speaking. It weighed her down, pressing in from all sides. Her hands tightened into fists, and she crossed her arms over her chest.

"I'm sorry, Father. I don't know how to do this. I"—her throat closed up—"I wish you were here."

Ellayne ran her fingers along the stone she had carved. The tips of her fingers glowed with warm light, spurred on by her magic, and it lit up the words.

In loving memory of His Majesty, King Butch Maudit—Wise Ruler, Devoted Husband, Beloved Father.

Her head bowed. "You deserved more," she said, closing her eyes.

Besides the breeze twirling around her in circles, she didn't hear anything, which was why she jumped a few inches in the air when a hand touched her shoulder.

"Armannii!" she said, clutching her pounding chest. "What's wrong with you?"

"Sorry, Queenie." He stepped back and put his hands in his pockets, staring down at her. "I forgot I had silencing runes on my shoes."

Ellayne took a deep breath, calming her magic down after it flared up from the scare. Armannii watched her hands as the faint glow faded. "Why are you here?"

"You wanted me to tell you when the kid got back." Armannii raised an eyebrow.

"And?"

The elf shrugged. "He got back a few minutes after the lookout stopped you."

"How did you—"

Armannii wiggled his pointed ears with a smirk on his lips.

"Right. Obnoxious hearing." She rolled her eyes. "Did he say anything?"

"Yeah, and then I came here."

Ellayne watched Armannii's silver eyes for any flicker of gold that would indicate he was lying to her. "What did he say?"

"He needed to do something before the council meeting," Armannii said, crossing his arms over his chest. "I let him go so I could update you."

Biting her lip, Ellayne held back the question she wanted to ask. *Was he alone?* Instead, she nodded. "Well, I suppose we should go back to get ready for the meeting."

"If you need some more time—"

"I'm fine. Let's go."

The path back to the village was almost all downhill, and since Ellayne had no desire to engage in small talk with Armannii, the return trip took less time. Her mind raced—something it hadn't stopped doing for what felt like weeks now.

Her thoughts fell on Kade. He was different somehow, not the man she'd confided in two weeks earlier—the day after her father died. Ellayne knew full well Kade had things he was dealing with, yet his constant disappearances were grating on her like sandpaper. He'd vanished multiple times since he'd recovered from his fight with his best friend turned enemy. Kade would simply leave for hours on end, and the part that irritated Ellayne the most was that he would completely avoid her questions when he returned. If he ever answered, it was some lie about checking the surroundings. She knew it was false because she had placed lookouts around the area, and after questioning them about Kade, none of them ever saw him patrolling.

Ellayne ran her tongue along her front teeth, shaking her head. The thought of her best friend keeping secrets from her stung. She clenched her jaw, remembering that half the time he had not returned alone. Dayla had been with him. She hated the thought even as it crossed her mind. *Kade would tell me, right? If they were—*

"Queenie?"

"Hmm?" Ellayne didn't bother to look up from her focus on the ground. The sun rose behind them, casting their shadows far ahead. The elongated shapes of their silhouettes kept her attention.

"Your listening problem has worsened, apparently."

"Apparently."

"Have you decided if you're sending them?"

Ellayne remained silent, waiting for more information. With so many plans and queenly duties swirling around her head, it was difficult to pin down which one he was referring to.

"The group that's supposed to go north to the Coves, led by Matt and Dayla? Is any of this ringing a bell?" His tone rose in pitch with each statement. "We need to keep recruiting, and the Coves are too far for you to go, especially since you need to lead here. And—"

"Right." She nodded. "I haven't decided yet. Can we discuss it in the meeting?"

"Yes." He paused, his eyebrows furrowing when she looked back at him. "Are you all right?"

"I'm fine. I just—I just have a lot on my mind."

"Don't we all."

She caught herself as her footing started to slip down the slope of the hill. One ridge separated them from the town, and after climbing the last incline, the sandstone buildings spread out in front of them.

The rising sun danced off the shards of glass in the main street, spraying rays of colored light all over the sandstone bricks. She noted the change in lookout, now a young woman with short white hair and luminescent wings fluttering on her back. Ellayne smiled at the woman, who inclined her head in response.

"Good morning, Your Majesty," the lookout said.

"Morning."

"The last group from Pingbi should be coming in today," Armannii said, pausing to talk to the woman.

"I'm aware, Ovair." The woman popped her hip out and narrowed her eyes at Armannii.

"All righty then." He nodded, continuing down the road to where Ellayne waited for him.

When they were far enough away, Ellayne raised an eyebrow at Armannii. "What'd you do to get on her bad side?"

Armannii snorted. "I'm on everyone's bad side at some point. She'll get over it."

Ellayne didn't point out that he hadn't answered her question. "Is Dayla still—" She stopped asking when Armannii shook his head.

"No. She left with Kade a few minutes after he got back."

"Oh." Ellayne bit the inside of her cheek. *Of course she did.* She breathed through the annoyance—annoyance she didn't want to have toward either of her friends. "And she didn't say—"

"No."

"Peachy." Ellayne sighed, pushing open the front door to the building where she had been residing for the past two weeks.

Since a majority of the structures had been destroyed in a raid, many people were sharing space under the same roof, especially if the building still had one. In the more destroyed part of town, makeshift tents had been set up. Ellayne shared her living space with three other people: Dayla, Kade, and Armannii. The two men stayed in the downstairs room, and Dayla and Ellayne shared a bedroom upstairs. One of the outside walls no longer stood intact thanks to an explosion of dark magic. Armannii had used a door from an abandoned building nearby to try to seal it up as much as possible; however, light from the sunrise still sent rays through the cracks around the door.

"Do you want me to go find the kid?" Armannii asked, handing her a cup of tea.

She sipped it, trying not to turn her nose up at the bitter taste. No matter what she or anyone else did to it, tea always tasted like boiled weeds.

"No." She put the cup on the table, fully intending to "accidentally" leave it there. "He'll probably be back soon." Although, with Kade's inconsistency, she wasn't so sure the statement was true. "And before you say anything, I know we can't start without Kade. He's part of the council."

"Ah, yes. The council." Armannii's ever-present smirk returned, pulling at the sides of his mouth. "You're not upset he left with a certain siren, are you?"

Ellayne glared at him. "Dayla has helped us nonstop from the moment we got here. Of course I'm not upset."

"You're lucky you're not an elf."

"It's not a lie."

"Really lucky."

"Shut up."

"Whatever you say, Queenie." He wiggled his eyebrows at her.

Ellayne shook her head, striding to the back of the house where the staircase led up to her bedroom. Since she had found her father's declaration that proclaimed her as rightful heir to his throne, she, Armannii, and Kade had held their council meetings up in the room she shared with Dayla, and she didn't want to start a meeting with any underclothing lying around.

"I'll be up in a bit," Armannii said as she left the kitchen.

"Don't rush."

Chapter Two

he window across from the door let in a breeze, not because someone had left it open but because the glass that once lined it had shattered during the battle in Bolee. The fragmented glass no longer lay scattered on the floor, though Ellayne didn't take her boots off in case more shards ended up in the bottom of her feet. She wandered around the room picking up her few items and placing them back in her bag—a bag she'd borrowed from Kade a few months earlier.

It wasn't the dark spattering of dried blood on the flap that held her gaze but instead a necklace chain wrapped around the strap. The shiny silver matched the one around her neck, and besides the initials on the back, the medallions on the chains were identical. The image engraved on the front—a dragon struck through with a sword—reflected light at her as she unwrapped the chain.

Flipping the medallion over, she ran her thumb across the two letters inscribed on the back—DM. A sigh escaped her lips, and she brought the medallion over to the window to examine it with better light. Unlike her own necklace, there was another item on the chain: a small mirror.

She didn't bother looking in it, knowing full well that the person she wanted to see in the reflection wasn't there—the same person she visited every morning since he died in her arms. Her father. The mirror held no value now. Not since she had freed him. Still, she weaved the chain between her fingers, glancing out the window at the street below.

People gathered at one of the buildings across the main road, coming together to repair one structure at a time per her orders. With another group of rebels arriving from the destroyed remains of Pingbi, Bolee would be well past full capacity. In light of that, she had assigned most of the town's inhabitants, at least those who weren't in combat training, to the task of preparing for new arrivals.

Ellayne leaned against the frame of the window, watching the people work. Some used magic, lifting fallen beams or bricks with a few flicks of their hands, while others made a fire line to pass materials in and out of a building. She smiled to herself as she tracked their progress, not because they were repairing the town— although that helped her breathe easier—but because of the variety of people working in harmony. Ellayne had yet to meet another person in the town with light magic like hers, but still, the image of those with dark magic and rune magic working beside those without, and even more so, human working with nonhuman, gave her a sense of peace within the tumult always stirring in the back of her mind.

The sun shone fully above the horizon, and a rainbow reflected on the wall across from her. A beam of light struck a sparkly tiara sitting on the desk behind her—her mother's tiara. Placing the medallion necklace on the desk, she picked up the tiara and ran her fingers over the diamonds. Memories of asking to try on the tiara when she was a little girl floated through her mind. Her mother's answer had always been yes.

On the desk near the medallion lay a folded piece of parchment with dried bloody fingerprints all over it. It was the declaration her father had given her mere moments before he'd died—one naming her queen. She put the tiara back on the desk and gazed at all three objects, one to represent each member of the family she'd lost.

"He's coming." Armannii's voice by the doorway made her jump for the second time that day, and she glared at him. He snorted and nodded toward the window.

Ellayne strode to the window and searched for dark hair. It didn't take long to spot Kade walking down the main street. Her eyebrows dipped for a second as she watched Dayla keep up with his long stride, sticking to his side.

"Careful, Queenie." Armannii leaned back on Ellayne's bed, his head resting against the wall. "You're turning green."

"And you're going to turn black and blue if you don't shut it." Ellayne pointed at him, turning her attention away from Kade. "He's going to be here in a minute, and you better drop whatever this is." She waved her hands in a small circle.

"Only if you promise to stop moping every time you see them together."

"Armannii, I will hurt you."

"No you won't." He wiggled his eyebrows and rubbed his hand up and down the scruff on his chin. "Because I'm the only one who knows how you feel."

"You're right"—Ellayne stuck her hip out to the side, folding her arms across her chest— "I won't hurt you. I will *kill* you if you don't stop." She wore a bold smirk on her face, looking down her nose at him. For less than a second, her heart stung; she had given the same attitude to her older brother when he had picked on her during their childhood.

"You wouldn't do that either. I'm too valuable."

"You think too highly of yourself."

"I can second that." Kade grinned as he walked into the room, closing the door behind him. Dayla must've stayed down on the main level. "Why are we talking about Armannii's highly inflated ego?"

"Doesn't matter." Ellayne uncrossed her arms, straightening her posture. "Where were you?"

Kade shrugged and sat down on the edge of Dayla's cot. "I went to check on the west border near the Cylan River. The lookouts there have been keeping an eye out for any movement on the water or south near Cyanthia. Nothing to report yet."

Ellayne refrained from pointing out that she had intentionally assigned a man from each post to update her at the end of every day. Not only that, she could tell Kade was lying, though it wasn't about their enemy's movements; that much was true. His eyes continued to shift to the ground, and he ran a hand through his curly hair. His false statement had to do with his whereabouts instead.

"I guess we're starting this meeting then, huh?" Armannii asked, leaning forward from where he sat. He waited for Ellayne's nod of approval. "All right then, I'll start. I took your suggestion and went with a few others to put up more wards in the south. The king, of course, would be able to break through if he put his mind to it, but we should be safe from Blanndynne and her mutt."

Kade tensed up, and Ellayne bit her lip. "I'm sure they won't be coming back right away. My brother seems to have the same thing in mind that we do: getting help," Ellayne said, doing what she could to turn the conversation away from Kiegan. The two weeks separating Ellayne from the last time she had seen her brother, Blanndynne, and Kiegan were not nearly long enough to forget that he had almost killed Kade. It did not surprise her when Kade had to take a second to resolidify his facial features in stone.

"That's good," Kade said, his voice just as steely as his expression. "We can use all the protection we can get. It's not exactly the wisest thing hiding out here in the Fields, but if the wards can make it look like we aren't here, then we should be safe for the meantime." He rubbed his shoulder, a habit he had picked up after his old best friend had ripped it open to the bone with a sword sizzling with magic lightning.

"Right." Ellayne nodded. "And I assigned a group of ten rebels to head west into the Black Forest. They will begin putting up wards for a secondary campsite. Just in case he decides to strike."

"Wise decision," Armannii said. "And I don't think it's a matter of 'if' Diomedes attacks. It's a matter of when."

"You're probably right." Kade stopped rubbing his arm, leaning back so that his tunic went taut across his chest.

Ellayne knew he had been training—helping to teach the rebels to fight just like she did when she got the chance—but she was not expecting to see the lines that his muscles created beneath the fabric. He had been lanky and tall when she first met him, but ever since their time in the Dark, he had bulked up. She pinched the inside of her palm to distract herself, squinting at his mouth to catch what he was saying instead of letting her eyes stray any longer. What good was she to her people if she spent her council meetings staring at her best friend?

"I heard word that the king has groups moving far east to cut us off from the north," Kade said, tilting his head to the side. "Which would spell bad news."

Ellayne leaned against the wall and turned her attention to Armannii. "He has allies up near the Elemental Mountains, doesn't he?"

"Unfortunately for us, yes." Armannii nodded. "There is at least one town in what used to be the northern kingdom that allied with him back when he became king five years ago. They have well-trained mercenaries, which would make sense as to why he'd send people up there."

"That was my mother's domain, so it doesn't surprise me he's turning to them. They hated the war on magic and would continue to support your brother even if they knew what he was doing to the rest of the country. Did you know—" He paused, sneering at nothing and no one in particular. "I heard from a guy the other day that three people in Cyanthia were beaten to death simply because they didn't have magic. Happened right in the middle of the street in broad daylight." Kade's eyes turned cold as he glared at the wall behind Ellayne. "Your brother is going to start up another war all right, but it's just going to be the opposite of the first Split."

Armannii sighed, scratching the top of his head. "Well, when the pendulum swings as far as it did for the first war, it's no surprise that some individuals want it to swing the other direction just as far, if not farther. King Kylian did the entire country a disservice by beginning the war, and probably in more ways than we can even see now." Armannii pursed his lips, flicking his eyes between them. "Your children's children are going to have to deal with the consequences of the first Split. But if anything, that just means we need to work harder to prevent another hundred-year war from happening."

"Right, easy peasy," Kade scoffed. Some of his curls fell over his eyes as he tilted his head down. "And what miraculous plan do we suddenly have to stop that from happening? Because last I checked, there's still an evil murderer on the throne of Phildeterre, and we have nothing near powerful enough to take him down."

"That's why we're all here, Kid." Armannii's voice was soft, yet it held an edge to it—a warning. "We're here to figure out what our best move is and how we can end this with as few casualties as possible."

Ellayne watched Kade, gauging his reaction, but he still hadn't looked up. The only change in his posture happened when his shoulders and back tensed. "Clearly *that's* effective. Did you not see what he did to Pingbi a week ago? Every building was in ashes."

"I saw the destruction, but we couldn't have known it was going to happen." Ellayne spoke as gently as she could, careful not to make him any more upset. She could already feel his dark magic riling up her light magic, and it made her fidget to stay comfortable. It didn't feel right to be at odds with her best friend, but the magic made it so.

"That was my home, Ellayne," Kade said, his voice breaking a bit as he finally looked up and made eye contact with her. "And your brother destroyed it."

"Kade, I—" Ellayne's words caught in her throat. How was she supposed to apologize for something she couldn't have predicted? She hadn't taken a torch to the small farm town. Catching herself, she took a deep breath before her hackles could rise any farther; that was the last thing this council meeting needed—her temper. "I'm sorry. I really am. If I had known, I would've stayed until the next day and fought my brother there. But I didn't, and now the only thing I can do is take care of the Pingbi refugees and try to find a way to end all this."

"I know how to end this," Kade muttered, but before Ellayne could say anything, Armannii pulled some of the tension out of the room with an easygoing smile.

"All right then." He held up a finger to shush them both, and then, distracted like a child, he turned his focus to the grime under his fingernails. "You should probably be aware that your brother has known about the sorceress's connection to the north for a while. We met the would-be ruling family of Byshan when he was looking for a way to end the war. He made quite a few alliances with them when he became king since they helped him take the throne." Armannii picked at his nails, glancing over to see both Ellayne and Kade staring at him. "What?"

"That's probably something you should've mentioned earlier," Kade said as he leaned forward and rested his elbows on his knees. "It's kind of important."

"I would've, but my other council members decided to stray from the subject." When neither Ellayne nor Kade returned his grin, he erased it from his face and straightened up. "Look, this information doesn't change our situation. Both Diomedes and Queenie are looking for allies. For both parties, there are more productive places to look than others. The king's most likely allies just happen to lie in the north."

Kade opened his mouth to respond, but Ellayne held up her hand. "You're right. It doesn't matter in regard to our own search for help. However, we should be prepared for mercenaries from the north to fight alongside my brother."

"I suppose the question then is whether we should send a group up there to cut Diomedes's men off, right?" Armannii folded his legs to sit cross-legged. Ellayne held back a grin, amused to see a man in his thirties sitting like a six-year-old.

"Might give us a better chance when we eventually go to battle. I'd rather not have to fight highly trained mercenaries on top of the entirety of the royal guard," Kade said, nodding in agreement.

"No." Ellayne shook her head, a frown wrinkling her forehead. "Not until we have confirmation that my brother is actually sending for help in the north. I'd rather not risk lives for—"

"But he'll already have the mercenaries if we wait for confirmation," Kade argued. "We can't risk him getting any stronger. Not when he already has the entire country terrified of being blasted into oblivion for even mentioning your name."

"I know, and like I said, I'm sorry about Pingbi, but—"

"And if you hadn't noticed, Ellayne, his new queen has unbelievable power up her sleeve. You heard what Blanndynne did last week at the royal wedding, right?" He waited for her to respond, but after a deep sigh meant to contain her growing annoyance, Kade continued. "She *bewitched* two Dark Soldiers who were caught trespassing in Phildeterre to dance until their feet were bloody and disfigured, and then she had them beheaded. And do you know why? As a gift to her new husband. Those are my father's men, Ellayne! I knew them. I trained with them. They were good soldiers, and she killed them for some sort of power show. I don't know how much longer I can sit back and—"

"Where did you hear this?" Ellayne asked, her tone even despite the fact that her stomach was turning. She knew Blanndynne was capable of villainy, but these actions were twisted and evil.

Even though it had been some time since she found out his lineage, it remained strange to hear Kade speak so calmly about his father. Like his constant disappearances, the topic of his father happened to be yet another subject Kade avoided discussing with her.

Ellayne turned her attention back to Kade, shaking off the image of Kade standing next to his father in the Dark Castle throne room—a younger replica, the spitting image. Instead, she focused on the royal wedding, which had been announced a few days after the secret event had actually happened. It didn't surprise Ellayne; her brother was a private man. Although she was sure Blanndynne was probably disappointed at the lack of opportunity to have all of the country's eyes on her.

"Kade," she said, her eyebrows creasing as she watched him. "Tell me how you heard about what happened."

"I—" Kade hesitated, his jaw tightening. "I heard it when I was off checking the—"

"That wedding was supposed to be private, open only to the king's council and a few members of the king's court. How did *you* hear about it?" Ellayne asked, her voice dropping lower. She herself had only heard about the wedding when the information spread through the country that the king had officially taken Blanndynne to be his queen. A false queen according to the bloody parchment next to Ellayne, but still. At least Blanndynne had a throne and a castle to rule from.

"Look"—Kade put up both hands—"it doesn't matter where I heard it. What matters is that it happened. She's powerful, not to mention the fact that she has Kiegan and his dark magic wrapped around her finger. And Diomedes himself has stronger magic than anyone has ever seen."

Ellayne clenched her hands into fists behind her back, controlling the growing warmth by taking deep breaths, just like Armannii had been training her. Each breath in, she let the warmth ease her mind. Each breath out, she focused on loosening her muscles. She wasn't supposed to push her magic away like she had tried before, but instead she was to acknowledge its presence and ask that it remain under her control, assuring it that she would use it if need be. Afterall, magic was, as Armannii said, like a stubborn yet loyal child.

"I understand that, Kade. And I know that you want to find a way to get Kiegan back; we both do. But—"

"But we can't just sit here and wait for Diomedes to attack us first, Ellayne. Not after what he did to Pingbi." Kade rubbed his shoulder again. It had almost healed completely, but she could tell it still bothered him, especially when he got fired up.

"Of course not," Ellayne said as she narrowed her eyes at him, already straining to remain calm after what seemed like Kade's third referral to something she already considered a heavy loss.

And it was still something she couldn't change. "But in regard to sending people north to block my brother's men, it would be reckless. I would be sending inexperienced fighters right into the dangerous and deadly hands of people who have been trained in combat for years. Not to mention we don't even know if they're there, or how many there are. I think—"

A knock on the door cut Ellayne off.

Dayla poked her head in. "Sorry, E, but there's someone here who wants to see you."

From the first sound of Dayla's voice, Kade straightened up. He rolled his shoulders back, lifting his chin and sitting with posture that would've impressed Ellayne's father. In the blink of an eye, Kade became the perfect image of royalty. A prince, at least from the outside. Ellayne felt a wave of turmoil as she fought off a negative reaction to Dayla's sudden appearance. There was a battle in Ellayne's mind as she tried to keep control over her facial expressions.

She faced Dayla, forcing a smile on her face. "Who is—" Ellayne stopped when she saw an older woman with salt-and-pepper hair tied up in a large bun. Square glasses magnified her birdlike eyes as Linetta, Ellayne's aunt, walked into the room. "Linetta!"

The woman held her arms open, and Ellayne rushed into them. "Hello, sweetheart." She squeezed Ellayne. Unlike the first time Ellayne had hugged her, Linetta did not smell like old parchment and tea; instead, she gave off the smell of campfire and sweat.

"Did you just come in?" Ellayne asked as she pulled back.

Linetta nodded. "Brought in a group of seven others from Pingbi. I've been making sure they get settled, just like you said. When I heard that you were here and not off running this place, I wanted to see you. Unfortunately, it was before I cleaned up." She shrugged. "I figured my niece wouldn't mind if I'm a little disheveled." Linetta glanced around the room. "Sorry to interrupt."

"It's all right." Kade offered a warm smile to Linetta, all anger and frustration completely erased from his face. "It's good to see you again." He stood up and shook her hand, bowing his head in respect. "Thank you again for your help with the refugees."

"Of course." She patted his hand in hers, but after a second of holding it, she frowned. "Are you all right?"

"Fine." He pulled his hand away and kept a smile on his lips, albeit a strained one.

"Linetta." Ellayne tugged her aunt's hand, pulling her toward Armannii. He rose to his feet when she led her aunt over. "This is Armannii. I've been so busy these last two weeks that I don't think I've had the chance to formally introduce you two. Armannii helped break my curse."

"Among other things," Armannii added, a grin on his face. He put his hands on his hips and wiggled his eyebrows twice at Ellayne. Although she returned his gesture with a skeptical look, she knew he was right. The elf had his obnoxious moments, but they were few and far between compared to his wise and heroic moments. Not that she would *ever* tell him. He would never let her live it down.

"I remember you," Linetta said, her eyebrows furrowing in the middle of her face. "You came into the shop and showed me a piece of paper. But . . . I don't quite remember what happened after that."

"Nice to meet you." Armannii shook her hand. "I left afterward."

Ellayne glanced at his eyes, and though they remained silver, she had a sneaking suspicion that he wasn't telling the full truth.

"Right." Linetta blinked a few times. "I suppose you did." She turned toward Ellayne.

Even though Linetta could no longer see Armannii's face, Ellayne could. And he smirked at her. *He used his mind-wiping rune on her. I'd bet my mother's tiara on it.* She kept her features relaxed even though she wanted to scold the elf.

"I'm sorry"—Ellayne focused on her aunt—"but we're having a council meeting. Can I find you in a bit?"

Linetta squeezed Ellayne's upper arms with gentle hands. "Of course. I'll see you later. It was nice to meet you, Armannii, and to see you again, Kade."

They waited until she shut the door before they started talking.

"It's great she's been helping the other rebels," Kade said as he sat back down on the edge of the cot. Though the interruption had come in the middle of their council meeting, it seemed to have been for the best, as if it reset them all back to amiable perspectives. That, however, wouldn't last long if Ellayne's suspicions were correct.

"It is." Ellayne rubbed the medallion around her neck with the back of her thumb. "And as much as I'd like to talk to her, the three of us should get back to the council meeting."

Armannii sat back down, and he mirrored Kade on the opposite bed, placing his elbows on his knees.

The elf spoke next. "I believe the discussion was about whether we should send a group to potentially cut off Diomedes's forces from connecting with allies in the north."

"It's too much of a risk."

"Taking out your brother *is* a risk." Kade didn't hesitate.

"We aren't trying to 'take out' anyone." Ellayne frowned at Kade, who narrowed his eyes back at her. "We're trying to get him off the throne just like your father asked me to." She held up her hand to prevent Kade from cutting in. "And don't you dare start asking me what we're going to do with him afterward. I told you that's something I'll figure out when I need to."

"You need to figure it out now, Ellayne. People are depending on you." Kade bit his lip as he watched her.

"You think I don't know that?" Her voice rose several notches, but it came out more as a strained whisper. "Between my father's death and my brother's takeover, these people—my people—are the only thing I've been thinking about. You think I don't know what they want?"

"I've been thinking a lot about it, and with everything your brother has done and the way the country is beginning to turn on those without magic, I think my father may have had a point. The safest thing for Phildeterre *and* for the Dark is to make sure Diomedes doesn't hold the throne any longer. You know as well as I do, maybe better, that Diomedes needs to—"

"Don't." Ellayne pointed at him, and warmth raced to her hand, lighting it up with magic before she could even think about taking deep breaths. "Don't you dare finish that sentence."

"Die."

"How dare you?" She stomped across the floor and paced the room, flinging her hands out to the sides as she spoke. The veins beneath her skin were glowing faintly. "Just a few weeks ago you convinced your father that I didn't have to kill my brother. Why are you so eager for me to take his life now?"

"He's a murderer, Ellayne! And he's doing nothing politically to ease tensions after the Split. It's been five years, and we're about to see the opposite of that war begin because he's too busy trying to hunt you down, too busy to make any sort of legislation to help these people, *your* people. What's wrong with you? Why are you protecting him?"

"The same reason you're protecting your father, Kade. Dio's family. He's my brother. I'm not going to kill him."

"Diomedes killed both of your parents." Kade's voice continued to rise. "My father isn't perfect, but he hasn't done that."

"The Dark King has killed plenty of other people. Right, Armannii?"

"Leave me out of this, Queenie." Armannii held his hands out in front of him, shaking his head.

"My father—"

"Killed people for trying to feed their families," Ellayne said. "You've only known him for a little while, and you're defending him like he's some sort of saint. I've known my brother for my entire life, and this is not him. Something happened to him five years ago to give him magic, and I just have to figure out what that was so I can get him off the throne. *Without* killing him."

Kade stood up, and the room dropped several degrees, even with Ellayne's magic pumping heat into it. His magic easily overwhelmed hers. He stood in front of her, staring down his nose. The vein in his neck pulsed and his muscles tensed. Each of them kept their hands clasped as fists by their sides.

"My father does what he needs to do to stay in his position." Kade jabbed a finger in the direction of the window, keeping his eyes fixed on Ellayne. For the first time in a while, the dark magic in his veins traveled up his arms and past his sleeves. Within a few seconds, even his neck was beginning to show trace amounts of darkness beneath the pale surface. Ellayne could tell he was struggling to maintain control.

"What you just said"—Ellayne lowered her voice—"doing what needs to be done to benefit yourself, is selfish. I'm trying to do what's best for my subjects, and sending them on a suicide mission, unprepared and untrained as they are, is something I'm not willing to do. That, Kade, would be selfish."

The room continued to drop in degrees as Kade's eyes darkened even more. They stared at each other, locked in a silent contest, still only a foot apart. Darkness pooled in his hands, and the inky veins traveled up his forearm as black mist swirled off and dissipated. Kade's jaw tightened, and hers did too. As she glared at him, her cheeks fired up, and out of her peripheral vision, she saw them glow.

"Hey now." Armannii got to his feet and stepped between them. "Both of you need to calm down. Kid"—he jerked his chin toward Kade—"go for a walk. And Queenie"—he turned his attention to her—"stay here and take a breather."

Chapter Three

llayne stood at the window, tracking Kade's figure as he stormed out the front door beneath her. He looked back over his shoulder, and his body tensed when he caught a glimpse of her through the broken window. She remained there even after he disappeared behind a building. Ellayne allowed the light breeze to soothe her; however, it was not as effective as she'd hoped, and she called her magic to her hand.

Find my aunt and tell her to meet me up here, she whispered in her mind, and after a second thought, she tacked on a please at the end. A stream of light magic twirled and twisted from her fingers. It flitted out of the building through the window, and she couldn't help but grin as she watched it travel in the air above the main street. It glistened in the sun, which held a spot halfway between the horizon and the highest point in the sky. The magic spiraled into a building nearby, and several minutes later, Linetta walked out.

She headed straight for the house Ellayne sat in, and soon enough, she knocked on the door. Ellayne told her to come in, and she hugged her aunt again.

"I got your message. You're getting better at that. I assume it has something to do with all those hours spent training with your elf friend." Linetta sat down next to Ellayne on her bed, and Ellayne nodded. "Your meeting ended sooner than I thought it would."

"I agree." Ellayne rubbed her temples, sighing.

"What happened?"

"It's complicated. Kade—"

"He's different." Linetta didn't verbally ask, but Ellayne took it as a question.

"Very much so. He didn't know he had dark magic until recently, and it's been—"

"Confusing, I'm sure."

Ellayne nodded, rubbing her fingers over a silver bracelet on her wrist. "He wants me to get my brother off the throne."

"Isn't that what you want?"

"By killing him."

"Oh." Linetta reached over and grasped one of Ellayne's hands in hers. "I assume you don't feel great about that part."

"Can't say I do." Ellayne closed her eyes, shaking her head. "It's just . . ." She sighed. "My brother used to be one of my closest companions when we were children. At least, that's how I remember it. And it's like, I know he's ruined my life. He killed my mother and my father. He put a curse on me that was supposed to last forever. And yet, I can't fathom the idea of killing him. However, it seems to be what everyone—what Kade—wants me to do. But he didn't used to think that way. When we were back in the Dark Castle, Kade agreed that I shouldn't have to kill my own brother. But after the battle here, after he almost died, it's like something changed."

"Has he explained what has changed his mind?"

Ellayne shrugged. "He mentioned how my brother poses a dangerous threat to Phildeterre, especially those without magic. He hasn't put legislation in place to help the country begin healing from a war he forcefully ended over five years ago, which has made prejudices grow. And, well," Ellayne said, pausing as she collected her fragmented thoughts. "He heard somewhere that two people he knew were brutally killed at the royal wedding."

"That's awful, and I'm sure the loss of his companions has hurt him deeply. Not to mention his home being destroyed a week ago. Your friend is certainly dealing with a lot." Linetta pushed her glasses up the bridge of her nose.

"And that's another thing. Pingbi." Just the name of the town felt like a dark stain that refused to come clean no matter how much she scrubbed it. It was a mistake that seemed to meet her in nearly every conversation. She had failed. People had died. And it felt like there was nothing she could do to make it better—not with the town lying in dusty ruins. Ellayne opened her mouth, but no words came out. Her face tightened, and she felt the threat of tears.

"Ellayne, look at me," Linetta said, her voice calm. Ellayne obeyed, biting the inside of her cheek to keep any moisture from reaching her eyes. "You are not responsible for the destruction your brother caused in Pingbi. There was no way you could have known."

"I know that, and that's what I tried to tell Kade. But I . . . I don't know if I believe it. Some part of me should've known that signing on to support our cause would put them on the target list for Dio. I should've known that word would get back to him, but I didn't know it would happen so quickly. And I should've been there to protect them. So many people died, and others were hurt. None of the buildings were left standing, and I—"

"Do you blame yourself for what happened to Bolee before you arrived? The destruction that happened here?" Linetta's question caught Ellayne off guard.

"I, well, no." Ellayne frowned. "I didn't know what had happened and—"

"Think about it, sweetheart. What happened in Pingbi is not all that different. You didn't make those people ally with you just like you didn't form the group of rebels that stood up against your brother here. You've done a wonderful job of stepping into your leadership, but you need to understand that people are making their own decisions. And every decision has consequences. When something like Pingbi happens, we must mourn it, use it as a learning experience, and try to do better in the future."

Ellayne let out a breath she hadn't realized she was holding as the tiniest of weights lifted off her shoulder. She knew somewhere in the back of her mind she would always count Pingbi as a failure, a scar that would never fully heal. But her aunt's words had helped, at least a little.

"Thank you, Linetta. I-I really appreciate that. I think I needed to hear someone else say it." Ellayne tucked a piece of hair behind her ear. "And with Kade, it's just that I'm worried about him. I guess I'm concerned that he's not thinking straight."

"Like I said, it sounds like he has plenty on his plate, enough to make a normal person change moods dramatically. But am I right in assuming you think it has something to do with his magic?"

"Can it do that? Mess with people's minds? That's what my father always said, but I know I shouldn't exactly trust his judgment when it comes to magic."

"Best that you don't." Linetta squeezed Ellayne's hands. "I suppose if it's imbalanced, magic can alter a way of thinking. But it's not just dark magic. All magic requires balance."

Ellayne's eyebrows furrowed again, and she pulled her hands out of Linetta's. "What do you mean? Balance of what?"

"I don't know exactly, but your mother studied it when her best friend went dark."

"Emmalee." Ellayne breathed the name of her mother's best friend and Kade's mother. Ellayne resolved to let Kade share the secret of the parentage, though the idea of telling her aunt tempted her.

"She was such a sweet woman, always bringing Evie and me cakes when my father wasn't around."

"Do you think it was magic that made her do the things she did?"

"To some extent, yes." Linetta pushed her glasses back up the bridge of her nose when they slid down. "But magic is nothing without a vessel."

Ellayne stayed silent, reflecting on what her aunt said. After a while, a question formed in her head. "What about rune magic? It's not passed down by family lines like light and dark magic, and it's not contained within a person. How does it exist without vessels?"

Linetta chuckled. "Your father really prevented you from learning anything about magic, didn't he?" Her aunt's voice stayed soft, and if anyone else had said it, it would've sounded condescending. "You're right that both light and dark magic are passed down, but you must remember that they are passed through *human* lines. Only humans can possess light and dark magic. Nonhumans like your elf friend and so many others have magic running through their veins, it's just not light or dark magic. However, I've heard that it could be a weakened version of one or the other. But that's why nonhumans use runes. It's the only way they can manifest the magic within themselves. The amount of magic in them is often not concentrated enough to do magic without the runes. Of course, everyone is different, and there are exceptions to what we know being recognized every day. Genies are a wonderful example. They aren't human, yet they somehow wield both light and dark magic at the same time. If you research magic, it continues to break the very rules it created."

"You're right. My father didn't prepare me for any of this." Ellayne rubbed her temple, adding the information Linetta was explaining to the list of things she needed clarification for when she trained with Armannii the next time. She smiled when she imagined her aunt's bookstore, which had unfortunately been burned to the ground during a raid. Her aunt must've learned everything she was sharing from those books. "What about when a nonhuman marries a human with light or dark magic and they have children? Would they end up only being able to do runes? Or would they have light or dark magic?"

"One or the other. Or neither." Linetta tilted her head. "You could have children who could only perform magic with runes, or you could have children who have one or the other type of magic. Or you could have a child with no magic. Always a possibility."

"And if a person with light magic married a person with dark?" Ellayne felt the blush rise to her cheeks the second she asked the question, and it deepened when an image of Kade sitting across from her with his tight shirt popped into her head.

Again, Linetta let out a soft chuckle. "Same deal. Light, dark, or nothing."

"But that's probably pretty rare, right? Because of the antagonism between those two types of magic." Ellayne couldn't help the clutter of words tumbling out of her mouth any more than she could stop the nervous laugh. "I mean, you don't know of any couples like that, do you? It's—"

"Rare, yes. But not impossible." The grin on her aunt's face was vaguely reminiscent of the smirk Armannii gave her any time he referred to Ellayne and Kade. "And the relationships, few as they are, tend to be the strongest I've ever read about. When in harmony, light and dark magic have a power that surpasses most. It's a beautiful, albeit uncommon, type of relationship."

"Right," Ellayne said, rubbing the back of her medallion. Her desire to change the subject grew with every passing second. Thankfully, her aunt seemed to understand.

"You know, there was a reason you reminded me of Evie when you walked into my shop."

"I look like her." Ellayne nodded. "I know."

"Not just that." Linetta smoothed out her skirt and folded her hands in her lap. "You have her spirit and her stubbornness. But most importantly, you have her heart."

"How do you know?"

"After everything your brother has done to you—to your family—you still don't want to kill him. That is exactly how your mother would've responded."

"But Emmalee—"

"I don't know what happened on that mountain, but I know that your mother came back a different woman. There wasn't a day that went by that she didn't mourn the loss of her friend."

"You agree that I shouldn't kill Dio then?"

"I'm not going to tell you what to do. But I will say this." Linetta stood up, walked to the desk, and picked up the tiara. Placing it on Ellayne's head, she raised Ellayne's chin with the tip of her finger. "I know you will make the right decision, not because of who your parents were, but because of who you are."

"Where is everybody?" Ellayne asked when she walked down to the kitchen an hour after Linetta left.

Armannii leaned back in his chair, his feet crossed on the table. He shrugged. "Kade's still out on a walk, and Dayla left soon after." He tossed another bite of a roll in his mouth. Dayla must've made them during their meeting because the house smelled like yeast from the moment Ellayne walked out of the bedroom.

"I guess we should've talked about her. Matt too." Ellayne sat down across from him. "I'm going to send those two and a few others up to the Coves. The more people who know we need help, the better chance we have."

"Glad you made a decision about it." Armannii raised an eyebrow. "But it doesn't have anything to do with Dayla and—"

"No. It doesn't."

"Still a bad liar."

"I—"

"But it doesn't matter. It's a wise choice."

Ellayne rolled her eyes. "I have a question for you, but I need you to answer honestly."

"You'll know if I don't."

"Do you know what's going on with Kade?"

Armannii stopped chewing on the piece of bread and tucked it into his cheek when he spoke. "What do you mean?"

She wasn't sure how to phrase it. *He's been gone a lot. He snaps quicker than he used to. He won't honestly say where he's going.* None of those words managed to make it out of her mouth.

"Well . . ." She took in a deep breath. "He seems different."

Armannii nodded. "He *is* different. He's been different since we were in the Dark."

"I mean recently. Since we got here. Has he been acting strange around you?"

"I guess." He swallowed his bite. "But you're going to have to ask a better question to get a better answer."

"Right." Ellayne glanced toward the door. Even as she had entered the room, she had questioned whether to bring Kade's sudden change in behavior up with Armannii, and with the response the elf had just given, she decided against pursuing it any further. "Well then, I'm going to go see how the new residents are doing. I also need to meet with some of the lookouts, check in on combat training, and discuss the state of our food and supply rations with someone. I'll be back later."

"Queenie?"

She was already by the door when she looked back at him. "What?"

"Try to remember to breathe at some point."

The last thing she saw before she closed the door was Armannii's smirk.

Somehow, in the midst of checking on the people in the town, Ellayne got roped into helping with the building reconstruction. The monotony of passing bricks down a line of people provided more time to reflect than she desired.

She was in the middle of replaying her conversation with Linetta when a woman with two short horns and dirty-blond hair tapped Ellayne on the shoulder.

"Your Majesty?" She spoke in a wavering voice, and when Ellayne finally glanced at her, she nodded toward a young man standing a few feet away.

"Mattias." Ellayne passed one last brick and left the line. The people scooted in, filling the gap she'd left as she approached the man. "Is everything all right?"

"It's all fine, Your Majesty." He bowed but stood straight when she waved her hand off to the side. "I went in to report to Mannii about how my trainees are doing, and he mentioned you wanted to talk to Dayla and me."

"Did he?" She fell in step beside him, and they started down the main street. "What exactly did Armannii say?"

Matt, who stood at the same height as Ellayne, lifted and dropped his shoulders in a shrug. "He just said to talk to you."

When she first met Matt in the Dark Castle, it had been hard to make out his appearance because all of the Dark Soldiers wore the same armor head to toe, almost always covering their faces. But he had since ditched the armor and instead wore a white tunic. The sun reflected off it, lighting up his face. Though he was strong and built like many other soldiers she'd met, his face remained rounded, not angular like Kade's or Armannii's.

"I need your help, and Dayla's too." Ellayne steered him to the town square where the lightning post was situated. It stood above every roof, and the metal gleamed in the sun. Matt remained silent, letting her continue to give her orders. Out of everyone she was in charge of, Matt made her feel the most like a royal. She wasn't sure if it was because he always addressed her with the same respect and honor she had seen the royal guards give her parents or if it was because he had never once questioned an order she had given. "I want to send a small group to the Cyro Coves to recruit more people. Dayla is from there, but I want to send her with some protection, which is why I want you to go with her."

"From what I understand about Dayla, she could certainly take care of herself if need be. Of course, I'm sure she will deeply appreciate your concern, Your Majesty. I would be honored to help. When do we leave?" For a second, a glint shone in his eyes, and he smiled at her, but he seemed distracted by something she'd said.

"As early as you can. I'm sure you have three or four others you can take with you, right?"

He nodded curtly, his hands braced behind his back as he gave her his full attention once more. "Of course. But you'll have to put someone else in charge of my combat trainees. Armannii thought I would be the best fit for the ultimate beginners since a few of the other soldiers are less patient. I've taught them what I can so far, and I've seen progress. But we started a little over a week ago, and these people need a lot of guidance."

Ellayne sighed. *They aren't the only ones.* "I'll have Armannii find someone else to do the training. I really appreciate this, Matt."

"It's my pleasure. Anything's better than working for the Dark King." He paused. "Speaking of the Dark King, where's his son? I meant to speak with him yesterday, but he disappeared before I got away from training. I had a few questions for him."

Her hands warmed, and she covered them with the fabric of her cloak to keep the magic from being seen—a habit she'd picked up when the magic had first manifested.

"You and me both. But I don't know." She forced her inflections to be as normal as possible. "If you see Kade, let him know I'm looking for him."

Matt inclined his head. "I will. Is there anything else, Your Majesty?"

"I suppose there's no need to tell Dayla all of this. I'll let her know when I see her later; however, if you see her in the meantime, send her to me. Okay?"

"All right, I'm going to—" He stopped and leaned around to look at something behind her. "Hello, Your Highness. We were just talking about you."

Ellayne turned and took a step back when she found Kade standing only a few inches behind her. With how jumpy she had been the last few days, and with all of the crunching glass on the ground, it was impressive he had managed to sneak up on her like that.

"I guess that's why my ears were burning," Kade said, and although he smiled, it didn't reach his eyes. "I heard you were looking for me. Is that correct?"

Matt nodded. "Yes, Your Highness." He glanced at Ellayne and then back at Kade. His eyebrows creased for a second, but then he took a breath and his facial expressions went back to neutral. "I'm sure I'll find time to speak with you in the future."

Kade stood taller, the same way his father had when he'd tried to get information out of Ellayne through intimidation. Only, his face was kinder, and the longer Ellayne watched him, the more she thought he held the stance of her own father over his own. A posture of regality. All he was missing was a crown. However, few others in Bolee knew about Kade's true lineage. Kade had made it known early on that he preferred it remain quiet, not because he was ashamed, he said, but because there was enough excitement having the queen of Phildeterre gracing the town. He thought it would be wise to keep people's focus on the battle at hand. Still, he resembled his father a bit more every day.

Matt inclined his head, his hands still clasped behind his back. "I was just leaving, but I'll send Dayla to you if I see her. Your Highness, Your Majesty." He saluted to Kade and bowed to Ellayne before swiveling on his heels and leaving them alone.

Chapter Four

our Highness," Ellayne mocked, curtsying. "Can we—"

"Talk? Yeah, that's why I came to find you." He shoved his hands in his pockets, glancing over the top of her head. His gaze must've been tracking Matt's receding figure, and then it flicked to a few other people before he peered down at her again. "But I'd rather go somewhere else."

"Like?"

He jerked his head to the left, and she walked beside him. With everything she had been managing, she'd barely had time to see him besides a few council meetings and chance encounters when passing through the house. Her hands felt sweaty, but even after the big blowup from the meeting earlier, she was relieved and thankful to be with him. Despite their rocky start when they first met, it hadn't taken her more than a few weeks to realize how much she could trust him and he'd become her closest friend. Just being around him made the world seem a bit lighter, although that could've been the afternoon sun.

Kade led her off the main street, and soon they left the town behind. The glass grass beneath them crunched as they made their own paths through the Glass Fields of Phildeterre. With the sun directly above them, Ellayne felt perspiration forming as little beads on the back of her neck. It was a nice feeling to get out of town and away from all the responsibility it held . . . until Kade opened his mouth.

"Why do you need to see Dayla?"

She knew he was trying to start small talk, but Dayla was on the list of things Ellayne wasn't thrilled to discuss with him. "I'm sending her, Matt, and a few others up to the Coves for more recruits."

"Is that safe?"

Ellayne scoffed. "Nothing about our situation is safe. But that's why I'm sending Matt and three or four others. That's actually what I was talking to Matt about."

"Is that enough people? Can't you send—"

"Kade, stop." She planted her feet and crossed her arms over her chest. "Why did you come to find me? I sure hope it's not to question every decision I'm making. That's getting old. Fast."

He clenched his jaw but didn't say anything as he turned to face her.

She shifted, moving her hands to her hips. "Look, I wanted to talk to you too." She sighed, blinking a few times before continuing. "Kade, I need you to be honest with me about what's going on in your head right now. Two weeks ago I thought, well, I thought we were okay, you and I. I mean, have I done something to upset that?" Ellayne watched his stone features. "It's just, well, I'm . . . I'm worried about you."

With an eyebrow raised, he said, "You're worried about me?"

Ellayne frowned. "Of course I'm worried about you! You nearly died because Kiegan tried to kill you. Now you go goodness knows where, and when you return, you refuse to tell me the truth about where you've been. It's infuriating." She balled her hands into fists. "I thought we were the kind of friends who talked to each other, or at least argued until one of us realized we were being stupid. Am I wrong in thinking that?" Her gaze darted from one side of his face to the other, but nothing seemed to change. "Well, am I?" Her stomach knotted as she struggled to read his body language, or lack thereof—although, she supposed that would help him when it came to ruling.

Every muscle in Kade's body tensed, and darkness trickled into his hands as he crossed his arms over his chest. His steady glare made her want to take a step back, but she held her ground. He may have changed, bulked up and begun blocking her out, but she wasn't about to take that lying down.

"It's not a bad thing for me to care about you, you know," she added. She hated that he wasn't saying anything. *It's like talking to an angry wall,* she thought as the seconds drew on. *Or a rock. Or a piece of steel. Or—*

"My life has flipped 180 degrees, Ellayne," he finally said, his breath shuddering. His low voice cut through her. "Everything has changed."

"I said the same thing when I broke my curse, but Calder pointed out how wrong I was." She bit her lip, remembering Dayla's older brother who had died to keep Ellayne and her companions safe. "Not everything has changed." She stepped closer to him. "I'm still here." She repeated Calder's words. "I'm still here for you, you big idiot." Ellayne tried a tiny smile, but he didn't return it. "If you'd let me. But you keep pushing me away like I've somehow turned into your worst enemy."

"That's not what I'm doing."

"Then what are you doing? Because to me it looks like you're turning into—"

"My parents?"

"No," Ellayne snapped. "Why do you think everything has to do with who your parents are? You're not your father. You're Kade, my best friend, and I'm so sick of you pretending like you're not!"

"I didn't find you to get chastised," he muttered.

"Then what?"

"I came to tell you that I'm going to be gone for a day or two. I wanted to let you know beforehand."

The words came out so fast, it almost seemed like they pushed Ellayne, making her take a step back. "What?" All of the energy she'd felt when yelling at him fizzled out. "Leaving? For where? Why?"

Kade rubbed the back of his neck, tilting his head until he was looking at the ground. "I didn't want to leave for that long and not tell you I was going. I didn't want you to—"

"Worry? Of course I'm going to worry. Please don't go. If it was something I said, I—"

"I have to go."

"Why?"

"I'll tell you later."

"When?"

"Someday." He rolled his lips inward, frowning. "If it means anything, I'm sorry I've so clearly hurt you. I never wanted that." With a step forward, he closed the space between them and pulled her into a hug.

She wasn't ready for it, and he pinned her arms to her sides when he wrapped his around her. Just like every time they touched before, any place his skin made contact with hers sparked and left a tingling sensation behind.

A sensation that always left her wanting more.

Once he made sure she was headed in the right direction to get back to the town, what with her terrible sense of direction, he left her, walking in the opposite direction. It hadn't taken her long to recognize he carried nothing with him—no bag, no supplies, nothing. She watched him, shielding her eyes from the sun. *Where could he possibly be going? Without me.*

His absence made the walk back to the town feel longer, and she dragged her feet on the ground. *With all this sneaking around, I wouldn't be surprised if he was going to see—*

She froze in the middle of a valley, glancing back in the direction Kade had gone. *His father. He must be going to see the Dark King. But why hide it?* Ellayne rubbed her shoulder. *And why hide it from me?* She wondered if it had to do with the agreement she had made with the Dark King to remove her brother from the throne—an agreement she had yet to fulfill.

Ellayne continued to question Kade's words and actions all the way back to the village. She pondered how she hadn't thought of the Dark King as a reason for his disappearances. Armannii had said that his father was looking for Kade or had at least sent men. Ellayne stopped where she stood in the valley of a field, a cold thought filling her until she shivered: What if the two men Blanndynne had killed at the wedding were there searching for Kade? That would explain why he had been so upset. Knowing him, he probably blamed himself for their deaths just because he was in Phildeterre with her instead of the Dark with his father.

She continued walking back to Bolee, and as much as she hated it, there was another thought pestering her. Ellayne had found ways to avoid it, mainly by busying herself with queenly duties. But she was alone with no company but her thoughts. Before she could stop it, she began thinking about Kade and Dayla.

He'd spent more time with the siren than he had with Ellayne in the past two weeks. Jealousy crawled up inside her, taking her thoughts and mind captive in its sickly green claws. It made her think horrible things about a woman she happily called her friend. And the more she tried to fight it, to make it go away, the more it turned its attention to her. It left her contemplating every fault, every flaw, frailty, and failure she possessed.

To make her self-doubt worse, Dayla ended up being the one who greeted her back at the house.

"Have you seen Kade?" the siren asked, mixing a vile of a light blue liquid around in circles. "He's supposed to take this last draft of medicine to help the scars fade on his shoulder."

Ellayne glanced from the shiny glass container to Dayla. "He just left."

The conversation with Linetta she had earlier about offspring from parents of different magic backgrounds left Ellayne staring at Dayla, wondering if the siren's children with Kade would possess only rune magic or Kade's dark magic. She dug her nails into the palms of her hands to stop her straying thought from getting any further.

"Do you know when he'll be back? He needs to take this today."

"He's gone for the next day or two. Guess those scars are inevitable." Ellayne started up the stairs but didn't make it far.

"Wait," Dayla said, causing Ellayne to turn around midstep. "Matt said you wanted to talk to me."

Ellayne nodded, rubbing her temples. "Right, sorry. I've got a lot on my mind."

Walking back to the table, she nodded for Dayla to sit down. The siren continued to swish the container in circles as she took a seat across from Ellayne. *Cal used to do that when we talked,* Ellayne thought as she watched the siren swirl the vial.

"I totally get it. The last few weeks have been chaotic. What's up?"

"I have something I need you and Matt to do." Ellayne rubbed her temples in small circles, encouraging the headache forming to go away before it achieved critical mass.

"What?"

"We need more recruits or we don't stand a chance against the king, so I need you, Matt, and a few others to go to the Coves to get some more people. I wanted to send you because—"

"I'm from there." Dayla nodded. "That makes sense. And Matt will offer protection. It sounds like a good idea."

"So you'll do it?"

"When the queen asks you to do something, you do it."

Stop spending so much time with Kade, Ellayne thought. *Now there's something your queen asks you to do.* She shifted in her seat, forcing away the idea of the two of them together. Dayla's question brought her back to the conversation.

"When do we leave?"

"That's up to you and Matt, but I'd prefer within the next few days."

"All right. I'll meet up with him after I'm done with this." She held up the medicine. "It needs a bit of heat; do you mind?"

Ellayne held out her hand and took the vial from Dayla. It wasn't the first time the siren had asked for Ellayne's help with something she was brewing up. In fact, the two of them had spent a fair amount of time together, enough for Ellayne to see the ways in which Dayla had grown since her brother's murder. It wasn't difficult for Ellayne to think of her as a friend unless a certain dark-haired prince was thrown into the equation.

Warmth filled her core as Ellayne focused on pulling the magic to her hands before telling it to heat up. Soon enough, air rose in tiny bubbles from the bottom of the vial, and Dayla stopped her.

"That should do it." She took it back with two fingers, flinching at the temperature. "Thanks. Cal was always better at making this potion. I've messed it up three times already today." Dayla's voice was softer, and Ellayne tilted her head down.

"He was good at what he did," Ellayne said as she rubbed the back of her neck.

"I'm sorry, E," Dayla said, pausing to stick her tongue in the side of her cheek. "But I may have overheard part of your council meeting. And I—well, I just don't understand."

Ellayne raised an eyebrow, her hands gripping her legs under the table. "I'll ignore the fact that you were eavesdropping on royal matters. What don't you understand?"

Dayla's shoulders sagged. "Everything in me wants revenge on the man who ordered Cal's death. I see the captain's face in my nightmares, and each time I'm too late to stop Cal's execution. Every time I have the nightmare, I kill the captain. I need to avenge my brother's death."

"I know where you're coming from, but—"

"That's the thing, E. I know you know where I'm coming from because the king killed your mother and father, among other things. You should be fantasizing over ways to end his life, but you're clearly not. Why don't you want to see the man who killed your parents meet the same fate?"

"It's more complicated than that. The man who killed Cal was a stranger to you. Dio is my brother, and—"

"Brother or not, sooner rather than later, you're going to need to realize that he is a monster and your people and country come first. You have to accept that you're the queen. We rely on you. You can't keep running away from that."

"Dayla, that's enough." Ellayne stood up. "You have no idea what you're talking about. There's more to it than killing and murder. So, if there's nothing else, I'm going to go upstairs for a while."

Dayla opened her mouth, but before she could say anything, and before Ellayne made it to the stairs, Armannii raced into the house.

"Queenie," he panted. "You need to see this."

"What is it, Armannii? I was about to—"

"The Black Forest is on fire."

The speed rune on Ellayne's shoes had her flying over hills with ease. Armannii kept pace beside her, and they sprinted toward the growing cloud of smoke over the trees on the horizon. The smoke billowed in the wind, blowing toward Bolee and the Glass Fields. The acrid air burned Ellayne's lungs, and she coughed as a reaction.

The Cylan River came into view and stretched out over the horizon, a barrier between them and the fire drawing near. Ellayne and Armannii stopped when they reached the riverbank.

"How is this possible? How did it start?" Ellayne asked, craning her neck from side to side. No one else was around the riverbank. *There should be at least two lookouts here*, she thought. "Aren't there enchantments and spells to prevent this from happening?"

"The wards can be cancelled out with magic; it just needs to be stronger than the magic that laid them down in the first place." Armannii put his hands on his hips. "Do you think it's him? Diomedes?"

Ellayne nodded. "Who else would it be?" She ran her fingers through her hair. "But I don't know why unless—" Realization struck her. "You have to get back to the town and warn them. This might be a distraction. He may be trying to strike Bolee."

"He would . . ." Armannii clucked his tongue. "But what about the fire?"

"I'll figure something out, but you need to go. Get people ready in case of an attack."

"You got it." He turned but looked back at her. "Be safe."

"You too."

Chapter Five

llayne's eyes watered from the smoke, and the air grew warmer by the second until a thin layer of sweat covered her forehead. Water rippled in front of her as she stood on the steep bank of the river. The Black Forest lay opposite her, calling for help from the fire destroying it from the inside.

Shaking her hands by her sides, she scrunched them into fists and relaxed them again as magic rushed down to her fingertips. Ellayne craned her neck for something she could use against the raging flames. Unfortunately, there was nothing but glass fields on her side of the river. She knew glass wasn't going to stop the fire. A sparkle from the Cylan River caught her eye, and a plan began to form.

Raising her hand in front of her, she watched light begin to coil around it, dancing toward the edge of the water. *Come on,* she thought, urging her magic. *Stop the flow.* When the water continued to sweep right over the insignificant wall her magic created, she dropped her hand with a grunt. For a second, the water built up, but it released and the river leveled out.

She directed her magic at the Cylan River again. This time she raised both hands, palms out, and focused on the center of the water. She knew from experience how cold it was. As she called on her magic, she imagined the tendrils of icy liquid slamming against the barrier she was putting up. The mental image hit her, and she took a step back.

Her magic pulsed as the water pounded against her blockade. Each second she held her hands out, the water surged upward against the invisible dam. *Now what?* She lifted her chin, squinting at the top of the sloshing tower she'd created. It would've easily reached the top of the lightning post back in the village, possibly towering a few stories above it.

Go, she thought, pushing her hands out straighter than before. The liquid tower dispersed at her command, spiraling upward into the sky in a watery cyclone. As soon as the dam left, the river began to flatten back out with more water from the sea.

Ellayne's hands shook, trembling out of her control. But it wasn't just her hands. Every part of her body quivered. Her eyelids felt heavy as her magic carried the water. The cyclone lifted over the trees of the Black Forest, traveling toward the plumes of black smoke hovering above the horizon. *Almost.* Ellayne's hands dropped when the water reached the center of the fire, causing the droplets to disperse over the blazing treetops.

Even from where she stood, the sound of sizzling and crackling intensified, but it was followed by a hollow ringing in her ears. The horizon tilted to the side, rolling in front of her eyes. Ellayne stumbled, her equilibrium distorted. Her body felt heavier, and though adrenaline still pumped through her veins, it seemed that was the only thing keeping her upright. And it was fading. Fast.

The world spun when she lost her balance again, though this time she fell forward. Her boots slid on the slick mud at the edge of the riverbank, and without the ability to right herself, Ellayne toppled into the river below.

The shock of the frigid water slapping Ellayne in the face spiked her adrenaline level once more, and she kicked her feet to reach the surface. *Seriously?* She burst to the top of the water. *How is this happening again?*

Help me, she called to her magic, but no response came. *Help,* she thought again, thrashing her legs to stay afloat. The current yanked at her, drawing her toward the center of the river. Her feet couldn't touch the bottom, and every few seconds the water sucked her underneath its icy clutches.

Ellayne used her arms and legs to fight against the current. Her mind raced faster than the water carrying her when she recognized the harsh truth that Kade wouldn't be there to save her this time. She was on her own. Alone. She coughed out a chestful of water when she resurfaced and used her hands to spin around, looking for the closest shoreline.

"Swim with the current." She remembered Kade's words the last time she took a dip in the river. That time it had been Kade's idea. *"Swim diagonally toward the coast, and let the current push you."*

Swiveling around, she faced the direction the river urged her. Marking the Black Forest on her right, she swam with the current to the left—the side she fell in. The Cylan River propelled her downstream, but she used it to gain enough speed to break out of the strongest part of the current.

Her lungs ached from the amount of water she'd inhaled and the amount of oxygen she hadn't. *Keep going,* she repeated to herself in a rhythmic pattern. The muscles in her arms and legs grew weary, and the adrenaline from the initial fall faded. *Don't stop,* she screamed at her feet every time they slowed down.

Ouch. Ellayne winced when her hand jammed into something hard. She blinked residual water out of her eyes, grinning at the sight of the wall of dirt that made up the riverbank in front of her. The water was still too deep to touch the bottom, but ahead of her sat a few boulders sticking out of the river. *Just make it to the rocks.* She skimmed along the riverbank, staying as far away from the undertow as possible.

Ellayne sped closer to the boulders, realizing too late that she was going to smash into them. The impact knocked the wind out of her, and she grimaced as her face grated along the rock. The part of the boulder under the water was slick, causing her to slip right past it. With only two more boulders to stop herself on, she readjusted, sticking her feet out in front of her so she floated on her back instead of her stomach.

Her knees bent as she prepared to hit the next rock. For a second, she was able to grasp the lower half with her legs, but once again she slipped off. Spinning to the side, Ellayne tried to straighten herself for the final rock. Her last chance. She reached for the surface.

The top of the final boulder was as slick as the submerged section, but unlike the first two, there was a crevice underneath. She stuck her boot inside and hoisted herself up, using the current to push her. Using what little strength remained in her arms, she wiggled onto her stomach. Ellayne coughed out more water as she collapsed on top of the rock. She stayed on her belly, too tired to flip over to her back. The only part of her body still in the water was her feet, and the water pushed against them.

With the sound of the river rushing past her, and with a sizable amount of water in her ears, Ellayne struggled to hear any sound from the fire in the Black Forest. Every part of her hoped that she had succeeded in slowing the fire as she let her eyelids close. Concern filled her for those living where the flames had struck. As her mind drifted in and out of consciousness, she pictured the villages she had visited in the Black Forest—villages that might very well be in ashes. Hundreds of faces flashed in her mind of people she'd met in her travels through the forest; however, one face stood out the most.

Almond-shaped eyes and teal-tipped hair. Gills on the side of his neck and cheeks that turned pink whenever he misspoke. Calder. The thought of him brought back a memory she tried to stay away from. But in her exhausted state, and after her recent conversation with Dayla, she couldn't stop the memory from playing behind her eyelids.

"Your resistance toward our search is considered treason. You are hereby condemned to death." The words the captain of the royal guard had said sent more shivers down her spine, and all she could do was lie there. Helpless. *Just like Cal.*

The sword had sliced right through his back, piercing him through and through. Dayla's screams echoed in Ellayne's mind. *My fault, all my fault Cal is dead.* She squeezed her hands into fists but didn't have the energy to keep them that way.

Her feet, still in the freezing water, grew numb, but not as numb as her mind. She pushed against the memory of Calder's murder, fighting against every ounce of emotion trying to overwhelm her. *I'm sorry, Cal,* she thought, shivering on top of the boulder. *I'm so sorry.*

Being out in the air, soaking wet, left her lips trembling and her body shaking. The roaring river grew to a deafening point. Somewhere in the thunder pounding her ears, she heard someone calling her name. Then silence.

Chapter Six

 roaring noise in her head woke Ellayne. She reached her hand up to her pounding skull, steadying it as she sat up where she lay. The light in the room came from a window—a broken window. *How did I get back here*? Her bag sat in the corner of the room she and Dayla shared. She squinted her eyes, urging the tiny hammers in her head to stop slamming against her brain so she could get out of the cot without falling to the ground.

"E!" Dayla scrambled up from the floor where she had been sitting cross-legged. "You're up!"

"Not so loud," Ellayne said, cringing as the headache worsened. "How am I here? Last I remember—"

"I found you," the siren responded, positioning herself at the end of the bed. She twirled a piece of hair around her finger. "Armannii came back and told everyone to prepare for a possible attack. I could feel something happening with the river, and when I asked where you were, he sent me to go check on you."

"You're the one who found me?"

"I had to swim up and down the river quite a distance before I found you passed out on a boulder. I—"

"The fire. What about the fire?"

Dayla shook her head. A grin spread across her lips. "How'd you do it?"

"Do it?"

"Put it out." Dayla leaned back against the wall, keeping her pale blue eyes on Ellayne. "I felt the essence of the river change for a minute or two, but then it went back to normal. When I found you, the fire was out, at least from what I could tell at that point. And sure enough, a few people who were in the forest scouting for you came back a few hours ago and said that the fire was over."

"I—" Ellayne rubbed her fingers in small circles near her temples. "I did it? But how?"

"That's what I want to know." Armannii leaned against the doorframe, and his entrance left Ellayne's brain spinning again.

"There was no attack?"

Armannii shook his head. "And it's a good thing too. Everyone here was scrambling. Any attack would've left this place in more shambles than it already is."

Ellayne leaned her head back against the bed frame, closing her eyes as she took a deep breath. "What is he doing?" When she opened her eyes, Armannii fully entered the room and sat on the edge of Dayla's bed.

"Your brother?" Armannii asked, shrugging. "Your guess is as good as mine."

"Except it's not." Ellayne sighed. "Because you know this version of him better than I do."

"Well—"

A knock on the front door downstairs cut Armannii off.

Dayla rose to her feet. "I bet that's Matt," she said, glancing toward Ellayne. "I told Matt I'd accompany him to find a few more people to go with us to the Coves. But if you need me to stay—"

"I'm fine." Ellayne forced a smile. "Thank you for finding me and bringing me back here. I really appreciate it, Dayla."

"Matt helped," Dayla said as she walked to the door. "I couldn't carry you myself."

"Tell him thank you for me."

Dayla nodded and left the room, closing the door behind her.

"You handled that well," Armannii said, his voice low in case Dayla could still hear.

Ellayne raised an eyebrow. "Handled what well?"

"Your incredibly obvious jealousy."

If it didn't hurt her head so much, she would've rolled her eyes. "She saved me and brought me back here." Ellayne's headache intensified when she remembered the harsh way she had spoken to Dayla before she had left for the river. Despite that, the siren had still cared enough to try to find her. The thought left the taste of shame in her mouth as it mixed with the bitterness of jealousy.

"Actually, she said you had already gotten yourself out of the water. However"—he held up a finger to keep her from interrupting him—"I'd like to hear why you went for a swim in the first place."

"That stupid river has tried to kill me three times now," Ellayne muttered, pushing the blanket down to her lap.

"Well I doubt it jumped up and swallowed you."

"I was trying to stop the fire." Ellayne ran her hand along the back of her neck. "But once I sent a wave of water over it, I felt completely exhausted. It was like—"

"You were completely drained of your energy."

"Exactly."

"How much of your magic did you use?" Armannii asked, switching from Dayla's bed to the end of Ellayne's. He sat next to her. "Can you call on your magic now?"

"I haven't tried." Ellayne stared down at her hands in her lap. "Not since I woke up at least."

"Do it."

"Now?"

Armannii nodded. "It's important."

She closed her eyes as she took a deep breath. With Armannii's guidance and training, Ellayne did what she had been practicing over the last two weeks. As she tried to call it forth, she followed the directions he gave her on the first day of training. *Please show yourself,* she thought, knowing her magic responded best to a polite tone of voice. *Hello? Are you there?*

A frown formed on her face when the cold emptiness inside her continued. *Where are you?* she asked, keeping her breathing steady despite the rising anxiety.

"Well?"

She shushed Armannii, clutching her hands into fists as she made the next plea. *Please show yourself!* Still no response. Her lower lip trembled. *Please.* Ellayne's heartbeat pulsed behind her eyelids, and the hammers that created her headache when she first woke up were back, banging away at the inside of her head.

"Ellayne, calm down. Just stop," Armannii said, his tone more serious than normal. He placed his hand on her foot, and she opened her eyes to stare at him.

"What happened? What's wrong with my magic?" Ellayne shook under Armannii's grasp. "Why won't it respond?" Her chest tightened, and breathing became difficult as her level of panic rose.

"Sometimes magic takes a while to gain back its strength when it's been pushed to its limits. It can become dormant."

Ellayne gasped. "No," she whispered. "No, no, no. Not now. Not when I need it to remove Dio from the throne."

"Take a deep breath." Armannii took his hand off her. "I'm not saying that's what happened."

"But it might be?"

Armannii wouldn't quite meet her eye as he took a deep breath and said, "It's a real possibility, but it's not even the worst-case scenario, so I wouldn't worry yourself. Not when you've already got enough to focus on."

She couldn't stop the sob that came out of her mouth. "Armannii, I can't take on Dio—"

"I said not to worry about it." He tilted his head when he looked at her. "Even if it is exhausted to the point of being dormant, it could return when it's back to full power. It just might take a while."

"How long?"

"It could be a few hours, it could be a few years." He kept going even when she let out a terrified gasp. "It could even remain dormant for the rest of your life. But as long as it's there, then you shouldn't have any nasty side effects."

"You mean my magic could be completely gone?" Ellayne's breaths came out ragged, and it became increasingly difficult to take them. "What if my magic is gone?"

Armannii scratched his chin, and it took a few seconds before he answered her question. But when he did, he kept his silver eyes locked on hers. "Then you could go insane. Or worse. But you shouldn't jump to that conclusion yet. Yeah, you can be a little nuts sometimes, but I'd be able to tell if something was actually wrong. At the moment, you seem fine, and I'll just keep an eye on you." He offered a small smile, but it did nothing to help stop what felt like the room caving in on her. "And for now, we'll consider it dormant unless it proves otherwise."

Ellayne held back a whimper, instead forcing her spazzing lungs to take in a steady breath. "How do I get my magic to come back if it's in a dormant state?"

"I'm unaware of any ways to spark it back into action," he said, but at her hiccup he added, "but that doesn't mean there isn't a way."

Despite her high anxiety levels, Ellayne wasn't crying. Instead, her mind raced through different options of how to bring her magic back. She had always seen the best results when she didn't push it away and instead treated it like a child, helping it grow and asking it to obey politely. She remembered the last time it didn't respond to her because she had pushed it away for so long. A lolang—a reptilian wolf beast—had almost killed Kade because her magic had ignored her.

But she knew something that made her magic spark more than politeness.

"Make me mad," Ellayne said, her shoulders rolling back as her posture straightened.

"What?"

"Say something about Kade and Dayla, or insult my parents. Just say something that will—"

"No."

"Armannii!" Ellayne rose to her feet, ignoring the throbbing in her head. "Do something to make me angry right now or I'll—"

"As much as I consider myself an expert at ticking you off, I won't do it. Your magic will come back with time." Armannii stood up too. "Besides, I can tell by your tone of voice that you're already annoyed. There's still no magic. You can't force it."

"Please just—"

"No, Queenie. And I mean it. I'm not going to make you hate me just so you can chance jump-starting your magic."

"But what if it's actually gone?" Ellayne said, folding her arms across her chest.

Armannii bit his lower lip. "I told you I'd watch for signs, and I will. But at this point, you shouldn't jump to that conclusion."

"You have to help me."

He shook his head, placing his hands on his hips. "If your magic is completely gone, you'll lose your sanity within a day or so. If we get past that point and you're still—well—you, then we'll go from there. But honestly, Ellayne, you need to calm down. You're not doing yourself or anyone else any favors by panicking."

"Armannii, I order you—"

"I've got to go make plans with Matt and the other combat trainers." He stopped midstride toward the door. "I'll send someone to look after you in the meantime."

"Please—"

"Good job stopping the fire, Queenie," he said over his shoulder. "I'm proud of you."

Ellayne paced the room while waiting for Linetta to show up. *Come on,* she shouted in her head. *Why aren't you working?* She tried time and time again to call on her magic, but each time she felt like she was only talking to herself.

A soft knock on the door pulled Ellayne out of the emptiness inside her, and she opened it to find her aunt.

"Armannii told me what happened." Linetta pulled Ellayne into a hug, wrapping her arms around Ellayne's waist. "How are you feeling?"

Ellayne rested her chin on her aunt's shoulder, bending over to compensate for the several inches of height difference. *How am I feeling?* She pondered the best way to tell her aunt that she was falling apart on the inside.

"I'm fine," she said, stepping back from Linetta. She led her aunt to her bed, and they sat down side by side.

"I highly doubt that." Linetta patted Ellayne's knee. "You don't have to put on a brave face for me, honey."

With a sigh, Ellayne closed her eyes. "What all did Armannii tell you?"

"You saved many people in the Black Forest by putting out the fire, but it had some consequences. He didn't specify what they—"

"My magic is gone," Ellayne said as she opened her eyes, the words tumbling out faster than she meant them too. *Not the smoothest explanation of my situation,* she thought as she watched her aunt's reaction. "He said it might be dormant."

Linetta pinched her lips together, nodding slowly. "It was a big task. A delayed restoration of magic should be expected."

"But I can't help wondering what I'll do if it's gone forever. How am I supposed to face Diomedes without it? I mean, I was already at a disadvantage before, but now . . ." Ellayne's voice rose in pitch, and her posture straightened. "I can't beat him even when I have my magic, let alone without it. I don't stand a chance; Phildeterre doesn't stand a chance."

Her aunt considered her words, not contradicting her or telling her everything was going to be okay. Instead, she stayed silent, and the ambient noises surrounded them in a bubble. People outside spoke in muffled voices, wind whistled through the broken window, and floorboards creaked below them.

"There is plenty to worry about," Linetta said after a while. "You're up against someone much more powerful than you, and you've lost one of your weapons, so to speak. But your mother was in a similar position when she fought against the sorceress, and she didn't give up just because her magic receded into hiding. In fact, after the specific battle where she lost her magic, she told me that was when she figured out how to remove the sorceress's threat."

Ellayne's ears perked up at the mention of her mother, and the mention of the sorceress left her with the image of Kade walking away from her. She shook her head to focus her thoughts. "What do you mean? My mother lost her magic too?"

"No, not permanently. But in one particular clash, she expended her magic too much, and it went dormant. Probably like yours. She came to me in tears, saying similar words to yours, always concerned about the country more than herself."

Ellayne didn't argue even though she didn't agree. She knew full well that her own first concern had been for herself, and the concerns for the country had come later. Guilt flooded through her, adding to the tumult in her head. Of course her mother had been concerned about the country first. She was sure her father would've been the same if he had been in a situation like them. Yet another item to add to the list of things that made Ellayne feel inadequate when it came to taking the mantle of queen.

"I told her what I'm going to tell you now. You are more than your magic. You are wise, you are determined, and you are passionate. Put those things together and find a way to fix this—with or without your magic. Everybody has a weakness, magic or not."

She questioned the validity of her aunt's statement. Did her brother have a weakness? It didn't seem like it. She knew she needed to talk to someone who knew more about this version of her brother if she was going to find that out. Ellayne ran her thumb over the royal medallion necklace hanging just above her tunic.

"But what if—"

"Don't focus on the what-ifs; focus on the present. You're needed here."

Ellayne sighed. Cal had said the same thing. "I needed to hear that. Thank you." She grasped her aunt's hand and gave it a squeeze. "I'm glad you're here."

Chapter Seven

e's got to have a weakness, Armannii." Ellayne rubbed her temples with her fingers as she paced the floor in her room. "Think harder. We have to find a way to take him off the throne. Especially now with my magic dormant. We have to outthink him."

"If I thought any harder, Queenie, my head would explode." Armannii sat cross-legged on her bed, holding his head with his hands. "Ask me how to take down a vampire, and I'd tell you a wooden stake, or if you're me, a wooden arrow. Ask about a werewolf, and I'd tell you a weapon coated in silver. And for a genie, the same, but with jade. But once Dio got his magic, he was unstoppable."

"He can't be unstoppable," Ellayne snapped, pausing in the middle of the room to glare at him. "He can't." Her voice broke, and she cleared her throat as she continued pacing. "We have to be missing something."

"We're not." Armannii ran his hand over the back of his neck, groaning as he did so. "When your brother caught word that there was a way to get magic if you weren't born with it, he became obsessed with the idea. I was skeptical because I didn't trust the source, but the more we looked into it, the more it seemed like a real thing. However, it came with a price. After we failed to end the war peacefully, your brother had this demented idea that if he got magic, he could end the war, could even change the world and make it better. I went along with it because the war was against people like me. I guess I was trying to look out for myself." He rubbed his cheek, scratching the scruff.

"Where did you hear about the opportunity to get magic?" Ellayne asked as she sat down on Dayla's bed across from him.

"I took your brother to an old . . ." He paused, gritting his teeth. "An old adversary."

"Otto?"

Armannii had a painful smile spread tight across his lips, and he sighed as he shook his head. "You've met him. You know how crafty he is. I left him alone with your brother because Diomedes asked me to. That was my mistake. Otto wormed the idea into Diomedes's head until he was certain him gaining magic was the only way to face your father and end the war. So, that's what we did. We headed to the Elemental Mountains and you can see how that turned out. The object, the dagger you trapped him in after you broke your curse, left him with no eyes, dark magic, and an awful personality" Armannii let out a deep breath.

"Did he ever explain how it all happened?"

"Not to me." Armannii shook his head. "And like I said, he was too powerful to stop after that. The only reason I got out of the castle after he cursed you was because he let me go."

"Because you were friends."

Armannii scoffed. "I don't think your brother possesses the capacity for any sort of relationship now that he has magic; it consumed him. When I realized how broken he was, I hesitated. Told him he was nuts and that I didn't sign up for murder."

Armannii snorted, but he continued to frown. "He threatened me. Said he'd kill me if I ever stepped foot into Cyanthia again. So I left, and that's when I decided you were my best bet to taking care of him."

"None of this is helping me figure out a way to stop him." Ellayne sighed, rubbing her eyes with the heels of her hands. "How are we supposed to even the playing field and remove him from the throne if we don't even understand how the dagger gave him magic? This would be so much easier if we knew what we were up against, you know? Find out if fighting him is even worth it." She pushed harder on her eyelids until she saw flashing lights. "If I had known this was what he would become, I would've tried harder to reach him," she muttered.

"A lot of good that would've done. He was all but determined to go dark side." Armannii exhaled loudly as he stretched his back. "You aren't a seer, Queenie. You couldn't have known this was coming."

"What?" Ellayne pulled her hands away from her face and pointed a finger toward Armannii.

"Sorry to burst your bubble, but you can't see the future." He leaned back, smirking. "But boy would that be nice. Imagine the things we could do if—"

"Focus, Armannii. Maybe that's a good plan. Figure out the future. What if we visit a seer? They've got to know what's up with my brother, right? Maybe—"

Armannii shook his head. "It's a nice thought, and it must run in the family. Your brother and I went to see the last seer of this generation."

"And?"

"And nothing. Diomedes killed him."

Ellayne sat up straighter. "Why'd he do that? Did the seer say anything before—"

"I wasn't in the room when he talked to him." Armannii paused, his forehead wrinkling. "When I got back, the seer was already dead."

"Oh. Then I suppose that's a bust. Unless—" Ellayne stopped talking as a memory flashed across her mind.

"What's a seer?" Six-year-old Ellayne had asked her brother as she flipped through the pages of a book about magic. They were in their father's private office where he kept the banned books—a private office that was free to invade when their father was away on business. The books on magic, however, were always in limited supply, even in there.

"Someone who can see the future," Diomedes responded, chomping on an apple he stole from the kitchen. "For a fee, they will tell you more about yourself than you want to know."

"How do they know the future?"

"Magic, of course."

"Wow." Ellayne's small hands moved over the drawing of an old woman in a cloak holding a book the size of three or four bricks. "And I thought this was a big book," she said as she pointed to the one she was looking through on the floor of their father's office.

"As soon as they make a prophecy—"

"What's a prophecy?" she asked her brother, who raised an eyebrow at her.

"It's something that will happen in the future."

"Whoa."

"And when a seer makes a prophecy, it's instantly written into a book like the one in that illustration."

"So they're writers too?"

"No." Diomedes shook his head. "The words are written down by magic, which bind the seer to the book. All of the prophecies one seer makes will be written in one book that can never be altered or destroyed.”

“Never?”

Her brother nodded. “Never. It’s a protected book.” He put his feet up on his father’s desk as he reclined in the chair. Being ten years older than her, he was already sixteen and very accustomed to sneaking into places he shouldn’t.

“But why is it protected?”

“Because some people don’t like what they hear when they talk to seers, and they try to change the future. But you can’t. No matter what road someone takes, the prophecy will come true. The book has a powerful spell of protection on it so nobody can try to mess with the future.”

The memory faded as Armannii waved his hand in front of Ellayne’s face.

“Are you still awake, Queenie?” he asked, chuckling when she smacked his hand away.

“The prophecy book,” she said, tucking a strand of hair behind her ear. “We need to find the prophecy book connected to the seer you and my brother went to.”

“How will we find it?” Armannii asked.

“I thought you had connections.”

“Fair enough.” He snorted. “I’ll see what I can find out,” he said, standing up. “And in the meantime, our little band of rebels could really use your guidance when it comes to combat training.”

“That’s still incorrect, Lydia,” Ellayne said. She wore a smile, but it was forced. “You can’t hold the weapon that way.”

“Why not?” the young werewolf replied, a growl rumbling beneath her words. Out of all of the rebels in the combat training program, the youngest girl gave Ellayne the most trouble. It probably had something to do with her family, all of whom were dead according to the young girl. Ellayne had overheard her conversation with some of the other trainees earlier. If Lydia really was an orphan and all alone, then at least she and Ellayne had that much in common.

"Because you lose your power. This type of sword is meant to be held with both hands, not just one." Ellayne tried to correct her in the way she imagined she would if she had a younger sibling she could teach fighting to. Just like Dio had for her.

"It looks better if I use one."

"And you'll be dead faster too," Ellayne said, keeping her tone as steady as she could, though it was getting increasingly difficult.

Clearly, anger or annoyance was not the way to restore her magic because training the untrainable was pushing her to the edge of rage. She watched the blond girl grip the sword with both hands, rolling her eyes at Ellayne as she did so. Dio never would've let Ellayne get away with a look like that; he would've knocked her on her rear end before she knew what was happening, and he would've done it all with a grin plastered on his face.

Each thought that drifted back to Dio left her feeling drained. He wasn't dead, but she would never get to spar with him for fun again. No. The only duels left in their future seemed to Ellayne like they would end bloody for one or the other, if not both.

"All right." Ellayne turned to the other nineteen people in the training session, steeling herself against the thoughts of her brother. "Face your partners. Partner A, strike to the right, and B, block it. Slowly now, everyone. I want to see you practice this ten times, then switch roles."

She kept her eyes on the duos as they followed her orders. A sense of hopelessness settled over her, and she sighed as she watched the awkward way most of the people fought. Metal clashed against metal, and for the beginners, wood against wood.

Yet despite most of the attacks being parried, every once in a while someone would holler after being hit in the arm by their partner.

Three different sessions later, Ellayne said goodbye to the last of the trainees and headed back to Dayla's house. She entered without knocking, and walked straight into the middle of a meeting.

"Your Majesty," a young man around her age said, rising to his feet when she walked in. She recognized him from somewhere. "Welcome back."

"Yeah," she said, nodding to him. "Thanks. What's going on here?" Ellayne directed the question toward Dayla, who sat in a chair next to Matt. Five people sat in the common room.

"E, these are the three people who are going to come with Matt and me to the Coves," Dayla said, nodding to each person. "Finn, Jesper, and Millie."

Finn's blond hair curled around his face. His square glasses made his eyes appear enlarged, and freckles danced across the bridge of his nose. His face was familiar to Ellayne, and it took her a few seconds to place him. He had been in Pingbi when Ellayne first visited there with Kiegan and Kade. He must've arrived with the others from the destroyed town in the Level Plains.

Jesper was the opposite of Finn; he had dark hair and skin, but his eyes were bright green. He nodded to her when she glanced at him.

"A pleasure, Your Majesty," he said in a deep voice. He appeared closer to Armannii's age, at least ten years her senior.

Millie had gills on the side of her neck—gills exactly like Dayla's. Ellayne inclined her head toward the new siren. She had red hair that cut off around her chin, but what caught Ellayne's eye was Millie's left arm. It ended in a stump at her elbow. Ellayne caught herself staring and forced herself to flick her eyes equally between the three new recruits.

"Thank you for assisting Dayla and Matt on this journey," Ellayne said, standing as tall as she could. Her father had always made ruling seem easy, but speaking with authority was not as natural for her as it seemed to be for him. "When will you leave?"

"Tomorrow morning," Matt responded. "We've made a plan, and Dayla has prepared how she will present your invitation to ally with you to the other sirens. It should only take us a few days, and then we will hopefully return with more able hands to join the fight. We were just finishing up by discussing supplies."

"Take what you think you'll need," Ellayne said, placing her hands on her hips. "I want this to go as smoothly as possible."

"Thank you, Your Majesty," Millie said. Her voice was much higher than Ellayne expected. "We will recruit as many of our people as we can." She nodded toward Dayla.

"Your dedication is greatly appreciated, Millie," Ellayne said, smiling. "All of yours." She made sure to make eye contact with each one of them individually. "Now, if you'll excuse me, I'm going to go wash up."

"Good evening, Your Majesty."

"Bye, Queen Ellayne."

"Thank you, Your Majesty."

"Good night, Your Majesty."

"I'll see you in a bit, E."

Chapter Eight

*ow has it already been four days since Kade left?* Ellayne thought as she helped the young werewolf, Lydia, with her footing for the twelfth time that day. *Where is he, and why hasn't he come back yet?*

"I can't hold my foot that way," Lydia whined. "Why can't I just do it this way?"

Ellayne sighed. "As I've said before, you're more balanced when your foot is partially turned outward. If you keep it straight like that, you'll lose your balance, giving your attacker the advantage."

Kade had the same issue. She remembered their time spent training together in the Dark and the progress he made once he became the Dark Prince. The Dark Soldiers' training left him able to hold his own in a fight. Unless that fight was against his old best friend, Kiegan.

"Come on, Your Majesty," Lydia said, waving her hand. "I'm going to let you try to hit me."

"What an honor." Ellayne rolled her eyes, stepping into her battle stance without a second thought. A smile crossed her lips as she remembered the first time she had challenged her brother when he was training her years ago. Ellayne had a feeling this was going to end the same for Lydia as it had for her. She warned herself to go easy, not wanting to embarrass Lydia like her brother had done to her in front of some of the royal guard. However, she was aching to fight someone, even if it was only for a teaching moment.

Ellayne swung her weapon, a wooden pole meant to represent a sword, and was pleased when Lydia reacted fast enough to block her. She nodded her approval, blocking when Lydia tried to catch her off guard. Just as Ellayne suspected, once Lydia attacked, she took an extra step, trying to regain her balance. Seeing her opening, Ellayne spun and, as gently as she could, hit Lydia in the torso.

The werewolf growled but backed away. "Fine, I'll work on the footwork."

"Right, now who's next?" Ellayne asked, turning back to the onlookers. A few people stepped back, avoiding direct eye contact with her. "No volunteers?"

"I'll take a swing at it," Armannii said behind her. "It's been a while since we dueled. You've picked up a few tricks. Maybe you'll be able to beat me this time."

Ellayne scoffed. "I remember the fight differently." She tossed the pole up and caught it by the end. "I seem to remember taking you down."

"Oh do you?"

Ellayne chuckled. "All right, Armannii. Let's see if you're past your prime."

The elf motioned for Lydia to hand him her weapon, which she did. "Bring it on."

The onlookers formed a circle around them, big enough that the two people dueling could swing without hitting someone but small enough that Ellayne and Armannii were in close quarters. Armannii made the first move, attempting to distract her with an extra flourish to his strike. She stepped out of the way, countering by swinging her weapon at him. He blocked it, shoving her backward a step.

"Not bad," he said, grinning.

"Trying to blind me with your perfect teeth? Not going to work." Ellayne laughed, jumping out of the way when he swung low.

"Worth a shot."

Armannii lunged, but Ellayne twirled out of the way, landing back in her striking stance. His back leg was still exposed from his lunge, but Ellayne had a feeling he'd left it there a second too long to see if she would strike. It was reminiscent of the duel Armannii had been referencing. And it was a trap—one she didn't fall for. Instead, she moved to the left, away from his leg.

He chuckled as he too went back to his original stance. Back and forth they went, striking and blocking, dodging and weaving around each other in a deadly dance. With her heart racing, Ellayne swung low, leaning back as he brought his weapon inches from her face in order to block her. With her staff caught by his, he forced her to step back. As she did so, he twirled his staff, spinning hers out of her hand.

With his weapon pointed at her face, she put her hands up, pressing her lips together as she shook her head back and forth.

"For someone who prefers a bow," she said as he lowered his weapon and she put down her hands, "you are quite handy with a sword."

"Yes." He tossed the weapon to the nearest person. "Yes I am."

"Your Majesty, Ovair." A young woman came up. Ellayne recognized her wings, marking her as the lookout with a grudge against Armannii.

"What's going on, Marigold?" Armannii's voice lost the arrogance it carried only seconds before. "Is something wrong?"

The woman ignored his question, instead talking to Ellayne. "Your Majesty, there is a dryad here by the name of Elowen who wishes to speak to you. You and Ovair." She cast a glare in Armannii's direction.

Ellayne and Armannii met Elowen in the middle of the town square. The dryad had green dreadlocks down to her waist, and unlike in the Black Forest where they had first met, her warm brown skin stood out in the bright light of the Glass Fields. During their first encounter, Ellayne had not noticed the scrawling dark vines that covered Elowen's arms and legs in tattoos. They were elegant and mesmerizing.

"Hello, Your Majesty." Elowen bowed as Ellayne and Armannii approached. "How are you?"

"I'm fine, thank you, Elowen. What brings you here? Is something wrong?" Ellayne motioned for them to sit on a bench nearby.

Elowen followed her over and they sat with their knees angled towards each other. Armannii stood to the side of Ellayne, casting his shadow over her.

"I heard through the mycelium that you were the one who stopped the fire raging in the Black Forest, and I wanted to come confirm that this was indeed true." Elowen cast her gaze first at Ellayne, then at Armannii.

Ellayne glanced at Armannii and nodded. "I did."

"Well then, I came to thank you, and on behalf of my other brothers and sisters in nature, I wanted to pass on a piece of information that Ovair was searching for." She nodded toward

Armannii. "My siblings and I heard a rumor you are seeking a prophecy book from the last seer of your generation. Is that true?"

Armannii responded first. "It is. Do you know its location?"

Elowen regarded him with steady eyes. "I do."

"Where? Where is it?" Ellayne asked, her voice louder than she intended. She lowered it, placing a soft smile on her face. "It's very important we find that book."

"Of course." Elowen nodded. "Unfortunately, I cannot retrieve it for you. It is in a place even I dare not go."

"Where is it?" Armannii asked.

"It is in the castle of Cyanthia. King Diomedes had it brought there after he seized control, and as far as anyone knows, it never left."

Ellayne and Armannii exchanged looks as she ran her thumb along her necklace. *Peachy.* Ellayne groaned inwardly. *How am I supposed to get it now?* One look at Armannii's face told Ellayne he was feeling the same wave of defeat. His eyebrows furrowed, his shoulders slumped, and he rubbed the back of his neck.

"You're sure that's where it is?" he asked, his voice low.

"We are sure. Yes." Elowen nodded. "The book of prophecy you seek is hidden somewhere in the castle. I do not know specifically where he keeps it, but I have heard that he has the genie read a specific passage every day."

"How do you know all this?" Ellayne asked. "I can't imagine my brother is broadcasting this information publicly."

"I have friends in many places, Your Majesty. Including the castle of Cyanthia."

"You have friends there?" Armannii raised an eyebrow. "As in friends who could help us get in?"

"For their safety, I must decline. There is nothing but trials and death if they reveal themselves as traitors to the current king."

They will face those anyway, Ellayne argued in her mind. But she kept her mouth closed and nodded. "Thank you for this important information, Elowen," Ellayne said before Armannii could pressure her into helping.

He cleared his throat. "Yes, thank you. And thank your brothers and sisters as well. We greatly appreciate your aid."

"Of course." Elowen rose to her feet. "Now, if you'll please excuse me, I am dying to get back to the shade of the Black Forest."

"Travel safely."

A few hours later, Armannii and Ellayne sat in the common room of the house. With both Dayla and Kade gone, the emptiness was nearly overwhelming. She leaned back in her chair, closing her eyes as she waited for Armannii to respond to her question about entering through the secret passageways.

"I don't think so," he said, rubbing his finger and thumb along his chin. "He's going to be on higher alert since the last time I snuck in. All of the passageways, especially the one from the stables, are going to be riddled with royal guards."

"Then what do you suggest? Because you've shot down everything I've said."

"Well—"

"And we need to get this book fast. The longer we wait, the more time we give him to attack first. And I can't very well protect my people without my magic. Magic trumps sword."

"I know that, and I agree. We need to do this fast. But if we go in and get caught, we lose everything. Your people need you. We should send someone else in your place so—"

"Absolutely not. Sending people to the Coves is one thing, but even then, I was sending someone who was from there. Dayla knows the Coves; I know the castle. I can't send someone in who doesn't know where every closet is or how to gauge the distance of the guards patrolling using only their footsteps. Sending someone in, especially now, would mean death. You heard what Kade said about those two Dark Soldiers. I doubt Blanndynne or my brother are going to give any mercy to a couple of spies."

"I see your point." Armannii sighed. "But if the two of us are going in, it makes things more complicated. Your brother may not have eyes, but I doubt there's a single royal guard who doesn't know what you and I look like. They've had our faces plastered on posters for weeks now. Hired an expert portrait painter to do it. Although, I gotta say, I'm definitely more handsome in person."

"Focus, Armannii." Ellayne rolled her eyes. "Maybe we could wear disguises. I could dress up like a maid or something, and you—"

"That's great and all, but that doesn't change your face. They'd arrest the both of us before we even made it halfway past the first shop in Cyanthia."

"Well, you're the expert in runes. Shouldn't there be one that can alter our appearances?"

Armannii paused, and both his eyebrows rose. "I can't be too sure, but I could look into it. There's a shop nearby that has some books on runes. I vaguely remember a rune that alters the appearance of the person it is inscribed on, but the details are fuzzy, and you don't want to draw a direct rune on your skin if you can't remember every single curve and dot. That's a mistake I will *never* make again." He shuddered. "Couldn't speak for a week," he muttered under his breath.

"And that must've been a relief to all your friends," Ellayne said in a teasing voice.

He sneered at her, then stood up, tapping the table with two fingers. "I'll be back in an hour, hopefully with a rune that can help. And if I'm not, assume some royal guard saw my beautiful face and brought me straight to your brother."

"Yeah, let's hope not."

An hour later, Armannii found Ellayne as she was addressing a few of the lookouts to the north. They had come to report a sighting of royal guards, which left Ellayne struggling to keep the look of fear out of her eyes. That was *not* something she wanted these people to see.

"Have the soldier in charge up there double the number of patrols," Ellayne said, resisting the urge to reach for her medallion. "If anything else happens, come straight back to report."

"Of course, Your Majesty," one of the two men said. He couldn't have been more than sixteen, and his companion wasn't much older.

Ellayne nodded to them when they left at the same time Armannii entered. He saluted them, and when they saluted back, she realized they must've been Dark Soldiers who had abandoned their positions to join her. Armannii and Matt had pointed out quite a few soldiers in similar situations, but most of them had been assigned to lookout posts around Bolee and the Glass Fields, meaning she didn't get to know them as much.

"Good news I hope," Armannii said as he joined her at the table. "Because I certainly have good news."

"Then maybe you should go first because that was definitely not good news."

"I prefer bad news first, so you start." He put his feet up on the table, leaning back to look at her.

Ellayne leaned back in her chair too, allowing herself to slouch for the first time in a while. "It was confirmation that Diomedes went to the north for aid. They spotted royal guards passing into the Albanistic Desert."

"Well, it's not great news, but it's not really a shock either. We were already guessing he was doing that. Now we know for sure."

"I just hope it doesn't cause any problems for Dayla and Matt. They're up north too; farther west, sure, but still. The royal guards and the mercenaries in the north could definitely be a source of danger for them if they're caught."

"It's best not to worry about things you can't control," Armannii said, running a hand through his hair. "Besides, I think you should focus on where you want to search for the prophecy book when we get into the castle."

"So you found a rune that could work?" Ellayne took a deep breath, shifting her focus from the danger she had possibly placed her friends in to the dangers that were now staring her down.

"Of course I did. Was there ever any doubt? And I found another rune" —he pulled a piece of parchment out of his pocket— "that will copy everything on the page it is laid on. That way we don't have to figure out how to lug an enormous tome out of the castle because that would definitely be conspicuous."

Ellayne eyed the parchment, nodding in approval. "Great job. Now we just need to figure out where to find the book and how to figure out what prophecy is even about my brother."

"You love ruining my good moods, don't you, Queenie?" Armannii chuckled as he put the parchment back in his vest pocket. "But lucky for you, I came with even better news. I ran into Linetta, literally. She's okay but was definitely a bit startled. Anyway," Armannii said with a grin, "I mentioned the seer's book, and she rattled off a couple of interesting tidbits of information. You know, I think she was probably lonely in that bookstore with all that knowledge and no one to share it with. Ever since you introduced us, she has tried to talk my lovely pointed ears off about something or other."

"Armannii, the book?" Ellayne raised an eyebrow, trying to get her friend back on topic.

"Right. Well, she said that the quickest way to find the exact page you're looking for is to spill your blood on it. You're related to Dio, whose prophecy you're looking for, so it should, in theory, open to the correct page by itself with a little bloody motivation. Just like most magic, it responds to blood."

"So you want me to cut myself and, what, bleed on the cover?" Ellayne scoffed at him. "You really think it'll open to the right page if I do that? That seems a bit risky, doesn't it?"

Armannii bobbed his head. "I think we're about due for some good luck, like a book magically opening to the prophecy about your brother. Don't you think?"

Ellayne bit her lip. "What if we get caught?"

"Could you *be* any more pessimistic?"

"Best not to ask that question. What?" Ellayne held out her hands in defense. "I'm just trying to find all the holes in this plan before we start it so that we don't end up in the castle with nowhere to run and a powerful royal couple trying to kill us."

"All right. Well, we'll find the fastest escape route and get out, or we'll go down swinging." He took a deep breath. "What do you think?"

"I think we better get ready because we've got one shot at this, and I don't want to mess it up."

Chapter Nine

he last time Ellayne had seen the castle, she had been escaping with her curse broken and her identity restored for the first time in five years. Her thoughts were filled with memories of that night as she stared at the silhouette of the Cyanthian castle on the horizon. The towers stood out like needles in front of the three moons setting on the horizon.

"The servants and guards who don't live in the castle will be arriving soon," Armannii said beside her. His silver eyes reflected the low light when he turned to look at her. "We should do the runes now because running this close to town might get us caught."

"Right." Ellayne held out her wrist, watching Armannii pull his rune pen out of his vest. "It's not going to hurt, right?"

He let out a low laugh. "No, this isn't like the healing rune. It may feel itchy, and you may get a bit light-headed, but that will fade away. You'll know the rune is fading when you feel unbalanced and disoriented."

"Lovely," she said, watching him copy a rune from a piece of paper in his other hand.

"I also want you to put this on, but only after the rune takes effect." He handed her a metal cuff meant to dampen magic, which she recognized from the Dark.

"Why? My magic isn't showing," Ellayne said.

"If we run into your brother, he will most likely be able to sense your magic, no matter if it's dormant. Better not to risk it, even with a different identity."

"Won't the cuff counter the rune?"

"If you put it on too early, yes. You'd be stuck somewhere between how you normally look and the new face the rune is giving you. But if you wait, and the rune is drawn correctly, which it is, then you'll be fine. I'm *very* good at drawing runes."

"Your humility is showing."

Armannii snorted. "You should know, though, that there's a good chance the rune won't last as long as normal because of the magic-dampening cuff. You need to be ready for it to fade and for you to go back to your charming little self at a moment's notice."

"So I could be standing in front of my brother and switch back without any warning?" Her voice rose a bit as she tried not to picture the terror of that potential situation.

He shrugged. "In theory."

He wasn't lying about the rune being itchy. In fact, he'd completely undersold it. From the moment he completed the symbol on her arm, Ellayne wanted to scratch it, wanted to peel the skin off her arm. And as the seconds ticked by, it only got worse. She leaned against the nearest tree as the blood drained out of her face. "Why are runes so uncomfortable?"

"Is it really that unpleasant?" Armannii paused in the middle of drawing his. "The rune book I found it in said it shouldn't be too bad—just a minor annoyance."

"Why don't you finish yours and tell me if this is minor." She squeezed her eyes shut, hoping the world would stop spinning if she did. Closing her eyes helped a little, but she still used the tree to hold herself up.

"I mean," he said, causing her to open one eye, "it's not comfortable, so to speak, but it's not as terrible as you're making it seem. Oh—" He paused when Ellayne spun around and vomited behind the tree. "I guess it is that bad for you."

"You think?" She grimaced as she wiped her mouth with the back of her hand. "Why isn't it affecting you like this?"

"I don't—oh, I know." He handed her a handkerchief. "It's because your magic is dormant. And—"

"And you can't draw runes on people with no magic," Ellayne finished, squinting at him as she righted herself. "You couldn't have thought of that before you put the rune on me?"

"It never crossed my mind." The man in front of her shrugged, but the more she stared, the less he looked like Armannii. At least, not until she focused really hard on his eyes. His normal chestnut hair grew long and became white blond. It fluttered over his eyes, nearly blocking them from sight. But that wasn't the only thing different about him. His jaw, which used to be a harsh line covered in stubble, softened and rounded out, completely changing the shape of his face. His nose shrank, making his mouth appear bigger. *Or maybe it is bigger*, Ellayne thought, lost in the distraction of the appearance-changing rune. He was also shorter by a few inches. *Either that,* she thought, *or I've grown.*

"This is amazing," Ellayne said, looking down at her hands to find that the rune elongated her short fingers, as well as the rest of her limbs. Her hair, once long and blond, was now shoulder length, frizzy, and quite red. "But why are your eyes still silver? It's kind of a giveaway if they shift to gold when we have to lie to get in."

"Elf eyes reveal truth no matter what. My eyes aren't going to change because of some old rune, especially one that is creating a façade for us to hide behind." He shrugged, still grinning. "But at least the bangs will help hide it. Come on, we should go," Armannii said. Even his voice changed, rising several pitches. "We need to get there when the others do. It'll give us more of a chance to fit in."

"And you have the sheet of parchment with the mind-wiping rune, right? Just in case?"

"Best contingency plan we have." Armannii patted his pocket. While his clothes now appeared baggy and too large, her tunic no longer reached her knees and barely covered her behind. Even her trousers felt tight. She was thankful for the cloak even though it too hung several inches above the ground now.

"I've never been in the streets this early in the morning. It's quite bare," Ellayne whispered as they made their way along the streets of Cyanthia. The stalls were closed, not yet open for the day even though the horizon was lightening with the approach of the sun.

"I heard people went into hiding after the attack on Pingbi. No one wants to get on the bad side of a king with dark magic," Armannii replied.

Even after the conversation with Linetta, Ellayne still cringed at the mention of the destroyed town. No matter how many times she reassured herself that there was no way of knowing her brother was going to strike—no matter how many times she repeated that she was doing all she could for the remaining villagers, no matter how many times she had caught herself before she heaped a pile of blame on her own shoulders—she couldn't move on. The stain, the scar, the guilt was still there, hanging like a dark cloud over her shoulder. Her first big failure as queen, branded on her country for everyone to see. She shivered.

Ellayne felt eyes on her, but with all of the closed shutters, she wasn't sure where it came from. It sent goose bumps trailing along her skin, and she rubbed her arm as she kept pace with Armannii.

"We're almost there," Ellayne said, nodding toward the large wall surrounding the castle. "We'll need to go—"

"Around the back," Armannii said. "I know. Servant gate it is. Let's hope it has less security," he muttered, gesturing toward the eight royal guards positioned in front of the main gate.

"Yeah," Ellayne agreed. "Let's hope."

They made their way around the wall of the castle, keeping their heads down whenever they passed anyone. That worked until they came across the two guards at the back of the castle.

"You two," one of the guards barked. "Remove your hoods and identify yourselves."

The first guard was taller and rounder than the other. The shorter one was older by at least twenty years, his hair gray near his temples.

"Let me talk," Ellayne mumbled to Armannii. "My name is Elowen Beam, and this is my—"

"Let him introduce himself," the other guard ordered, cutting Ellayne off. "He's got a tongue, doesn't he?"

"I'm Mika," Armannii grunted. "Mika Jace."

"What is your business here?" the first guard asked, glancing between the two of them.

Ellayne resisted the urge to look at Armannii and check his eyes. They had to be gold, but hopefully the guards didn't notice because of the long bangs covering them.

"We work here," Ellayne said. "I'm a maid, and Mika works in the kitchen with Trina." Ellayne started to question whether the head chef she remembered still resided in the castle. Her brother could've removed Trina, in which case Ellayne had just given them away. Anxiety crept along the back of her neck, and she forced herself to stop before the emotions associated with the thoughts spilled onto her face. Her heart pounded inside her ribcage, but she offered a pleasant smile on the outside.

She glanced at Armannii and was surprised to see how rigid his jawline was as he watched the two men. When she turned her attention back to the guards, she tried to figure out what was making Armannii so tense. They weren't hostile, at least not at the moment. In fact, besides the sharpness in their voices, their eyes were relaxed, maybe even a bit too calm. Like they were looking at her and Armannii, but not really.

"All right," the second guard finally said. "Go in."

"Thank you," Ellayne said, not hesitating to follow Armannii through the gate.

As soon as they were out of listening distance, Armannii answered Ellayne's question before she could even put it into words.

"They were bewitched," he muttered. "And I'd bet you my bow it's Blanndynne. She's really good at it. I've seen her do it before. But usually it isn't this obvious."

"What do you mean?"

"If someone is bewitched well, you normally wouldn't know. Their eyes were glazed over like they weren't in full control of their own minds. That's a sign of a few things; either the enchantment is weak, fading, or the bewitched person is fighting against the hold of the spell. People with very strong wills are often the hardest to control, and their eyes will almost always be a little cloudy. So those guards were either fighting tooth and nail against the enchantment, or the spell is fading and whoever placed it needs to refresh it before they get out of it."

"How many of them do you think are like this?"

"Knowing your brother and Blanndynne, I'd guess most of the royal guard. Diomedes killed the council members who didn't agree with him, but he wouldn't have wanted to waste so much time destroying the royal guard and searching for loyal replacements. He probably had Blanndynne put them all under an enchantment to shift their loyalties over to him."

"That's awful."

"And it means that even if you grew up here, it's doubtful you'll find any sympathizers to stand with you if worse comes to worst."

"Well then," Ellayne said, sighing, "let's make this quick."

"Are you sure it's going to be in the office?" Armannii asked when she came out of the servants' quarters wearing the appropriate garb: a gray dress that went down to her ankles, a full-body apron, and a strip of cloth that covered her frizzy hair. She left pieces of hair out around her face, hoping that the bright color would deter anyone from second-guessing who she was.

"I'm pretty sure," Ellayne responded, stuffing her cloak and tunic into the bag Armannii held open. She had left her pants on underneath the dress, not bothering to take them off since they were short on time.

"We may only have one shot at this," Armannii said, handing her the piece of parchment enchanted with a rune to replicate any page of a book on which it was placed. She put it in her apron pocket.

"I know. I think the office is the most likely place, but if he's having Blanndynne look at it every day, the other place it may be is the throne room."

"That's riskier on all accounts."

"Right." Ellayne nodded. "Which is why I'd prefer we check the office first."

"I think the first thing we need to do is figure out what part of the castle he's in. Then we know where to avoid."

"Shouldn't he be in his chambers? It's still really early and—"

"When he got his powers, he stopped sleeping, at least from what I could tell. I bet he's already up." Armannii and Ellayne entered one of the main corridors.

Noticing another maid, Ellayne nodded to her, keeping her gaze low. *Please don't stop us, please don't stop us,* Ellayne pleaded in her head.

"Hello," the young woman said, and Ellayne forced a smile. The woman's eyebrows furrowed as she looked between the two of them. "Are you new?"

"Is it that obvious?" Armannii asked, plastering a grin on his face. The woman turned her attention away from Ellayne and placed it on the elf instead. "I've never been here before. Lovely place, really. My friend here is supposed to relay a message to the king. Do you know where she can find him and where I can find the kitchen?"

Ellayne silently thanked the disguise rune once again for giving Armannii long bangs. His lie hadn't tipped the woman off when his eyes changed color. And even though Ellayne knew Armannii was only trying to get the woman to go away and give them time to search, it still felt like he was serving her up to her brother when he mentioned that she was searching for him.

The woman narrowed her eyes even more. "What kind of message are you passing on?"

"It's supposed to be for the king's ears only, I'm afraid," Ellayne said.

"How did you come across this message?"

"My brother." *Technically not a lie.* "He wanted to update the king, but his messenger, well—" She stumbled, but Armannii was there to help her.

"The messenger wasn't in good shape," he said. "We live in opposite buildings in town, and I saw the guy collapse on her front doorstep early this morning. Came to see what kind of delicious reward I could get for my help."

The maid eyed both of them, but after taking a deep breath, she nodded down the hall. "His Majesty is in the throne room. I can take you to the kitchen for your 'delicious reward,' " she said to Armannii. "I was heading there to prepare the king's breakfast."

"Well—" Ellayne started, but Armannii cut her off.

"That would be wonderful," he said, grinning. "I hear the head chef makes the best apple pastries. Is that true?" Armannii asked, following the maid down the hallway they had just come from.

Being left alone in the corridor, Ellayne began to panic. How could he just leave her? What was he doing? Ellayne reached up for her necklace but remembered that she had left it back in the house in the Glass Fields. Instead, she twisted the bracelet around her wrist over and over again. If Dio was in the throne room, then the office was clear for her to search. With a deep breath, Ellayne continued in the direction she and Armannii had been going when the woman stopped her. *With any luck, I'll get the book, get the elf, and get one of Trina's pastries before I leave.* She snorted. *I can't believe I'm thinking about pastries right now.*

Ellayne followed the hallways, remembering each turn from her childhood. It had been over five years since she had lived in the castle, but the map of it still existed in her mind. Kade had been trying to map the castle, and Ellayne remembered correcting him. Her mind wandered to him and whether he was safe or not. He had been gone two—almost three—days longer than he said he would be. Trapped in a wave of worry for her friend, she didn't look up in time to see the person standing at the end of the hall.

"What are you doing in here?" The false queen of Phildeterre, Blanndynne, stood at the end of the hallway, right next to the door to the king's office.

Chapter Ten

 ello," Ellayne said, and remembering who she was speaking to, she curtsied. "Your Majesty." *Of all the people I could run into.* Ellayne kept her sight on the floor, not daring to make eye contact with the genie.

"I asked you a question," Blanndynne said, and out of her peripheral vision, Ellayne could see her turn her nose up.

"I was told to come fetch some linens from the closet up here," Ellayne responded, still keeping her eyes fixed on the floor. "The head maid said the linens in the closet downstairs are all with the laundry."

Blanndynne glared at her. "Oh really? Is that so?"

"Yes, Your Majesty." Ellayne dipped lower in her curtsy. She forced every muscle in her face to smile at the woman who did not deserve to wear one of her mother's crowns. Ellayne thought of the way her maids responded to her when she was living in the castle. Short answers. That was the key.

The queens stared at each other, Ellayne finally making eye contact. Blanndynne's eyes narrowed, her eyebrows creasing in the middle.

"Do I know you from somewhere?"

"I've been in the corridors, Your Majesty. Perhaps—"

"Quiet." Blanndynne waved her hand. "I didn't ask for your excuses. Besides, if you're dawdling while looking for the linen closet, you may as well remake all of the beds on this floor. Strip the sheets and take them to the laundry. Then clean the windows because a few birds met an unfortunate end. I also need you to scrub the floor in my bathing room because I dropped a pot of perfume in there. Oh, and on that matter, I need a new jar of perfume."

"Of course, Your Majesty. I—"

"I wasn't finished," Blanndynne snapped, her beady eyes bearing down on Ellayne. "When you finish with that, the eastern hall needs sweeping on the third floor, the ashes need to be cleaned out of the guest rooms in the north wing as well as the south wing, and one of my husband's guests spilled a glass of wine over my favorite settee. Remove the stain on the rug as well."

A pair of patrolling guards stared at Ellayne as they passed, saluting the queen, who barely waved them on. Ellayne made note of where they went. If Diomedes kept the guard rotation the same, they wouldn't be back for at least ten minutes.

Ellayne didn't respond verbally but instead dipped into another curtsy. She kept her head down, hoping for any kind of distraction shy of Armannii or herself getting caught. It appeared Blanndynne had not changed from the time she watched Ellayne during the curse. There was still a mile-long list of chores she was ready to hand out, only now it seemed she had more victims to force into labor.

"Well? What are you waiting for? An invitation? Get started. Oh, Kiegan my dear."

Not only did Ellayne's ears perk up at the mention of her old friend, the man himself showed up, coming around the corner dressed in royal guard garb.

"I thought I heard your voice," he said, kissing Blanndynne's hand and bowing. "I came to fetch you. King Diomedes requires you in the throne room right away."

"Of course." Blanndynne fluttered her eyes at him, but just as quickly, she turned her icy glare to Ellayne. "Are you going to be so insolent as to not give Marshal Greene the honor he so deserves?"

Kiegan lifted his chin as he looked down at Ellayne. It became very difficult to swallow as she curtsied again. He looked so much more regal than he had the last time she'd seen him. It was hard to compare the man in front of her to the one who had found a way to smile at every opportunity when they first met. There was no smile on his face now, and she doubted there had been one for a while.

"My deepest apologies, sir." Ellayne tried to keep her voice as pleasant as possible, but that proved to be a difficult task when all she heard in her head was the hurt in Kade's voice as he told her about the two Dark Soldiers Blanndynne had killed. *Danced until their feet were disfigured and bloody.* It made Ellayne want to shiver, but she tightened every muscle to keep from reacting. Ellayne lowered her chin, trying to humble herself as much as possible before the two of them.

"I assume you've got a number of things to see to," Kiegan said, his words clipped. "I suggest you begin. Neither the king, queen, nor I tolerate anything less than hard work. Understood?" He waited for her to nod before adjusting his gaze to Blanndynne. "The king is waiting for us, my lady," Kiegan said, nodding toward the hallway he'd emerged from. He glanced at Ellayne, but only for a second. In that moment, Ellayne's eyes caught a glimpse of something that made her stomach tighten. His eyes had been unfocused, almost a little cloudy.

Could it be . . . ?

Ellayne struggled to keep her face neutral until both Blanndynne and Kiegan had turned their backs. They left without another word to her, making small talk as they went.

With another check down each corridor, Ellayne entered the king's office, closing the door behind her.

The banned books on magic no longer hid behind the map on the wall, where they'd been stored during her father's reign as king of Phildeterre. Instead, Dio left them on display in a bookcase near the desk. However, besides a few items on the desk, including what looked to be an ancient knife, and a large painting of a dragon— her brother's favorite mythical creature—hanging on the wall, everything was eerily similar to the way the office had looked when it had belonged to her father. Ellayne refrained from touching anything. In the back of her mind, she knew there was a small chance that he had placed a spell on the room to keep people from stealing. It was best to only touch the book when she found it.

Standing in front of her father's old desk, Ellayne fought back memory after memory of sneaking into the room with her brother and of all the times the two of them were called back into the office when their father returned. One particular memory stood out as she stared at the map on the wall.

"Tell them that I will get back to them in the morning," her father had said to a servant when they walked in, escorted by the royal guards who'd caught them. The servant bowed before leaving the room.

Ellayne had been about nine years old, and her brother was nineteen. It was only a few years before he met Armannii. The map had looked bigger back then, an entire world she had yet to explore. She kept her eyes locked on the map, not daring to make eye contact with her father. Ellayne knew his look of disappointment.

"Do you know why I had you brought here?" her father asked, taking off his reading glasses and rubbing the bridge of his nose.

"Someone snitched on us," Diomedes said.

"Now why would someone snitch on you, and for doing what?"

It was a very good parenting technique, getting his children to confess to something before even telling them what they were in trouble for.

"We have one of the books from in here," her brother admitted, pulling it out from behind his back.

"And why did you take it?" King Butch asked, taking the book and placing it on his desk.

"Because."

"Because why?"

"Because you won't let us read it otherwise," Ellayne said before her brother could answer. She remembered the look on her father's face, his eyebrows raised and his mouth partially open. Of course, he evened out his features within a second.

Her father clasped his hands under his chin. "Do you know why?"

Ellayne shook her head back and forth, blond curls falling in front of her face. "No."

"It's for your protection," he said, and then he made eye contact with Diomedes. "Both of your protection."

Diomedes stiffened next to her, and Ellayne stared up at her brother, wondering why he appeared so angry.

"Son, as consequence for your actions, you will work with the new guards, training them in combat." Ellayne's father turned his attention to her. "Laynie, you will spend your free hours helping the maids with the sewing."

"But—"

"You are dismissed." He rubbed his head again. "Both of you."

Ellayne blinked a few times, wishing more than anything that her father was sitting across from her at the desk, even if it was to discipline her. Since the fire in the Black Forest, she hadn't had time to return to her father's grave—to talk to him about everything on her mind—and the weight of missing him left her sighing.

Footsteps in the hall made her jump, and she moved behind the door. Biting her lip, she waited for them to walk in, for it to be her brother, and for it all to be over. But the footsteps kept going past the door.

Breathing out a sigh, she refocused her attention on finding the prophecy book. *If I were an enormous book of prophecies, where would I be?* She moved around the room, tilting her head from side to side to evaluate the possible spots it could be hiding. After searching the obvious places where it could be seen without moving something, and finding it in none of those places, Ellayne sorted out which locations would be the most viable to hide the book. She made a list in her head, knowing there was a chance that once she started touching things, some sort of warning would be magically sent to her brother.

She resolved to check the desk first. The top drawer was the only one she opened because it was the only drawer big enough to compensate for the sizable book. Ellayne moved as fast as she could, pulling the drawer open, scanning it, and finding nothing but parchment and writing supplies. The cupboard behind the door where her father used to keep his maps was next. When she opened it, it appeared her brother hadn't bothered to change what was being kept there. *If not those places, the only other option in this room is . . .*

"Yes," she breathed, pulling back the map to find the prophecy book hidden in the secret compartment in the wall. But as she reached for it, a wave of nausea fell over her, and she stumbled backward. Concerned she'd set off an alert, she fought against the swirling in her head and grabbed the book.

It was just as heavy as she suspected, and with the continuous waves of disorientation, she tripped and fell with the book in her arms. Landing on her wrist, she let out a cry before biting her tongue. *Stay quiet,* she ordered herself. *Don't make more noise than necessary.*

Her arm felt irritated, and though she wondered at first if it was from something covering the book, she realized what was happening when she saw her reflection in a glass vase. She squinted her eyes, trying not to throw up all over the office. The red hair was fading, straightening out, and growing. She could feel the clothes getting bigger as she tripped on the hem of the dress.

Remembering the rune-enchanted parchment in her apron, she favored her injured wrist as she heaved the book onto the desk, no longer worrying about making a mess. Frustration filled her when she realized she hadn't thought to bring a knife even though Armannii had mentioned that she would need her blood to get to the correct prophecy. Her spinning gaze landed on the decorative knife near where she had placed the book, and she pulled it out of the gem-covered sheath. Why her brother had decorations in his office when he had no sight to enjoy them with was a mystery to her, yet one she was thankful for as she did a hatchet job of cutting her arm open. Drops of her dark blood spilled onto the cover, and for a second Ellayne held the knife back, thinking it hadn't worked.

However, a second later the cover slammed open by itself. The entire desk vibrated from the book, and Ellayne stumbled back, dropping the knife. The air in the room was still, yet the pages flipped as though a wind blew them. Words blurred together as they flew by on the yellowed parchment, though she wasn't sure if they were blurred because of the speed the pages were turning or because of the rune making her sick as it revealed her true identity.

The pages stopped moving, landing flat. Ellayne hesitated before she took a step forward. There was no way to tell if the prophecy was the right one, if the blood had even worked. And what was worse, she couldn't check even if she wanted to because the words wobbled on the page when she attempted to read the prophecy because of the irritating rune on her wrist.

Knowing there wasn't much time before she was found out, she pulled the parchment out of her apron and laid it flat on the page with the words. She checked to make sure the parchment had copied the book with a quick glance. Once she saw an exact replica on the paper, she tucked it back into her apron. Her head spun worse than before, and Ellayne tripped as she teetered toward the door.

Have to find Armannii, she thought as she stumbled out of the office. No one was out there, but she could hear footsteps. Unfortunately, due to her reversion back to herself and the aversion to the rune, she couldn't tell what direction they were coming from. *I need somewhere to hide.* She dragged her arm along the wall to stay upright, begging the coolness of the stone bricks to revive her faster. The footsteps were getting louder, and with the confusion the rune created, it sounded like they were all around her. She held her breath as someone came around the corner.

"Queenie," Armannii whispered as he approached her. His hair was still blond, his disguise in full swing still. He caught her with one arm and supported her, using the other arm to pop something into his mouth. "Did you find it?" he asked, his voice muffled from something smelling vaguely familiar.

Chapter Eleven

hat's wrong with her?" one of the guards asked, watching Ellayne with a pinched expression as her nausea increased.

"She's dealing with a stomach bug."

"You're lying," the guard said as he pointed a finger at Armannii. "I can see it in your eyes."

"Really?" Armannii grinned. "How so?"

"They changed to gold," said a female guard. "Which means you're an elf."

"I'm flattered you find me so handsome as to stare into my eyes, but is now really the time?" He readjusted his grasp on Ellayne.

"I just meant, well—"

"Shut up," the guard in front ordered the female guard, who nodded her head to the point where Ellayne thought it might fall off. "You two are under arrest for trespassing in the—"

"In my pocket," she said,
apple pastry?"

He grinned. "I got you o
first," he said, rubbing a few cru
clean-shaven, unlike his normal sel
survive." Armannii pushed his bangs
about how obnoxious the long hair was.

"Do they know we're here?"

"Oh, we know," said an unfamiliar voice so
Ellayne.

Armannii turned, and Ellayne turned with him to fi
ten guards blocking the hallway.

"Well, this could be an issue," Armannii said, breathing o

"Yes." Ellayne nodded even though it made her head hurt more. "Yes it could be."

The guard stopped talking, and many of them backed up when, for the second time that day, Ellayne threw up.

"Well done, Queenie." Armannii chuckled as he pulled her back down a different hallway. The guards pursued them, but when the one in the lead slipped in the puddle, it caused a domino effect behind them.

"It was my plan all along." Ellayne rolled her eyes but regretted it when the hallway spun in front of her. "How do we get out? The passages are all—"

"Can you stand by yourself?" he asked, coming to a stop in front of a window.

"Maybe."

"It'll only be for a second." Armannii peered out the window, nodded, and pulled out his rune pen. "Give me the paper with the prophecy," he said, holding out his hand.

Ellayne did as he said, wiping her mouth off with the back of her hand after she handed him the parchment.

Armannii traced a quick rune on the paper and handed it back to her. "Put it in your pocket again, then step back." He put his rune pen away and ran to the other side of the hallway. A small pedestal with a vase on it sat against the wall. There were others like it spaced down the corridor. Armannii lifted the pedestal, grunting as the vase slid off and shattered.

Though Ellayne knew from experience that the pedestals were heavy, Armannii lifted it above his head with little effort. He slammed it against the glass in the window. A crack appeared.

"What are you doing?"

"You wanted a way out, so I'm making one," he said, bringing it down for a second time. The spiderwebbing spread, and with a third hit, the glass shattered. He used the pedestal to break off the jagged edges.

"But we're on the second floor, you've got to be insane to—"

"Aim for the pond," Armannii said as he yanked her to the window. "And if you miss, bend your knees and roll."

"Armannii, I—"

Her sentence ended in a scream as he pushed her out the window. The sky and the water below her blurred together, and she didn't have time to close her mouth before she hit the water.

The impact burned the parts of her that hit, and she sucked in a lungful of algae-filled water before reappearing at the surface. With another splash, Armannii popped out beside her. The green bacteria from the water clung to his white blond hair.

Her boot got stuck in the mud as she waded toward the side. "A warning that you were planning to throw me out of a second-story window would've been nice, you know," she sputtered, squeezing her hair out as he traced speed runes on both of their shoes.

"I figured 'aim for the pond' was a heads-up. And if I had given you a full warning, then I wouldn't have had the chance to hear you scream bloody murder on the way down." He grinned up at her. "Besides, we made it out."

"But what about the prophecy? The parchment is probably ruined now because of—" She stopped talking when she reached into the soaking-wet apron and pulled out the parchment. It was completely dry and undamaged.

"And you doubted me," Armannii said, a smug smile still plastered on his face.

"What about my incentive?" Ellayne asked, putting the prophecy back in the apron.

"It was either the pastry or the prophecy." He shrugged, standing up. "Sorry," he said, pulling the mushed, soggy pastry out of his pocket. "But on the plus side, we just need to clear the gate, which I recommend we do now."

He zipped off toward the servants' gate in a blur. Emptying her stomach and the surprise swim helped clear away the rest of the disorientation from the rune, and judging by the effects of the last rune drawn directly on her skin, she was thankful the speed rune was drawn on her boot instead. *No one needs me running faster than the eye can see when I can't see myself.*

Catching up with Armannii in a matter of seconds, they ran through the gate just as someone gave the orders to close it.

"Not bad, Queenie. Not bad." Armannii chuckled just as his hair started to get shorter. "You make a pretty good thief."

"Your Majesty," the lookout said when they reached the town in the Glass Fields. "What happened to you?"

Ellayne glanced at Armannii. "You couldn't have given me a warning that my appearance would cause concern?"

"When you show up, there's always cause for concern," Armannii joked, nodding to the man with horns growing out of his head. "She's fine, just needs to wash up."

The man watched Ellayne carefully, but she smiled and nodded.

"I'm fine," she reassured him. "Glad to be back. Did I miss any important reports?"

"No, my lady. But your friend Kade wanted me to tell you to go straight back to your house," the man said.

Ellayne's eyes widened. "He told you that himself? As in he's here? In the town?"

As soon as the lookout nodded, Ellayne raced toward the house, and with the speed rune still on her shoes, she reached it in a matter of seconds.

"Kade?" she called out as she entered, turning her head from side to side to catch a glimpse of him.

"Ellayne?" His voice came from the bedroom, and a second later he walked out.

Unable to control herself, she ran to him—at full rune speed. She crashed into him, causing his arms to wrap around her, and they hit the floor with a thud. She had a bit more of a cushion, landing on top of him, but they both groaned. Ellayne leaned her head against his chest, listening to his pounding heart. Kade rubbed the back of his head with one hand, steadying her with his other.

"I suppose I'll come back later," Armannii said, and when Ellayne glanced back, he was grinning the widest smile she'd ever seen on his face.

"I just—" Ellayne started to say, but he cut her off.

"I'll be back in a few minutes. If you could both be in an upright position when I do get back, that would be great." He turned and sped away.

"I didn't mean to tackle you," she said, sitting back on her heels as he slid out from beneath her. "I have the speed rune on my shoes and—"

"It doesn't matter." His dimple popped out, and for the first time since he'd left, her stomach flipped in a good way. "I'm happy to see you too. But why can't I feel your magic?" He ran his fingers from her shoulder down to her hand. "It normally sends this, well, I guess I could call it a shock, through my body, but I don't feel— oh." He held up her wrist with the magic-dampening cuff. "This would explain it. Is there a reason you're wearing it?" He paused for a second, his nose wrinkling. "And why do you smell like you were swimming in a bog?"

"It's a long story," Ellayne said, taking the cuff off and tossing it behind her toward the table in the common room. It missed and rolled toward the wall. She shrugged. "I'll fill you in on it later, but—"

"Ellayne." His hand was back on hers, and his eyebrows furrowed even more than they already had been. "I still can't feel it." He rubbed small circles into the back of her hand, then flipped it over. Kade traced the lines down Ellayne's palm, sending chills from her wrist all the way down her back. "Why can't I feel your magic?"

"It's—it's gone. Well, dormant, as far as I know." Ellayne sighed, pulling her hand away. She pushed against her thighs and stood up. The speed rune on her shoes had her at the table in the blink of an eye.

Kade followed suit, and they sat down after Ellayne picked up the magic-blocking cuff. She ran her finger around the inside ridge again and again.

"What happened while I was gone?"

Ellayne snorted, putting the bracelet on the table with more force than she had intended. "What happened?" She had no idea where to begin. "Well, for starters, the Black Forest caught on fire, I put it out, and apparently I expended my magic to the point of causing it to go dormant. And then—" Ellayne stopped when Kade's jaw clenched. "What is it?"

"Nothing," he said. "Keep going."

"No." She shook her head. "Tell me what's going on. Why did you just tense up?"

"Just keep going." He looked away from her, and even though she couldn't sense it like she used to, she saw the darkness of his magic flowing down to his hands under the table. "Tell me what I—"

"No." Ellayne crossed her arms and leaned back on the table. "I'm not saying another word until you tell me why you got so upset just now."

"Ellayne, don't—"

"What are you so afraid of me finding out? Because that's what this is, right? Fear? It's fear of something. And you not telling me is driving me insane because I thought . . . But apparently I was wrong." Ellayne stood up, shoving the chair behind her. "If we were friends"—she pointed her finger at him—"you would've told me the truth by now."

"Ellayne, stop," he said, his voice less ferocious than before.

She shook her head, turning around. "I'm done with this, Kade. Do you understand how excited I was to see you? How much I missed you? And then to have you show up with the same ridiculous amount of secrets and lies. I'm not going to put up with it. I'm done. If you don't want to tell me why you've been acting so weird, fine. But I just know that I—"

Kade stood up fast enough that the table scooted away from him. "I started the fire."

"Wh—"

"I started the fire. It's my fault that your magic is dormant."

Chapter Twelve

llayne's heartbeat pulsed so loud she could hear it. "What do you mean you're the reason my magic is dormant? You started the fire?"

"Listen to me." Kade held out his hands, which were entirely black from his magic.

"I'm listening," Ellayne said, crossing her arms over her chest. "But you better tell me everything, or I'm walking out of here right now."

"Can we sit down again and—"

"Kade!"

"Fine." He closed his eyes and took a deep breath. "Like I said, I started the fire in the Black Forest."

"Why?"

"Will you let me explain without interrupting?" he growled, and she narrowed her eyes at him. "I set the fire because . . ." He sighed, and it sounded like all of the air inside of him came out in one breath. "Because my father asked me to."

"What?"

He held up a finger, and Ellayne closed her mouth. "All those times I've disappeared? I've been going to see him. He's been helping me understand how my power works. He's been training me. And he's trusted me with some jobs. It's really the only way he'll let me stay here instead of going back to continue my training in the Dark. And since he's been in Phildeterre—"

"He's here? In Phildeterre? Where? Why didn't you tell me?"

"Because—"

"He should have declared his presence to—"

"To whom?" Kade said, his chin jutting forward. "To your brother, the monster? Or to you? Phildeterre isn't exactly in a position to host royalty at the moment. And I told you what happened to those two Dark Soldiers. But what I didn't mention was that they were with me, helping me, and when the royal guards showed up, they sacrificed themselves so that I wouldn't be caught. They're dead, and I—"

"You should've told me."

"I agree—"

"No, you should've told me. Wait." Ellayne furrowed her eyebrows. "You agree?"

Kade nodded, closing his eyes. "I should've told you after I went to see him the first time, but—" He reached up, rubbing his scarred shoulder.

"But keeping secrets is so much more fun, right?" Her lip sneered, and she ground her teeth until they ached.

"No, but you were safer if—"

"My safety is none of your concern."

Kade's lips tightened into a thin line. "Your safety is my *only* concern."

Ellayne ignored the way her stomach turned, covering it with her arms. "How does setting the Black Forest on fire keep me, or my people for that matter, safe? It sounds a little contradictory, doesn't it?"

"One of the jobs got out of hand."

"Out of hand? Kade, you could've burned down the whole Black Forest! How in the world did you think—"

"Ellayne," he said, his voice a warning once more. "Just wait. Please." His dark eyes softened. "I didn't mean to cause such destruction, but when I tried to rein in my magic, I couldn't. The fire got out of control, and I stopped focusing on managing the flames and instead tried to get people out of there. Then, before I knew it, the fire was out. I didn't know who did it or how, but I was ecstatic. It was a miracle. But now, hearing that . . . that this terrible thing I did, it hurt you." He paused and ran his fingers through his hair multiple times. "I-I just . . . I blame myself for you losing your magic."

She took a deep breath. "Well, this won't come as a surprise, but now I blame you too."

With the speed rune still on her boots, Ellayne left the house before Kade was able to form a single word. She didn't cry as she ran. However, the wind blowing in her eyes still had her blinking back tears.

What's wrong with him? What's wrong with me? Why didn't he feel he could trust me? Ellayne stopped at her father's grave, leaning against the stone. *Why would he turn to his father? What if he had gotten himself killed?* She let the hot air from the noon sun burn down on her, not bothering to search for any shade, not that she'd find any nearby.

"Why do I care so much?" she asked the grave. "On second thought, don't answer that."

"I could answer it for you," Armannii said, causing her to jump where she was. "But I think you'd rather I didn't."

"What are you doing here?" Ellayne said, wrapping her arms around herself.

"I followed you." He squatted down, placing a crystalized flower next to King Butch's grave. "How often does your father answer your questions, might I ask?"

"What do you want, Armannii?"

"I wanted to talk to you."

"About?"

"The kid," he said, standing up and brushing off his hands. "You don't know the whole story."

"What? And you do?"

Armannii nodded. "And you should hear it before you go racing away."

"Then tell me," Ellayne said, planting her feet shoulder distance apart. "Because I'd really like to know why in the world you, of all people, are siding with Kade and the *Dark King*. He wants you dead, remember?"

"Oh, I haven't forgotten. But this isn't for me to tell," he responded, matching her stance and placing his hands on his hips. "It's *his* story." He nodded behind her.

"Ellayne, I wasn't finished." Kade's voice made her spin around. He must've been practicing rune magic and drawn his own speed runes because it hadn't taken him long to catch up despite the distance she had put between them.

Kade's eyebrows were furrowed, and his jaw was clenched, but his eyes weren't angry.

"I don't want to hear—"

"Listen to what he has to say. It's in your best interest." Armannii placed a hand on her shoulder, but she shrugged it off.

"You don't get to tell me what to do," she said, raising her chin.

"My father wants revenge." Kade tucked his hands into his pockets.

Ellayne stopped backing away from the men and planted her feet. She placed her hands on her hips. "What do you mean? Revenge for what?"

"Isn't it obvious?" Kade asked. His magic, which had calmed down during his run over to the grave, returned to his hands. His face darkened as he lowered it, glaring at the ground. "He wants the culprits who persecuted his people to pay. A lot of them are here in Phildeterre. Or at least . . . they used to be."

"You killed them?"

"No, but—" It was a whisper, carried away by the wind of the Glass Fields. Kade's shoulders drooped, and he closed his eyes. "I did what he said to do."

"What?" Ellayne reached up, cradling her elbows in her hands. "What do you mean?"

"He said I could help. That I could make a difference. It's . . . it's hard to explain."

Armannii scoffed as he shook his head. "It's actually the easiest thing to understand at the moment."

"Armannii—" Kade started, but Ellayne cut him off.

"Then you explain it." She popped her hip off to the side. "Because I'm about to leave if you don't."

Kade's magic flared, but he grasped his hands into fists and tucked them behind his back. He stood tall, his posture straight. "Fine. Tell her."

The elf glanced between the two of them, then stuck his hands in his pockets. "The Dark King has the names of people who entered the Dark to cause chaos and hurt his subjects. He wants the list to be crossed off by punishing those who persecuted his people, but the list rarely gets shorter because these kinds of ruffians almost always have friends who react by causing more damage.

By having the kid hunt them down, the Dark King is sending a message that he will not let the crimes they committed go unpunished, that the things they did are terrible enough that he sent his own son to rectify the issue. Not only that, but the king's own presence here gives these people even more of a threat because you know as well as I do that it's been at least a generation or two since a Dark King has stepped foot in Phildeterre."

"That's absolutely ridiculous." Ellayne shook her head. She flicked her gaze between the two of them. When neither of them spoke, she sighed. "Armannii, I'd like a word with Kade . . . alone."

"All right, but first . . ." He bent down and undid the speed rune on Ellayne's boots. "No running away, Ellayne," Armannii said in a whisper only she could hear. Then he ran off in the blink of an eye.

She kept shaking her head as she tried to process what was happening. *How could Kade just go along with it?* Her mind raced as she tried to rid it of the image it painted of Kade as a malicious errand boy for the Dark King. She didn't want to see him that way. More than anything, she just wanted to see him as the prickly cartographer he used to be—as her best friend. But that man, just like his cartography shop, was gone.

Ellayne whirled around and faced Kade straight on. "Sending your son to murder your enemies? That's insane."

Kade's shoulders went rigid. "I told you, I'm not killing them. I told my father I wouldn't."

"Then what? You're setting their houses on fire? And oh, maybe their neighbor's and the entire northeast part of the Black Forest? Kade, how could you? These are *my* people. You're hurting *my* subjects."

"Maybe, but what about my father's people? Are they supposed to just be beaten down with no justice in sight?" Kade lifted his chin. "You're not the only one who's looking out for others, Ellayne. When I stepped into this role, I took on the same amount of responsibility you did, but the difference is I'm not going to sit around and wait for things to get better."

"So what, you're just taking your father's vengeance into your own hands? How is that any better? How is that any better than what my brother did? How is that just?"

"It's more just than letting these criminals walk around like there isn't a serious consequence to their actions. And don't you dare compare me to your brother." Kade clenched his jaw but took a deep breath before continuing. "My father said you'd have an issue with it, which is why he asked me to keep it quiet."

"And you didn't think there was anything wrong with that? Kade, I may not be ruling from a castle, but this is still my country, and there are still rules. If I remember correctly, your father is a stickler for rules. He should know this." Her voice went up another notch.

"He does know, and—"

"And what's more, I'm assuming it's not by chance that he's here in Phildeterre right before things are about to go sideways."

"My father wants your brother off the throne as much, if not more, than you do." Kade crossed his arms over his chest. "Believe me, there is no underlying scheme here."

"If your father wants Dio gone so bad, why hasn't he offered help? That would be the right thing to do. He's got plenty of soldiers, and I'm sure he's got little birdies telling him just how much we need the help. But instead, he's shown up in my country, begun hunting my people, and revealed no indication that he has any intention of helping. Excuse me if I'm offended by his lack of respect."

"Because you treat him with so much respect yourself?" Kade said, scoffing. "He freed your father, and you barely said thank you."

"I'm sorry. I was a little preoccupied with the fact that my father was in front of me for the first time in five years. And how was I supposed to thank the man who seemed to break you?"

"Break me?" Kade's voice got louder.

"Kade, you were sobbing when you learned about your parents. On your knees, bloody and bruised from being beaten into submission by your father. How in the world could I have any respect for a man who did that to my best friend?"

He stepped back, rubbing his chin. It appeared he hadn't shaved since he'd left, and he had the start of a beard coming in. "If I could forgive him and move forward, then you need to as well. If we're going to have any chance at getting back to the friendship we had, I need you to accept not only me but my father too. Ellayne, I haven't asked much of you, but I'm asking you to do this." His voice was softer, and he caught her gaze, locking it with his. "Please," he said, stepping toward her and gathering one of her hands in his. "Please, Ellayne." He held her hand captive, resting it on his chest near where his heart beat wildly.

How could he take control of her mind so easily? With one look—one touch—she wanted to agree, to apologize for everything she'd said. His dark gaze melted her, turned her to a useless puddle.

But she couldn't.

She had to stay strong.

Because this wasn't just about the two of them, as much as she wanted it to be, dreamt it could be.

It was about her country. Her people.

Though her outer appearance remained solid, inside she felt herself crumbling into pieces. She didn't want to do it, but she knew she had to. Ellayne pulled her hand out of Kade's.

"I'm sorry. As much as I want you here by my side, I—" She licked her lips before continuing. "I don't think that's wise anymore. You . . . you need to leave. All of you." *Stay firm,* she told herself. *Don't break.* It took an incredible amount of self-control not to take the words back—to try to make him forget she'd even said it. But it was too late.

"What?" Kade's jaw dropped, but he regained the steel nature on his face. "You can't be serious. Leave where?"

"Go back to the Dark with your father. Don't come back. At least"—her heart squeezed in pain at the look of betrayal on his face—"not until this is over."

"Ellayne." He reached again for her hand, catching it before she could move away. "Don't do this. I told you I was trying to keep you safe—"

"Safe? Kade, hunting down my subjects and hiding it from me has nothing to do with keeping me safe. Whatever this is, it's not about me. If you want to keep me safe, then you'll leave. I have enough to deal with concerning my brother. I don't need more conflict, especially not with the Dark King. What he's doing, what *you're* doing, is absolutely illegal, and if I didn't have my hands full, it would be one of my first concerns. My country is in more danger with you and your father here than it is without."

His cold hand dropped hers, and he took a deep breath, his chest filling and expanding his stance. "I would've thought that of all people, you'd understand. You know how persecuted the people in the Dark are. I thought you, being as loving as you are, might understand. Might sympathize. But I guess I was wrong." He shook his head, sending a dirty look in her direction. "I—" He let out a dark chuckle. "I can't believe I thought we'd see eye to eye on this. But you've only ever seen my father as another enemy." He tilted his head up, closing his eyes. "You should know, Ellayne, that if you treat someone like they're the bad guy long enough, they're going to start to believe it. But I never thought you'd be the one to do that. I thought you were the type of person to try to uncover what's really true. I mean, that's why you won't kill your brother, right? Because you think he might have a shred of decency left? But if I asked you to give my father the same benefit of the doubt, you'd scoff and turn your back. I see that now."

"Kade, I'm not turning my back on you. I—"

"That's *exactly* what you're doing, Ellayne." He jabbed a finger at her. "And the sooner you realize it, the better. You know, I understand why my father didn't want me to say anything. He was right. You couldn't understand even if you wanted to."

The sun bled down on them, basking them in a burning glow that felt like flames. Ellayne bit her cheek. If her magic hadn't been dormant, she would've felt it matching the sun's heat. "I'm sorry, Kade. But this is what's best for my country."

"If this is what you want, Your Majesty, then I guess this is goodbye." His nostrils flared as he shook his head. He bowed mockingly.

"Goodbye, Your Highness." Her voice was completely devoid of any emotion. Ellayne waited until he disappeared on the horizon before slouching.

Chapter Thirteen

hat was harsh, Queenie," Armannii said as he came up beside Ellayne. He kept his eyes in the direction Kade had disappeared. "He didn't want to add more to what you're already dealing with, so he—"

"Enough, Armannii." Her voice was terse, even to her own ears. "You shouldn't even have been listening. And I don't need a lecture. Not from you."

"Are you sure? Because I think you could use a bit of wisdom since you just sent away the man you—"

"I don't understand how the two of you could keep this from me, especially since it concerns my country. *My* people. You two are supposed to be my trusted council! How am I supposed to trust either of you when you've been hiding this?" Ellayne raised an eyebrow, and Armannii shoved his hands in his pockets.

"It wasn't for me to say, Ellayne." Armannii followed her as she made her way back to the town. "And the kid didn't want to hurt you."

"Then he should have been honest from the start instead of sneaking around behind my back and expecting that to be a better option than being up-front with me. And that's a lousy excuse. Neither he nor his father did what was right in this situation."

"You know me. I'm the last person to jump to the Dark King's defense, but I understand where he's coming from in this case. Sure, he's going about it the wrong way, and you have a right to be ticked about it. But Kade was right too." He paused and waited until she looked at him. "Your judgment of the Dark King is biased. And your father and I are fully to blame for some of that. I've struggled for years trying to forgive that man for murdering the woman I love. Years, Ellayne. And every time I got close, I balked. For some reason"—he pushed his hand through his hair and then ran his thumb along his chin—"I got this idea in my head that if I forgave him, it made what he did okay and that it would somehow give him power to hurt me again. But I was wrong. And you know who showed me that? You."

"What?" Ellayne folded her arms across her chest.

"You had absolutely no reason to even give me the benefit of the doubt after what I did. But Ellayne, you forgave me. Really, truly forgave me. And you showed me how relieving that forgiveness is, for you and for me. So I've forgiven him. Not that he needs to know. And you know what? I'm okay. I can sleep through the night without nightmares of Kit dying at his hands, and I don't feel like strangling the nearest person at the mention of the Dark King anymore. The kid's request isn't just for him or his father. If you give the Dark King a fair chance, like you gave me, like . . ." He paused, sighing. "Like you're giving your brother, then you're going to feel the freedom it offers just as much."

"I hear what you're saying, I really do. But it's not that easy. You proved to me that you were worth forgiving. The Dark King may have freed my father, but he doesn't seem to do anything for free. There's always a price with him. My father said so himself."

"And do you think the Dark King somehow proved to me that he was worthy of forgiveness? He was still planning to kill me. Probably would still love to be given the chance." He tilted his head and shielded his eyes from the sun. "Look, Ellayne. I'm saying this to you because I know you're not stupid. You're one of the wisest people I know, and I'm pretty wise myself. If we wait for everyone to prove that they are worthy of forgiveness, that they have rectified themselves, we'll be waiting forever. Forgiveness should be given whether it is asked for or not. I'm not about to stroll up to Kade's father and tell him I forgive him. But in my heart I have, and that's the most important part. You taught me that."

Ellayne didn't know what to say. Her lip trembled, and after the roller coaster of emotions since she had returned with Armannii to Bolee, it was all she could do to keep from bursting into a sobbing mess. "I-I messed up, didn't I?"

"That's your call, but if you want my opinion—"

"I do."

"Yeah. You messed up. But you can make it right. He's not gone yet. If what Kade said is true, they're camping out north of the main portal. It'll take a while for them to get all of the Dark Soldiers organized. You have some time. We can go back into town, take a look at the prophecy to see if it's anything useful, and go from there. Plus, I have a feeling there might be a bit more wisdom you could learn from your aunt. Sound good?"

Ellayne took a deep breath, closing her eyes as she bit her lower lip. "Yeah. Just give me a second to process. I'll meet you at the house."

Back in Bolee, Ellayne read from the parchment, squinting when the elegant curves of the letters swirled together into cursive. At some point during the silent walk back into town, her head had started pounding, and it hadn't stopped. After the first few lines, she picked up on the lyrical nature of the prophecy, and her tone followed suit.

> *A nest with two eggs—divergent, opposed;*
> *An egg breaks open—an infant exposed.*
> *One bird without feathers—jealous and flightless;*
> *Another born colorful—scared of bias.*
> *Steal feathers from others—a price is paid;*
> *How to open the eyes—a life slayed.*
> *No longer bare, but worthy—powerful;*
> *Feathers of one are natural—bountiful.*
> *A crack in the ground—opening wider;*
> *A clash of feathers—one survivor.*

"You've got to be kidding," Ellayne said, crossing her arms over her chest. "It's a poem? I hated poetry when I was being tutored."

"From what little I know about prophecies, they are almost always in poem form," Armannii said, leaning over her to read it again.

"That's just great." Ellayne sighed, sitting down next to the table. The chair creaked beneath her, and she rolled her eyes. "Now we have to decode it somehow."

Armannii ran his finger along the paper, reading it for the third time. "Maybe we should shove Diomedes into a 'crack in the ground.' That would solve a lot of our problems."

"Even if that is a key of some sort, he'll just find a way to get out. His magic is powerful."

"True." Armannii sat down opposite her. "I've seen him fly on occasion, so maybe a crevice wouldn't be the best."

They stayed silent, each of them taking turns reading and rereading the prophecy. But with the argument with Kade still playing repeatedly in the back of her mind, it was hard to focus. Ellayne twirled her bracelet around and around her wrist. Eventually, she rested her elbows on the table, placing her face in her hands.

"This is worse than being tutored because there's so much more riding on this than just my father's ire if I fail."

"I think you and Diomedes are the two eggs and later the two birds."

"Why?"

"Because your brother didn't have magic and therefore was 'featherless,' and you were born with magic."

"Since when are magic and feathers the same thing?"

Armannii rolled his eyes. "It's metaphorical, Queenie. You're not actually a bird, last I checked, and neither is your brother. But you were born into the same family—"

"I hadn't noticed." Ellayne rubbed her eyes with her hands.

"It may be important here. This prophecy isn't just about Diomedes; it's about you too."

"So what if it's about me?" She rested her cheek on her hand and looked at him. "We just need to find out why Diomedes got upset enough to kill the seer so we can exploit that. It doesn't really matter what it has to say about me."

"But what if it's connected?"

"Hmm?"

"His destiny and yours." Armannii pointed to the last line. "What about this? It says there can only be one survivor. If this is about the two of you, then you should care."

"I'm not killing my brother, Armannii," Ellayne said, her posture straightening as annoyance bubbled back to the surface. "I feel like I've said this a million times, but I'm not going to murder Dio. I—" She faltered. "I can't. Especially not without my magic."

"That's not what I'm saying." He shook his head. "But you have to consider that one of you may not make it through this. There may only be one—"

"Survivor. Yeah, I get it." Ellayne groaned. "However, that doesn't help us. Dio probably assumes it's going to be him. And at this rate, so do I." She pushed back from the table, standing up.

"You really shouldn't think that way."

"How else am I supposed to think?" Ellayne lifted her hands and gestured around. "We are not in a good place here, Armannii. He has things we could only dream of having. Our men couldn't fight a stray cat, we hardly have enough resources to provide food and housing, and my magic is dormant."

Armannii wasn't watching her. Instead, he was rereading the page. For some reason, that annoyed her, and she gritted her teeth.

"I'm going to find Linetta."

"Mhmm," was the only response.

I messed up, Ellayne thought as she walked through the streets. *I shouldn't have sent Kade away. I need him now more than ever.* She kicked a piece of rubble to the side, listening to the way the clang echoed off the buildings nearby. People were heading home for dinner, which meant the town was hers to wander alone. That was, until she found the person she was looking for.

"Ellayne." Linetta grinned as she approached her niece. "What's wrong?"

Ellayne shook her head. "Honestly? Everything, as dramatic as that sounds."

"Well, that's going to need some explaining." Her aunt led her to a nearby bench, and the two of them sat down. "What did I miss?"

I banished my best friend, the man I— Ellayne cleared her throat. "I've had a rough day."

"But I heard that you found what you were looking for when you went into Cyanthia."

"I did." Ellayne nodded, folding her hands in her lap. "But it wasn't as helpful as I thought it would be. It's not the how-to-peacefully-remove-your-evil-brother-from-his-tyrannical-reign that I had been hoping for."

Linetta pressed her lips together. "And?"

"It may be valuable, but it's going to take more time to figure out how we can use it to our advantage, which we don't have—"

"You're still not telling me something." Linetta's eyebrows furrowed, creating more wrinkles than she had normally. "You're easier to read than your mother."

Ellayne ran her tongue along the front of her teeth. "I had to make a hard decision today, and—" Her voice cracked. "It was a mistake."

"What was your reason for making it?"

"Well ..." Ellayne bit her lip. "I wanted to protect the country." She opened her mouth to continue, but the words dried on her lips. *He kept a huge secret from me and it hurt.*

"Then your heart was in the right place."

But it wasn't, Ellayne argued in her mind. *Even if I want to believe her, I can't.* She recalled the anger—the betrayal—she had felt when he revealed what he had been sneaking away to do. But then she remembered the look in his eyes. She had betrayed him too, had failed to give him and his father a chance at redemption. "It's more complicated than that." She sighed. "I—" She choked. "I sent Kade away."

Linetta straightened up. "Oh?"

Ellayne shifted on the bench, wringing her hands together. "He told me that he . . . he started the fire in the Black Forest."

"Did he say why?" Linetta asked, pushing her round glasses higher up on her nose. "I only spoke with him a bit when you all came to my bookstore, but he didn't seem like the kind of person to do that maliciously."

"He did it under someone else's command," Ellayne said. She questioned whether she should tell her aunt who Kade's father was. "He said it got out of control."

"That was apparent. Who told him to do it?"

With a sigh, Ellayne closed her eyes. "His father."

Linetta stayed silent, letting Ellayne take the time she needed to gather her thoughts.

"He's the Dark Prince. But none of us knew that until we were in the Dark."

"And I take it that this information doesn't sit well with you."

"It was fine until he started acting differently." Ellayne slouched, ignoring all of the training she underwent as a little girl. "He would disappear and not tell anyone where he was going."

"Do you know now where he was going?"

Ellayne nodded. "His father is apparently somewhere in Phildeterre, and he was going to see him. The Dark King had Kade hunting down his enemies. I'm not quite sure exactly what he did with them, but it wasn't good. His father sent him after my subjects, Linetta. I-I couldn't let him do that. It's illegal and wrong. I wanted to protect my country."

"Are you sure he was hurting them?"

Ellayne shook her head, then tucked a strand of hair behind her ear. "But I can't imagine he was bringing them flowers. And what with the fire . . . I mean, this is the Dark King we're talking about. My father may not have been at war with him, but they weren't on the best terms. And I just don't want to think about Kade doing his bidding. Not when Kade—" She stopped, unsure what she was intending to say. *Kade is my best friend. Kade is one of the few people I thought I could trust. Kade is the man I—*

"You care deeply for him." If it hadn't been Linetta who said it—if it had been Armannii or anyone else—Ellayne would've denied it.

Her lip quivered. "Yes."

"And you feel you've made a mistake in sending him away?"

"Didn't I?"

Linetta didn't respond right away. "Your mother had to make some hard decisions when it came to Emmalee. But there may be a difference. You need to consider what is driving Kade. Is it revenge like Emmalee? Or is it something else, something you can understand and agree with?"

Ellayne recalled Kade's words, but she still couldn't picture how in the world he could justify his actions. And why had he used her as an excuse? How could hunting down his father's enemies protect her—keep her safe? What had the Dark King said to make his son believe he was right in following his orders? She still had so many questions. Ellayne covered her face with her hands. "I messed up," she said, her voice hitching in her throat. "I shouldn't have sent him away."

"Take a breath, Ellayne." Linetta placed a hand on Ellayne's back. "You still have time to undo what's been said."

"I need to find him and apologize. I can't let him go."

Linetta held out her hands and pulled Ellayne to her feet. "Then you better get going."

Chapter Fourteen

ou shouldn't go alone. Let me go with you," Armannii said, tucking an arrow into his quiver. The tip of it glittered with green for a moment, and Ellayne's distracted mind wondered what material made up the arrowhead. The thought continued after seeing the other arrows he placed in the quiver: silver, gold, wooden, and a few others carved with runes.

"No." Ellayne stopped putting her canteen in her bag, nodding to his weapons. "You stay here and keep training everyone. I need you in charge." She tied up the bag, scanning the room for anything she might've missed. Her sword leaned against a nearby wall, and she walked over to grab it.

"But you're the queen. These people need to continue to see you leading them. Not me. Although, I'd probably look irresistible in a crown . . ."

"I *am* leading. This is called delegating, and my father did it all the time. Besides, the Dark King will kill you as soon as he lays eyes on you, whether he knows you've forgiven him or not." She attached her sword and sheath to her belt. "And I need you alive if I'm going to remove Dio from the throne."

"That's a fair point, but your people need your guidance; they need you alive. Here. It's not safe for you to go out alone. Not when half of the country is sided with your brother."

Ellayne waved her hand. "Elowen is going to meet me at the edge of the forest. I won't be alone. I'll have her." *And soon enough, I'll have Kade.*

"You should know this isn't right. You're royalty, and you really should take a few others with you. Seriously," Armannii argued, but he laid his weapons down on the table. "I should be going with you."

"If half of Phildeterre is sided with my brother, then the other half is sided with me or . . . at least sided against him." Ellayne picked up the bag and put it over her shoulder. "It shouldn't take too long, especially with a speed rune on my boots." She nodded toward him. However, he didn't move.

Armannii placed his hands on his hips. "You haven't mastered how to control the speed rune so you can walk for an extended amount of time without the speed kicking in. How do you expect to take the rune off when you don't want it anymore?"

"Easy." Ellayne plastered a grin on her face, wiggling her eyebrows as she reached down and took her boot off.

"So you're planning to walk around the Black Forest with bare feet when you no longer want the rune? That sounds like a brilliant idea, Queenie." He rolled his eyes. Pulling his rune pen out of his vest, he took her boot and drew the speed rune on the sole. He did the same for the other one when she handed it to him.

"I've wandered the Black Forest without shoes before. It's not pleasant, but I don't exactly have time to learn how to do runes at the moment, do I? And these are still the only pair of shoes I have with me. I don't have time to go find someone with my shoe size. I've already wasted enough time staring at that stupid prophecy, and—"

"Fine." He crossed his arms over his chest. "But I don't like this idea. And as soon as all of this is over, I'm adding runes to the ever-growing list of things I need to teach you during our little training sessions."

"Why?"

"Because I'm not your rune slave, Queenie." The corner of his mouth turned up into a smirk. "Even if you want me to be."

Ellayne chuckled. "All right. You can teach me rune magic after this nightmare is over." A dark thought crossed her mind, and she questioned if she'd be able to do rune magic with her own trapped in a dormant state.

"While I'm gone, make sure training is continuing to progress, and the woman in charge of rations may want to set up a meeting with me. Tell her I'll speak with her as soon as I get the chance, or you could deal with the shrinking amount of supplies we have. But if nothing else, make sure the people from Pingbi are getting settled. I meant to go speak with their leader, but—"

"You've been busy. I'm sure she'll understand. I'll make sure she knows you've thought of her and her people."

"Thanks, Armannii. I appreciate it."

"Queenie?" Armannii said just as she was about to open the front door. "Give the kid a little bit of slack when you see him. He's under a lot of stress too."

"We all are."

 "Hello, Your Majesty." Elowen bowed when Ellayne met her on the edge of the Black Forest. She had her dreadlocks pulled into a knot on the back of her head.

"Hi, Elowen. Thank you for meeting me." Ellayne nodded to the dryad. "The Dark King is still here, right?"

"Yes," she said, pausing as she glanced at Ellayne's boots. "You have speed runes. Good. That will help us cover ground, but we should go. They're very near the portal, and there isn't much time before they cross back into the Dark." Elowen turned back and entered the trees. Instead of having her speed rune drawn on any shoes she wore, Elowen drew her speed rune directly on her ankle.

"How did they get through the portal?" Ellayne asked, keeping up with Elowen as the trees blurred around them. "Doesn't my brother have men on this side guarding it?"

"I don't believe the Dark King gave the royal guards much of a choice."

"So he killed them?"

Elowen didn't respond, but the silence was enough of an answer. Ellayne struggled to swallow. She wasn't upset over the loss of a few royal guards, but she thought of the two guards who were bewitched. If the ones at the portal had been under a spell, then they would've had no choice but to follow their orders even if they didn't want to.

And then there was Kiegan. His eyes had been glazed over, just like the guards' eyes. Armannii had said that meant a weak or fading spell, or it could mean he was fighting it, that somewhere inside his mind, he was a prisoner to Blanndynne or whoever had placed the enchantment. But then again, maybe Ellayne was only seeing what she was hoping to see. Maybe she only thought his eyes were cloudy because she was hoping his decisions were not his own. She let out a sigh as she continued to run with Elowen.

In the low light, it looked like Elowen was gliding over the forest floor. The ease with which Elowen navigated through the trees contrasted directly with Ellayne, who tripped on root after root. As soon as the leaves blocked out the sunlight, Ellayne felt the heaviness of the darkness around her. Wind whispered through the branches as they went.

They slowed down, Ellayne watching Elowen for changes in speed. *I always take the sun for granted.* Ellayne groaned inwardly as she pushed a branch out of her way only to have it break near her hand.

"Please be careful." Elowen turned when she heard the snap. "We are approaching the center of the burn scar, and the trees around here are struggling to heal as it is without opposing outside forces."

"Right. Sorry."

Light poured in through scraggly branches up ahead, and Ellayne could see the damage from the fire better. *A fire Kade set*, Ellayne reminded herself. The flames had left the tree trunks charred black—blacker than the normal dark shade of bark. The farther in they went, the higher up the damage went until it broke through the uppermost branches.

"This is terrible," Ellayne said, coming to a stop behind Elowen. Her words came out breathy, and she had to remind herself to close her mouth and stop gawking. *How did he do this?* She stared upward, spinning in a full circle as the light of the sun poured down on her through the skeletal trees. Ellayne wondered how she had managed to stop the blaze. The remains of the forest left her feeling cold from the inside—something even the sun couldn't fix. She missed the warmth of her magic, and it left her feeling heavier than before.

"This way, Your Majesty," Elowen said, standing near a fallen tree. Even upturned, the width of the trunk was still taller than Ellayne. "The forest is like this for quite a distance."

And she was right. It seemed like the damage done from the fire Kade started went on for miles. The farther they went, the more impressed Ellayne was that she'd put out the flames. It was becoming clearer why her magic was gone. When they took a moment to rest, Ellayne ran her hand along the edge of a burned trunk, and it tinged her fingertips black.

"A few of my sisters were lost in this tragedy," Elowen said in a low voice. Her words had Ellayne glancing at her. "They were trying to put up more wards to protect the trees, and they didn't get out in time."

"I'm sorry, Elowen," Ellayne said, crossing her arms over her chest. "It should never have happened."

"I heard that some man with dark magic started it. Was it the king?"

Ellayne shook her head and took a deep breath. "No. I originally thought he may have started it as a distraction to attack us in Bolee, but he never attacked."

"So you don't know who started it?" Something about the way Elowen clipped the ends of her words left Ellayne's stomach uneasy.

"Well, I—" Ellayne stopped when a branch broke nearby. "Did you hear that?" she whispered, grasping the hilt of her sword and spinning in a circle.

Elowen's ears perked up, and she laid her hand on the nearest tree trunk. Closing her eyes, her hand began to glow light green. A split second later, her eyes shot open, and she motioned for Ellayne to follow her. The speed runes kicked in, and once more the trees blurred together.

"Men with weapons," Elowen said over her shoulder.

"Royal guards?"

"Couldn't tell." The dryad leapt over a fallen branch, and Ellayne weaved around it. "It's harder to see through burned trees because their connection is weaker."

The news that her dryad friend—and probably all other dryads—could use the trees to see had Ellayne making a mental note to mind her actions when she was among the trees. It also made more sense to Ellayne as to how Elowen knew Kade was still in Phildeterre. They kept running until Elowen slowed to check another tree.

"We aren't being followed," she said as she lowered her hand. "But we're nearing the portal."

"That's good, right?"

Elowen nodded. "However, I'm afraid I can't go much farther. I have no desire to meet the Dark King."

"I don't blame you." Ellayne pulled her braid around to the front and twisted the end of it around her fingers. "I don't really want to see him either."

Elowen pointed in the direction they were headed. "If you keep going this way, you should find your friend."

"Thank you, Elowen."

"Of course. And if you should need me for any reason, all you have to do is place your hand on a tree and call to me. I will hear it."

"Really?" Ellayne placed her hand on a tree. "That's incredible. One more thing before you go," she said, remembering her literal run-in with Kade back in Bolee. "Could you cancel the speed rune on my boots for me? I haven't learned yet, and—"

"Of course." Elowen bent down, and a moment later Ellayne could walk without traveling ten or more feet in a second. "Take care, Your Majesty." The dryad stood and bowed. "Good luck."

Ellayne kept her hand on the hilt of her sword all the way up until she heard the indiscernible mumbling of male voices. She grimaced as she peeked around a tree trunk. A group of at least forty Dark Soldiers stood in clusters between trees, but all of them wore the attire associated with their position: head to toe black metallic armor. Kade never dressed like a Dark Soldier, so she doubted he was among their ranks. But she also didn't see him anywhere else.

Craning her neck, Ellayne scanned as far as her eyes could see into the darkness for any sign of Kade but found none. Instead, her eyes focused on a few soldiers who were headed in her direction.

"—heard something," one of them said, his voice distorted by the helmet. "It was over this way."

"It could've been a squirrel," a different one said, and their voices got louder with every step in Ellayne's direction.

She gripped the hilt of her sword, knowing full well she would only be able to take on a few. *Not forty*. She bit the inside of her cheek. Regret for not letting Armannii join her added to the clamminess of her hands. Ellayne held her breath. *This was a mistake*. The footsteps drew nearer, and Ellayne moved as quietly as she could into a better fighting stance. A few moments of silence passed. The only things Ellayne could hear were the other soldiers in the distance and the sound of her heartbeat pounding in her ears.

"I told you it was just a squirrel," the second voice said. "There's nothing here. Let's go."

Leaves on the forest floor rustled. Ellayne's lungs burned as she trapped the air she had inhaled, only releasing it when the footsteps faded away. She leaned against the tree trunk, shaking with adrenaline. *That was a close—*

"Well, well, well." A hand grasped Ellayne's shoulder, spinning her around and pinning her against the trunk. "We seem to have a little spy on our hands."

Chapter Fifteen

ook what I found behind a tree over there." The Dark Soldier who apprehended Ellayne shoved her in front of the forty Dark Soldiers she had been watching. He took her sword, holding it so that it stuck her right between the shoulder blades.

"I told you it wasn't a squirrel," one of the men said, elbowing the soldier next to him.

"Definitely not a squirrel."

Ellayne held her chin high, keeping what regal air she could despite the humiliation of being surprised from behind. "I need to speak with the Dark Prince," she said, rolling her shoulders back.

"Do you now?" One of the men in front of her stepped forward, his armor clinking as he crossed his arms over his chest. Unlike with the royal guards, Ellayne couldn't tell who the highest-ranking Dark Soldier was; however, since this one stepped forward, she assumed it was him. He towered several inches above her. "And what makes you think you have the right to address His Highness directly?"

I am the queen of this country, and he is my best friend. Ellayne found it simple to think the words, but they never made it past her lips.

"His Highness doesn't make it a habit of speaking to people like you."

Oh really? A long list of snide remarks trailed through her head. "Ah, so you know him personally then?" Ellayne asked. However, she barely had time to raise an eyebrow before the soldier backhanded her. She stumbled sideways, clutching her face. Despite the throbbing sensation in her cheek, she let out a brief sigh of relief at not being skewered on her own sword, which a soldier still held to her back despite her movement. However, after a nod from the soldier in front, Ellayne glanced behind and saw the soldier lower her weapon.

"I suggest you watch your tongue," the Dark Soldier who had hit her said, his voice dripping with irritation.

You think? "Of course." She inclined her head to him. "My apologies." Her cheek stung, but she let go of it and straightened her posture again. "Where is the Dark Prince?"

"That's none of your—"

"In conference with the Dark King," a different soldier said, earning himself a punch to the shoulder.

"Shut it," the soldier in front of her snapped at the one who had spoken.

"Right. Sorry, sir."

"What do we do with her?" a new soldier asked.

Despite the helmets covering their faces, Ellayne could feel all eyes on her. She begged her cheeks not to redden, but they disobeyed her. *How do I get out of this? There are too many of them. Why didn't I bring someone with me? Do I identify myself?* She raced through questions, annoyed when almost all of them returned unanswered.

"I have an idea," the soldier who'd slapped her said. The way his voice turned silky, like he was smirking under the helmet, left her skin crawling. He took a step toward her, and she matched it by taking a step back—a step that landed her backed up against another soldier.

Ellayne's eyes widened as they closed ranks around her. Both her heart and mind raced, pounding in her chest and head. *Think, Ellayne, think.* She put her hand out to keep space between herself and the nearest soldier, but he grabbed her wrist, twisting it to the side.

"Let go of me," she ordered, but the demand didn't come out as powerful as she'd hoped. "Don't touch me."

"Or what?" the soldier holding her said, closer to her face as he towered over her. "You're outnumbered."

Ellayne did what she could to control her breathing, but the closer they got, the harder it was to suck in oxygen. Her body trembled, and there was nothing she could do to stop. *Help,* she thought, unable to voice the words. *Please help me.* Another hand grabbed her other wrist, and though she tugged against it, they were stronger. *Please,* Ellayne begged, screaming inside her head. Seconds ticked by, and they drew ever closer. *Help.*

Warmth exploded from her core, coursing through her. *Yes.* She balled her hands into fists. *Finally.* Her magic filled her, bringing with it overwhelming comfort. *Protect me,* she thought, appealing to her magic.

"What is—" The soldier didn't have time to finish the question before a flash of light and heat radiated from Ellayne, and then there were no more hands on her. In fact, the nearest soldier was at least ten feet away. Just like the first time her magic had manifested, her skin glowed.

Ellayne called her magic to her hands, and an orb of light hovered over each one. She felt lighter than air, and the relief at the return of her magic nearly had her in tears. *Thank you,* she thought over and over again.

"Lay a hand on me again and I'll make you regret it," she said, spinning to stare down as many as she could.

One of the soldiers at the front got to his feet and pulled a sword from the sheath hanging at his waist. He pointed it at her. "You can't take on all of us."

He was probably right, but Ellayne didn't show anything that would make them think she agreed. "Doesn't mean I won't try." She tossed one of the orbs of light up into the air, catching it with ease.

More of the Dark Soldiers directed their weapons at her. She was surrounded by them again, though they stayed several feet away. And unlike before, Ellayne didn't feel nearly as vulnerable with the warmth of her light magic pulsing through her.

But with the return of her magic, Ellayne also sensed the dark magic around her. More than one of the soldiers possessed it, either that or—

"What's going on here?" a familiar voice boomed behind her.

"Your Highness." The soldiers around her lowered their weapons and bent down on one knee, bowing.

Ellayne spun around. She dropped her hands to her sides, and the orbs of her magic disappeared, though her hands continued to radiate light.

Kade dressed like he had in the Dark Castle, wearing a silk tunic underneath a military jacket. A silver crown intertwined with his dark curls, and just like in the castle, his dark eyes bored into hers.

"An explanation," he said, still staring at her. "Now," he barked.

A soldier stood up to address Kade, and by the sound of his voice Ellayne discerned he had been the one who had slapped her.

"We found her spying from the trees over there and took her into custody."

"You"—he pointed to the soldier who'd addressed him—"get everyone in order. We're leaving in a few minutes." He narrowed his eyes at Ellayne. "You, get your sword and come with me."

Ellayne nodded, taking a shaky breath as she stepped away from the group of men. She picked up her sword, which had been discarded by the soldier who'd taken it, and slipped it into her sheath. Ellayne fell in step behind Kade as he stomped into the forest. He didn't talk as they walked, and Ellayne ran over what his first words might be until he finally said them.

"Leave," he said, spinning around.

"What?"

"That's what you told me," he said, keeping his arms straight by his sides. His hands balled into fists, and she felt the repulsion to his magic. After the absence of it for so long, she was grateful to be feeling anything. "What are you doing here? Making sure I'm following through? Because I fully intend to—"

"I'm sorry."

"Excuse me?"

"Kade . . ." Ellayne bit her lip. "I'm sorry for sending you away. I was hurt and upset, and in the moment it seemed like the best decision for my country . . . for me. But I was wrong. I-I should've tried harder to understand. I still don't, but I don't want to lose you. If you think your father deserves a chance, then I owe it to you to give him one. I'm sorry. I really am."

His eyebrows furrowed. "You weren't wrong." He glanced around, probably checking to see how alone they were. She wondered if he knew about the dryads using the trees to watch the forest. He probably did. "It's safer if my father and I leave. You had a point. What I was doing is against the laws and certainly against any treaty we have with you. I should've thought it through. I think you're right. The best thing for your country is for us to leave immediately."

"You can't leave." Ellayne stepped forward and tried to hide the hurt on her face when he backed away from her.

"I've already made the decision." He clenched his jaw. "The portal is being opened as we speak."

"I messed up, Kade." Ellayne closed her eyes, sighing. "I shouldn't have been so rash. I was wrong to send you away, especially after such a terrible fight."

"But you did."

"I'm sorry," she said again, and this time her voice caught in her throat. The warmth of her magic was there to soother her, but it wasn't helping as much as she'd hoped it might. "I don't want you to leave. Kade, I need you to stay. I can't do this without you. I—"

"Your magic is back," he said as his hands unclenched. His change of subject surprised her. "When did that happen?"

"Just a few minutes ago, when your soldiers—" She paused when his features darkened. "Doesn't matter."

"What did they do?" His tone sounded menacing. "Did they hurt you?"

Without thinking about it, Ellayne's hand went up to her cheek, which still throbbed from being slapped. "No, I'm fine. I—" She gasped when he stepped forward and grabbed her wrist, pulling her hand from her cheek.

If it was possible, his eyes darkened even more when he examined the mark on her skin. His dark magic pulsed coldness into her wrist, which overwhelmed the normal spark between them. He lowered her hand to her side, then raised his hand again and ran his fingers over her cheek, sending wave after wave of shivers down her spine.

"Who did this?"

Ellayne reached up and covered his hand with hers, bringing both of them down to their sides. She wrapped her hand around his, letting the buzz between their skin give her the courage to say what she wanted to say. "It doesn't matter," she said, her voice softer than intended. "What matters is that you come back to Bolee with me. I can't face Dio without you. I don't want to face anything without you."

"Ellayne—"

"Hello, Your Majesty," yet another familiar voice said from only a few feet away. "It's been a while."

Chapter Sixteen

t was as if the Dark King had appeared out of thin air. Kade dropped her hand like it was on fire, clasping his hands behind his back and straightening up at the sudden appearance of his father. He inclined his head, bowing as the Dark King stepped forward.

In the low light of the Black Forest, the Dark King's hair seemed to be less gray. It made him appear younger than Ellayne knew him to be. He wore a dark green cloak with fur around the collar, and his crown was twice the size of Kade's. Each finger had at least one ring on it, reminding Ellayne of the one Kade wore that had made the Dark King realize he was his son in the first place.

Remembering his attention to formalities, Ellayne curtsied. "Hello, Your Majesty," she said, lifting her chin. "Up until a little while ago, I was unaware of your presence in my country."

"My apologies." He nodded his head. "Due to the conflict between you and your brother, I thought it best not to distract you from your priorities. And what with your father dead"—his lip quirked upward—"I didn't want to cause you more strife."

Ellayne bit her tongue, a habit she'd picked up when she spent several weeks in the Dark King's castle. She took a deep breath, feeling her magic swell within her, but she reined it back. Not because she felt like he deserved it, but because Kade had asked her to give him a chance.

"In the future, Your Majesty, I request that you formally present yourself when you are in my country."

"I will keep that in mind," he said, an eyebrow lifted in a way that made Ellayne want to hit something; it was just something about his personality. He acted as though he were so much wiser, so much better than her, and it continually rubbed on her. "However, we were just about to leave."

"So I heard," Ellayne said, glancing at Kade, who bobbed his head down once.

"I ordered the men to prepare to return," Kade told his father. "They should be ready by now."

"Why don't you go make sure, Son?" The Dark King had a lilt to his voice, and Kade's eyes widened.

"I—"

"Now." The king kept his focus on Ellayne. "I'd like a word with Her Majesty." He glared at his son for a second. "Alone."

Kade rolled his shoulders back, nodded, and with one last glance at Ellayne, strode off in the direction of the soldiers.

"I take it you haven't forgotten about our deal?" The Dark King drew Ellayne's attention away from Kade's receding shadow.

"I haven't." Ellayne stood as tall as she could, but the king still towered over her. "I fully intend to remove my brother from the throne." *And I'm in a better position now that my magic is back,* she added in her head.

"And since you have returned to your country, how do you intend to do that?" He crossed his arms over his chest.

Ellayne copied his stance, crossing hers as well. "I'm deciding the best way to do so without wasting lives."

"And?"

And my brother seems invincible. She bit her cheek. "I'm making some progress."

"But you have yet to act on any plans you have made?"

"Why are you here?" Ellayne asked, popping her hip out to the side. "I can't remember the last time the Dark King himself came to Phildeterre. You always sent representatives when my father was king, and he did the same. Why come in person? Why now?"

"My son was only supposed to take you and your father to the portal. He was not supposed to cross through into Phildeterre. As a concerned father, I crossed through to make sure he was okay."

Liar, she thought, biting down on her tongue harder than before. This "understanding" thing was proving to be more difficult than she had anticipated, and she fought for control over her facial expressions. "I'm sure Kade has appreciated your concern," Ellayne said in a voice dripping with feigned sweetness.

The Dark King's smirk hesitated for a second, but he recovered. "Of course. I care about the well-being of my kin. He's the only heir I have."

Ellayne rolled in her bottom lip, catching a piece of skin with her teeth. "And was that the only reason for your visit? Or did you come with news that you were intending to volunteer your men to aid me in the upcoming battle with my brother?"

He took a step toward her, and though she wanted to back up, she held her ground. The Dark King looked her up and down, pausing when his eyes landed on the medallion around her neck.

"As much as I'd like to help, I have already lost two of my men to that monster in the last month, and I have no intention of offering any more sacrifices. Not when you have not shared any clear indication of a plan. We would be fighting blind, so to speak."

"I would think, Your Majesty, that if removing my brother's threat were as important to you as you make it sound that you would realize something of that importance might just be worth dying for. I'd die for it, and so would the people fighting with me."

He tilted his head to the side as he regarded her with a careful gaze. "My son thinks very highly of you. That much is clear." He stroked his chin with a few fingers as he considered his next words. "So I have another proposition for you."

"Oh?" Ellayne raised an eyebrow. "And what would that be? More assassination requests perhaps?" She couldn't help the sarcasm as it leaked out of her, yet inside she was trying so hard to give the man a chance. Ellayne knew she was failing.

His jaw clenched the same way Kade's did when he got annoyed. "Not quite. I'm in possession of something that might aid in your monumental task."

"Besides your large army?" She waited for him to answer, but he simply nodded. "I'm listening."

"I can't tell you here. Not when there are eavesdroppers." He nodded toward the nearest tree.

"Then where?"

"In the comfort of my own home, of course."

Ellayne's mouth opened. "I don't have time to go to the Dark," she said. "I'm one step away from full-on battle with my brother. If I leave, it will give my brother ample opportunity to win the battle with little to no fight. That's out of the question."

"I should think you would be willing to make some time for this particular deal, especially when you are up against as formidable an opponent as your brother."

"What do you want?"

"Excuse me?"

"You don't offer anything without something to gain in return—that much you've proven. So tell me what you want."

The Dark King lifted his chin. "I believe you know."

Ellayne tilted her head. "Do I?"

He nodded. "My son confessed to me what your reaction was when you found out about what he has been doing. I figured you'd be displeased. I believe it's safe to say I was correct. My desire to right the wrongs done to my people does not sit well with you."

She kept her mouth shut, waiting for him to be up-front. It didn't take long for the Dark King to continue.

"You understand the need to protect your subjects, do you not?"

"Clearly, but—"

"And you want to rectify the past and make a better future for them?"

"Of course. But—"

The Dark King grinned. "Then please explain to me why you are so opposed to my desire to do the very same thing." His eyes stayed narrowed on her, watching as she tried to come up with an answer suitable to present to a king.

"Your Majesty," she finally said, "I completely understand the need to protect my people." Ellayne tilted her face up.

"I would think so."

"But what you are doing is hunting down *my* subjects without conducting any sort of trial. These people may have done horrific things. With the past as it is, I don't doubt it. However, by returning to Phildeterre, these people are under my protection. And I believe you know that." She switched her weight to her other foot, popping her hip out to the other side.

"Do I?"

She nodded once. "You follow the rules. It's the only means I can see to justify the way you treat your subjects. And if I had the opportunity to go through the current treaty between my country and yours, I believe there would be a few agreements you are breaking by sending your son after them. What you have done is illegal, and as I told Kade, it would certainly be at the top of my priority list if I weren't dealing with Diomedes. But I get the feeling you knew that, and that's why you've shown up now. I don't have time for your twisted idea of justice, and you know it."

The Dark King considered her, rubbing his thumb along his chin. "Interesting."

"Look, Your Majesty. Despite his deceitfulness, I trust your son, probably more than most people in my life at the moment. He asked me to give you the benefit of the doubt, to try to see eye to eye with you. He respects you and asked me to do the same. And I'm trying. However, I'm sure you can see how your clear disregard for the treaty between Phildeterre and the Dark makes your son's request a difficult one. I have no desire to see the agreements between our two realms fall to pieces. In fact, I have every desire to work more closely with you once everything with my brother is over. I do see the value in our alliance. I do see the value in your subjects. And I do see the value in continued growth between us.

"You and I both put our subjects first. I respect that about you, Your Majesty. But what I can't, nor will I ever, support is a king who tries to undermine my authority by seeking to give out vengeance under the guise of justice, harming my people while hiding it from me. *That* is unacceptable. I may be young, but I know better."

In the moments after she said it, she could sense the air around her getting colder. His magic flared up, but unlike his son, he had better control over it. Hers acted up in response, and she slowed her breathing to calm it down.

"I see." He placed his hands behind his back. "That is unfortunate." He tilted his head down, looking at the forest floor. "Is there any way to change your mind?"

"Into letting you hunt my people?"

"If that's how you'd like to pose it, yes."

"No," she said.

"Then I suppose I will be on my way." He turned, leaving the way Kade had. "If you change your mind, I'll be in my castle. And so will my son."

"Kade needs to stay here," Ellayne said, taking a step forward.

The Dark King spun around. "The only way he is staying is if you allow me to continue in my endeavors."

"I will not. But I need Kade here to remove my brother from the throne."

"Then you need to figure something else out." He paused, then added. "And I'll make sure to send your regards to the king's mother for you."

Ellayne couldn't process his words before he disappeared into the darkness. *The king's mother?* Her eyes widened, and she sprinted in the direction he had gone, but she found no trace of him. *The old queen? My father's first wife? Dio's mother?* She called on her magic to light the area around her, but even when she went back to the trees where the soldiers had gathered, she could find no one.

Everyone was gone.

The silence of the forest filled her with more adrenaline. Ellayne placed her hand on the nearest tree, concentrating by closing her eyes.

"Elowen, I don't know if you can hear me, but I need help. Please come find me. And someone needs to tell Armannii to meet me at Cassandra's. We are going to the Dark." She spoke the words aloud, feeling absurd talking to a tree. *I just hope she heard,* Ellayne thought as she continued walking in the direction she remembered coming from.

How was Diomedes's mother still alive? Ellayne played the Dark King's words over and over in her head as she stepped over large roots and pushed branches out of her face. She was glad Elowen had removed the speed rune because she knew it would be easier for Elowen to find her if she was moving at a normal pace.

As she traveled through the trees, Ellayne tried to remember what little fragments she'd heard about Queen Lenora—King Butch's first wife. *Mouselike; that's how my mother described her in her journal,* Ellayne remembered. The only person Ellayne had heard talk about the first queen was her son, Diomedes. A memory drifted into her mind of a conversation she'd overheard when she was younger.

"You act like she never existed!"

Diomedes and his father were in the middle of an argument, one which Ellayne listened to through the wall when she was eight years old.

"Watch yourself, Son," her father warned, his voice muffled through the door. "I've told you before, you don't know the full story."

"Then tell me. I have a right to know what you did to drive my mother away."

Ellayne sat outside the room, keeping one ear pressed to the wall. She didn't have to worry about the guards patrolling; they never had enough courage to ask what she was up to. It wasn't quite like being invisible—they certainly noticed her sitting on the floor of the corridor—but they never approached her.

"I'm not going to talk about this right now," her father said, and Ellayne could hear the paper rustling on his desk. Her brother must've interrupted him. "I've got two hearings tomorrow, and if you keep barging in here, I'm not going to have time to look over these cases. How is that fair to my people?"

"I don't care about your people," Diomedes said, his voice dropping low so Ellayne had to strain to hear. "I want to know why my mother didn't take me with her when she left. Why was I stuck here with you?"

Ellayne could hear her father sigh, and his chair squeaked. "Your mother wasn't in her right mind. The sorceress, she . . . she tricked your mother into following her."

"That's a lie. This is only because you hate magic."

"The sorceress and her magic were dangerous, Son." Her father's voice was stronger, yet it lacked its normal power. "You asked for a reason, and I gave it. Now go."

Scurrying away from the door, Ellayne ducked behind a pillar, watching her brother stomp out of her father's office. The memory was so vivid, she could remember the cold marble against her skin, and as she continued through the forest, she placed her hand on her shoulder, warming it with her magic. With her mind focused on the old queen, she didn't notice the uneven ground beneath her boots, nor the dryad in front of her.

"Your Majesty?" Elowen appeared, stepping out from a tree. "You called?"

Ellayne nodded. "I'm glad it worked." She leaned against a trunk. "I need you to take me to Cassandra's. I assume, since you know this forest better than most, and since you know Armannii, that you are aware of it?"

"I am. And I sent one of my sisters to get the elf. He should meet us there." She glanced around. "The Dark Soldiers are gone?"

"Yes, and I need to go in after them."

"All right." Elowen bobbed her head. "I assume you need the speed runes redrawn?"

"I would appreciate that, yes." Ellayne waited for Elowen to stand back up. "Ready to run?"

"Of course, Your Majesty."

Chapter Seventeen

"vair should be at the portal," Elowen said as she slowed down. One of her dreadlocks fell out of the knot, and she tucked it back in as they walked around the trees.

Every once in a while, the dryad would pause, reaching out to place her hands on the trunks. Ellayne wondered if she was watching for Armannii or checking to make sure their surroundings were safe.

"Speed runes are my new favorite thing." Ellayne didn't think much about what she'd said until Elowen chuckled. It came out as a tinkling sound, and Ellayne smiled. "Horses take so long," she added, thinking of Curry, Kade's horse. "It took us hours, if not days, to travel around here just a little while ago."

"They are quite convenient," a male voice said, and Armannii stepped out from behind a tree near Ellayne, making her clasp her hand to her chest and step back.

"Do you really have to make me jump out of my skin every single time?" Ellayne glared at him. He shrugged, a smug grin plastered on his face.

"I'll be leaving now, Your Majesty." Elowen inclined her head. "But you know how to reach me."

"Thank you again, Elowen." Ellayne stepped forward, surprising the dryad as she pulled her into a hug. "I'd actually be lost without you."

"Of course, Your Majesty." She came away from the hug grinning. "I'm sure I'll speak with you again."

Ellayne waited for her to disappear into the trees before she turned to Armannii. Remembering why she'd called him there, she started with an apology. "I'm sorry, but we have to go back to the Dark."

"No apologies needed, Queenie." He shrugged, jiggling the arrows in his quiver. "I was born there; I have no qualms about going back."

"Good." Ellayne took a deep breath. "Because Diomedes's mother is alive, and the Dark King knows where she is. I intend to find her and get her to talk Diomedes off the throne."

Armannii didn't miss a beat. "I was not expecting you to say that, but it's the best plan we've had so far."

"And that is the nicest compliment you've ever given me." Ellayne smirked. "Let's go."

The tree concealing the secret second portal was easier to find with Ellayne using her magic to light the area around them.

"So it just came back?" Armannii asked as he drew a rune to open the passageway on the trunk. He had already taken off her speed runes.

"Exactly. One second I was surrounded by Dark Soldiers, and the next my magic knocked them all away."

"You're just full of good news today, aren't you?" he said, stepping back and allowing her to enter the tree first.

"I suppose." She paused, waiting for him to seal up the entrance behind them. "It wasn't entirely good. The Dark King wouldn't let Kade stay here unless I let him continue hunting the people on his revenge list."

"And what's a Queenie supposed to do without her Dark Prince? Ouch!" He flinched when she punched him in the arm.

"And he wouldn't give me any information about the queen unless I came back to the Dark and agreed to the other terms."

"I understand not wanting to return to the Dark, especially for someone who loves the sun as much as you."

Ellayne struggled to breathe as the sickly sweet aroma coming from the sap on the walls filled her nostrils. But try as she might, she couldn't hold her breath long enough to make it to the end of the tunnel. The back of her neck felt damp by the time she heard the guardian's voice call out to them.

"Back so soon, Ovair?" Cassandra's high-pitched voice echoed in the hall before they even reached the first room. When they entered, the guardian nodded at them from her seat in a rocking chair positioned in the corner. "After what you told me about your last trip, I would've thought you'd want to stay away a bit longer."

"Consider me a glutton for punishment," Armannii joked, but she didn't laugh.

Cassandra's appearance didn't match her personality; it was something that had caught Ellayne off guard the first time Armannii brought her to the portal. Despite being over two hundred years old, Cassandra and her twin sister, Verina, looked no older than eight. They were identical. Both girls wore their long red hair in two braids. That day, Cassandra wore a lilac dress, which went down past her knees. The fabric lit up with runes forming a beautiful pattern, especially to Ellayne, who couldn't recognize any of them. But Cassandra's eyes captured Ellayne's attention the most; there were no pupils nor irises. Her eyes were completely white.

"Hello, Your Majesty," Cassandra said, rising to her feet when Ellayne stepped farther into the room. "Welcome back."

"Thank you," Ellayne said, adjusting her tunic so it wasn't stuck to her back with sweat anymore. "We need to use—"

"My portal." Cassandra nodded. "I figured that was the case. No one ever comes just to visit."

Ellayne felt a twinge of guilt and made a mental note to visit Cassandra and Verina for the sake of visiting when the war with her brother was over. *That is, if I survive,* she added, thinking suddenly of the prophecy.

"Of course, you'll have to take my test." The guardian led them to the next room, where Armannii pulled a stool out for Ellayne and then placed one in the center of the room for himself.

"Right, let's get it over with then," Ellayne said as she sat down on the stool.

Cassandra pulled her rune pen out from behind her ear, approaching Armannii first. With nimble fingers and a steady hand, she traced a rune on his wrist that pulled him into his head. As soon as she finished drawing his rune, Armannii's body stilled, and his eyes closed. Ellayne watched him breathe steadily as Cassandra wrote the rune on her wrist.

In one blink, Ellayne no longer sat on the stool in the same room as Cassandra and Armannii. Instead, blackness surrounded her. Just like the first time, the ground reflected her image. She let out a relieved sigh when she felt the cold metal of her sword resting on her hip.

Ellayne walked out into the darkness. She was semi-aware of the fact that Cassandra was rummaging through her mind, picking and choosing what would make the test personal and challenging for Ellayne specifically. Just as she was about to test whether Cassandra could hear her thoughts, she came across a door.

Dark wood went several feet above her head. Nothing else appeared in the distance, and after Ellayne checked around, she approached it. With one hand on her sword, Ellayne turned the handle and pushed.

The first thing she heard was whimpering. She ripped her sword from her sheath in a flash, pointing it at the back of a man who aimed his own weapon—a loaded crossbow—at two teenagers huddled together.

"Lower your weapon," she said, projecting her voice as much as she could. Her hand stayed steady, and it hovered a mere inch from the attacker's spine.

"No," the man said. From the back, he was not familiar to Ellayne, and after he spoke, she confirmed that he, along with the trembling targets, were all strangers to her.

"Put it down, and we can discuss this like adults," Ellayne said again, this time poking him with the very tip of her sword.

One of the teenagers, a girl, started to cry. "Please d-don't kill us."

"W-we didn't do anything," the boy next to her added, pulling the girl closer.

"Is that true?" Ellayne asked, and they both nodded.

"It's me or them," the man said, holding the crossbow up and aiming. "I suggest you choose fast."

Ellayne's heart raced as she recognized the choice set before her—kill or let him kill. She took a step to the side, keeping her sword raised.

"It doesn't have to be that way," she said, inching around so she stood to his right side. He had dark hair, but it got lighter on the ends. What stood out the most was a scar that ran from his right cheek all the way down his neck. "You can lower the weapon, let them go, and—"

"Make your decision," he said, not taking his eyes off his prey.

"Please," the girl said, and she turned her face to hide it in the boy's shirt.

"Three." The man started counting. "Two." He lowered his gaze to line up the shot.

In a split second, Ellayne made her decision, leaping in front of the two teenagers. As if in slow motion, the arrow sliced through the air and landed in her chest.

But before the pain of being shot could hit her, she gasped, waking up from Cassandra's test.

"Seriously?" Ellayne asked, dropping her head into her hands. She rubbed her eye sockets, applying pressure until she could see shapes in the air that weren't there.

"Always a surprise with you, Your Majesty." Cassandra grinned, though her eyes were closed. She stood in front of Armannii, her hand raised near his face.

"I finished before him?"

"There's a first time for everything," the guardian replied. "Now if you'll remain quiet, he should be done soon."

Ellayne nodded, shivering as the afterimages of the test faded from her mind. Being in the testing room again, sitting in the silence, left her mind vulnerable to the unwanted image of the first test she had taken—a decision she had not wanted to make. In her head, she saw the consequence of her choice—Kade falling off a cliff with her unable to save him. She forced it away, focusing instead on Armannii.

His breathing was not as peaceful as when he'd first entered the test, which made sense with how the guardian ran them. Instead, he breathed inconsistently, shaking every once in a while. Sweat pooled at the back of his neck, and she could see his bottom lip quivering. As she ran her hand over her bracelet—one Armannii had used to help break her curse what seemed like ages ago—she wondered what his test was like. By the way he was reacting to it, she hoped for his sake it would end soon.

"All right then," Cassandra said, stepping back from Armannii, who sucked in air and leaned forward when his test ended. "Follow me to the portal."

Ellayne stood up, but Armannii didn't move from his bent-over position. "Armannii?" She placed a hand on his shoulder, but he shrugged it off.

"Go," he said, his voice cracking. "I need a second."

"I can wa—"

"No. I'll be there in a minute."

"Come, Your Majesty." Cassandra nodded her head toward the tunnel that led to the portal room.

Ellayne hesitated, but after another glance at Armannii, she followed behind Cassandra.

Chapter Eighteen

ou're not going to tell me what you showed him in the test, are you?" Ellayne asked as she waited with Cassandra in the portal room. The energy and magic from the portal drew Ellayne's focus as she asked the question. Runes covered the walls, and the dark and light magic that held the portal together danced and swirled on a podium in the center of the room.

"No," the guardian said, putting her hands behind her back. "He can tell you if he so desires." Cassandra kept her eyes on Ellayne. "Just like I won't tell him what happened in your test."

"I suppose that's fair."

"Why did you do it?" Cassandra's question caught Ellayne off guard, and she furrowed her brow as she turned to look at the little girl.

"Why did I do what?"

"Jump in front of the two people instead of killing the person trying to harm them?"

"I didn't know the people. Who am I to decide who lives and dies when they're all perfect strangers?"

"I suppose that's one way of looking at it." Cassandra pressed her lips together. "But as many times as I've run that test, you are only the second person to choose the option of self-sacrifice."

Ellayne stood up straighter. "Only one other person did what I did?"

Cassandra bobbed her head up and down. "Curious, don't you think?"

"Who was the other person?"

"It was a young man quite a few years ago."

"What was his name? Would I know him?"

"Let's go, Queenie," Armannii said, ducking into the room.

The guardian's lips quirked up in a rare smile. "Tell my sister I need my favorite bowl back," she said as Ellayne gripped Armannii's arm.

"Of course." Ellayne nodded. "Thank you, Cassandra," she said as they stepped into the portal.

It felt like the floor dropped out from under her, and it was all she could do to hold on to Armannii's arm. Her fingers and toes tingled, and something in the spinning dark and light flashed. She closed her eyes to keep from getting sick, trusting Armannii to lead her through. *I forgot how much I hate this,* she thought, squeezing the elf's arm tighter.

Then it was over, and they crossed through the sister portal.

"You could've held on without your nails," Armannii muttered, rubbing his forearm where her nails had left little crescent moons on his skin.

"Sorry," Ellayne said, squeezing her eyes shut and rubbing them with the heels of her hands.

"Hello, you two!" Verina greeted from the same part of the room Cassandra had stood in. "It's so good to see you again."

"It's good to see you too, Verina," Ellayne said, pulling her hands away from her face to smile at the second guardian. Visibly, the only difference between the two happened to be that they kept their rune pens behind opposite ears. "Your sister says she wants her favorite bowl back."

"I'm sure she does." Verina grinned.

The ongoing joke of borrowing each other's things and reminders to do chores came from the fact that the twins couldn't cross the portal themselves. If they did, the magic keeping the portal stable and the guardians alive would shatter. They stayed in contact using the people they sent through. It was yet another reason Ellayne hoped for an opportunity to visit them just for the sake of visiting.

"Have you heard whether the Dark King returned to his castle yet?" Armannii asked, straightening his quiver on his back.

"He hasn't yet returned, but he should arrive soon. His men had transportation ready as soon as he reached this side," Verina said as she led them out of the portal room, through the testing room, and into the entry room with the rocking chair. Even the twins' homes were identical. "You weren't thinking of going there, were you?"

"Unfortunately, we have to," Ellayne said, crossing her arms over her chest. "Whether we want to or not."

"But the Dark King wants your head, Armannii," Verina said, her white eyes widening. "You can't seriously be considering going into your enemy's territory."

Armannii shrugged. "It wouldn't be the first time."

"It could be your last," the guardian said, putting her hands on her hips.

"Aw, are you worried about me, Rina?" Armannii smirked.

"Of course I am. Why wouldn't I be?"

"That's sweet of you," he said, winking at her.

"We should go," Ellayne said, nodding to the tunnel leading out of the tree. "And hopefully we'll be back soon."

"I hope so." Verina waved as they left the room.

And hopefully we'll have a few extra people with us, Ellayne added to herself as she followed Armannii out.

"Seriously, Queenie," Armannii said, finishing the sight rune on her neck before they entered the Dark. "As soon as we have a bit of quiet time, I'm teaching you runes."

"I'm not arguing," Ellayne said, letting her hair back down. She pulled the hood of her cloak up over her head. "It would definitely come in handy."

After tracing the same rune on his own neck, he opened the entrance with his pen. "Keep your sword out this time."

"Don't lead me under any lolang burrows and we'll be just fine," Ellayne said with a sneer, remembering the sting of the wolf-dragon's claws when it ripped through her shoulders.

He snorted, equipping his bow with an arrow. "We'll head to Matt's house first. There's something there I think might come in handy."

Chapter Nineteen

ell me again why we're stopping here instead of going straight to the Dark Castle?" Ellayne said, leading the way down the staircase of Matt's tree. It was the second time she had been there, and she felt more comfortable than she had the first time, especially after meeting Matt in person.

"Let me ask you this, Queenie," Armannii said when they got to the entranceway. He motioned for her to move her hair so he could remove the sight rune. "What were your plans to get into the castle?" His pen tickled her neck, and she scratched at it when he was finished.

"I hadn't quite come up with one yet."

"No surprise. And better yet, how do you know the old queen is even in there?"

"Well, I don't. But the Dark King said he'd give her my regards, which is what made me think she's there. Plus, he probably keeps his bargaining chips in a place easy to access, right?"

"Fair point."

As the rune faded, she saw him undo his sight rune and then open the door. Within a matter of seconds, he activated the runes in the main living area. The light blinded her at first, and she blinked back tears.

"Well, I thought of a plan because I suspected you wouldn't," he said, and through blurry eyes, Ellayne could see exactly what he meant.

"How did you get these?" Ellayne asked, walking straight to the two sets of Dark Soldier armor propped up against one of the walls.

The rigid metal was strong enough to hold its shape, so it appeared that there were two soldiers waiting to ambush them. One of the suits was shorter, just about Ellayne's height.

"Didn't I tell you? I still look excellent in Dark Soldier armor." He grinned, putting his bow and quiver down on the kitchen table. The room, as well as the rest of the home, was rounded; there wasn't a corner in sight.

"You used it to sneak out of the castle when . . ." Ellayne's words trailed off. "When I left you. Armannii—"

"Don't worry about it." He shrugged, putting his hands in his pockets. "I knew I'd get out of it. I always do."

Ellayne ran her hand through her hair, pushing it away from the side of her neck. "I should've tried harder to get him to let you go."

Armannii grinned. "Put that regret into something we can use now. Let's focus it on not getting caught this time."

She bit her lip and nodded. "That's a good plan. But how do we get in? The Dark King still wants your head mounted in his foyer. What do we do, just walk in the front door?"

"Sounds fine to me," he said, distracted by rummaging through his bag. "And if that fails, we have this." He pulled out a piece of paper.

Ellayne leaned forward to look at it. Her mind went blank. She blinked. *What was I just thinking about?* She furrowed her eyebrows, running her hand over her bracelet, which lay crooked on her wrist.

"What just—"

"Ready to go?" Armannii asked, tucking a sheet of paper into his vest.

That paper . . . Ellayne scratched her head. "What just happened?"

"Mind-wiping rune." Armannii smirked. "You must've stared too long at it."

Ellayne frowned, then shrugged as she straightened the bracelet. "Maybe next time you shouldn't shove it in my face."

"Fair point." He paused as he glanced at the armor, frowning for a millisecond.

"What?"

Armannii shook his head. "Nothing. Come on, we should—"

"No. What's wrong?" Ellayne stepped forward, placing a hand on his arm.

He looked back at her, inhaling deeply. "You know me. It's nothing important."

"If it managed to make it to your expressions, then it's clearly not nothing. And besides"— she sat down in a chair at the table— "we're about to go on a risky mission, and we need our heads to be clear."

With another glance at the armor, he turned his back on it and sat down at the table with her. "I suppose you have a point."

Ellayne waited in silence a little longer, letting him take the time he needed to collect his thoughts.

"I've never really struggled with Cass's or Verina's tests before. It always seemed clear what decision I had to make. But this time . . ." He hesitated.

"It wasn't as easy," Ellayne finished for him, and he bobbed his head.

"The test almost always has Kit in it because they know how important she was to me. How important she still is. But the test had nothing to do with her this time. Instead, it was about . . . about other mistakes I've made." He rubbed the bridge of his nose with his fingers. "When I turned my back on your brother, I turned my back on Blanndynne. We had, well, I guess you could call it a complicated relationship."

"Like with Kit?"

"No," he said, shaking his head. "I loved Kit. I always will." A soft smile crossed his lips. "To this day, she's the only woman I've ever loved. So with Blanndynne, it was different. I cared for her, sure, but it was only in a friendly way. Maybe at first I found her attractive, but the more we spoke, the more I wanted to protect her, like a brother might. She was so ambitious, and I supported her in her desires. It made sense. Before we freed her, the entirety of her existence was pleasing other people—being used by them and then getting tossed away like rubbish when they had their fill of wishes. When Diomedes made it clear she could focus on herself and her desires, I think it went to her head.

"It didn't seem to affect what we were doing—trying to end the war on magic. At least, not at first. But then Diomedes got his magic, and I think she saw him as a source of protection so she'd never feel weak and used again. When she chose to go with Diomedes instead of me, I knew she was making a mistake. After the Elemental Mountains, your brother didn't seem to care about anyone, even the people we were supposedly trying to fight for. I knew he wasn't going to help her grow or give her the attention she needed. I regret leaving her behind. It's my fault she's working with Diomedes."

"How is it your fault?"

"I don't know. It just feels like it is. If I had given her the care she desired, maybe she would've chosen a different path."

"And the test? What does that have to do with the armor?" Ellayne asked, nodding toward the item that had seemingly sparked the conversation.

Armannii ran his fingers over his jaw, making a scratchy noise from the scruff. "Nothing, I guess. It just made me think of the mistakes I made while I wore it as one of the Dark King's men. I was faced over and over with a choice: kill or be killed. And in the test at Cass's, I guess I just realized that I might have to make that decision again, but this time with Blanndynne. Cass had me make the choice: kill or be killed. And I know I've made plenty of mistakes, but I couldn't do it. I couldn't kill her in the test. Not when I believe she could still change. What if all it takes is someone talking to her?"

"I understand," Ellayne said, sighing. "Probably better than anyone. I can't—I won't—kill my brother. I don't know why. I just . . . I believe he's still got something good in him."

"It's a grim thing, to take a life."

"I thought you said you hadn't?"

"I haven't, but I know the time will come. Every choice we make is bringing us closer to war, and our enemies have no qualms about killing. I don't want to, but I will protect you even if that means taking a life. Even if it means taking *her* life."

"You know I'd never ask you to do that, right?"

Armannii nodded. The two of them sat in silence, neither moving. Ellayne wasn't sure how long they stayed like that. Eventually, she glanced at the armor, and in the rune light she could see her reflection in it.

"You'll have to help me get this on," she said, going to the armor and sliding her hand over the metal. It was cool to the touch. "I haven't had much practice with full armor."

Her friend straightened up, rising to his feet. Just like every time he had broken his walls down, they went right back up as soon as the conversation was over. *But maybe not quite as high as before,* she thought.

"They didn't teach you that in princess training?" Armannii said, walking over to the smaller armor set. He lifted the helmet off and placed it on the table.

"Must've skipped that lesson."

Piece by piece, Armannii took the set apart and reconstructed it on Ellayne. Each part added weight until Ellayne was sure she would collapse, getting crushed beneath it.

"How am I supposed to move in this?" Ellayne's voice echoed inside the helmet, and she flinched. "It weighs as much as I do."

Armannii chuckled. "I would draw a rune on it to help with that, but it's partially made from magic-repellent metal."

"But I can still sense my magic." She pulled at the warmth in her core, drawing it to her hand and forming it into an orb of light. "See?"

"That's why I said partially," he said, rolling his eyes as he started putting his armor on. "It's a low enough percent of the metal that runes don't function on it, but dark, or in your case light, magic can."

"Why block rune magic but not the other two?" Ellayne asked, doing her best to sit down in the clanging armor.

"It's a way of controlling the mass of the Dark King's soldiers. No tampering with the armor. It puts all of his soldiers on even fighting ground."

"Except for people with light or dark magic." She frowned under the helmet. "That doesn't seem fair."

"Since when did you think the Dark King played fair or let his men play fair?" Armannii had already donned half of his gear, but he cocked his head to the side. "However, you just brought up a very fair point."

He pulled two cuffs off the belt of his suit of armor, motioning for Ellayne to hold out her hands. Armannii took off her glove and clamped one of the rings around her wrist, then the other on the same wrist. Ellayne felt her magic disappear.

"How is this a good idea?"

"There are very few, if any, Dark Soldiers with light magic. It'll be a dead giveaway. Sorry, Queenie." He smirked as he put her glove back on. "I know you just got it back, but it'll have to wait." He handed her the key to the cuffs he'd put on her. "Probably don't want to lose this," he said, grinning when she glared at him.

"Where should I put it?" Ellayne asked, holding the key in her gloved hand. She could hardly bend her arm, and not a single pocket was visible on the armor.

He pressed his lips together, his forehead wrinkling. "Hmm." He took the key back. "Maybe I'll keep it in my vest."

"And if we get separated and I need to use my magic?"

"Right," he said. "Good point. What about tying it up in your hair? Then it's hidden by the helmet, and you can get to it if you really need to."

After five more minutes, the key was well hidden in Ellayne's blond hair, which was tucked up into the helmet. Armannii wore the full suit, and so did Ellayne.

"Are you taking your bow?"

Armannii shook his head. "Too obvious. Besides"—he lifted the sword that came with the armor, which Ellayne had too—

"these are basically standard for the Dark Soldiers, and it might tip them off that we don't belong if we show up with other weapons."

"Does that mean my sword—"

"Stays here too." He nodded, the helmet shining in the light.

"Are we coming back?"

"That bow is my baby," he said, pointing to his weapon. "There is no way I'm leaving her behind."

"Okay." Ellayne chuckled at Armannii's vehemence. "Ready?"

"Let's go find us a long-lost queen, Queenie."

The Dark was even more difficult to navigate with the armor on. The helmet inhibited her sight, taking away her peripheral vision. It also distorted the sounds around her.

"I hate this metal nightmare," she grumbled, tripping for what felt like the fiftieth time. "How much farther?"

"Not far." He waited for her to catch up. "If you could struggle a bit less, it might be better for our cover. Just by the way."

Ellayne stuck her tongue out at him, but not only could he not see because of the helmet covering her face, she also licked the metal inside. She rolled her eyes. *Of course that just happened.*

"Straighten up," Armannii said, stiffening a second later. "I hear other Dark Soldiers coming. And don't say anything. There are more men than women in service to the king, and it's more of a giveaway if they find out you're a girl."

She nodded. "Understood."

"Walk side by side with me, and do your best to stay in step. It's not as important out here, but once we get inside—"

"Why are you two out of your area?" a male voice barked from somewhere up ahead.

Ellayne stood as tall as she could, squinting through the trees. Finally, two Dark Soldiers dressed exactly the same as them stepped out, their hands on their swords. It was hard to keep an eye on Armannii because of the blocked peripheral vision, but she managed to copy him as he also moved his hand to his sword. When he relaxed, she did as well.

"We weren't on patrol, sir," Armannii said in a lower voice than normal. It already sounded different with the helmet, and the drop in pitch aided in covering his true voice. "We are reporting back from the village of Wisp Willows."

"And what exactly are you supposed to be reporting?" the taller soldier asked, glancing between Armannii and Ellayne.

"The Dark King heard reports that some of the king of Phildeterre's men infiltrated and were planning an attack. We were sent to check the truthfulness of the claim."

"And?"

"We thoroughly searched the village but found no sign of King Diomedes's men."

Ellayne breathed easier knowing Armannii was free to lie as much as he wanted because the helmet hid his eyes. With a smirk, Ellayne wondered if his eyes would ever turn back to silver since every word out of his mouth was false.

Having watched the royal guards in the training grounds growing up, she knew she could copy their stance. However, she was unsure how much of the royal guard training lined up with the Dark Soldier training.

"Very well," the taller one said, removing his hand from the hilt of his sword. "Continue on."

"Thank you, sir," Armannii said, saluting.

With only a quick glance at his motion, Ellayne did her best to copy what he did.

"Sloppy salute, soldier. That better be fixed the next time we cross paths," the Dark Soldier said.

Remembering her promise to Armannii that she wouldn't talk, Ellayne stuck her tongue out—not as far as to lick the inside of the helmet again—but nodded. She straightened up and rolled her shoulders back.

Armannii marched off in the direction they were going to begin with, and Ellayne couldn't help but notice that the Dark Soldiers kept their helmets pointed in her direction.

"He was right," Armannii said in a low voice when they were out of hearing distance as well as out of sight. "That was an atrocious salute."

Instead of talking—she didn't want to risk someone like an elf overhearing—she smacked him on the arm. Their armor clanged together.

"Next time keep your wrist straight, your elbow at forty-five degrees, and make sure your boots are together," he said, and the lilt in his voice made her think he was grinning.

He's loving this too much. She pressed her lips together, refraining from smiling. *This is the last time he is ever going to be allowed to order me around like this.* She lengthened her stride as much as she could but still struggled to keep up with Armannii's long legs.

"Remember," he said as the Dark Castle finally came into view as a great looming shadow in the distance. "Copy me, and we might just make it out alive."

Chapter Twenty

pen it," ordered one of the Dark Soldiers at the main gate. The man in charge of the entrance obliged, and a loud creaking sound reverberated inside the helmet when the gate opened.

I can't believe it worked again, Ellayne thought after Armannii repeated the lie he'd previously told the other soldiers. *Now we just need to find someone who knows where the queen is.*

Ellayne followed Armannii's lead, saluting the Dark Soldiers when they passed by.

"Better," Armannii said under his breath. "But don't tuck your thumb underneath next time."

The front doors opened, revealing the grand hall lit with a combination of runes and lanterns. Two Dark Soldiers greeted them inside, and Ellayne made the suggested corrections to her salute before following Armannii down a hallway.

"Where do you think they'd keep her?" Ellayne said, risking a whisper when they turned down another empty corridor.

"Either the dungeon or a tower," Armannii said. He paused in the alcove of a doorway. "But at some point, we have to be ready to accept that he may have been baiting you and be ready to bail."

"I'll accept it when it can be proven true, until then—"

"Good," an unfamiliar voice said behind them. "I'm glad I found someone else."

Ellayne and Armannii whirled around, saluting when faced with yet another Dark Soldier.

"Sir?" Armannii stood upright, and Ellayne rolled her shoulders back to appear taller.

"Go to the Dark Prince. He has requested a few men to report to him."

Ellayne refrained from asking why, letting Armannii inquire instead.

"He didn't say, but my guess is to take out some aggression. He's in the training room."

"Aggression, huh?" Armannii's voice held a lilt to it, and Ellayne knew he was hiding a smile under his helmet.

The Dark Soldier nodded. "Things didn't end well in Phildeterre. I heard a rumor from a few who returned, and they said there was a woman involved."

Ellayne's cheeks warmed, and she bit her tongue to keep from responding.

"Is that so?" Armannii's tone made her blood boil. "Then I suppose we better go help His Highness out."

"Be careful though," the man said as he was about to continue down the hallway. "I heard he sent quite a few men to the healer. Uses his magic to get an upper hand ever since His Majesty started training with him personally."

"Thanks for the heads-up." Armannii nodded, saluting one more time. The Dark Soldier repeated the motion, then left. "I know where we're headed."

Leaning around the corner, Ellayne made sure the soldier was well out of range before responding. "Do you think it's a good idea to find him?"

"Not find him. Fight him."

"Are you—"

"Besides." Armannii strode away from her, and she had to jog to catch up to him. "I want to see if I can still knock him on his royal backside."

"That has nothing to do with why we're here."

The elf paused and tilted his helmet down at her. "What were you planning to do then? Walk up to the Dark King and ask him where she is?"

"Well, no. But—"

"Then go with this, and we might just get what we're looking for as well as a chance to beat the kid at combat."

Ellayne rolled her eyes but didn't respond.

"If you agree, I'll even let you take a shot at him."

"You'll *let* me? Why would I even want to do that?"

"To get rid of any pent-up annoyance you have at him."

She shook her head. "I'm not angry at him anymore. We talked. We're good."

"You're not upset that he wasn't honest with you about what he was doing since he healed from his fight with Blanndynne's mutt? That he was tracking down your subjects and making them regret being born? That he burned down a huge section of the Black Forest? That he's the reason your magic went dormant?"

"Armannii, sh—" Ellayne looked around, her concern about being overheard filling her with chilling anxiety.

"Or maybe because you're jealous of all the times he chose to talk with Dayla instead of you."

"Quit trying to rile me up." She did what she could to cross her arms over her chest, but the armor clinked together, too bulgy to allow for much bending. "I'm not falling for it."

"Not even if I told you that I wasn't the first person he told about his father's illegal activities? Even if I told you she knew about it first?"

Ellayne faltered, her hands dropping to her sides. Even with the magic-dampening cuffs, she could feel the warmth of her magic creeping down her arms toward her clenched hands.

"That's not true." Ellayne gritted her teeth together. "Why would he tell her before me? I'm his best friend. He hardly knows her!"

Armannii glanced around. "Keep your voice down," he muttered; however, even then she knew he was smirking. "She did know. It's one of the reasons they disappeared together every time he came back. He confided in her, and she in him."

"So they're close," Ellayne whispered. "That shouldn't make me mad. He's allowed to confide in whomever he wants. He's an adult."

"But it does make you mad."

"Yes." She shook her head. "I mean no." There was a moment of silence. "I don't know."

"So you're sure you don't want to go take a little bit of that confusion out on the kid?"

I shouldn't be this fired up, she thought as she tried to rein in the heat traveling through her body. For all she knew, the only thing they did was talk. And the two of them were just friends, so none of it should've mattered anyway. Her teeth ached from how hard she was grinding them.

"Fine," she said. "We'll go find him, but only because he might know where Dio's mother is."

"Sure." Armannii nodded, leading the way. "That's the *only* reason we'll go see him."

"Enter." Kade's voice boomed from the other side of the training room door when Armannii knocked.

"Say nothing," Armannii whispered to Ellayne before pushing the door open.

Ellayne clenched her jaw as soon as they walked in. Kade stood in the middle of the training room—a room he'd brought her to the last time she was in the Dark Castle. He wore a light gray tunic and dark blue trousers. It left him looking less like a royal prince and more like the Kade she knew. Except for the darkness in his eyes.

"Grab one." Kade nodded to a barrel with several training sticks.

"I'll go first," Armannii said, dropping his voice to a lower pitch again.

"Couldn't care less," Kade muttered, grabbing a staff of his own. "As a fair warning, I will be using my magic."

"By all means, Your Highness." Armannii bowed, and to Ellayne it appeared dramatized. If Kade noticed, he didn't say anything.

Ellayne stepped back, standing by the door. She knew Armannii was capable, having fought him herself. But she still clenched her hands into fists at the thought of her friends fighting, let alone Kade using his magic.

"Ready?" Kade asked, pushing his hair out of his face.

Armannii had half a second to nod before Kade lunged. Holding back a gasp, Ellayne watched Armannii step aside. With another step, he stood next to Kade, bringing the weapon toward

Kade's leg with a whack. The Dark Prince grunted, stumbling to the side as Armannii leapt away.

"Fine," Kade growled, and his hands darkened with magic. "Reset."

Ellayne questioned how Armannii was moving as quickly as he was with all of the heavy armor. She leaned against the wall, cringing any time one of them landed a blow. *If Kade asks to duel me . . .* Ellayne shuddered.

"Again," Kade said, his eyes locked on Armannii, who had hit him in the back after spinning out of the way of Kade's attack. His arms blackened with magic up to his elbows, but he had yet to use it.

Armannii nodded, taking a few steps away. His stance was perfect: feet aligned for stability, knees bent for agility, and weapon held in the most convenient spot for movability. The elf tracked Kade as he began walking in a circle. A blast of dark magic flew over Armannii's left shoulder, and he moved to the right just as another missed where his chest had been.

Ellayne sucked in a breath, taking a step forward. She made up her mind to say something before Kade struck Armannii with his magic, but as she took another step, Armannii shook his head at her.

Kade didn't notice as he flung another blast of magic at Armannii. The elf jumped out of the way, landing near a few mats. Not giving Armannii much time to prepare, Kade spun a rope of dark magic at Armannii, who rolled on the ground to avoid it. His armor clanged when he ended up with his back pressed against the brick wall. Kade raised his hand again, and an orb of darkness hovered above it.

"You win," Armannii said, dropping his weapon, which clattered when it landed on the ground. He rubbed the shoulder he'd landed on when dodging the last blast of magic. "No need to finish me off."

The Dark Prince's shoulders froze, and he lowered his hand. "Right." He looked over his shoulder and pointed his weapon at Ellayne. "You." He tilted his head. "You're up."

Peachy.

Chapter Twenty-One

rmannii patted Ellayne on the shoulder when he handed her the weapon.

"Remember what I told you before we came," he said.

I should just tell him, she thought as she turned to face Kade. *I should just tell him, and then we can do what we actually came here to do. Who cares if he told Dayla about his father? I shouldn't be annoyed by that . . . but I am.*

"Ready?" Kade wiped his sweaty forehead with the back of his hand.

Ellayne nodded, and even with her hands shaking, she blocked his initial strike. The sound of the wood cracking together echoed around in the helmet, and Ellayne cringed. *How do they fight like this?* She swung her leg out, but Kade realized and leapt backward. With the weight of the armor, Ellayne didn't straighten up fast enough, and Kade took advantage. He swung his staff down, leaving Ellayne no other choice but to roll away.

I can't beat him with this armor, she thought, using the wall to push herself to her feet.

"Are you new?" A small smile appeared on the edge of Kade's mouth. "Because you fight like you've never worn armor before."

"Something like that," Armannii responded for her.

Ellayne held the weapon out again, fixing her stance as Kade approached her. *I never should've agreed to this*, she thought, raising her weapon to block his. *This was a mistake.* She swung her staff, but he blocked her and twisted his weapon so she almost lost her grip. *I have too much of a disadvantage.*

"Have you ever used a sword before?"

His insult had her glaring at him through her helmet. Everything in her wanted to respond, tell him that up until a little while ago he hadn't ever used a sword. But she held her tongue. He tried to strike again, but she spun out of the way and used the momentum to elbow him in the shoulder.

"That wasn't as bad," Kade sneered, and Ellayne sidestepped when he went for her again. "I'm sure you'll improve with training."

You certainly did. Ellayne winced when the staffs cracked together again. An image of the last time they sparred entered her mind, and she smirked when she remembered knocking him on his smug behind. The annoyance of Kade's banter left Ellayne feeling warmer inside the suit of armor, and she wished she could wipe the sweat off her forehead before it trickled down and lit her eyes in fiery pain.

"Are you going to try to hit me, or are you just going to stand there?" Kade asked, straightening up from his stance.

His change in footing drew her eyes to his boots, and a slight smirk stretched into a full smile when she saw her chance. With a step to the right, she baited him and held the weapon up to block his strike as she charged. The armor took the blunt force as she rammed her shoulder into his rib cage, using her shorter height to her advantage.

They both grunted when she collided with him, but because of his faulty footwork, the Dark Prince was the only one to hit the ground. Ellayne rolled her shoulders back. She pointed the tip of her staff directly at Kade's throat.

"All right then." He pushed himself up on his elbows when she backed up and lowered the staff. Kade tilted his wrist toward her, and a blast of dark magic shot out of his hand, barreling toward her chest.

With the weight of the metal, Ellayne didn't move fast enough, and she caught the burst in the center of her torso. The staff clattered to the ground as Ellayne flew across the room. A scream erupted from her lips but ended as soon as her body slammed against the wall. Her brain rattled around in her head when the helmet made contact with the brick, clanging like a bell. On the moment of impact, she felt a crack in her chest, and a second after landing, she found out why.

Breathing was near impossible.

Flinging her arm across herself, she tried to ease the screaming fire inside her chest. Her head throbbed. She could only see through one eye because the helmet had twisted; through it she could see three versions of Kade rising to his feet. Multiple visions of Armannii spun in front of her as he knelt down, still wearing his helmet.

"Well, that was exciting," he said, offering his hand to help her sit up.

Ellayne knocked it away. "Shut up," she wheezed. Ellayne cringed when her fragmented ribs shifted as she coughed. "Get this stupid helmet off."

"Wait, what are—" Kade started to say, but he stopped when Armannii slid Ellayne's helmet off.

"You almost had him, Queenie." Armannii grinned when he took his helmet off as well. "Just needed to watch out for that dark magic."

"Are you insane?" Kade rushed to them and knelt on Ellayne's other side. His hands shook as he ran them through his hair. "What are you two doing here? Why on earth would you not tell me? I could've . . ." His voice trailed off as he gripped her by the shoulder, and together he and Armannii helped prop her up against the wall. She kept her arm across her chest, sucking in sharp breaths whenever she moved in the slightest.

"It's a long story." Ellayne groaned, tilting her head back and leaning it against the cool brick wall. The number of versions she was seeing wasn't going down. "Not one I want to tell with a concussion."

"Ellayne," Kade said. "I'm sorry. I didn't know—"

"That was the point, Kid," Armannii said. He took his gloves off and pulled his rune pen from somewhere inside his armor. "Help get the chest piece off her."

"No," Ellayne said, shaking her head. "I don't want that stupid healing rune."

"You're going to need it if we're going to do what we came here to do."

"No." She closed her eyes. "That rune is evil, and it hurts more than this."

Kade shifted next to her. "Why are you here? You shouldn't be. It's not safe, especially for you, Armannii. What's the paper for?"

"Queenie, open your eyes," Armannii said, ignoring every word coming out of Kade's mouth.

Ellayne hesitated when she heard parchment rustling but opened them anyway. Her mind went blank the moment she saw the paper Armannii held. All she could see were swirling lines in the rune, twisting and turning in a mesmerizing way. The emptiness in her head refreshed her, lightening the load she hadn't realized she was carrying. But it finished too soon.

She blinked. The top half of her armor lay to the side of her, and her torso didn't feel like it was shattered by a hammer—or a brick wall.

"What did you—" Ellayne rubbed her head, sitting up straighter. "You used the rune on that paper to—"

"Distract you from the pain of the healing rune by wiping your mind? Yeah." Armannii stood a few feet away with Kade. "Figured it would be easier than fighting you on it."

"You were right," she said, getting to her knees. A dull ache throbbed in her torso, but it was nothing near the searing pain when the ribs first broke. From past experiences, she knew the worst of the healing rune was over, but she still rubbed her rib cage to ease the soreness.

"Ah." He smirked. "My three favorite words."

"Oh, be quiet," Ellayne snapped. "It's your fault I got blasted across the room in the first place."

"I'm not the one with dark magic," Armannii said, nodding his head toward Kade. "He's the one you should take that up with."

Ellayne tucked a strand of hair behind her ear as she glanced at Kade. His lips pressed together into a straight line, his hands on his hips. A vein stood out on his neck, emphasized by his clenched jaw.

"He wouldn't have hit me if he knew who I was," Ellayne said, turning back to Armannii. "How much did you tell him while I was out?"

"Not much."

"You two shouldn't be here," Kade said. He stepped forward. "I could've killed you."

"You gave it your best effort," Armannii said. "That's for sure."

"I'm serious." Kade lowered his voice. "You need to leave. Now."

"We can't." Ellayne shook her head. "We need to find someone first."

"Who? Who in the world could be so important that you two would risk your lives by sneaking in here?"

Ellayne glanced at Armannii, who shrugged. "Okay, this is going to sound ridiculous, but I think Dio's mother is here somewhere."

"Wait." Kade leaned to the side. "Your father's first wife? You think she's here? In the Dark?" He scratched the side of his head. "Isn't she supposed to be dead?"

Armannii sat down on a crate. "Supposed to be. Yes."

"But she isn't," Ellayne said. "Not according to your father."

Kade's jaw clenched again in response, but he remained quiet.

"He tried to make a deal with me. When I refused, he taunted me by letting it slip that Dio's mother is still alive and that she's in the Dark somewhere." Ellayne smoothed her hair, twisting a piece of it back into her braid.

"What deal?"

Ellayne took a deep breath. "He'd allow you to stay in Phildeterre if I would grant you permission to continue hunting my people from his petty list of targets."

Kade's shoulders tensed. "Right."

"So," Armannii said, drawing out the word. "Are you going to help us, Kid? Or should we go find another Dark Prince to assist us?"

"Help you how? I don't know anything about the old queen."

"Well then." Armannii stood up. "I'll help you get that armor back on, Queenie, and we'll just be on our way."

"What?" Ellayne asked, her eyebrows meeting in the middle. "But—"

"You're just going to go?" Kade interrupted her.

"Go look for the queen," Armannii said as he grabbed the chest piece of Ellayne's suit and put it over her head. "Yes. We don't have much of a choice." He strapped each piece of armor to Ellayne, and besides the clinking of metal, the room remained silent.

Ellayne met Kade's gaze, and they stared at each other. His eyes widened, his pupils dilating bit by bit. After a few seconds, he closed them, sighing. Kade's features continued to soften, yet his muscles remained tensed.

"I'll help you," he said, opening his eyes as he placed his hands on his hips. "But only because I know you're stubborn enough that you won't leave until you find what you're looking for."

"Who," Armannii corrected, handing Ellayne her helmet. "Who we're looking for."

"Thank you," Ellayne said, first to Armannii, then to Kade. "Where do we start?"

Chapter Twenty-Two

llayne walked side by side with Armannii a few strides behind Kade. He stood tall, the crown in his dark curls reflecting in the light of nearby torches and runes. None of the Dark Soldiers noticed two fakes in their midst as long as Armannii and Ellayne acknowledged them when they walked past. Ellayne thought back to Kade's suggestion. *Towers first, then dungeon.* Though the healing rune had helped with her ribs, her head ached, especially when there was any sort of loud noise.

She flinched when a nearby door slammed, and a Dark Soldier came around the corner.

"Ah, Your Highness." He saluted. "I was just coming to look for you."

Kade paused, and Ellayne stopped next to Armannii. She hated how the helmet blocked most of her vision. *Not tactical at all,* she thought as she did her best imitation of standing at attention.

"What is it?" Kade asked. "I'm in the middle of something, Criss."

"I apologize, but His Majesty would like a word with you."

"Now?" Kade kept his voice steady, but Ellayne could tell by his tense shoulders that he was upset. "As I said, I'm doing something at the moment."

The Dark Soldier bobbed his head. "I'm afraid he was insistent. If you'll just follow me . . ." The soldier turned, and it gave Kade enough time to glance back. His eyebrows furrowed as his gaze darted between Armannii and Ellayne.

What do we do? Ellayne bit her lip. Her mind raced as she tried to figure out if the Dark King was onto them or not. *We haven't been here that long,* she thought. Questions zipped through her head, but in less than a second, Kade faced forward and followed the Dark Soldier. Ellayne risked a glance at Armannii, who nodded. Ellayne grimaced as she fell in step with the elf.

"What does my father want?" Kade asked.

"I was not at liberty to ask, Your Highness."

"Right. Of course."

Ellayne forced her lungs to breathe in a normal pattern, but the idea of being exposed scared her—not for her sake, but for Armannii's. There was no way the Dark King would let him escape another time.

"He's right in here." The Dark Soldier stopped at a door where two other Dark Soldiers stood on either side. He saluted.

"Thank you," Kade said, then addressed the two false soldiers behind him. "You two, go to the west tower. I'll find you again when I am through with whatever this is."

Armannii saluted, and Ellayne remembered at the last second to copy. Ellayne turned as sharply as she could manage without tripping over her feet and continued down the hallway with

Armannii. When they were out of earshot, Armannii whispered to her.

"I have a feeling we're on borrowed time. We need to check the towers, and we need to do it fast."

Ellayne nodded but said nothing on the off chance someone was nearby.

"Follow me," he said, and he led her down a few hallways until they came to a staircase.

She recognized it right away and risked speaking. "I remember this tower. This is where the Dark King kept me after he moved me out of the dungeon."

"There are only two rooms in this tower. If you took up one, then maybe the person we're looking for is in the other. Come on."

After several flights of stairs, Ellayne made Armannii wait while she caught her breath.

"It's like . . . carrying . . . another . . . person . . . on my . . . back," she wheezed, leaning over to place her hands on her knees. "How did you . . . do this . . . for so many . . . years?"

"Easy." Armannii leaned against a wall a few steps above her. "I'm in better shape than you."

"Are you calling . . . me fat?"

"If the oversize shoe fits, Queenie." He snorted when she smacked him, the metal in her glove clanging against his arm.

"Jerk," Ellayne said, her eyes narrowing at him. "Let's keep going."

"You sure you won't keel over?"

"Shut up."

Armannii continued chuckling under his breath when they had to stop for her a second time. Finally, they reached the top.

"When they kept me here, there were guards stationed outside this door," Ellayne said, nodding toward the room in which she'd been held.

"Probably means no one is here," Armannii said, pulling his rune pen out. "But we should still check."

He tried to draw the open rune on the door, but nothing happened.

"It's magic repellent, genius," Ellayne said. "Even I knew that, and I wasn't the captain of the Dark Soldiers."

"Then how do you suggest we get in? Hmm, Queenie?"

Ellayne stepped forward and tried the doorknob. It twisted with a creak, and she pushed. The door opened, and Ellayne wished Armannii could see the smug grin spread across her face.

"Like that?"

"Uh-huh," he said. "It's empty." He shut it after stepping in to take a look at the room. "But it's good to know that while I was getting beat to a pulp by the soldiers, you were being treated like royalty."

"I *am* royalty, and you sound bitter."

Armannii didn't say anything else as he approached the second door. He tried the handle, but it wouldn't budge. "Now what do you suggest?" he asked, his voice dripping with amusement.

"Try a rune." Ellayne shrugged. "I only said the first one was magic repellent. This one may not be."

He pulled the pen back out and traced the open rune on it. Nothing happened, just like the first time. "We need a key to get in."

"That much is obvious."

"And typically only high-ranking soldiers carry keys," he continued.

"So we need to find one and somehow convince him to open the door?"

"Unless you have a better idea."

With all of their back and forth, Ellayne didn't hear the steps on the stairs until after Armannii was pushing her toward the first door. He opened it without it creaking and closed it just as quietly once they were inside. Holding a finger up to his lips, he stopped Ellayne before she could ask what else he'd heard with his super hearing. Armannii pointed for her to get behind him. They stood to the side of the door, flat against the wall, and he drew his weapon.

Ellayne's muscles stiffened when the handle of the door turned. Armannii held the sword out so whoever walked in would be caught with the tip of the weapon in their face. Holding her breath, Ellayne watched the door open.

"Put it down, Armannii," Kade said, entering and closing the door behind him. "It's just me."

"That was fast, Kid." The elf put his sword away, and Ellayne stepped out from behind him. "What did your father want?"

"That's irrelevant," Kade said, his eyes shifting to Ellayne.

"Sure it is," Armannii muttered.

Ellayne reached up and took her helmet off, enjoying the fresh air. "We can't get into the room next door. Do you have a key?"

Kade pulled a ring of keys from his pocket. "I do, but I think I have something better than a key."

"Oh yeah?" Ellayne raised one of her eyebrows. "What would that be?"

"I know where my father is keeping the queen."

"What are we doing here?" Armannii's voice was hoarse when he whispered to Kade. "Isn't the Dark King nearby?"

Kade opened a door with his keys and ushered them in. It seemed to be a small meeting room with a table and a few chairs. Raising his fingers to his lips, he lowered his gaze to Ellayne. "I'm sorry, Ellayne, but he knew you would be coming. I had to tell him."

Realization slapped Ellayne across the face. "You sold me out?"

"Ellayne, sh." He motioned for her to lower her voice, but with the anger boiling up in her, she could not, nor did she want to, oblige.

"You told your father I'm here?" She reached for her sword, but he caught her hand.

Armannii was faster. "What did you do, Kid?"

Kade's face darkened as he stared down Armannii's sword. "You need to leave," he said, his voice low. He still had his grip on Ellayne's glove, and she could feel the metal getting colder. "I didn't tell him you were here, Armannii, and if you know what's good for you, you'll get out."

"I'm not leaving her here," Armannii said, moving the sword closer to Kade's face.

"Trust me," Kade said, and he let go of Ellayne to raise both hands up by his head. "My father won't hurt her, but he won't hesitate to kill you."

Armannii lowered the sword an inch but continued to point it at Kade. "You don't know what he'll do. She was trespassing on his land. He's not—"

"That's enough. Leave. Now."

Ellayne turned her head from Kade to Armannii. Her hands shook from anger, and the last thing she wanted to do was go reveal herself to the Dark King. But the fear of losing Armannii was stronger.

"Go, Armannii," Ellayne said, sighing. "I need you alive if we're going to get Dio off the throne."

"Queenie, this isn't a good—"

"Please." Ellayne placed her glove on the flat part of his blade, lowering it down to his side. "I need you, Armannii."

She couldn't read his face because of his helmet, but he nodded. Stowing his sword in its sheath, he turned on his heels and walked away. Ellayne waited until the door closed before whirling around to face Kade.

"I can't believe you," she spat. "You—"

"You should take your armor off. My father will be less than thrilled if he finds out how you got in here." He stood up straight, switching his gaze from the door to Ellayne.

She pulled the helmet off, shoving it into his stomach. "You're despicable."

"I'm trying to make sure neither you nor Armannii get killed. A little appreciation would be nice. Your half-baked idea wasn't going to end well. Besides, this way you have a chance to build a relationship with my father and me, and"—he held up a finger to shush her before she could argue—"Armannii gets out alive."

Ellayne glared at him as she fiddled with the clasps on the armor. Her frustration only grew when she couldn't get it off.

"Here." Kade placed the helmet on the table. "Let me help."

"No." Ellayne stepped away, her stubbornness rolling off her in waves since her magic could not.

Kade inhaled deeply, closed his eyes, and then closed the space between them. Ellayne stood still, stewing in annoyance as he unfastened each piece of armor and removed it from her body. She felt like a child. He probably saw her as a child. Ellayne clenched her hands into fists, and Kade seemed to notice as he removed the vambrace from her left arm.

"You know, this would be a lot easier if you would relax."

"Shut it, Kade," she growled, looking away from him. She had no desire to let his powerful gaze mess with her emotions. For once, she was glad her magic was being dampened by the cuffs because the spark between them wouldn't interfere with her vexation. She wanted to be mad—wanted to feel the heat rise to her cheeks—not because she was staring at her best friend's muscles but because he had sold her out to a father he'd barely known for two months.

"You can be mad at me all you want as long as you know this was the only way your little suicide plan wouldn't end in tragedy." His words tickled the hair by her neck as he undid the gardbrace on her shoulder. "Whether you thank me or not, I did this for you."

Ellayne bit her tongue, refusing to speak for the rest of the time they were in that room together. Instead, she concentrated all her focus on keeping her features as neutral as she possibly could, which was difficult when his fingers grazed the side of her waist as he lifted the chestplate off or when he gently touched the nape of her neck lifting another piece. Each touch was a battle for control—for neutrality.

"All right. That's the last of it. I'll have someone come return this to where it belongs, and my father will never know. Now, let's go," Kade said, clasping his hands behind his back. "My father is waiting for us."

Ellayne felt a growl erupt from her throat, but Kade didn't seem to notice. She fell in step behind him, and though she knew he was only two feet from her, Kade had never felt farther away.

Kade paused at the door he had gone through to see his father. The soldier who had been there before was no longer present, and with a glance over her shoulder, Ellayne steadied herself for what was about to happen.

"I know you're upset with me, but—"

"Open the door, Kade." Ellayne looked away, no longer wanting to see the way he was watching her.

"Ellayne, I'm—"

"Now." She seethed, clenching her hands into fists again. Ellayne peeked at Kade out of her peripheral vision.

Kade's exhale was strong enough to blow some of his curls away from his forehead, but they fell back into place as he pushed the door open.

"Welcome, Your Majesty," the Dark King said, his posture overly casual from behind a large black desk. He lifted his chin as he smirked at her, his rings glittering in the rune light as he gestured toward a chair across from him. "Please, have a seat."

"Your Majesty." Ellayne curtsied even though she had no desire to. "And I think I'll stand, thanks."

"As you wish." The Dark King nodded toward Kade, and his son joined him, standing beside the desk. "I seem to remember you asking me to present myself when entering your country. I would've expected you to do the same. I can't say I'm thrilled at the idea of you sneaking around my castle."

"I'm sure that's upsetting, Your Majesty," Ellayne said, biting her cheek.

"To say the least. How did you get in?"

"I have my connections." Ellayne kept a straight face as she repeated one of Armannii's favorite responses to her questions.

"And I have a feeling you won't be revealing those connections to me, now will you?"

Ellayne shook her head.

"Right, well, let's get down to business. Shall we?" The Dark King clasped his hands under his chin, resting his gaze on her. "Why did you sneak into the Dark and into my castle?"

"I thought you already knew the answer to that," Ellayne said, shooting a glare at Kade.

"I do, but I'd like to hear you say it."

What a surprise, she thought, and the urge to roll her eyes returned. "I need Lenora to get Diomedes off the throne peacefully."

"So, you still have your heart set on removing your brother in a nonviolent way then?" He waited for her to nod, which she did. "And you somehow think your father's previous wife will give you some sort of advantage?"

"You seemed to think so, Your Majesty. Need I remind you that you're the one who brought her up?"

"That I did." He waved a hand in dismissal of her statement. "And you'll remember that you rudely refused to offer me what I wanted."

"I-I remember," Ellayne said, hating the way she stumbled through the words. She tried to channel the power her father had when running his council, but it left her feeling stiff. Her father would never have gone in person. Neither of the kings did. But, she supposed, times were clearly in need of a change. Maybe this was it.

"So, have you slinked your way into my kingdom to accept my terms? Because I assure you, there are much better ways to get on my good side than breaking into my castle." His eyes darkened. "I did *invite* you to join me here. That was not, however, an invitation to trespass."

Ellayne squared her shoulders, using the emptiness created by the pause in the conversation to think about her next words. She had told Kade she would try, and despite her annoyance at her friend in that moment, she wasn't about to give up on him or his father. "I understand, and I apologize. It was wrong of me to do what I did, and I ask your forgiveness."

The Dark King tilted his head to the side, not responding. But then he nodded. "Go on."

"I am willing to discuss a new treaty in which our two countries can cooperate when it comes to judgement and trials, thus allowing you *legal* methods of procuring justice. But I can't work the details out until after the chaos with my brother is over. If you agree, in exchange, I want Lenora to come with me to Phildeterre."

"You drive a hard bargain there, Your Majesty."

"How is that a hard bargain? It's exactly what you asked for," she said, unable to keep the shock from her voice.

"Not exactly." His voice lilted. The pause left Ellayne shaking as she waited for him to agree or reject her proposition. "But I'll accept."

"I deeply appreciate this, Your Majesty. Thank you," Ellayne said, her posture straightening. She ignored the small smile that crossed over Kade's lips. Residual anger still echoed through her veins. "Where is she?"

The Dark King rose to his feet and crossed the room to stand in front of Ellayne. She always seemed to forget how tall he was until he was peering down at her. "Before I take you to her, I must give you a warning."

"Oh?"

"I may not understand your desire to remove your brother peacefully, but what I do understand is the risk. You can't stay trapped in whatever fantasy you have of redeeming the king. Not when reality is banging the door down. If you don't come to this conclusion soon, you're going to face more loss than you can bear. Your brother is gone, and the sooner you realize that, the sooner you can end this once and for all."

Ellayne gritted her teeth as she looked up at him with her eyes narrowed. "Thank you for the warning, Your Majesty." She could barely get the words out.

"Of course." His lips pulled up into a grin. "Now, if you'll follow me, I'll take you to Lenora."

Chapter Twenty-Three

ou are relieved of your station." Kade nodded to the Dark Soldier standing at the top of the final staircase leading down to the dungeon.

"Your Highness?" the soldier said in a deep voice. His helmet turned as he took in the Dark King and Ellayne, then looked back to Kade.

Kade glowered at the soldier. "It wasn't a request." He lowered his voice.

"Go," the Dark King said, waving his hand.

The Dark Soldier turned his attention from the Dark Prince to the Dark King before nodding and going up the stairs to the main floors of the castle.

"This way." Kade grabbed a torch from the wall and walked down the last flight of stairs.

The stale air brought with it memories of being held prisoner in the cells that lined the elongated room. Ellayne shivered involuntarily.

"Two, two, there were two." The interruption of a scratchy female voice made Ellayne jump.

I know that voice, she thought, peering into the darkness. Ellayne strode past Kade and walked straight to the last cell against the wall. Nothing moved. Ellayne readjusted where she stood, placing her hands on the bars to see if her hunch was correct.

From the darkness, two hands reached out, snatching hold of Ellayne before she could move away. The hands that held hers captive and pressed against the bars were chained together, the metal clinking when it tapped the cell. Though it was dark, Ellayne didn't need the torchlight to know that the hands belonged to someone who was older than she was. The skin was rough, scratching against her hands. Though they were bony with large knuckles, the grip remained tight.

Ellayne sucked in air when the prisoner grabbed her, and she tried to pull away. Her heart raced, and she didn't have time to process as Kade stepped forward and slammed his fist against the bars. The sound echoed around the dungeon and rattled Ellayne.

The hands released, and Kade pulled Ellayne back from the cell by the wrist.

"Are you all right?" he asked, his voice low. He still held her wrist, and he waited for her response before he let go.

"I'm fine," Ellayne said. "Startled is all."

"This is her?" Kade tilted his head to look into the cell. He had placed the torch in the holder on the wall, and the light flickered yellow. Even with the light, though, it was hard to see.

"Yes." The Dark King stayed by the doorway, his face in shadow from the angle of the torchlight.

Ellayne listened as the woman muttered under her breath. It was the same phrase over and over again, the same words she'd spoken when Ellayne was held in the cell next to her.

"Two, two, there were two. Two peas in a pod. Two eggs in a nest."

Kade tilted his head as he peered through the bars in the cell. "How long has she been here?"

"Since the battle between Her Majesty's mother and yours in the Elemental Mountains. I took several prisoners from Emmalee's army right before the final battle."

"But why?" Ellayne asked, turning to face the Dark King. "Why hold her prisoner for so long?"

He tilted his head. "Bargaining chip for the future. She was one of Emmalee's closest confidantes."

"So she's been here all this time?" Ellayne glanced toward the woman. She felt sympathy for her, knowing the misery of the cells firsthand, although for a shorter amount of time. Ellayne couldn't begin to understand the old queen's agony, having been in there for over twenty years.

"I'm going to go back to my office. I have alerted my men to your presence. I will inform them that you, Your Majesty, will be leaving with *one* other person." His eyes flitted to Kade when he emphasized the number.

"Of course, sir." Kade nodded his head.

"It's been a pleasure doing business with you, Your Majesty," the Dark King said, returning his gaze to Ellayne. "And let's both promise to be a little more courteous next time we're visiting each other. Sound like a plan?"

"Yes, Your Majesty. Thank you." Ellayne inclined her head, waiting for him to disappear up the stairs.

"Ellayne," Kade said as soon as he deemed his father out of listening distance, "I'm sorry I told him about you, but—"

"Save it, Kade." Ellayne held up her hand. "I don't want to hear your excuse."

"Listen anyway." He grabbed her hand and lowered it to her side. "As soon as I realized it was you two, I knew I needed to make sure you were going to get out of here safely. Both of you. I knew that the only way that was going to happen was if I sent Armannii away and told my father you alone had come in after the old queen."

"You could've ruined everything, Kade! He could've trapped me down here again, and don't you dare say he wouldn't because he did it in the past. He could've sent me away empty-handed. He could've—"

"But he didn't," Kade said, dropping her hand. "He gave you exactly what you wanted."

"Well—"

"And you're both safe." Kade crossed his arms over his chest.

Ellayne bit her cheek, trying to think of something else to be mad about, but she could find nothing. "Fine. It worked. Congratulations."

Kade sighed, closing his eyes. "You're still mad at me, and I accept that." He lowered his voice and stepped closer. "But you have to understand that I will always do what's best for you first."

She looked to the side, not wanting to meet his eyes. Ellayne didn't trust her own resolve to stay firm. Her eyes followed his hands as they went to his hips, and a ring of keys jingled on his belt. "Whatever. Let me in there with her."

Kade stiffened and shook his head.

"Absolutely not." Kade moved his hands away from his keys. "We don't know what she's capable of. She could hurt you."

"Kade, she's an old woman. I bet she's harmless."

"She just grabbed you," Kade argued, gesturing toward the cell with one hand outstretched. "You have no idea what she could do to you if you went in there. And you wouldn't have your magic."

"I already don't have it." Ellayne pointed to the cuff on her wrist. "Hence the reason you didn't know it was me."

"This isn't a good idea. You don't know what my father did to her. She's clearly not right in the head."

They stayed silent, listening to the prisoner muttering behind the bars, the sound echoing around the stone walls. She must've been shuffling around, agitated by the visitors outside the cell.

"Two, two, there were two. Two, two, there were two."

"How else am I supposed to get her out of here if I don't go in to see her?" Ellayne asked.

"Well—"

"Please, Kade." Ellayne lowered her voice to a whisper. "If I can get her to remember who she is, maybe she can get Diomedes to step down or at least distract him enough to get the upper hand."

Kade shifted his eyes to the cell, then the floor by his feet. "Fine, but I'm coming in with you."

"Okay." Ellayne nodded.

Kade opened the cell with his ring of keys. It took him a second to get the door open because the keys got stuck, and she could feel adrenaline seeping into her blood. She processed what it could mean to get Lenora on her side. All Ellayne would have to do was get her to remember her son. Then she could return to Phildeterre and finally get Diomedes off the throne. *Somehow,* Ellayne thought as she bit her lip. The door slid open.

Ellayne stepped in first, putting one hand out in front of her to guide her way. She didn't want to run into anything. She heard the prisoner shuffling against the back wall, but the woman had stopped muttering.

"Hello?" Ellayne said, keeping her voice to a low volume. "Queen Lenora? Is that you?"

No response came as Kade stepped in behind Ellayne, sliding the door shut except for a tiny crack. When everyone stopped moving, the dungeon filled with silence. Only the sound of water dripping in a different cell echoed in the darkness.

Even with the light coming from the torch behind her, Ellayne couldn't make out the prisoner. Despite being in the darkness, her eyes did not adjust fast enough to see the shadow in the corner lunge at her.

Ellayne gasped as she slammed into the wall. She struggled to breathe as she reached up to pull the two weathered hands off her neck. They squeezed her windpipe, and she choked as she wrestled against the old woman. She couldn't move, stuck between her attacker and the stone wall.

"Please," Ellayne squeaked as the hands tightened. "Stop."

"Ellayne!"

Kade's silhouette moved toward them, and Ellayne sucked in a breath when the hands around her throat released her. She bent over, bracing her hands on her knees as she sucked in air. In the low light, her eyes landed on Kade, who gripped one of the prisoner's wrists with his hand. The prisoner froze in place, her sight focused on Kade.

"Are you all right?" Kade asked, his attention still on the prisoner, though Ellayne knew the question was directed at her.

"Fine," Ellayne said, standing straighter. "I'm fine."

The old woman still hadn't moved, and neither had Kade. They stared at each other in the dim cell.

"She said I'd know when you came," the prisoner said, and unlike before when she'd spoken, her voice was not gravelly.

"Who?" Kade asked.

"Your mother, of course."

Kade rolled his shoulders back, narrowing his eyes at her. "What do you mean? She knew I'd come?"

"She would've told you herself, but" —her head snapped sideways to glare at Ellayne— "she killed her. She killed Emmalee."

Ellayne's mouth opened, but no words came out. Her eyes widened, and she glanced between the old woman and Kade. It wasn't the first time someone had mistaken her for the late queen. *But it is the first time I've been choked because of it,* she thought as she raised her hand to her sore throat.

"Tell us your name," Kade demanded, ignoring the prisoner's previous comment. Ellayne knew he was asking simply to confirm her identity. But after attacking Ellayne and identifying Ellayne as Evangeline, there was little doubt in Ellayne's mind.

"You don't know?"

"Answer me," he said, his voice strained.

"I am Queen Lenora."

Chapter Twenty-Four

llayne shifted where she stood, unsure where to look as her eyes finally adjusted to the lack of light. Kade still held on to Lenora's wrist, keeping his arm rigid so she could not move away. *What changed?* Ellayne thought as the old queen opened her mouth to speak and once again it wasn't nonsense.

"Your mother knew you'd inherit her power," Lenora said, her attention on Kade's grip on her arm. "But she did not say you would be this powerful."

The only reason Ellayne could see Kade's magic rippling was because it made his hands and the old queen's forearm disappear in blackness despite the glow from the torch.

"What do you mean?"

"I know the metal in the dungeon dampens magic, yet yours reveals itself nonetheless. It's exactly as your mother planned it."

Kade tilted his chin down. "Planned it? Planned what?"

"For her offspring to possess some of the strongest dark magic in history. That's why she chose the Dark King to be the father."

"Kade," Ellayne said, stepping forward. The old queen hissed at her, making Ellayne recoil.

"Then you went and stole any hope Emmalee had for a future." Lenora went to lunge for Ellayne again, but Kade yanked the woman across the cell, standing in between the two women.

"Lay another hand on her and I'll make sure you regret it." His voice was low, and Ellayne strained her ears to hear what he said next. "Is that understood?"

The woman didn't answer, at least not verbally, and from where she stood, Ellayne couldn't see Lenora behind Kade's broad shoulders. The question of why the old queen's sanity had returned haunted Ellayne, and she bit her lip, glancing toward the stairway out of the dungeon.

"We should leave," Ellayne said, stepping back so he and Lenora could pass through the cell door first. She closed the cell behind her, and it locked automatically.

"Follow me," Kade said, his hand still around Lenora's wrist.

"Why are you taking me out of this dreadful place?" Lenora directed her question at Kade, ignoring Ellayne's presence altogether. "And why now?"

"Now is not the time," Kade responded, glancing from Ellayne to the staircase. "Once she gets you out, she'll explain what's going on."

Lenora stopped before she reached the first step. "I'm not going anywhere with her. She's evil. She's the enemy. She's—"

"She's going to get you out of here, and you're going to listen to every word she says. Understand?" Kade's voice was measured, but his glare was nothing but ferocious.

Lenora didn't argue, but she did cast Ellayne a sneer. *My mother was right,* Ellayne thought as she stared at the old queen. *Lenora does have beady eyes. Dio's lucky he only inherited his mother's hair.*

Ellayne followed them up the stairs, letting Kade lead the way with the torch in one hand and Lenora's wrist in the other. He hadn't let go once since he pulled her off of Ellayne. She wondered if it was because he thought the old woman would make a break for it or attack Ellayne again. Either way, Ellayne appreciated that it left her with one fewer thing to worry about, except for the fact that she knew it would just be her and Lenora eventually. That thought gave her goose bumps.

"Keep silent," Kade said to Lenora as they approached the top of the dungeon entrance. There were no Dark Soldiers at the door, which had Ellayne letting out the breath she hadn't known she had been keeping in. She knew that the Dark King had alerted everyone to the fact that she was there, but she didn't want to have to talk her way out of the castle.

"The main entrance is this way." Kade left the torch at the archway to the dungeon.

"I'll follow you," Ellayne said, earning a glare from the old woman. A memory of her mother popped into her head at the sight of Lenora's sour face. *Mother always said to be careful because one day my face might freeze that way.* Apparently, no one told Queen Lenora. Ellayne couldn't help but smile at the thought of the old woman being unable to change her unpleasant facial expressions.

Ellayne fell in step behind Kade and Lenora as the three entered the hallway, straight into the path of two Dark Soldiers on patrol.

"Your Highness," one said after saluting. "Beg your pardon, but what are you doing with this prisoner?"

Ellayne's spine straightened, and she clenched her jaw. Seconds seemed like minutes as she waited for Kade to respond.

"My father didn't inform you?" Kade raised his chin. "She is leaving with the queen of Phildeterre immediately."

"Of course, Your Highness," the second said, nodding his head. "I didn't recognize Her Majesty." He inclined his head toward Ellayne.

"As you were, soldiers."

"Of course, Your Highness," the first soldier said. He clicked his heels together and stood taller.

The Dark Soldiers said nothing further and instead saluted, following the corridor in the opposite direction. Ellayne waited until they were out of earshot before speaking.

"Thank you."

Kade released Lenora to rub his eyes with the back of his hand. "I can only take you as far as the main gate. Then it's just the two of you." As soon as he was done, he made eye contact with Ellayne. "Are you going to be okay?" He gripped Lenora again, though this time it was around her upper arm.

"We'll be fine," Ellayne said, though she didn't believe it.

"All right. Then we'd better go."

"How much farther?" Ellayne asked, facing forward after checking behind them. Every time she turned around, she expected a horde of Dark Soldiers to be chasing them, but every time the hallway remained empty. After sneaking in, it felt strange to simply be waltzing out the front door.

Kade kept his eyes on Lenora, who bent over, catching her breath. Ellayne remembered how out of shape she herself had been after a little while in the Dark King's dungeon. Though she knew the old woman hated her, she still felt sympathy for the strenuous journey ahead of them.

"It's not that much farther, only another hallway or two." He pushed a curl out of his eyes and readjusted his grip on Lenora. "Come on."

Ellayne's steps seemed to echo in the empty hallways, and though she knew she was safe with Kade there, she wished there were a way to make her footsteps silent. *Like a rune.* She grimaced. *I seriously need Armannii to teach me rune magic.* The thought of the elf made her chest tighten, and she hoped he was safe too.

They entered the main hallway, and Ellayne laid eyes on the intricate carvings on the front doors. Soldiers stood on either side, and when Kade inclined his head, they opened the doors.

"Open the gate," Kade called to the soldier in the watch station above them. There was an echo of his order, and while he waited for the command to go through the chain of soldiers, he let go of Lenora, who rolled her shoulders back. "Remember what I said earlier." Kade glared at the old queen. "If you lay a finger on Ellayne, you'll regret it."

Lenora sneered at Ellayne, then nodded to Kade. "Understood, Your Highness." Her voice was filled with rotten sweetness.

There is no doubt in my mind, Ellayne thought as Kade turned to face the opening gate, *this woman wants me dead.*

"Good luck, Ellayne," Kade said, stopping short of stepping through the opening. "I know you can do this."

Ellayne turned to face him, watching the way the torch on the gate lit up his face. "Thank you, Kade. I-I wish you could come with me." She lowered her gaze, feeling the weight of leaving another friend in the Dark Castle again. "I don't want to do this without you."

Kade reached out and placed his hand on her shoulder, causing her to look up at him. "I know."

Before she knew what she was doing, she reached forward and wrapped her arms around his torso. She wished he would hug her back, but he didn't. Part of her wondered if it was because his men were watching; she could feel their gazes even though she couldn't see them.

Biting her lip, Ellayne pulled away and turned around. Lenora scowled at her but said nothing as Ellayne started off into the Dark. She didn't dare look back, knowing it would pain her too much to see Kade left behind. Lenora kept in step as they ventured farther into the trees and away from prying eyes.

When she felt they had gone far enough away not to get Armannii caught, Ellayne paused behind a tree. Lenora watched her as she unwound her hair from the key to the magic-dampening cuffs. Her fingers shook from the cold temperature, limiting her dexterity as she undid her cuffs. Ellayne made sure to keep an eye on Lenora, not wanting to turn her back to the old woman. When she finally released the cuffs, she hooked them to the belt that should've been holding her sword, but it was back at Matt's house. That was a big no-no for the Dark, and she knew it as she tucked the key into her trouser pocket. The warmth of her magic sent pleasant shivers up and down her skin, and she welcomed it back. Focusing on Armannii, she told him in a message where they were, asking him to meet them quickly. As soon as the wisp of light left Ellayne's hand, Lenora cringed away.

"I don't know how you managed to bewitch Emmalee's son, but you will not do the same to me."

Ellayne ignored the woman's words, instead keeping her attention on Armannii so the message would get to the right person. *Come on, hurry up, Armannii.* Leaves shifted, but the elf did not appear.

"I don't know what evil you have planned for Emmalee's son—"

"I have nothing of the sort planned. Now would you be quiet?" Ellayne's voice came out louder than she wanted it, and she cringed as her voice spread among the trees. "How did you even know who he was?" She managed to lower the volume back down to a whisper.

Ellayne held a glowing orb in her hand as a light source, so she was able to see Lenora lift her hand. Concerned the woman was going to hurt her, Ellayne braced herself for an attack that didn't come. It took a second for Ellayne to realize Lenora wasn't attempting to hurt her. The old woman held out a dark stone around her neck. "Emmalee gave this to me so I would recognize her offspring when the time came."

Maybe that's why she's not spouting nonsense anymore, Ellayne thought. Her mind filled with different types of spells the sorceress could've placed on the necklace, though the list was as limited as her knowledge of magic. It distracted Ellayne—so much so that she didn't see the person watching her from the branches above until he revealed himself.

Chapter Twenty-Five

o you found her?" A familiar voice rang out from the branches above them, startling Ellayne. Laughter followed it, and Ellayne glared up into the branches as she relaxed her hands from the fists she'd tightened them into. "I've been waiting for ages, Queenie. I was beginning to wonder what had happened to you."

Ellayne relaxed when the elf jumped down from a nearby tree. "You got here fast."

"You said to come quickly." He shrugged. "So I did." Armannii placed his rune pen on her neck and traced the sight rune. When he finished, he turned to the old woman, his armor squeaking. "You must be Queen Lenora." He bowed from the waist to the old woman, who stood still nearby.

"I am. Who are you?" She eyed him warily.

"My name is Armannii," he said as he tucked the rune pen away.

"And you're a Dark Soldier?"

Armannii chuckled. "No. I just find their fashion choices to be exquisite." When Lenora didn't laugh at his joke, Armannii cleared his throat. "Right, um, well. We better get going."

Ellayne glanced back to where the gates separated her from the man she missed more than she'd ever say. Her heart ached to go back for Kade. The muscles in her legs twitched as she resisted running back and begging to see him again. But the Dark King had made it clear; Kade was not coming this time. Ellayne felt sick to her stomach as she turned her back on the Dark Castle and followed Armannii and Lenora.

The queen stayed next to Armannii and well away from Ellayne as they walked back to Matt's house. But Ellayne didn't mind. She wasn't in a talking mood as her thoughts fell on the man she had left behind in the castle. When had life become so complicated? Though it was outrageous, she almost missed the peaceful bliss of having her memories gone every time the Curse of Infiniti reset her.

In the back of her mind, she knew she should be celebrating the victory. She had Lenora. She hoped that would help resolve the issues with her brother peacefully. He might even come to his senses. However, she wasn't naive. She knew her father and mother were gone forever. There would be no going back to the way things were before her brother got his magic. But maybe there could be a new normal. And maybe, just maybe, her brother could be a part of it.

But then again, the warning the Dark King had given her echoed through the blissful image she had created of the future, shattering it. She didn't want to think of her brother as a monster, yet did he not act as one? And as she walked around the tangled trees, her eyes played tricks on her, hiding brief glimpses of her brother through scraggly branches, a ghost stalking her with every step she took.

Ellayne watched Armannii take off his armor, and when the last piece clattered to the floor of Matt's house, she cracked her back by turning side to side. "I'm glad I didn't have to walk back here in that ridiculous armor. I seriously sympathize with all the Dark Soldiers. At least the Cyanthian armor is lightweight," she said, cracking her neck.

Armannii went to sit at the small kitchen table with Lenora, who kept her beady eyes locked on Ellayne. It made goose bumps travel up and down Ellayne's arms.

"It's not that bad once you get used to it. It's actually kind of unfortunate you lost the other set. Never know, could've come in handy in the future again," Armannii said, picking at dirt under his fingernails. "And now I think you have some explaining to do to our friend here." Armannii gestured toward Lenora, who still hadn't taken her eyes off of Ellayne.

"Right." Ellayne sat down across from the old woman. Her face appeared more wrinkled in the light shining down from the ceiling, and a rash grew up the side of her neck. She sat up as straight as she seemingly could, but there was a natural hunch to her shoulders. Besides a red scarf tied into her dark hair, everything else she wore was a dirty tan. The skirt was a darker brown than the tunic, but they were both stained and ripped in some areas. The smell coming off her was rancid: a mixture of urine and body odor. But the woman didn't seem to notice.

"My name is Ellayne—"

"Lies," Lenora hissed. "Every word you utter is a lie."

"Hey now," Armannii said, placing a hand on the table between them. "I suggest you wait 'til she's finished to insult her.

It would be in your best interest." Though he spoke with a smile, his tone remained stern.

Lenora raised an eyebrow, her eyes dancing between Ellayne and the elf. But she didn't say another word.

"As I was saying, my name is Ellayne, and I am King Butch's daughter." *Probably better if I don't mention my mother outright,* she thought. Lenora had made it abundantly clear that any mention of Evangeline would provoke an attack. "Phildeterre is in dire need of your services, madame." Ellayne did her best to smile, but it came out more as a grimace. "Diomedes, your son, is leading the country into war again. He will stop at nothing until he has complete control over Phildeterre, no matter how many lives it may cost."

Lenora didn't interrupt, but she did lift her chin, tilting her head to the side. Ellayne took a deep breath.

"We need your help to prevent him from destroying the country and all who live there."

The old woman sneered. "And what do you expect me to do?"

"Well . . ." Ellayne rubbed her fingers over her bracelet underneath the table. "Since you are his mother, and knowing how much he cares for you, I propose that you talk him out of his foolish plan. Talk some sense into him. I think—no, I know—he will listen to you."

Armannii nodded along to what Ellayne said. *Please say yes.* Ellayne restrained her face, not revealing the dire nature of her request.

"What do I receive in return?"

"Your freedom and your son." Ellayne didn't hesitate. "Once you talk Dio down from the throne, we will offer you safe passage with him wherever you desire to go."

Lenora clicked her long fingernails on the table. With a big yawn, she said, "You are asking a lot of me. I have not been in

Phildeterre, let alone seen my son, in over twenty-five years. I must think on this and will make a decision later. But as for now, I am tired."

"But—"

"Of course, Your Majesty," Armannii said, bowing his head. "You must be exhausted." He stood up, his chair screeching as he did so. "I'll show you to your room." He offered his arm to Lenora, and she took it.

Once they were gone, Ellayne slumped down in the chair. The fact that she didn't know whether it was day or night left her body tired and confused. A yawn escaped her lips, and she rubbed her eyes with the backs of her hands. It felt nice to keep her eyes closed, and she wondered when she'd last slept.

The chair across from her squeaked, and she looked up to find Armannii staring at her.

"If you aren't going to fall asleep, I'd like to hear what happened after the kid sent me away in the Dark Castle." He leaned back in the chair and folded his arms across his chest.

She nodded with a sigh. It didn't take her long to fill him in because he stayed quiet until she was finished.

"I'll be honest," Armannii said as he snorted. "I never would've thought to solve that problem diplomatically."

"Until Kade sold me out, neither would I." She rolled her eyes, but something about the statement weighed heavy on her. "Shows the kind of queen I am."

"Your brother was never a fan of diplomacy either."

"I remember," Ellayne said, a glimmer of a smile on her lips. "I remember all the times he left the castle before the meetings. He'd sneak out and—"

"He and I would go to a pub or—"

"Cause trouble in town." Ellayne raised an eyebrow, and Armannii laughed.

"I remember one time we snuck into the back of a tavern, and I distracted the staff while your brother switched every single label on their spices in the back. When we returned the next day, I had the saltiest sweet roll you've ever tried. We couldn't stop laughing, and when they figured out it was us, we were never allowed back again."

Ellayne smiled, remembering the mischief she and her brother had gotten up to when they were younger. "When I was five and Dio was fifteen, my parents went away on business for a week. Dio snuck me into the throne room, and we made a fort with the thrones and the curtains around the area. He and I spent three days in there reading. I'm sure there's still a stain where I spilled my grape juice on the bottom of one of the curtains. We would've gotten away with it if the maids hadn't come in to clean the room to prepare it for our parents' return."

Armannii's smile faded, and his eyebrows furrowed. "There are moments where I forget everything has changed. I get this desire to go visit him, to bug him about the stuffy outfits he had to wear in court, or to visit our old stomping grounds." He scratched his chin. "Then I remember."

"I know. I-I want him back." Ellayne lowered her head, feeling the strain of the long hours pulling at the muscles in her neck. "If there's a way to save him—to save all of them—I want to find it."

"And if there's a way, you'll be the one to pull it off, Queenie."

Chapter Twenty-Six

llayne wasn't sure at first what woke her up. She had taken Armannii's room after a suggestion from the elf. He had placed the queen in the room she had slept in the first time they stayed there, and they both thought it best that the two women stay far away from each other. Just in case.

Armannii slept in the room down the hall from the old queen, leaving Ellayne in the left corridor alone . . . until she woke up face-to-face with Lenora. The old woman's hand snaked out and covered Ellayne's mouth before she could get a word out.

"Sh," the old woman whispered. "I've got something to show you, Your Majesty." Her voice was soaked in sickly sweetness.

Chills ran up and down Ellayne's spine, and everything in her screamed that she should make noise. But what if Lenora had made a decision? Weighing the consequences, Ellayne didn't want to hurt the chance that she would help with Diomedes if she refused to comply. Ellayne sat up in bed, nodding to the woman so that she would release her.

"Follow me." Lenora tiptoed out of the room, and with one glance at her cot, Ellayne followed.

Armannii had lowered the light runes in the kitchen to a dim glow before going to sleep, but Ellayne was still able to see where she was going. Lenora pointed to the table, and Ellayne walked over to it, passing Lenora to do so.

Ellayne only realized her mistake when she felt the sharp point of a sword between her shoulder blades.

"We're going on a walk," Lenora whispered. "Outside."

"Lenora—"

"Hush," the old woman hissed, and she poked Ellayne on the back, making her move forward. "The cuffs. Put them on."

"But—"

"Now, daughter of Evangeline."

Ellayne couldn't turn to face Lenora, too afraid she'd wind up skewered on the end of the sword. Instead, she followed the directions given to her, grinding her teeth together as soon as she felt the light magic vanish from her body.

"Open the door," the old queen ordered, and Ellayne did. "Up the stairs." Each order came with the pinch of the sword on her back, and Ellayne flinched every time.

The winding staircase led to the door, which was sealed with a rune. "I can't open this one," Ellayne said, risking a glance over her shoulder. "I don't have a rune pen, and I don't know the rune."

"Step to the side." Lenora shoved Ellayne, still keeping the sword directed at her even as she pulled a pen out of her tunic. "I spent enough time in those cells to see many try to open them with the rune."

"But you don't have mag—" Ellayne's words cut off when she saw a rune begin to glow where the old queen drew it. "But how?"

"Go." Lenora shoved her through the opening in the tree, then sealed it behind her.

"How do you have magic? And where'd you get a rune pen?"

"I stole it off the elf. As for the magic, the Dark King tried to see if I possessed the gift, and when I didn't, he had experiments conducted on me in search of a way to infuse magic into those without. Emmalee was interested in a similar experiment, though she never would've tested it on a human until she knew it would work."

"Lenora, that's terrible. I'm sorry that—"

Lenora snickered behind her. "I don't need your sympathy."

"All right, so why don't you talk to me? Tell me where we're going. Tell me what you want." Ellayne kept her hands out in front of her, completely blind to the world. "I'm not your enemy here. I got you out of that awful dungeon. I was held as a prisoner there too for a while. Do you remember that? I was in the cell right next to you."

"Oh, I remember. You thought I was short a few marbles, didn't you? Thought I'd lost my mind? But that's what my mistress wanted you to believe, wanted everyone to believe."

Ellayne didn't say anything, not wanting to test the old queen's patience or sanity. Instead, she stepped carefully over a root, hoping Lenora would trip and fall. The old queen didn't. The farther they went, the more Ellayne searched for an escape route. She considered all possible distractions but found none that wouldn't conclude with her being run through with the sword. But a new thought overwhelmed her mind. She had no idea how to get back to Matt's tree even if she did get away. A chill ran down her back, and she shivered.

"My mistress knew I'd be a target when your mother and father finally killed her, so she gave me the only means of freedom she could. Insanity."

Ellayne refrained from pointing out that the only thing that had gotten her was twenty-five years or more in a dark dungeon cell. Instead, Ellayne said, "And she used the necklace you showed me as a means to break the spell she placed on you for protection? But how did the necklace know Kade was her son?"

"It's infused with the sorceress's blood. It will alert whoever possesses it to the presence of anyone who shares her bloodline. And the spell was created to break when one of her heirs returned to her most trusted friend—*me*. Only then could she be sure that I was in safe hands."

Without meaning to, Ellayne stopped, frozen by the words Lenora spoke. Pain sliced into her left shoulder when Lenora ran the sword into her. The cut wasn't deep, but Ellayne could feel the blood begin to ooze. With her hands chained together, there was no way to stop the bleeding.

Heirs? Her mind split between the news she had just been given and the stinging in her shoulder. The combination created a splitting headache.

"Keep walking," Lenora said, pushing her with the heel of her hand this time instead of the sword. "I didn't say you could stop."

"I-I'm sorry," Ellayne stuttered. "I just—I don't understand."

"I was there on the day she gave birth. Soon after, she died. Your mother murdered her."

Ellayne bit the inside of her cheek. *Don't respond. You'll only make this worse.* But the more she processed what Lenora was saying, the more she felt the growing storm of emotions interspersed with the fear she had experienced the moment the sword had poked her back in Matt's house. Now terror mixed and mingled with the curiosity that Kade might have a sibling, and then dread that the sibling might not be alive. Anxiety came to the forefront when she considered how she would tell him, and it all returned to an alarming realization that she might never get the chance.

"Emmalee was devoted to having more children after her daughter, Hazel, was taken from her. Some even called her obsessed with the idea. The thought of having more children was what drove her here, to the Dark and to the king. But when she left with what she came for, she did not expect that the fruit of her labor would bring twice the reward. She was overjoyed when she got to hold her son to her chest. It was the first time I saw a true smile on her face. But the midwife informed us that her task wasn't over yet. There was still one more to go."

Lenora paused in her explanation, and Ellayne took the chance to ask the question that had been burning since she'd realized Kade had a twin. "Girl or boy?"

"Two sons, which she sent into hiding with different people after placing a protection spell on them. She had no intention of letting their father know they existed, and with the impending attack, she wasn't going to lose another child, let alone two. She was unsure what would become of her when your mother and my ex-husband came to hunt her down."

Kade had a brother. A twin brother. The full impact of the truth had yet to hit her as Ellayne stumbled through the Dark. Rough bark scraped against Ellayne's outstretched hands, and she moved to the right to avoid hitting a tree. But even then, navigating the Dark now seemed easier than trying to find her way through all the thoughts and emotions in her head.

"There's not much I can thank your father for except my son, Diomedes, and Butch's attack on the town Emmalee's husband and daughter were in. If he hadn't killed precious little Hazel, Emmalee never would've become the strong leader she was. In fact, my mistress's sons would not have been born without the bloody part your father played because of his hatred and misunderstanding of magic."

"It wasn't his fault. And my father didn't hate—"

"Quiet," Lenora ordered, her voice brash and cold as she pushed the sword into Ellayne's back, causing her to yelp. "My ex-husband was a nightmare with a crown. His entire—*your* entire—family is a line of magic-hating monsters."

"I don't hate magic, Lenora. I *have* magic. That's why you asked me to put on the cuffs, remember? How could I hate a part of who I am?" It wasn't the first time Ellayne had asked that question, but it was the first time she had verbalized it. Since she had come to terms with the gift her magic was, she had wondered how she'd ever tried to hide that part of herself. It was one of the last things, besides a few journals and the medallion around her neck, that she had left of her mother. But while the writing in the journals would fade and the necklace might be stolen someday, her magic had only grown stronger with time; it had brought her closer to a mother she'd never be able to hug again.

"I'm sure your father despised you for what you are."

"You're wrong, Lenora," Ellayne said as gently as she could. "Dio thought the same thing, but you're both wrong. My father didn't hate magic. He loved my mother, and he loved me, magic included."

Ellayne screeched when Lenora kicked the backs of her knees, making her tumble to the ground. She barely had time to catch herself, slicing her palm open on something sharp.

"Your father was incapable of love. And you are an aberration that never should've existed. Turn around and face me on your knees."

"If you think so lowly of me, why tell me about Kade and his brother? Why share all of this with me, especially if you were planning to kill me all along? What about Phildeterre?"

"Phildeterre is going to be just fine when I return to my son and we rule together."

Ellayne would've been shocked if there were any part of her body not drumming with adrenaline. Her heart thudded in her chest, trying, it seemed, to break free and escape before it met an unfortunate end. But her body froze. *I need my magic. I have no weapon. Armannii doesn't know where I am.*

"You don't have to do this, Lenora. I told you, I'm not your enemy. I'm trying to do everything I can to keep Dio alive. He's my brother, and I—"

"*Half* brother, you insignificant little nit. You are worthless. Your mother was despicable, and you will die in the dirt where you belong."

The moisture from the ground soaked Ellayne's knees, but something Lenora had just said had Ellayne lifting her chin. "My mother was *born* to be queen. Even if she hadn't married my father and worn the crown, she had more royalty and grace in an eighth of her pinky finger than you have in your entire body."

Searing pain ripped across Ellayne's cheek, and she gasped as she pressed her fingers to her bleeding face. The initial pain of the strike was quickly followed by a burning sensation that brought tears to her eyes.

"You are *nothing*, daughter of Evangeline. Nothing except a reminder that my ex-husband lost his mind after I left."

Ellayne gritted her teeth, but when she blinked back the moisture in her eyes and looked up, she was startled to see Lenora holding the sword to her face. Not because of the weapon, which held a drop of crimson dangling at the tip, but because she could *see* the blood.

A faint glow surrounded them, and when Ellayne scanned the area, the tops of glowing mushrooms peeked back at her as they began to grow out of the trees around them. How far had Lenora taken her? Ellayne knew there were no mushrooms near Matt's house. Since she had been unable to see, she hadn't realized how far they'd traveled. Ellayne shifted away from a sprout near her knee, remembering the deadliness of the fungus. One touch and she would be dead in a minute or less.

Still holding her injured cheek—the sickening metallic smell and the warmth of her own blood was making her stomach turn—Ellayne glanced back up at the point of the sword, the tip now angled toward her chest. Lenora's malevolent eyes sparkled in the growing light.

"You're wrong about him. You're wrong about my mother. And you are most certainly wrong about me," Ellayne said, her voice bolder than she expected. "I meant it when I said I mean you no harm. You don't have to do this, Lenora. I—"

"Silence," Lenora snapped, lifting the tip of the sword until it touched Ellayne's chin. "I will not be swayed by anything Evangeline's offspring has to say." With those words spoken, Lenora swung the sword above her head, and Ellayne reflexively closed her eyes.

Realization settled in. She was going to die. Of all places, she was going to die in the middle of nowhere, lost in the Dark. Ellayne cringed at the stupidity she possessed in turning her back to the old woman; it had given her the upper hand. Ellayne had marched straight to her death. Barely hesitant. Foolish. Idiotic.

Questions raced through her mind in the milliseconds before the sword swung down. *Will Armannii look for me? Will anybody find my body, or will the fungus consume me before anyone has the chance? Will Kade ever know I'm gone? Will he ever know he might have a brother out there? What about my country? My people? Will I see my parents again?*

Each second moved in slow motion as Ellayne braced every muscle in her body for the strike that would certainly end her life.

Clank!

Metal clashed against metal, and Ellayne jumped at the echoing sound, which sent shivers down her spine and into her aching knees. What had happened? Had Lenora missed?

"Drop the sword, Lenora."

Kade. Ellayne's eyes shot open, and she squinted in the darkness for her friend. He stood beside them, his sword only inches from Ellayne's face. He had stopped Lenora. Their blades met in the middle, wavering as the old woman continued to push down.

How did he find me? Ellayne's mind raced as she released the breath she'd been holding, sucking in fresh air. Lenora's hands shook, and it took another few seconds before she slid the sword to the side and lowered it.

"Put the sword on the ground," Kade ordered, and he let his own sword drop from its position when she placed the weapon by her feet. "Good. Now come back to the house with us and—what are you doing? Stop!" Kade hollered, taking a step forward.

But he was too late.

"No!" Ellayne shouted as every hope of taking Lenora back to Diomedes disappeared in an instant.

Lenora took a step to the side, raising her hand. In one swift motion, she touched the largest mushroom on the tree. Neon pink slime covered her hand as she stumbled toward Ellayne.

Throwing her chained hands up in front of her face, Ellayne caught Lenora's poisoned hand before the pink slime made contact with her skin. But Lenora, unable to support her full weight due to the poison in her system, collapsed on Ellayne, who fell back to the ground. Ellayne kept the hand inches from herself and moved to the side to avoid lying on a mushroom beneath her on an exposed root.

Her heart hadn't stopped racing, and each of her breaths were quick and shallow to the point that she was getting light-headed. Lenora continued to try to touch Ellayne with the poisonous slime, but Ellayne used her legs to keep as much distance between herself and certain death. The strength in her arms was giving out though, and with each second that passed, more concern grew in her mind that a mushroom could sprout up beneath her at any moment. She needed to get up, but the dying queen's body weight pinned her to the forest floor.

"Ellayne!" Kade's voice cracked as he sprinted forward. He leaned his weapon next to a tree without the mushrooms and knelt down next to Ellayne.

With a grunt, he shoved Lenora off, pushing her onto at least three more mushrooms. Kade heaved Ellayne out from under Lenora's legs, the only part of her still touching Ellayne. Dirt covered Ellayne's trousers and tunic, but she sighed in relief when she saw a distinct lack of luminescent slime on the front of her clothing.

"You're good, you're clean. I don't see any residue," Kade said, checking Ellayne's back. "Are you okay? You're bleeding." He cupped her face, holding it steady as he pulled out a handkerchief. She winced when he dabbed at her cheek, turning her head to the side. Seeing Lenora's body, Ellayne struggled to swallow, and she went back through the conversation that had led to where she stood. "What are you—Ellayne, what are you doing? Don't!" Kade's voice went up in pitch when Ellayne broke free of his grasp.

Kneeling down beside Lenora's paralyzed body, she gently pushed the woman over, watching for any pink poison on the clothes. "I didn't want this," Ellayne said, her face scrunching up as she grimaced down at Lenora. "I'm sorry, Lenora. I don't know if you can hear me, but I'm sorry."

Bright pink veins spread over Lenora's skin, and her eyes became glassier by the second. Ellayne wasn't even sure if the woman had heard her apology, but she hoped she had. It was true. A line of foam leaked out of the old woman's mouth, and her chest no longer moved, frozen from the poisonous mushrooms.

"You were my only chance at removing Dio from the throne peacefully," Ellayne mumbled, using the back of her arm to wipe a stray tear from her uninjured cheek. "And now that you're gone,

I-I don't know what I'm going to do. I don't want to hurt him, Lenora. You may not believe me, but he's my brother, and I still love him."

Armannii's rune pen peeked out of Lenora's tunic, and Ellayne carefully pulled it out with two fingers, wiping the end with the poisonous goo on a clean section of Lenora's tunic. But before she stood up, another item caught her eye. The necklace Emmalee had given Lenora lay near the old woman's collarbone, and Ellayne avoided the bubbling foam draining down Lenora's neck as she took the necklace off.

"And I know you still loved Dio too. I just wish he had gotten the chance to see you." Ellayne sniffled, biting her bottom lip to keep from breaking down. "I wish you had given me a chance, Lenora. I'm so sorry." Ellayne's voice broke as she rose to her feet, Kade steadying her by gripping her elbow.

"Why did you take that?" Kade asked, nodding toward the necklace in her hand.

"I promise I'll tell you later. But I really want to go. I don't want to see what happens next," Ellayne said, her voice drifting off as she watched little spores begin to sprout out of the pink slime on Lenora's hand. "We should leave." She put Armannii's rune pen and the necklace in her trouser pocket, although it was a bit difficult with the cuffs still on and the cut on her hand still stinging from where she had landed on it when she fell.

"Here." Kade held out his hands, and Ellayne placed hers in his. He pulled out a master key for the cuffs and unlocked them, allowing her magic to flood back to her. "Are you okay?" he asked, stowing the cuffs and key with one hand while keeping both of hers in the other. "Did she hurt you anywhere else?" His voice was tight, contrasting with his soft eyes.

"My back is cut up, but we can worry about it later," she said, squeezing his hand with both of hers. "Do you think you can get back to Matt's from here? That's where we were when—"

"When what? She ambushed you, took Armannii out, and dragged you out here? Please tell me that's what happened and you didn't follow her like an idiot."

Although she could tell he was trying to make a joke, his timing was terribly off, and she pulled her hands away. "She tricked me, and I made a mistake. She got the jump on me. I, well, I was stupid. I didn't want to upset her because she was my only chance to talk Dio off the throne, and now—"

Kade sighed, and he pulled his own rune pen out of his jerkin. "Ellayne, you could've died."

"Actually," Ellayne said, moving her hair and leaning her neck to the side, "I would've died. If you hadn't shown up, she would've done what she came out here to do."

"And then what?" Kade's words were clipped, tickling her skin and raising the baby hairs near her ear as he traced a sight rune on her. "Did you stop to consider the vast number of people counting on you? What would've happened if you'd died?"

"But I didn't die, Kade," she said, straightening up and turning to face him when he finished. He was still leaning over, closer than she expected. The breath hitched in her throat.

"Well, you could've," he whispered, his sight dropping to her lips for less than a second.

"I. Didn't." Ellayne bit the inside of her cheek, also letting her gaze dip for a moment. It was silent, and for an instant she allowed herself to wonder what his lips would feel like pressed against hers. Sucking in quickly, Ellayne placed a hand on Kade's chest and pushed him back.

"Ellayne, I—"

"I'm fine. Really, Kade," she said, glancing to her hand when he caught it on his chest. She could feel his heart beating, and though it was steady, it beat faster the longer she held her hand there. After only a few seconds, it thundered inside his rib cage. "Please, can we go?"

With another squeeze of her hand, he nodded. Kade picked up the sword he had leaned against the tree, not letting Ellayne's hand go when she knelt down to pick up the one Lenora had used against her, cringing when the cold metal rubbed against the torn skin on the palm of her hand. Kade gently tugged her away from Lenora's quickly disintegrating corpse.

"You're sure you can get us back to Matt's?" Ellayne asked after only a minute.

"I used to make maps for a living, Ellayne. Of course I can."

Ellayne scoffed. "It's been a while. Maybe you're out of practice."

Kade paused, pulling her toward him, though not in a harsh way. "*Actually*, Your Majesty, I was working on a map of this area an hour ago."

Raising an eyebrow, Ellayne smiled, though it seemed out of place after what she had just gone through. "Oh really? And you're sure it was correct? There are lots of trees around here, and it is kind of hard to see at times."

"I'm *positive*." Kade's dimple popped out, and Ellayne watched his lips form the words. "Oh ye of little faith."

"All right, Prince Map Guy. Get us back there before Armannii sends every dryad and nymph to come find me." Ellayne lifted both of their hands, gesturing in the direction they had been walking. And with one final smirk at her, Kade continued navigating. "And while we're walking, it'd be nice if you told me what in the world you're doing here," Ellayne said. "Your father—"

"Doesn't know where I am. I left to come find you. He'll find out soon enough if he doesn't already know. I used the mycelium to ask around to see if you'd stopped at Matt's or gone straight to

Verina's. When one of the nymphs using the mycelium said they saw you out here with an old woman, I was worried."

"Well, now the only thing to worry about is the fact that I'm back to square one. I have no idea what to do next."

"We'll figure it out, Ellayne." He squeezed her hand as he led her over an exposed root. "Together."

His reassuring squeeze had the opposite effect on Ellayne as she remembered another part of her conversation with Lenora. At some point in the near future, she was going to tell Kade he had a twin, and there was no telling what he would say or do when she did. The necklace felt heavy in her pocket.

The longer they stayed silent, the more Lenora's death weighed on Ellayne, and she began to blame herself. Ellayne's shoulders slumped. One thought became very clear. The battle with her brother was almost unavoidable now. She would face Diomedes, and only one of them would live.

Chapter Twenty-Seven

llayne wiped another tear off her cheek, scowling at the wall across from her. Her muscles ached from training, she was pretty sure one of the bandages on her back had come loose and the injury had reopened, and the target she was practicing with was in worse shape than when she started. Her lungs burned, and a cramp formed in her side, but it all felt better than the throbbing going on in her head.

I can't go up against Dio; his magic is stronger than mine. I'd be dead in an instant. She used her elbow to smack the target, grunting. *Even if I have held my own in the past, ultimately, he'd win.* She hit it again. *I'd be dead.* Again. *He'd win.*

She grabbed a wooden staff from a barrel and swung it around. The more she considered it, the more it seemed the prophecy was right. One of them was going to die. And if she didn't figure something out, it was going to be her. Ellayne rammed the staff into the target. *And then my country is going to fall.* She gritted her teeth. *Like Pingbi. Like Lenora.* It would be all her fault. Ellayne repositioned her feet. *All my fault because I couldn't keep a stubborn old lady alive for more than twenty-four hours.* With a crack, she swung the weapon at the target. The post the target sat on wobbled, and she didn't wait for it to stop before striking again.

"How long have you been in here?" Kade asked from the doorway. He leaned against the curved frame, his arms crossed over his chest. His hair was fluffed higher on one side than the other, and he ran his fingers through it in an attempt to tame the frizz.

They had returned to Matt's house together, much to the surprise of a disgruntled Armannii. He was furious, but mainly at himself for letting Lenora get out. After thoroughly washing his rune pen, he left.

"Since Armannii went to get an update." Ellayne grunted as she swung around and struck the target.

"But that was hours ago."

"Your point?" She struck the target again, this time leaving a dent. Her brother would've broken it in half. She tried again.

Kade shook his head. "You can't blame yourself for what happened to Lenora." He stepped into the room and ran his fingers over another staff. With a tilt of his head, he picked it up and faced her. "It wasn't something you could stop. She obviously had decided she was not going to come back with us."

"I shouldn't have gone with her," Ellayne said as she directed her staff in his direction.

He circled her. "Well, yeah. That's just plain obvious. What you did was stupid." He lunged, and she dodged it.

"Rub it in why don't you?" She clenched her jaw, spinning to strike him on the opposite side. Kade avoided her.

"That's not what I was trying to do," he said, shaking his head.

"Really? Could've fooled me."

"I was trying to assure you that if she wasn't going to help us, then there was nothing you could've done to change her mind."

Ellayne sighed because some part of her knew he was right. But then who was to blame? The easiest answer stared back at her whenever she caught a glimpse of herself in a reflective surface. Since Lenora had died several hours earlier, Ellayne felt a heaviness bear down on her, adding to everything she'd been carrying since being named queen in her father's decree. She knew her father hadn't had any clue the weight she'd have to endure because of it. But that didn't take the grief and frustration away. The burden made every step difficult—slow. She had thought that by spending some time training, she might fix it, but it had only made it worse.

"If I don't figure something out, Phildeterre is going to be destroyed by my brother. Everyone is counting on me. I was the only one who could do anything to prevent that from happening. And now I've failed." She blocked his attack and returned with one of her own. "I feel like the only thing I've been doing since my father died is failing. My country, my people, and my parents."

"Stop that." He jumped to the side to avoid her. "You sound like you've already given up. But the war hasn't even begun yet."

"Oh yeah?" Ellayne raised an eyebrow. "People have already died because of Dio and his awful wife, and for all we know, Bolee is in shambles like Pingbi. For all we know—" She paused, her shoulders drooping. "Phildeterre has already fallen to Dio while I've been wasting my time here trying in vain to find a way to stop him."

"Are you kidding me?" He knocked her weapon away, nearly managing to land a strike on her before she moved away. "You can't be serious."

"What?" She hesitated for a second, frowning.

"You sound exactly as pessimistic as the day I found you in your room at the castle in a sobbing mess. You had all but given up then too. Then you know what happened?"

"Yeah. Armannii showed up, and together the two of you basically broke my curse without me because I was too busy losing my grip on reality."

Kade shook his head, scoffing at her. "*You* broke your curse, Ellayne. It wouldn't have broken unless somewhere in your fading mind you were determined. Magic requires action, but not thoughtless action. There's got to be intention behind it. Every time I learn a new rune, I have to master the intention behind it, not just drawing a complicated symbol."

"So? Maybe the last part of me wanted to break the curse. That shouldn't be a surprise. What does that have to do with what's going on now?"

"You've been walking around with a cloud over your head since your father died."

"Can you blame me?"

"Of course not. And you've handled it better than most people would." He offered her a small smile. "You once asked me to say one positive thing because you didn't think I could do it. To be fair, it was a lot harder back then. Ellayne, you're the reason I don't have to struggle to list the good things in my life. And now, in some bizarre twist of fate, the roles are reversed."

Ellayne went to lunge, but he moved out of the way, catching her wrist in his hand. He gave it a gentle twist, causing the weapon to clatter to the ground. At the same time he pulled her close, pinning her wrist to her back, he brought his stave up to her neck, a grin on his face.

"Now *you're* the pessimistic grump, and I'm asking *you* to tell me something positive."

"Are you serious?" Ellayne tilted her head, glaring at him. He pressed his lips into a bigger smile. "This is stupid."

He snorted. "Pretty sure I said those exact words when you asked me to do it the first time. Now, tell me something positive happening right now." Kade kept a steady grip on her when she tried to pull away. "Come on. I'll let you go as soon as you give me an adequate response."

"Or you could let me go now and we could keep fighting like adults. Just a thought." She grunted when he pulled her closer. He wasn't breathing hard, even after several minutes of dueling. "Fine. Lenora didn't kill me. Is that good enough?"

"It certainly is a plus." He lowered his voice, a glint in his eyes as his gaze washed over her face—a face that was sweaty and red. "It really would've put a damper on my day if you'd died."

"Yours and mine both. Now let me go," she said, rolling her eyes.

Before he let her go, he winked at her. In response, she stuck her tongue out. "Such a ladylike thing to do, Your Majesty." Kade released her, stepping back into a bow while she picked up her weapon again.

"Remind me again what all of that was for?" Ellayne said as she fell back into her fighting stance. He matched her, his footwork better than when she had fought him in the Dark earlier.

"It's supposed to be a lesson. You're a leader, Ellayne. And if my father has taught me anything, it's that people are always looking to their leaders. You and I, our parents, even your brother, we all have people watching us. If your people think they have no chance of coming out of battle alive, what makes you think they'll follow you?"

Ellayne bit her lip as she considered his words. "Your father told you that?"

Kade nodded as they circled each other. "He thinks you'd be a good queen, you know. He really does want you to come out on top."

"Really?" Ellayne knocked Kade's weapon away, moving when he struck. "I mean, that's great and all, but he does realize that his words mean nothing without action. He may want me to win, but he knows just as well as I do that I'd have a better chance with the Dark Soldiers fighting alongside us."

"I know that. And I've mentioned it to him in our meetings with the lead soldiers. They have no qualms about helping, but my father is concerned about the risk to his men. He knows your brother is powerful, especially with the violent displays he's given."

"But there's always a risk when you're trying to change something, right?"

"He wants to know there's a plan, that he's not just throwing his men into a battle where none of them come back. He cares about these men. Most of the ones I've talked to have been with him since they were children. Until I walked through his front door, I guess they were the closest thing to family he had. And Ellayne"—he blocked her, using the momentum to spin and let her stumble to the side, though he didn't strike when the opportunity presented itself—"I've gotten to know a lot of these men. Almost like . . . almost like they're my brothers."

Ellayne choked, and Kade must've seen the change in her demeanor because he lowered his weapon.

"What? What is it?" His gaze sucked her in, but the memory of what Lenora said lingered in her mind, smothering the moment with a sense of shame for having even waited as long as she had.

"Kade . . ." She stepped forward but hesitated. "Lenora said something, and—"

"Whatever she said doesn't matter now. She's gone, and it wasn't your fault," he said, but his words made her shake her head.

"No, this is important." Ellayne crossed the room, dropping the stave in the barrel. While she faced the wall, she took a few deep breaths. Fear and anxiety replaced the pleasant adrenaline of combat. It left her feeling cold as sweat ran from the back of her ear down her neck. When she finally turned to face him, she wrapped her arms around herself. "I shouldn't have waited this long to tell you. I-I'm sorry, Kade."

"Ellayne?" His expression darkened as he joined her by the barrel. He reached around her to put his weapon away, but his hand lingered on her shoulder. "What is it?"

Ellayne inhaled, drawing air in until it felt like her lungs would burst. "You have a brother." The words tumbled out, and she knew as soon as she said them that there was no going back.

Kade's forehead creased, his lips parting. "What?"

Rolling her lips together, Ellayne sighed. "Lenora said Emmalee had twin boys and that she sent them with different families to keep them safe before my parents . . . well, I guess before my parents hunted her down. I-I think you have a brother somewhere, maybe in Phildeterre."

He lifted his hand off her and ran both of them through his hair, turning so his back was to her. Kade's shoulders hunched, and he raised a hand to his chin. "So somewhere out there, I have a brother? A twin?" He spun around to face her again. "Did she say where?"

"I don't know," Ellayne said, shaking her head. Her heart still beat loudly, a thudding in her eardrums, but he was taking it better than she could've hoped. At least there hadn't been any magic outbursts yet.

Kade pushed his hand through his hair again, stopping halfway through. "How is this possible? How do I have a brother I don't know about? How do I find him? I have to find him, right?"

Ellayne nodded. "I think you should, and that's why I took this." She crossed the room to a crate on which she had left Lenora's necklace. "She said it has Emmalee's blood infused in it, and that's how she could tell you were her son. It was what woke her up from whatever insanity spell your mother put on her."

When Kade took the necklace, the dark stone on the center of the chain began to glow. Ellayne's eyes widened.

"It has a rune inscribed in it," he said as he held it right in front of his face. "Maybe Armannii will know which one it is."

She ran her hands up and down the sides of her arms. "I wish there were an easier way to tell you all of this. And I'm sorry I waited so long."

He looked down at her, but his eyes held no trace of anger, at least not toward her. "There hasn't been a better time than now. Thank you for telling me, Ellayne. Really," he said when she shrugged. "I know it just adds more to our plates, but I appreciate it. I really do."

"Are you going to tell your father?" She wasn't sure where the question had come from, but she didn't try to take it back. "Lenora said your mother didn't want either of you to ever meet him."

"I don't know," Kade said as he tucked the necklace into a pocket in his trousers. "It's a lot to process." He bit his lip. "And as far as I'm concerned, my mother has no say in what I do in regard to my father. He's here. She's not. That's just how it is."

"Of course." She tucked a piece of hair behind her ear. For the first time, she almost understood the loyalty Kade had begun to show his father. Was it not the same she had shown hers? The thought of her father left her longing to go speak to his grave, not because she wanted a response, but because it almost felt like she could organize her thoughts when talking to him. There was so much going on in her mind, she almost trembled at the thought of sharing the burden with her father. And once more, she found herself wishing he were there, giving her guidance. It hurt. The thought of him ached to her innermost core.

"We should go see if Armannii is back. Maybe he'll have some sort of insight into what we should do next," Kade said, and without another word—she wasn't sure she could've even spoken one without breaking down in that moment—she followed him out of the training room.

Armannii leaned back in his chair, rubbing the heels of his hands into his eyes. "Like I said, the nymphs said it's too risky to try to make it back to Verina's portal. The Dark King was furious you snuck away and has people everywhere searching for you." He pointed to Kade. "And Diomedes has men watching the main portal."

"So you're saying we're trapped here?" Ellayne's voice rose in pitch. This couldn't be happening, not when her country was about to go to war. She rubbed her thumb over her medallion. "I have to be there when we fight against Dio. I have to."

"Of course you do, Queenie. But for now, we're out of luck."

"And you're sure there are no other portals?" Kade asked, massaging his temples with his fingers.

"Oh, sure there are," Armannii said, rolling his eyes. "But not any that function." He turned his head to face Ellayne. "I'm sorry. I really am. But we're going to have to wait until we can leave."

"No," Ellayne said, shaking her head. "No. We can't waste time here. Not when Diomedes is so close to dominating *my* country." She began pacing the room, her hands on her hips. "No, there has to be a way."

"Well, unless you wanna magically make a portal yourself, then I don't see a way back." Armannii's words left Ellayne frozen midstep.

"Now there's an idea." She whirled around and pointed a finger at the elf.

Armannii's eyes widened, and his head tilted. "No." He shook his head. "That's impossible."

"It's clearly not." She waved her hand out to the side. "It's obviously been done before."

"By people who knew what they were doing," Armannii countered, rising up as well. He placed both hands on the table, leaning forward. His intense eyes matched hers as they stared at each other.

"He's right, Ellayne," Kade said, joining them by standing. "It's a risky idea."

"It's a good idea," Ellayne said, popping her hip out to the side and crossing her arms over her chest. "Even if it might be difficult."

"Might be? Are you insane?" Armannii furrowed his eyebrows. "You nearly lost your magic trying to stop a fire. This is going to take a lot more magic than that."

"And it's not something we could read how to do in some book. None of us have ever done anything like this before." Kade glanced between the two of them.

"But it won't just be me. It'll be all three of us. It has to be all three of us for it to work."

"Even so"—Armannii straightened up—"I wouldn't know what runes to write."

Ellayne stuck her tongue in her cheek as she considered his argument for a second, shifting her weight from side to side. "You'd only need a few. It only needs to stay stable long enough for us to get to Phildeterre."

"Are you serious about this?" Kade turned to her.

"Yes. The three of us are going to make a portal right here in the house."

Chapter Twenty-Eight

llayne continued to pace up and down the training room as Armannii flipped through a book he'd found in the house. Any time she spoke, he looked up at her with a glare in his eyes.

"Like I said, Armannii, it only has to stay open long enough for us to pass through. It's not a permanent thing." She rolled her eyes at his annoyed grunt.

"How are you planning to open the portal in the first place?" the elf countered. "It's your job as well as the kid's to open the portal, and if you can't do that, then I'll have nothing to keep open. So maybe start thinking about that."

As much as she wanted to respond with a witty rejoinder, she refrained. Instead, she went to go find Kade, who sat in his room alone.

"You aren't going to snap at me because I suggested doing a huge and possibly dangerous act of magic, right?" she asked as she leaned against the wall.

Kade glanced up at her, and she noticed the necklace glowing in his hands. "I guess I'd be lying if I said my mind wasn't somewhere else right now."

Ellayne crossed the room and sat on the edge of the cot with him. "Of course." She watched him fiddle with the chain, twisting it around his fingers. "You have every reason to be distracted. How are you coping?"

"Honestly? Better than I would have a month or so ago. But I feel like I've gotten to know my father, and I respect him in a way I wouldn't have thought possible in such a short amount of time. If that's how I feel about my long-lost father, I feel like my desire to find my brother is even greater." Kade paused, running his finger over the necklace. "Do you think my brother knows? About me, I mean. Or our parents?"

"I couldn't tell you even if I wanted to, and I want to." She placed a hand on his knee. "But I'm sure he's great like you, and maybe not as broody."

"You're one to speak." He bumped her with his shoulder in a playful manner as he tucked the necklace away again. Kade covered her hand with his, sending ripples of sparks up and down her skin. The smile on his lips wavered, and he frowned. "Ellayne, I had a thought, but it sounds kinda crazy."

"Crazier than what's happening in our lives right now?"

"About the same."

She stopped smiling, nodding for him to go on.

"I've been thinking, and I wasn't the only one who remembered there was another heir when Diomedes cursed you. I wasn't the only one to see things in books that weren't there for everyone else. And—"

"Kiegan?" Ellayne asked before he could continue.

"Is it all that unbelievable?"

Ellayne pressed her lips into a thin line, her eyebrows knitting together as she considered the idea. "If Emmalee placed a spell of protection over both you and your brother, then it would make sense as to why those things are true. And, well, you have similar features. I guess . . . I guess I could see it."

Kade nodded slowly, a pained look on his face. He let go of her hand, cutting off the sparks, and reached up to rub his scarred shoulder. "I don't know whether I want it to be him or not."

Images of Kiegan's cloudy eyes filled Ellayne's mind, and she bit her lip. She didn't want to give Kade false hope, just like she hadn't wanted to give it to herself. But since Kade had brought him up . . .

"How much do you know about being bewitched?" Ellayne asked, her voice quiet.

Kade cocked his head as he glanced sideways at her. "Not much. Why?"

It took her a moment to explain her and Armannii's escapade to the Cyanthian castle, but when she had briefed him, he already seemed to know where she was going.

"If Blanndynne placed the royal guard under an enchantment, she could've just as easily bewitched Kieg." Kade's eyebrows rose higher as he spoke. "That means he could have been bewitched this entire time."

"The key word there is 'could.' We don't know for sure. I could've just been seeing what I wanted so gravely to see. I haven't even brought it up to Armannii yet because there hasn't been any time and I haven't been sure."

"But it makes sense, doesn't it? The way he acted in Bolee, his lies. Ellayne, it could have been an enchantment this whole time." The excitement in his voice hurt Ellayne.

"I want it to be true too, Kade. I do. But we need to be a little realistic here. If Kiegan is your brother, which we still don't know for sure, and if he is bewitched, which we also don't know, then great, we might be able to get the old Kieg back. But we need to prepare ourselves for the case that he's not one or both of those. We can't let our guard down just on the off chance he might—"

"I understand what you're saying. I won't do anything stupid. But at some point, I need to know."

Ellayne nodded. "I hope we both find out. And soon."

"Okay, good." Armannii stood to the side of Ellayne, who gripped the strap of her bag with shaking hands, and Kade, whose steady eyes rested on Ellayne. They faced each other in the center of the room. "Now take each other's hands. No, Kid, yours go on the bottom."

Ellayne placed her hands on top of Kade's, reveling in the sensation of their skin touching. *Focus, Ellayne.* She chided herself as Armannii continued to prepare for them to open the portal.

However, Kade must've been thinking about the spark between their touching hands because he asked the question Ellayne had been meaning to ask Armannii for a while.

"Is it normal for there to be a buzzing sensation between people with light and dark magic when they touch?"

Armannii glanced up at them, his eyebrow arched. "You mean right now? Because it could just be—"

"No. It's every time she and I touch," Kade said, though he paused and turned his head toward Ellayne. "Right?"

She nodded. "Right. And it's only with you. When anyone else with dark magic touches my hands, I just feel their magic."

Sitting back on his heels, Armannii shrugged. "I have no idea. Could be some sort of mixture between magic and attraction."

Ellayne's cheeks burned, and she glared at Armannii. He wiggled his eyebrows at her from behind Kade. The elf lifted his chin, making direct eye contact with her while holding the most arrogant smirk she had ever seen—and she had seen plenty cross his face. She wouldn't meet Kade's eyes and instead tried to focus on regulating her breathing. Despite the restraint she placed on herself, she couldn't stop her eyes from flicking up to see how Kade had reacted to Armannii's statement. He was watching her with a small smile on his face.

"I suppose that could be a factor," he said, tilting his head to the side as he looked her up and down.

Her cheeks were on fire. Burning. Scorching. Maybe even glowing.

Kade's smile widened.

Dying for a distraction, Ellayne returned her attention to Armannii, who had gone back to work on the floor. He moved around them, marking the ground with runes she didn't recognize. The runes varied from simple ones with no more than three strokes to ones with over twenty.

"What do all of the runes do?" Ellayne asked, cocking her head to watch him draw one behind Kade.

"Some of them are for stability, some for navigation, others for protection," he responded as he sat back on his heels. He wiped the back of his hand across his forehead, which was glistening with sweat.

A thought crossed Ellayne's mind. "Does drawing runes take energy the same way that using light or dark magic does?"

"Not to the same extent, but yes." Armannii nodded. "And I can't remember the last time I drew so many runes with such high levels of magic required."

"It's a good thing you can," Ellayne said. "Because otherwise we'd be trapped in the Dark for who knows how long."

Kade nodded, still holding her hands in front of him. "Let's just hope we can do our part too. You know where you're going, right?"

"To the tiny house in the Black Forest," Ellayne said, bobbing her head up and down. "Aside from the castle, where we obviously can't go, it's the place in Phildeterre I'm most anchored to."

"Okay, but that means you'll have to lead. Armannii and I don't know that place as well."

Ellayne's stomach squeezed. "Wait, you mean I'll have to pull you two through? I don't know how to do that."

Armannii stood up. "It's easy enough. You just need to visualize the place you want to go, and don't stop. Remember to be determined about where you're going."

"What happens if I'm not determined?"

The space between his eyebrows crinkled, and he squinted at her. "There's a possibility we could end up in the wrong place, or each of us could end up in completely different locations. We could be lost somewhere between time and space forever. Honestly, since I've never created a portal of my own before, I don't know what it'll be like. The ones I've been to have existed for centuries and are directly linked, so it'd be pretty hard to stray off them."

"But since we're creating an unlinked portal, you may have to force a link to the tiny house," Kade said, finishing Armannii's thought. He squeezed her hands when her eyes widened. "Don't worry, you'll be fine. We all will."

Armannii wandered toward the entrance to the room and picked up his bow and quiver. While he was doing that, Ellayne leaned over and whispered in Kade's ear.

"I know you're trying to be all positive and whatnot, but what are the chances I mess this up?" She searched his eyes, but of course it was Armannii who responded, his back to them.

"Since it's your first time leading through a portal as well as creating a portal, I'd say the chances of something going wrong are higher than normal."

"Wasn't asking you."

He glanced over his shoulder, winking at her with his silver eyes. "I know. But I figured you might like an unbiased, truthful answer instead of whatever the kid would've told you."

Kade rolled his eyes. "Ignore him and focus. We can do this."

Ellayne bit her lip. "All right, are we ready?" She took a deep breath when both of the men nodded. "Here it goes."

Closing her eyes, Ellayne called on her magic. *I know this is going to be difficult.* She spoke to it like she would a child. *But it's important we open this portal and get all of us through.* A mixture of warm and cold air began spiraling around the room, but she blocked out the sound and focused again on creating the portal.

Heat filled her the more she summoned her powers, but another familiar sensation funneled in through her hands. A chill seeped into her, dampening the light of her magic. It was much stronger, and within a few seconds, she opened her eyes and dropped Kade's hands.

"What? What happened?" Armannii asked. "Are you all right?"

Ellayne rubbed her cold hands together, sending an apologetic look to Kade. "I'm okay. But—" Warmth returned to her fingers, and she couldn't help but notice the faint glow to her skin. "But the dark magic was too strong."

"Ellayne, I'm sorry," Kade said, catching her hands in his again. "I didn't mean—"

"Don't apologize, Kid." Armannii crossed his arms. "You're going to need to give it all you've got to create a portal. This is difficult magic, and it's not something you can go into with half the power. Sorry, Queenie, but you're just going to have to put more in to balance it out."

"But we all know his magic is stronger than mine."

Kade's hands tensed under hers, and she squeezed them. *Sorry,* she thought.

"I was putting all I had into it." She narrowed her eyes at Armannii. "What else am I supposed to do?"

"This was your idea," he said, clicking his tongue. "We could always wait until—"

"No." Ellayne shook her head. "Let's try again."

Before either of them could argue, Ellayne closed her eyes. With her focus narrowed on coaxing her magic into obedience, the heat from her core spread to the rest of her body. Even with her eyes closed, she could see a glow that was inevitably coming from her.

Just like before, Kade's dark magic came rushing into her through her hands. *Don't fight it,* she thought, *but don't let it overpower you. Match it. Work with it. Use its power to open the portal.* She fidgeted as the cold became almost too much to bear. *Please, Kade,* she thought, begging him to ease up a bit. *This needs to be balanced.* Somewhere in the room, she thought she could hear Armannii drawing more runes on the ground.

In some matter of time—she was too absorbed in focusing on her magic to notice how long—she no longer felt the opposing force of Kade's magic. A sense of peace settled over her, and without the distraction of the cold, she was able to focus on the portal again. She pictured the tiny house, a place she knew well from five years of being sent back to it every time the Curse of Infiniti reset her.

In the recesses of her mind, she pictured the worn-down wooden frame, the bedroom with only a bed, chair, trunk, and mirror, the room she'd woken up in multiple times without a single memory. Yet the memory of the room was crystal clear.

Some part of her brain recognized a hand on her shoulder, but she ignored it as she focused on the room and on the emotions it brought up. She took a step toward it, remembering the confusion of waking up with no identity. Another step at the utter despair of not being able to recall her own appearance. Step. Fear. Step. Hope. Step.

Freedom.

Ellayne collapsed on the ground as soon as the portal closed behind them. As with portal travel, her head spun, but the thing that made her feel the sickest was the residual coldness creeping up and down her arms. Kade bent down, and it took her a second to understand that his mouth wasn't just opening and closing. He was saying her name.

"Ellayne." He pushed a piece of hair out of her face. "Ellayne, can you hear me?" Panic reached across every feature on his hardened face.

How long have I been lying on the floor? she wondered, staring up into Kade's worried eyes.

"Why are there dark veins all over her? What did I do?" Kade's voice cracked, and Armannii's face joined him as they both stared down at her.

"Your magic was stronger than hers, so I drew a balancing rune back at Matt's. That's why you two were able to open the portal, but as soon as we crossed over, there was no balance rune and the amount of magic you were pumping into the portal spell and into her must've given her dark magic poisoning."

"What?"

"It'll fade, but it may take a while."

How long? Ellayne asked in her mind, but Kade asked the question for her.

"It'll probably only last for a few minutes, an hour at most. But she's going to be unresponsive until then. If I had thought to bring the magic-dampening cuffs, we could've used them to reduce the effects, but then again, maybe it would've hurt her magic and stopped it from coming back. All we can do is wait."

Peachy, Ellayne thought. But the other part of her couldn't help but be a little excited at successfully creating a portal to Phildeterre. *And Armannii thought I couldn't do it.* She wanted nothing more than to rub it in the elf's face, but she couldn't move.

Instead, Kade lifted her and placed her on a bed she knew well. Staring at the ceiling brought back memories—memories she didn't want to relive—of the time she'd spent under the Curse of Infiniti. So, rather than be haunted by the past, she eavesdropped on Kade and Armannii's conversation.

"Kiegan being under Blanndynne's enchantment was a thought that had crossed my mind. Just didn't want to share my theory without a little proof. But twins?" Armannii's voice came from the other side of the room. Ellayne assumed he was leaning back in the chair by the window because she could hear it creak under his weight. "Now that's one I didn't see coming."

Kade sat on the floor with his back to the bed. When he leaned his head back, running a hand through his hair, he brushed Ellayne's hand. The spark that went through Ellayne left her wanting yet unable to smile. *I can't even control my facial expressions. This is the worst.*

"You and me both," Kade said, his fingers brushing together and making a soft scratching sound. Ellayne recognized the sound and knew what he was doing. He had done it before. He was turning his father's signet ring around his finger. "It's like I keep getting thrown these curveballs that I don't have time to process because—" He stopped and shifted, probably glancing back at Ellayne. "Can she hear me right now?"

"Not sure." Armannii's clothes rustled, and he must've shrugged. "Why?"

"I just . . ." Kade sighed. "I just want to be careful about what I say if she can."

"And what would you say if she can't?"

Kade didn't speak right away. "I want to help her. At this point, I'd do just about anything for her. It's just, I keep trying to find time to figure out the mess my life has become. It's like juggling flaming daggers. Every time I try to go figure out who I am or what my life is headed toward, something more important comes up. Another knife is added, so to speak. And I'm left frantically trying to balance all of them. It sounds selfish, I know, I just—"

"Want to understand what your past, present, and future hold. I get it, Kid," Armannii said. "And I'm sure if you sat down and talked to her, she'd understand too. She wants what's best for you too, you know."

"I know she does. Believe me, I do. And I know my father isn't easy to get along with." Kade paused when Armannii let out a short, loud laugh. "But I could tell she was trying, back at the castle, I mean. And I appreciate it more than she'll ever know. But I think it's safe to say Ellayne and I, we've both changed. I'm not the same man who pulled her out of the river."

"Which time?" Armannii asked.

"I have more responsibility and power than I ever wanted. But the thing is, my father says I'm a natural. When he was in Phildeterre, I overheard him speaking with Criss about how quickly I picked everything up. I guess I surprised even him." Kade chuckled.

"Criss?"

"Yeah, I've been working with him the most because he's—"

"In charge. Yeah, I know. Criss took my position after I left. He plays by the rules. I'm sure he's a great teacher." Something in Armannii's voice, maybe the strain, left Ellayne thinking there was more to this Criss person than Armannii was letting on.

"But that's the thing; Criss wasn't in charge of me. The only one ranked higher than me was my father, and before we even left the Dark the first time, he put Criss and all of his men under my leadership." Kade cleared his throat at the same time the chair creaked. Armannii must've sat up straighter because Kade's next words were meant to reassure him. "It's true. I don't know why he did it, but—"

"Your father trusts you. That's a miracle in itself."

"You think?" Kade's voice went up. "You think he trusts me?"

"Well, he probably would if you'd stop running away every time he turns his back."

Kade didn't respond, and the room fell into silence. That meant Ellayne could only process what Kade had said, and the first half of it hurt because with everything he said, it became clear how much her issues had gotten in the way of his life, of his need for some of his own clarity. Of course he was trying to get to know his father. He had every right to. Ellayne wanted to apologize, but all she could do was lie there and stare at the ceiling.

Chapter Twenty-Nine

rmannii was dozing off in the chair and Kade was practicing magic on the floor when the dark magic poisoning finally began to subside. Although it seemed like it had been forever, Ellayne estimated that it had really only been half an hour.

The first thing out of her mouth was a thought that had crossed her mind after Kade and Armannii stopped talking.

"The mirror," Ellayne croaked, and Kade scrambled to his knees to lean on the bed next to her.

"Ellayne! You spoke." He gripped her hand in his, and a wide smile crossed his lips.

"The mirror," she said again. "Blanndynne."

In those three words, Kade understood what she meant. He jumped to his feet and kicked Armannii's boots, startling the elf.

"Why'd you do that?" Armannii slurred as he sat up. "I was almost asleep. Ah, Queenie's up," he said, watching Ellayne push herself up onto her elbows.

"We need to go, now," Kade said, moving the burlap curtain out of the way of the window. "Blanndynne had this mirror runed up so she could spy on Ellayne every time she was reset. She's probably already sent a group of royal guards this direction."

Armannii leapt to his feet, straightening his vest. "Of course she did," he said, looking out the window as well.

"I'm sorry," Ellayne said. "If I had remembered—"

"Doesn't matter now." Armannii craned his neck to see around the corner of the house. "If we leave now—"

"No." Ellayne cleared her throat as she heaved herself up into sitting position. Faint gray lines still traveled up and down her arms. It reminded her of when Kade had been healed by a young boy with dark magic, only dark magic in someone with light magic was apparently not a good thing.

"No? What do you mean no?" Armannii said.

"You go to Bolee ahead of us. Check to make sure everyone is okay."

"But—" Kade started, but she cut him off.

"I'm still too weak to run and probably will be for a little while longer." She paused, clutching her medallion. *At least I can still sense my magic though,* she thought. "Kade and I will follow after you as soon as I can."

Kade stepped forward. "I could carry you."

"We'd be too slow," Ellayne said. "And besides, I want to make sure the rebels are okay. We've been gone for so long that—"

"I understand," Armannii said. He was already drawing speed runes on his shoes. "I'll send word when I see how they're doing. Stay safe, and get out of here as soon as you can."

"We will," Ellayne said, swinging her legs over the side of the bed. "It's already getting easier to move. I'm sure we'll be right behind you."

"Take care of her, Kid," Armannii said, placing a hand on Kade's shoulder.

"I will."

Kade took Armannii's place in the chair as they waited for Ellayne's strength to return.

Lenora's necklace glowed softly in his hands, and every once in a while he'd look up at the window from it.

Ellayne wanted to bring up what he had said when she couldn't respond, but silence seemed louder than any coherent thought she could put together. After a minute, she cleared her throat, watching him from beneath her eyelashes. "I heard everything a little while ago. I figured you ought to know."

"Ellayne—"

She held a hand up, cutting him off. "And now it's your turn to listen," she said, watching him as he pressed his lips together, nodding. "I want to apologize, Kade. I never would've thought I'd cause so much trouble in your life, even in Kiegan's. I never meant for any of it to happen. In all honesty . . ." She snorted. "I didn't have much choice in who pulled me out of that awful river. But I hope you know I'm sorry for all of it. For ruining your childhood friendship with Kieg. For dragging you to the Dark after you begged me not to go. For pulling so much of your attention on myself because I was too blinded by my own problems to realize you had things you were dealing with. It wasn't—isn't—fair of me. And I'm sorry. I really am. And if I make it through all this somehow, I promise I'll try to work on my relationship with your father. I'm sorry I've struggled with it for this long." She paused to take a deep breath, rubbing her hand up and down her arm.

"You weren't meant to hear that. I didn't want to put any of what I told Armannii on you," Kade said, rubbing his finger over the surface of the glowing necklace. "You already carry enough. But thank you."

"It's me who should be thanking you. And Armannii, although I'm more reluctant to tell him because he'll tease me about going soft or something."

"Probably would."

"But it's true, Kade. Without you, I'd still be, well, here. Trapped for infinity." Ellayne sighed, tilting her head back to stare at the ceiling. "My father would still be under the spell, and my brother would be slowly destroying Phildeterre without anyone being the wiser. You changed everything for the better." She ventured a look at him to see half a smile on his face, although he was still looking down at the necklace.

"You've changed things too, Ellayne. And, whether you believe it or not, for the better." He finally looked up at her, and her stomach fluttered. "I mean, I have answers to questions I've asked for years and a father to answer them. I can do things now," he said, swirling a ball of black mist into a cloud formation above his outstretched hand. Little droplets of dark magic splashed down onto his palm and disappeared. "And I have you." He glanced down at the ground before quickly looking back up, gazing at her through the curls hanging above his eyes. "And you make it all worth it."

Ellayne tried not to show it, but every word he said had caused some sort of reaction with her magic, and her hands were glowing softly in her lap. For the first time since Lenora had died, since she had thought she'd lost all hope, she felt her insides begin to warm, and not just because of her magic. His words had left her feeling like she could take a full breath after being underwater for an extended amount of time.

"And I'm sorry," Kade eventually said, and Ellayne's head perked up.

"For what?"

"For poisoning you with my magic." He nodded toward the faint lines on her arms. They were darkest near her hands, but even those veins were a light gray now.

Ellayne let out a laugh, making him jump. "Are you kidding? We made a portal. A real, functioning portal. A little magic poisoning is the least of my worries."

"Even so, I'm still sorry." He reached for his sword, which leaned against the nearest wall. After a few seconds, he had the necklace tied around the hilt. He fiddled with it until the stone dangled. "Seems as good a place as any to keep it," he said when he caught her staring. "And if I get close enough to Kieg with it, maybe I'll catch it glowing."

"Right," Ellayne said, nodding. She had decided that she would allow herself to hope Kiegan was Kade's brother only if he truly was bewitched. Otherwise, she hoped the stone would stay dark if it made contact with the man who had betrayed them.

"And I think that time is now." Kade's attention was no longer on his sword but instead focused on something outside the window. "They're here." Kade stood up, moving the curtain farther back with a few fingers.

Her legs trembled as she stood up, but she regained balance and met him on the other side of the room.

"Well, she pulled out all the stops, didn't she?" Ellayne said as a line of royal guards surrounded the clearing. At the front stood two people Ellayne knew would cause more trouble than the whole group of guards.

"We could try to escape out the back of the house," Kade suggested.

Blanndynne turned her head to the side, a long ponytail swishing around as she nodded to Kiegan, who stood beside her. Kiegan raised his hands by his sides, and a ring of fire spread around the tree line. Ellayne stepped back from the window, covering her eyes as the bright flames grew taller.

"Never mind," he said, letting the curtain fall and cover the window once more. "What do you want to do?"

"How many guards do you think you can take on?" Ellayne asked as she situated her belt with her sheath and sword attached to it. Her hands shook, but every second energy returned to her. The adrenaline helped, she was sure.

"I don't know, maybe ten. And that's if they don't have magic themselves. But there have to be at least thirty out there, not to mention Kieg and Blanndynne. You can't honestly be thinking about trying to take all of them on."

"I am."

"But you're getting out of breath just walking around the room." He threw his hands up and let them fall by his sides. "How do you expect to win a battle like that?"

Ellayne shrugged. "I'm not seeing many other choices here," she said, and she tied her hair up into a bun. "I can't be sure why they're here, but I bet they're either going to kill us or bring us to Diomedes, which would be way worse. The only way we're going to get out of this is by fighting. Besides, I've wanted to knock that conceited look off Blanndynne's face since I saw her wearing my mother's crown in the castle." Ellayne sneered at the mirror, hoping Blanndynne could still hear her.

"But—"

"Let's go." She left the bedroom, cutting off whatever argument Kade was going to start. She waited for him to catch up before she opened the front door. With a deep breath, Ellayne walked out of the tiny house.

The fresh air revitalized her, but when she sucked in a lungful, the smell of smoke left her coughing.

"Hello again, Ellayne." Blanndynne projected her voice across the field with magic. "I thought that was you I saw in the mirror. How's your dark magic poisoning?"

"All but gone. I suggest you and your little mind-controlled army leave now, Blanndynne," Ellayne said, tilting her chin higher. "Or you'll regret it." She and Kade stopped in front of the line of guards, keeping at least thirty to forty feet away.

"You talk a big talk, but I know you're struggling just to stand," Blanndynne said. She crossed her arms over her chest and popped her hip out to the side. "You're not fooling me."

Kade stepped up beside Ellayne, his shoulder bumping hers. "Leave," he said, and Ellayne could feel the dark magic pooling off him in cold waves. He drastically lowered his voice, and Ellayne's ears strained to hear what he said next. "Get behind me when I count to three."

Instead of asking why, Ellayne followed orders, ducking behind him as soon as he counted. The cold intensified as Kade raised his hands, blasting a horizontal wave of dark magic that knocked the arc of guards—as well as Blanndynne and Kiegan— off their feet. Ellayne, overwhelmed once again by the dark magic, fell to her knees behind Kade, panting for breath. Her body shivered, her magic flaring as it tried to keep her warm.

"Ellayne!" Kade turned, dropping to the ground to check on her. "Are you—"

"I'm fine," she said, using his outstretched hand to stand back up. "Still recovering from earlier." Ellayne scanned the tree line, and although the fire was starting to grow again, the line of guards was scattered. "Good job," she said, brushing her knees off.

"Thanks, but now what?" He pulled his sword out, copying her motions.

"Now we fight," Ellayne said, twirling the hilt of her sword in an arc. "And Blanndynne's mine."

Blanndynne was barely on her feet again when Ellayne reached her. Dodging a blow from a nearby guard and countering it with her own, Ellayne took her first swing at Blanndynne. The genie spun to the side, and reaching inside her purple velvet jacket, she flung a throwing knife at Ellayne.

Block, Ellayne thought, and with a warm tingling from her hands, she placed a magic barrier between herself and the flying object. It clanked against the barrier, which then dissolved.

Armannii had taught her that move, and Ellayne was about to mentally congratulate herself when Blanndynne held out her hand, creating three spear-like items out of nothing. All three of them zipped toward Ellayne, and without the concentration needed to control her magic, the only thing Ellayne could do was brace for impact.

But the impact never came.

Instead, the spears stopped millimeters from her chest before shattering into pieces. Ellayne's eyes widened, and she cast a glance at Kade, but he was too busy fighting Kiegan in a cloud of dark magic to have stopped the spears.

"What just—" Ellayne mumbled, but something Armannii had said about genies trickled back into her mind. *She can't kill me with magic because she's a genie,* Ellayne realized, and a spark glistened in her eyes. *That's oddly comforting.* "Looks like the rules haven't changed, lucky for me."

"Worth a shot," Blanndynne spat, pulling two more throwing knives out of her jacket. "If I could use my magic to end you, this would all be over."

"Now where would the fun be in that?" Ellayne asked, taking out another guard near her with a blast of light magic. She sent a second guard hurtling toward a nearby tree. "How many of these poor guards do you have under your control? They are under your enchantment, aren't they?"

"At least half, if not more," Blanndynne said, a wicked grin across her face.

Ellayne spun her sword as she approached Blanndynne. The dry grass crunched beneath her boots, and the clinking of metal against metal sounded from the direction of Kade and Kiegan. *Thank goodness for Kade's initial blast, or we would be outnumbered and in more trouble,* Ellayne thought as she swung her sword to block one of the throwing knives flying toward her face.

"Wow, seems like my brother doesn't have any friends when you put it that way. Nope," Ellayne sneered after moving out of the way of another knife. "He needs his obedient little genie to mind control all of them. Must be fun to be at his beck and call."

"I'm not his slave. I did it for him because I respect him." Blanndynne ducked behind a tree as Ellayne swung. Ellayne barely had time to get another barrier up before Blanndynne came around the other side with a blade ready to slit her throat. The barrier, however, held.

"Too bad he has no respect for you." Ellayne kept a cocky grin on her lips as she backed up, keeping the barrier between them as she fell back into her fighting stance. "You're just his errand girl playing with crowns that don't belong to you."

Recognizing the disadvantage she had in her lack of projectiles, Ellayne raised her hand. She brought it down in one swift movement, and the tree Blanndynne stood next to followed her hand, moving a branch down and knocking Blanndynne to the ground with a crack. The genie didn't move, and a trickle of blood leaked out of her nose and the side of her head. Ellayne was about to go check on her when another sound from the battlefield stopped her cold in her tracks.

"Wait!" Kade's voice carried above every other noise, and, as it had many times before, it drew Ellayne's attention away from her present situation.

Turning her head, Ellayne watched Kade duck out of Kiegan's way, but instead of taking a very clear opportunity to strike his opponent, Kade stumbled away from him. Ellayne's eyes widened because she knew there was only one reason. Kade had gotten his answer. Ellayne sprinted out of the trees and into the clearing toward Kade, hoping to reach him before he did something stupid, but didn't get much farther than the tree line before a royal guard tackled her, pinning her to the ground as the wind came rushing out of her lungs from the impact. She coughed, trying to inhale more oxygen, but the guard pressed a knee into her chest.

"Get off," she grunted, pushing with both of her hands, her sword no longer nearby. The man wouldn't budge, and the pressure building behind her rib cage throbbed enough that she couldn't seem to grasp at the magic inside her.

Leaning down, he placed his hands around her neck, pinching until her airflow was all but gone. *Come on.* She fought to stay focused, but a rim of black filtered the outer parts of her vision. Her body felt tingly, and she thought she was hallucinating as the sky turned black.

"What?" the man above her said, and seconds later she could breathe again.

Choking on air, Ellayne kicked her leg out, tripping the man above her. He landed next to her, his head smacking the ground with a sickening thud. Ellayne sat up, clutching her hand to her chest as she stared at the sky, which swirled from blue to dark gray from a specific point. It wasn't a hallucination. The sky was turning back, and the sight of it made Ellayne's stomach turn. *That's right over the castle,* she thought as she staggered to her feet and regained her bearings.

"The queen is injured!" Kiegan hollered, running to Blanndynne. He blasted the fallen tree branch off the unconscious genie, carefully cradling her head in his hands. He picked a twig out of her hair, tucking a stray piece behind her ear. Bending all the way down, he lifted Blanndynne in his arms. A guard knelt beside Kiegan, tracing a speed rune on the marshal's shoes. "Our king is summoning us. Get back to the castle." He glared at Ellayne from fifteen feet away. The fire around the clearing dissipated, and the guards who were able to get up helped those who were injured and they disappeared into the trees. With one last scowl, Kiegan shouted, "It's time for war!" Then he and the remaining guards disappeared into the trees, all running toward the spot where the sky had gone dark.

Chapter Thirty

 ade." Ellayne reached him after returning her sword to her sheath. "Are you all right? It's him, isn't it? Kiegan . . ." Her heart raced in her chest as she waited for his response.

He still stood where the fighting had ended. Kade stared at the hilt of his sword, which hung limply by his side. He kept his back rigid, and when she got closer, she noticed his body trembling. Turning to face her, Kade's eyebrows furrowed and his eyes filled with conflict. Without a word, he dropped his sword and closed the space between them. He wrapped his arms around her, pulling her close. Kade rested his head in the crook of her neck, and she could feel his body shaking, and hers trembled with him.

Even though they had discussed it—had considered whether it could be possible—she still struggled to believe it was true. The shock was the only thing keeping her from crying. Kiegan was Kade's brother. Some part of her wanted the ignorance of not knowing. It was easier to be mad at Kiegan that way, to be furious that he had betrayed them and sided with her brother and Blanndynne. But how could she hate someone related to the person she cared most about in the world? And what if it wasn't even his choice?

Ellayne rubbed Kade's back as he took shaky breaths, and she squeezed her eyes shut. His soft sobs broke her heart, leaving her clutching him even tighter. The muscles in his back were taut, and he pulled her closer too. She ignored the throb of pain from the injury Lenora had given her, which was covered by a bandage on her back.

The only thing she seemed to be able to do was cling to the hope that Kiegan was bewitched, and she was sure that thought was running through Kade's head too.

But then, what if he wasn't?

What if he had truly chosen to stand against a brother he probably didn't even know he had? Ellayne had seen how their fight had ended. Kade hadn't been able to hurt Kiegan when he had the chance. And now, with the war approaching . . .

Kade released her, quickly moving his hand across his cheeks to hide any moisture. He adjusted his jerkin, sniffling in as discrete a way as he could manage. "I used to say we were closer than brothers. I just—all these years."

"I-I don't really know what to say." Ellayne stooped down to pick up the sword he had dropped. Before she handed it back to him, she held the necklace in her hand. "At least you know for sure now." The stone was heavy in her hand, dark and foreboding until Kade took the sword back and it lit up.

He clenched his jaw when he nodded, sticking his sword back in its sheath. "Are you all right?"

"Are you?" Ellayne asked, wrapping her arms around herself.

"Give me some time to get back to you on that," he said, and she could tell he was trying to be as lighthearted as he could. With a nod toward the unnatural sky, he sighed. "We should think about going. To quote someone I know, 'this isn't ominous at all.' "

Ellayne glanced at the tiny house sitting in the middle of the clearing behind them, clenching her fists. "Oh, to go back to simpler times," she mumbled under her breath.

"Your Majesty." A voice interrupted the silence of the clearing, and it came from a nearby tree.

Ellayne stepped toward the trees, her hand on her sword as she searched for the source, but she found no one on her first or second scan. She tilted her head to the side as she walked toward the voice. "Who's there?"

"My name is Fern." A woman only three inches tall stepped out onto a branch near Ellayne's face, causing Ellayne to jump backward. "Sorry, I didn't mean to frighten you, Your Majesty."

Ellayne tucked her hair behind her ear. "No apologies needed. How can I help you, Fern?"

The woman had red hair cut short to her chin and wore a dress that appeared to be made from foliage of some sort. Butterfly wings extended from her shoulders, and she used them to fly to a taller branch.

"The elf, Armannii, sent word through the Black Forest for you, and I'm here to deliver his message."

"Oh, of course." Ellayne nodded as Kade walked up beside her. *She must be a nymph,* Ellayne thought.

"He wanted you to know that the king destroyed Bolee in an attack while you were gone—"

"No," Ellayne whispered, her hand shaking as she raised it to her mouth. She felt Kade's hand rest on her shoulder, but even that couldn't stop the overflow of fear for her people rushing through her. "What happened? How many casualties?"

"No one was killed, thankfully, but the rebels had to move. They are in hiding, and I'm supposed to bring you to them."

Kade squeezed Ellayne's shoulder. "Thank you," he said, nodding to Fern. "Are you strong enough to run yet?" he asked, his voice lower and gentler when he spoke to Ellayne

"I'll be fine," she said. "Take us to them. I've been gone long enough."

Ellayne leaned against a trunk as she waited for her lungs to refill with air. *Okay, so maybe running across the span of Phildeterre wasn't a great idea.* She knew that, in hindsight, they should've chosen another place to land the portal, one that didn't require them to run low through the Level Plains and far west into the Black Forest. But that was the recommended path, what with Cyanthia being so close to the tiny house where they had landed.

"Are you all right?" Kade asked, bending down to look into her eyes.

"Peachy," she said between gulps of oxygen. "How much . . . farther?"

"We're almost there, Your Majesty," Fern said from a branch a few feet away. When Fern had traced a speed rune onto both of her wings and took off, all Ellayne could see—and what she was expected to follow—was an orb of glowing orange light, which was admittedly easier to see in the Black Forest rather than the bright, wide-open plains they had just come from.

"This area is familiar," Kade said when they passed an abandoned safe haven village. "We're somewhere across the Cylan River from Bolee, aren't we?"

"Yes. East of the burn scar." Fern nodded. "I'm impressed."

"I'm a cartographer," he said back, a half grin on his lips. "At least, I was until a couple months ago. Now—"

"You still are," Ellayne said. "You were bragging about your new map just a few hours ago."

"You're way off on your time there; it's at least been a day," Kade corrected, a crooked grin on his face.

"Whatever. Point being, you're just as much of a know-it-all now as you were then." The snide remark came with a genuine smile, and he nodded.

"Right. And you can't decipher left from right."

"That's not true." She scrunched her nose up.

Fern stopped by a grove of trees. "Sorry to interrupt, Your Majesty, but we're here."

Ellayne stopped running and rubbed her hand over the back of her neck, wiping away a layer of sweat. It was the first time she actually felt like she had run across the country when using the speed rune. Armannii hadn't been kidding—rune magic did take energy.

"Where exactly is here? I don't see anyone." She turned in a circle, calling on the rune Kade had drawn on her neck to see in the darkness. When she stopped turning, Kade removed the speed rune from her boots.

There were no signs of life between the trees, and Ellayne's eyebrows creased in confusion. Even her ears didn't pick up on any sounds out of the ordinary.

"The camp is protected by wards," Fern explained as she pulled out her minuscule rune pen. She marked up the tree she stood on, and a wave of magic rippled through the air. "They are stronger ones than in Bolee, meant for even more protection against enemies."

As soon as she finished, it was like a camouflaged curtain fell from the roof of branches, and a camp of at least four hundred large tents opened up in front of them, sporadically spread between the tree trunks.

"Your Majesty, you're back!"

"She's here!"

"Welcome, Your Majesty."

Voices spoke over one another as people stopped where they were in order to address their queen. Ellayne nodded to people, not seeing faces until her eyes landed on a familiar one.

"Lydia," Ellayne said, addressing the young girl she had trained. She smiled, but it felt forced as she continued to scan the growing crowd of people for a specific elf. "Where's Armannii Ovair?"

"Your Majesty." She curtsied, although it was sloppy. "I missed seeing you at training. The soldier who took over your lessons wasn't nearly as willing to take a joke." She rolled her eyes, and Ellayne snorted.

"I'm sure. But maybe the new trainer had a better chance at getting you to get your stance correct." Something about the young werewolf lifted some of the weight off Ellayne's shoulders, even if it was only for a minute while they were talking. When Fern had mentioned Bolee being destroyed, one of the faces that popped into Ellayne's head was Lydia's, and it was a relief just to be talking to her, to see all the people from Bolee and more moving around the camp.

"Last I saw Ovair, he was talking to the siren and the other Dark Soldier. The cute one."

Ellayne refrained from rolling her eyes at the way Lydia identified Matt. "Where were they when you saw them?"

"I can show you." She waved for Ellayne and Kade to follow her.

However, before they did, Ellayne thanked Fern for leading them there. The nymph's glow turned pinkish as she blushed, and she waved goodbye as Ellayne and Kade followed the young werewolf around the numerous tents.

"How long have you all been here? When did Bolee get attacked?" Ellayne asked, easily keeping stride with the shorter girl. Kade walked several paces behind.

"They attacked a day after you disappeared, but a few people found out ahead of time, so nobody was there when the king's men came."

"That's good." Ellayne grimaced. *I guess.*

Lydia stopped in front of a tent made from a beige fabric. "They should be in there."

"Thank you, Lydia." Ellayne gripped the girl's hand. "I appreciate it."

"Of course, Your Majesty," she said as she nearly fell over trying to curtsy again.

Ellayne waited for her to walk away before pushing back the flap of the tent.

"—could potentially be beneficial," Matt was saying as Ellayne and Kade entered. "Your Majesty, Your Highness, you've returned." He grinned and stood from the ground, where he'd been sitting in a circle with Armannii and Dayla.

Just as Ellayne was about to question why she couldn't hear them talking from the outside, she noticed a familiar rune on the sides of the curtains. *Of course Armannii soundproofed the tent.*

"Matt." She shook his hand. "And Day—"

She didn't finish the siren's name before she stumbled backward from the impact of Dayla's hug.

"E! You're back!" Dayla said as she stepped away. The first thing Ellayne noticed was a bruise that wrapped from one side of her neck to the other.

Ellayne gasped, her eyes widening at the healing wound. "What happened to you?"

Dayla's shoulders slumped, but not for more than a second. "We ran into some of the king's men, but I'm okay." She turned to

Matt, and a slight blush tinted her cheeks. "Matt made them regret it. And it actually ended up being a good thing. My people have always been on the more hesitant side of things when it comes to fighting. But when the king's men attacked, they saw the need."

"I'm glad you're okay," Kade said, offering Dayla a hug and nodding to Matt. "When I heard you were leaving for the Coves, I was worried about the risks."

"Like Day said, it ended up being a good idea, Your Highness," Matt said, and Armannii nodded as he finally stood up and joined the rest of them.

"It's true, Queenie. You made a good choice sending them." He leaned on Matt's shoulder, standing quite a few inches taller than him. "They came back with at least 150 more people willing to fight."

Dayla squeezed Ellayne's hand. "They had some questions, but I told them you're worth it."

"I'm glad you went," Ellayne said, smiling at Dayla. "I had no idea sirens had something against violence."

Shrugging, Dayla said, "Just because you and I have had an occasional brawl doesn't mean all sirens are like that. And before you say it, I know that's not what you meant. I was just joking." She patted Ellayne's hand. "Sirens have had rules about violence for hundreds of years ever since a civil war broke out. Now every child is taught to control outbursts of emotion that could lead to violence and not to use the siren song for selfish and harmful means."

An image popped into Ellayne's head of Kiegan cutting his hand with a knife while under Dayla's spell, and she frowned. That was certainly against the rules, but she didn't bring it up.

Instead, Dayla did. "I have a sneaking suspicion I know what you're thinking of, E, and you're right. I broke that rule on multiple occasions. Keep in mind, I may have been born in the Coves, but I was basically a child when Cal brought me to the Black Forest. I didn't grow up with a community of elders teaching me how to be a good little siren. I had a brother who dragged me away from my life. Of course"—her gaze dropped to the floor, and her voice softened—"he was only doing it to protect me. But still," she said, sighing. "I've had a very different upbringing than a lot of the sirens who came here with us."

"Well, I'm still grateful for what you all did." Ellayne pulled Dayla in for a side hug, nodding to Matt.

He bobbed his head. "And we were just talking about an option for when we eventually go to battle. Since we have a lot more sirens now, we can maybe use the Cylan River to our advantage since Cyanthia is so close to the river."

"Well, the time is now," Ellayne said, turning her attention back to Armannii. "Dio has apparently declared war."

"What? Already?" Dayla said from Ellayne's side. The siren cast a glance at Matt, who was looking at Kade.

"She's right," Kade said. "He sent a sign into the sky. Kiegan forced his men to retreat back to the castle in order to prepare for battle."

"While I'd love to hear what happened after I left, I think it's a bit more important to figure out what's going to happen next. Do you know where your brother's intending to do battle?" Armannii asked.

Ellayne shook her head.

"All right, then we must take the advantage we have."

"Which is?" Ellayne asked, rubbing her thumb across her medallion. She struggled to think of any advantages they had at the moment, even with the extra help from the sirens.

"We need to attack first."

Kade bit his lip, frowning. "Isn't that risky?"

"It'll be easier to send out different groups to surround the castle. Besides, the trees may give good coverage, but they would be awful to fight in. Matt"—Armannii focused his attention on Matt, who straightened up at the mention of his name—"I need you to get the other soldiers in charge of training and prepare the trainees for battle. Make sure people know what's happening and that they have weapons. Dayla, I'll leave you in charge of organizing the sirens. Do you think you can handle that? If not, Matt can help you."

Dayla glanced at Matt. "As much as I'd like to say I can, I think I'd prefer having someone who knows what he's doing."

"All right. Matt, once you alert the other soldiers, help Dayla organize the sirens. We will inform those in charge where they will be positioned as soon as we can. In the meantime, make sure people are fed and given what they need from the supplies we have. Anything to add?" He directed the question at Ellayne.

"To the best of your abilities, remind people that this is what everything has been leading up to. If we do this right, we prevent another hundred-year war from happening. Every single person out there has a chance to change the future, and it's important they know that."

"All right, save some for your address to the masses." Armannii chuckled. "But well said nonetheless."

By chance, Ellayne happened to glance over and notice Dayla and Kade making eye contact. *Not the time,* Ellayne reminded herself. *Bigger things to worry about, like the destruction of my country. Still . . .* She tried to hide the fact that she had balled her hands into fists by crossing them over her chest.

"Will there be anything else, Your Majesty?" Matt asked, halfway to the exit. He stopped, turning his full attention to Ellayne.

"No, thank you." Ellayne nodded.

Just as Matt and Dayla left the tent, a small orb of light flew in. "I have a message for the Dark Prince," said the nymph. It was a young man, and just like Fern, he had butterfly wings that kept him hovering in the air near Kade.

"I'll speak with you outside," Kade said, lifting his chin. He held back the curtain for the man, who flew out in a glowing green blur.

"Kade, wait." Ellayne tried to stop him, and he paused for a second.

"Trust me, Ellayne. I need to take care of this." He let the flap close before she could organize her thoughts and get another word out.

Chapter Thirty-One

llayne paced inside the tent, leaving Armannii rolling his eyes as he sat on the floor again. She talked with her hands as she ranted, raising them up to her sides and letting them slam down repeatedly.

"Of all times to be running off . . . Why does he keep doing that?" she asked as she turned to pace the other direction. Words tumbled out of her mouth before she could stop them. "I know he's got responsibilities, but—"

"But what? There shouldn't be a 'but.' He has responsibilities. Period." Armannii stared at her over the rim of his cup of tea. "He's next in line for the throne just like your brother was and like you were after. Don't you remember all the meetings and things Diomedes was in charge of?"

"I remember how many of them he shirked," Ellayne muttered, still pacing.

"The point is, while the kid has made his decision to stand with you against your brother, he's still the Dark Prince, and that requires some of his attention too."

"You're right. I shouldn't even be whining about this right now. We need to be figuring out a plan." Ellayne sighed, scratching an itch on her nose. "But, as much as I hate to admit it, I'm finding it harder and harder to believe that we have a chance of winning. Diomedes has trained guards on his side, not to mention he doesn't care how many people die. Blanndynne admitted to having over half of the guards under her control, so they're all basically meat shields. How are we supposed to win when I actually care about losing people? Not to mention the fact that I still don't want to kill my brother in the first place. And before you tell me that I have to, I know that. I know I'm the one who has to face him because of that ridiculous prophecy. And I know that only one of us will survive. And I know it will most likely be him because his magic is stronger than mine."

"Wow, Ellayne. Aren't you just a ray of sunshine?" Armannii snorted and then shrugged. "Your brother's magic isn't the problem."

"Oh really? When was the last time you took a blast to the chest? Because let me tell you, it doesn't feel good," Ellayne said, rubbing her ribs.

"What I meant is he can only be so powerful. As I've said before, magic is balanced by humanity. If there's all humanity, there's no magic. If there's all magic, there's no humanity to contain it, and it can't hold its form. So yes, your brother may have a ton of magic, but he's not all-powerful."

"Okay. Whatever that means." Ellayne sighed, waving her hand at what he said. "But he's still more powerful than me."

Armannii nodded. "And so is the kid and his brother, apparently." He had asked for the brief recap of what had happened at the tiny house and had barely blinked when Ellayne explained that their guess at Kiegan's lineage had been correct.

She narrowed her eyes at him. "You're not helping."

He held his hands up in defense. "All I'm trying to do is make the point that you've beaten the kid at combat before because you use your head. You don't give yourself enough credit. You're more capable than you think you are."

Ellayne sighed, squirming at the elf's positivity. Out of the corner of her eye, she saw the parchment on which the prophecy had been copied. Apparently, he had been reading it over earlier, and she wasn't surprised. If there were any answers as to how to get out of the situation she was in, she suspected it would be in the prophecy.

Armannii noticed where she was looking and leaned over to grab it. He placed it between them. Ellayne's eyes scanned the paper, reading the familiar lines—lines inextricably linked with her brother.

Armannii read it out loud in the silence of the tent.

A nest with two eggs—divergent, opposed,

An egg breaks open—an infant exposed.

One bird without feathers—jealous and flightless;

Another born colorful—scared of bias.

Steal feathers from others—a price is paid;

How to open the eyes—a life slayed.

No longer bare, but worthy—powerful;

Feathers of one are natural—bountiful.

A crack in the ground—opening wider;

A clash of feathers—one survivor.

"Makes just as much sense as the first time we read it," she said, sighing as she curled a piece of her hair around her finger. They had been staring at it for at least half an hour if not more. "And how is it supposed to help me defeat my brother? If anything, it just confirms one of us has to lose."

"So make it him," Armannii said, studying her face.

"Excuse me?"

"If one of you has to lose, make sure it's him."

"Oh yeah, because it's just that easy." She rubbed her face with her hands. "If it were that easy, I would've finished this in Bolee before he killed my father. Better yet, I wouldn't have been the world's biggest idiot and let him out of the dagger in the first place. If I hadn't been so stupid—"

"Your father would've been killed. And you might've been too," Armannii said, looking up from the parchment. "Besides, if you hadn't let him out, someone else would've." Leaning forward, he stared directly into her eyes. "This prophecy is right. One of you will come out on top, or else this will go on forever. Make sure it's you."

Ellayne rubbed the back of her medallion with her thumb, trying to muster up whatever smile she could. "No pressure or anything."

"No. It's a lot of pressure, but you can handle it. I know you can. You have to, for all our sakes."

Ellayne sat in the tent glaring at a close-up map of Cyanthia. Armannii had left several minutes earlier to check on the progress the troops were making. They had yet to decide where each group would go, and he had asked her to take a look at the map and start making decisions. It made sense. She probably knew the castle better than anyone else there. But still, anytime she came near making a decision about where to put a group, a haunting image of Pingbi in ashes popped into her head. Then an image of Lenora's dead body, her failures coming back to remind her that she was barely capable of leading as it was.

Rubbing her temple with one hand, Ellayne put down the moveable block of wood meant to represent Dayla's group, leaving it resting on the table with the rest of the pieces she'd yet to place. The only piece on the board was hers, smack-dab in the middle of the castle. Of that much she was sure.

But every time she picked up another piece, she hesitated, knowing it didn't just represent one but more than a hundred lives. How could she decide where to put them when she could be moving them right to their deaths? She sighed.

And when she forced out the thoughts of sending her people into danger, the empty space was immediately filled with the thought of Kade and what he was doing. Or Kiegan and whether he was bewitched. Or what her parents would've done in her situation.

But most of all, she thought of Diomedes.

How he had taught her most of what she knew about fighting. How he had been the person she looked up to for the first half of her life. How he had begged her to see the war differently from their father and his council. How he hadn't hesitated when he slit her mother's throat, leaving her body on the throne room floor. How he had sent her away to be cursed forever with no identity. How he had killed their father. How he was waiting for her in the castle. How she would face him. How she would have to take what she had learned from him and use it against him.

How she missed him.

Ellayne squeezed her eyes shut, gripping the table to keep herself grounded where she sat. There was no easy way out. The troops were limited and vastly outnumbered by her brother's men, and he held every upper hand with the power he possessed. He wouldn't even be weakened like the last time Ellayne had fought him.

"Ellayne, sweetheart, are you in here?" A new visitor peeked her head through the tent flap. Linetta offered a supportive smile, joining Ellayne in the soundproof tent.

"Hey," Ellayne said, standing to give her aunt a hug when she walked in. "What are you doing here?"

"Well, I'd be lying if I said I didn't want to see how you're doing. I heard that whatever you went off to do these last few days didn't go as planned, and I wanted to see how you're faring."

"Honestly? I'm struggling at the moment." Ellayne sighed as she sat on the ground with her aunt. "I've been staring at this map for a while, and I can't seem to figure out where to put everyone."

"Well, I'm sorry to say that I won't be of much help there. I haven't read many books on successful military strategies, sad to say."

Ellayne, to her surprise, chuckled. "Neither have I. But Armannii thinks it would be a good idea if I set up what I think should happen before he goes through and makes it all better. And I made the mistake of agreeing with him."

"Where's Kade? You did go after him, didn't you?"

"I did. And he's somewhere, but he had some things to see to, I guess." Ellayne fiddled with the hem of her tunic. "He didn't say what they were."

"And that makes you feel . . . ?" Linetta drew out the last word, waiting for Ellayne to fill in the blank.

"I don't know. I was frustrated, but Armannii made a good point. Kade came back with me, even against his father's wishes. He's clearly here to fight. Maybe I just need to give him space."

"I'm glad you've thought this through. But I think there's a part you're missing, maybe intentionally." Linetta lifted an eyebrow, her eyes kind behind her glasses.

"And what would that be?" Ellayne frowned, not sure she wanted to hear what her aunt was referring to.

Linetta smiled as she exhaled loudly. "You, my dear, sweet Ellayne, love him."

Ellayne's eyes widened. "I—" She tensed at her aunt's audacity. "I—"

"Come on now, Ellayne. You can lie to me, but you can't lie to yourself." She covered Ellayne's hand with hers. "But even if you don't want to go as far as admitting that, then at least admit that you care deeply for him, even if it is only as a friend."

I love him. I do. More than a friend. Her core warmed as magic tingled inside her. *I love Kade.* Admitting it to herself, Ellayne's chest tightened. She could feel her internal temperature rising, but whether it was from her magic or confessing to herself that she was in love with her best friend, she wasn't sure. It was like she could truly breathe for the first time since she had started to take an interest in him. It felt like years, but it had only taken a few short months.

And as she sat there, she remembered the moment she fell. After escaping the raid on Linetta's village together, they had traveled through a dark tunnel and walked for what felt like forever. But when they broke out of the forest, when the sun hit them, when they found the river near where they had met, it was just them. Kade and her. Alone. He had stared down at her with this look in his eyes, had promised to jump into the water again for her—something he had in fact done. And he had smiled, truly smiled. She knew now what the feeling stirring inside her had been. Attraction. Trust. Respect. But mostly love. Even with the curse nearly spread all the way to her heart, even though she was only a day or so away from having to start all over from nothing, he had made her smile. For just a second, he had stopped time. And she had fallen.

"—him. Then you can face whatever comes next," her aunt said, bringing Ellayne out of the inner confessions she was wrapped up in.

"What?"

"What part didn't you understand?"

"All of it." Ellayne's cheeks warmed. "I wasn't paying attention."

Linetta raised an eyebrow at her. "Oh really? Why not?"

"Because you're right. I love him." The words spilled out in a mess, and for a second Ellayne wanted to suck them back in as soon as they formed. "I mean—"

"Good." Her aunt beamed at her. "Then go tell him."

"Now?"

"What better timing than before a life-changing battle?"

"Um, I can think of a lot better timing. In fact, I could probably write a list of better times to confess feelings for someone. Starting with—"

"Ellayne?" The tent fabric muffled Kade's voice as it came through. "Are you still in there?"

Eyebrows creasing, Ellayne breathed a sigh of relief in remembering that whatever was said in the tent could not be heard outside. There was no way he had heard. At least, that was her hope as he stepped into the tent.

"You're back," she said, standing as her aunt did. "Is everything all right? You left so quickly, I thought something might be wrong." She watched his eyes go between Linetta and her.

"I need to speak with you," he said, avoiding her question.

"All right," Ellayne said. "What's going on?"

"Not here," he said, holding back the tent flap. "Sorry," he said to Linetta. "But I need to speak to her in—"

"Private," Linetta finished, a sly grin on her face. "I completely understand." She walked over to Ellayne. As she hugged her, she whispered in her ear, "Good luck. You can do this."

# Chapter Thirty-Two

llayne struggled to keep pace with Kade's long strides. "Where are we going? Why couldn't we have just talked back at the camp?" she asked, knowing she could have said what she wanted to say back in the seclusion of the soundproof tent.

"There's something you need to see," he said as they walked farther away from the campsite. "We're almost there."

"Well then, let's hope you can get us back to the campsite because I'm definitely going to be lost." She glanced over her shoulder, but due to the wards surrounding the camp, she was unable to see anything but the enormous trunks of the trees.

"Hello, Queen Ellayne," a familiar voice said from in front of her, making her turn her head so quick she nearly tripped over an exposed root. "It's nice to see you again." The Dark King stood in front of at least five hundred Dark Soldiers, all standing at attention in between and around the trees, which Ellayne could see because of the rune on her neck.

"Your Majesty?" Ellayne asked, freezing where she stood. "What's going on here?" Her heart pounded in her chest, and she tried to keep the shocked look from leaking onto her face. She bent down into a curtsy at the same time Kade bowed to his father.

"Well, as requested, I am presenting myself to the *true* ruler of Phildeterre, as per our last two conversations." He bowed his head, and to Ellayne's surprise, every single Dark Soldier behind him followed his lead, bowing their heads toward her.

"I-I welcome you then, but I must point out that your timing is extremely unfortunate. My brother has—"

"Declared that the war is beginning. Yes, I heard. And that is why I am here. Why *we* are here," he said, gesturing toward his soldiers. "May I have a word with you, Your Majesty?" The Dark King tilted his head to the side, away from the soldiers.

Ellayne nodded, following him, which she felt better about when Kade kept pace with her. When they were a little ways away, at least out of hearing distance, the Dark King turned to face them.

"I do not come here lightly, Your Majesty," he said, adjusting his cloak. "Just like my ancestors before me, I took staying out of Phildeterre business to heart. The treaties were enough to satisfy me. But that is no longer the case." He glanced at Kade, and for a second something softened in his dark eyes. "I see very clearly now that any future for the Dark will be directly linked to the outcome of the war here in your realm."

Although she was straining to keep her features neutral, Ellayne couldn't stop her eyebrows from knitting together. "I am deeply appreciative that you are here, Your Majesty. Deeply. But I'm still confused as to what changed your mind."

"You did. *Both* of you." The Dark King offered a small smile to Ellayne and then to his son. "From the moment my men brought you into my castle a few months ago, I could tell you were different from your family, Your Majesty. Not because of any prejudice or lack thereof for magic, but because I saw in your eyes you were determined. At the time, it was about freeing your father. But when you spoke to me a few days ago, I could see that, though you may lack the ability to plan"—he raised an eyebrow when she opened her mouth to argue, instantly making her shut it again—"you have determination. And you were right. If I want your brother off the throne, then I should do what I can to make that happen.

"And you, Son. You have shown me that maybe it is time for things to change, that there may be benefits for our people that we are missing by locking ourselves away. Of course, change is difficult, but I'm not too stubborn to see that it can be for the better. Your presence, as new as it still is, has taught me much about myself. Things, I believe, only having a child can reveal to a parent. Thank you, Kade."

A true smile crossed over Kade's face, and he nodded. He had his hands clasped behind his back, and his shoulders kept tensing and loosening, probably with excited energy that had nowhere else to go. She had felt the same way anytime her parents had complimented her, and a smile crossed over her face at her friend—no, the man she loved—receiving the same kind of praise from his father.

"Your presence here speaks powerfully to the kind of ruler you are," Ellayne said, standing tall. "I sincerely hope this war ends in our favor because I believe Phildeterre and the Dark have a lot to offer each other. And that is something I would hope to move toward as we build a new future."

"I would hope so." He extended his hand to her, and she shook it. "You, Ellayne Maudit, have done something not many people could've done. You have brought people from all walks of life together in unity, and you should be proud of that." The Dark King squeezed her hand before letting it go.

"Thank you," she said, stepping back next to Kade, whom she shot a quick look at. "I didn't do it alone. Which reminds me." She cleared her throat, lifting her chin. "As much as I appreciate your support in this war, I must emphasize that Armannii Ovair and any other Dark Soldier who has left your services is under my protection. They are free men here. Is that clear?"

The Dark King grinned, and she thought she could hear him chuckling. "I understand, and I admire the fact that you continue to put up with that elf. Shows the perseverance and patience you possess."

"He's been as much help to me as Kade. And that shouldn't shock you. I know he served you from a young age."

With a nod, the Dark King clasped his hands together, his rings clinking when they came in contact with one another. "He did. And to this day, the only person who has impressed me more is my own son."

"Well, isn't this nice?"

Ellayne and Kade spun around when Kiegan's voice came from behind them in between the trees. Her posture straightened, and she dropped her hand to the hilt of her sword. The tiny hairs on the back of her neck rose. When she saw Kiegan's eyes flick to the king behind her, she found herself shifting so she stood in front of Kade's father more—not that she could block the man who was just as tall, if not taller, than Kade.

"Kiegan?" Kade's voice lowered as he squinted at Kiegan's emerging silhouette. "What are you doing here?"

"I'm running a little errand."

"Who are you?" The Dark King tilted his chin upward, watching Kiegan with careful eyes.

"What?" Kiegan cocked his head. "My friends here didn't mention me? That seems a bit rude. I'm your other son. Came as a shock to me too, but I guess that's the truth, isn't it—Brother?"

Kade took a step back, his shoulders tensing. "How did you—"

"Find out? I heard your whole heart-to-heart with that elf before we came to you in the clearing. Blanndynne was just as surprised as I was."

"The mirror," Ellayne whispered, her hands shaking. She could feel her heart racing in her chest, and though she didn't want to risk taking her eyes off Kiegan, she glanced for a second to see how the Dark King was reacting.

His lips were thin, drawn in a straight line. When she looked at him, his gaze dipped down to her. He had gone very still. The Dark King clenched his jaw. "Another son. Are there any more I should know about?"

"Father, I—" Kade turned back to look at the king. "I hadn't had the chance to tell you. I haven't known for very long. I was going to—"

"Give you the great news," Kiegan said, a sneer still on his face. "Hello, Father. I'm Kiegan, and I do believe it's time we met." His eyes narrowed at the Dark King, a twisted grin plastered on his face.

"Your Majesty." Ellayne stepped back, her body still facing toward Kiegan, though her attention was on the king beside her. She lowered her voice a bit before she spoke next. "Kade and I have reason to believe he, like many of the royal guard, is bewitched."

The Dark King lifted his chin when he heard, cocking his head to the side. "Why are you here?" He spoke clearly, and Ellayne wondered if it hadn't been a mistake that he left off the word "son," something he had called Kade from the first time he had found out.

At his father's question, Kade stepped in front of Ellayne.

"I guess you could consider me the welcome party for our royal guests." He flung his arms out to his sides in a grand gesture.

"In other words"—Ellayne stepped out from behind Kade—"Diomedes sent you." She didn't know if she should try to convince Kiegan he was bewitched, but then a new question arose: Did he even know?

"Close." He shrugged. "It was my queen, actually. But that's neither here nor there."

"Ah, you mean the false queen, I presume?" The Dark King smiled. "Because Queen Ellayne clearly had no knowledge that you would be here."

Ellayne couldn't help the grin that crossed her face at the Dark King's comment. He really did support her as queen, and it filled her with a lightness she couldn't explain. To not only hear he approved of her leadership but to see him standing behind her, she almost felt like she was doing something right.

"How dare you?" Darkness seeped into Kiegan's hands, and sensing the temperature dropping, Ellayne's own magic flared up.

"His Majesty is right," Ellayne said, stepping forward next to Kade. She stood straight, rolling her shoulders back. "Both Dio and Blanndynne are unrightfully sitting on the throne. My father named me as the next heir."

"Your father's word means nothing. He's dead, and soon enough, King Diomedes will make sure you are too."

Kade's arms matched Kiegan's, covered in the dark mist of his magic. "Leave."

"Calm down, Kade." Kiegan's voice held a fake lightness. "I'm not here for her. The king wants to deal with her himself. I'm not even here for brother bonding time."

Ellayne's eyebrows furrowed. In the low light, it was difficult to determine if she was seeing things, but she thought Kiegan's eyes glazed over for a second—just like they had when she'd seen him in the Cyanthian castle. If what she had seen was real, then the enchantment was weakening, or even better, Kiegan was fighting it somehow. But only his eyes showed it.

The distraction of Kiegan's eyes left her unprepared for what happened next.

Kiegan's blast was aimed for Kade and Ellayne, but before she could protect herself, a wall of dark magic separated them from Kiegan's attack. When she glanced at Kade, his attention was fully on his father. The Dark King had protected them from Kiegan's magic.

The Dark King's focus rested on Kiegan, but he kept one hand directed at Kade and her, shielding them from Kiegan. When Kade took a step forward, his father's eyes shifted to him, and with a flick of the Dark King's wrist, both Kade and Ellayne flew backward and skidded across the ground. Kade groaned next to her, pushing up from where he lay on his stomach.

"Are you okay?" Ellayne asked, coughing as she regained her breath after having it knocked out of her.

"Fine."

The air around them was frigid, and the wind had picked up. A cyclone of dark magic swirled in front of them, hiding the two people standing in the middle.

"Father," Kade whispered as he jumped to his feet, heading straight into the growing storm.

"Kade, no!" Ellayne shouted, but her voice got lost in the wind. She watched him blast his way through the barrier of dark magic, right to the center of the storm his brother and father were creating. Ellayne covered her face as the wind hurled dust into her eyes. Concern for both Kade and his father left her feeling dizzy.

Using the tree to hold herself steady, she rose to her feet, pressing against the wind. But the sheer amount of dark magic in the air left her shivering. She clung to her magic to keep herself warm as she took small steps toward the storm. She knew she had to help, and she let that thought urge each step forward.

All she could hear were the sounds of shouts and branches cracking. Ellayne wanted to know what was happening—to have the reassurance that Kade and his father were all right—but there was simply no way to know. She was shivering. Freezing. Hopelessness settled in, weighing down the already difficult steps as she realized there was nothing she could do. All three of the men in the dark magic cyclone held stronger magic than hers individually, let alone when they all used it in conjunction. She leaned against a tree as tears began to form in her eyes. What if something happened to Kade? The thought of losing him left her clutching her chest, a mangled sob erupting from her throat.

The sound of the battle had drawn attention from the Dark Soldiers, and five of them ran up to her.

"Where is the Dark King?" barked the one who reached her first.

Ellayne pointed to the cyclone. "The Dark King and Dark Prince are in there fighting one of Diomedes's men. Please, you have to help them. I-I can't get any closer," she said, trembling.

Two of the soldiers sprinted toward the mass of dark magic but were blasted backward, landing with thuds against tree trunks. They did not get up again.

"Get more men!" the Dark Soldier nearest Ellayne hollered at the remaining two soldiers. They saluted and ran out of sight in the direction of the Dark King's troops. "How long have they been in there?" the soldier asked her.

"A minute or two, maybe more," she said, cringing as another wave of cold air struck her. "The other man tried to hit Ka—the Dark Prince and me, but the Dark King protected us. But then the man and the Dark King started fighting. The Dark Prince went in after his father."

"Why is Diomedes's man here?"

Ellayne shook her head, another sob coming out. She didn't want to form the words. Kiegan's malicious grin at the Dark King returned to her mind, and she squeezed her eyes shut. "He's here for the Dark King."

"No!" The scream came from within the dark magic cloud and echoed around Ellayne and the Dark Soldier.

Her blood froze.

The storm stopped, and a figure walked out toward them. Ellayne thought it was Kade until the man raised his hand and used magic to hurl the Dark Soldier next to her twenty feet away, sending him flying into a tree. The crack was deafening. Ellayne cringed.

Kiegan put both hands on his hips. "Try fighting King Diomedes now," he sneered, and before Ellayne could say or do anything, he raised his hands, and a wall of dark smoke separated them.

When it dissipated, the only thing in front of her was Kade and his father, who was lying with his head resting in his son's lap.

Chapter Thirty-Three

llayne's heart raced in her chest as she skidded onto the ground next to Kade. She could already see so much blood, not on Kade, but his father. It seeped into the neckline of his cloak, leaving a dark stain. "Is he—"

"He killed him." Kade's voice fell flat, and when Ellayne looked at his face, his eyes glistened with tears. "He killed our father."

The Dark King's head lolled to the side, and Ellayne felt the urge to vomit when she saw why. Kiegan had almost taken the king's head off with his sword.

"I tried to stop him, but—" Kade's voice cracked.

"Oh, Kade." Ellayne's lips trembled as she sat next to him, pressing her forehead into his shoulder. "Kade, I'm so sorry." Moisture filled her eyes for both of them. She wrapped her arms around Kade, and he leaned into her as real tears began to fall off his chin.

Kade turned, gripping the back of Ellayne's tunic in clutched fists as, for the second time that day, he cried into her shoulder. Only this time he was not silent. His breath was as uneven as the ground they sat on. He shuddered every few seconds, and she could feel wetness from his tears dampening her tunic.

She didn't care.

She was doing the same to him. Ellayne cried for Kade, for the short time he had spent with his father, for the time he should've had with him, for the things Kade hadn't yet learned, for the experiences he had yet to have as a son. She cried for the Dark King, for the brief time he had with Kade, for the changes she had seen in him since he met his son, for the adopted sons—his Dark Soldiers—he left behind, for his country, which he had cared for so passionately. She cried for the future.

Ellayne startled when a Dark Soldier hollered to a new group of soldiers approaching them.

"The king has fallen. Tell the troops." Two men split off and ran back the way they came. "Your Highness, are you or Her Majesty injured?" The remaining soldiers surrounded Kade and Ellayne.

When Kade finally pulled away, his eyes were red and raw. He cleared his throat, wiping his cheek on his shoulder. But the pain in his eyes was still there. Tears were still forming despite the new tenseness in his jaw. Kade shook his head. "We are fine. But my father—"

"Who did this?"

Ellayne answered for Kade, who she could feel trembling. "One of King Diomedes's men came and attacked him."

The Dark Soldiers stared at her; at least, she assumed they were staring at her behind their helmets.

"What are your orders?" one of them finally asked Kade. "We could send people after the murderer, and—"

"No." Kade squeezed his eyes shut, catching his breath when it faltered. "No, I want some of you to take my father's body back to the Dark. Prepare him for burial. If I don't come back, bury him in three days' time."

"But—"

"As for the rest of the men, prepare them to go to battle." Kade opened his eyes, rolling his shoulders back.

Ellayne ran her fingers over his back once more before she let go of him, rising to her feet. "Kade, you—"

"Go, Ellayne." He turned his attention to her. "Get your people ready. I'll deal with this. This is... this is my responsibility."

Two of the soldiers bent down and helped Kade up without jostling his father's body. Kade smeared blood on his trousers as he wiped his hands off, but that didn't seem to faze him given the intense glare he sent in the direction Kiegan had disappeared.

"Are you sure?"

"Yes. Go."

Ellayne's mind raced as she tried to navigate back to the rebel camp by herself. She paused in the middle of a step. She knew exactly why Diomedes had sent someone to kill the Dark King; he thought it would scatter the Dark Soldiers. But why Kiegan? It was cruel. Evil.

Sighing, Ellayne turned around, checking to see if she'd passed any landmarks she could recognize, but nothing stood out to her. She continued walking with only the hope that it was the right direction. And as she walked, she couldn't stop her mind from dwelling on what had just happened.

Kiegan had killed his own father. She shivered, even winced, when an image reappeared in her head of the Dark King, pale and lifeless in Kade's lap. The Dark King had come to help, and it cost him his life. Was that her fault too? She leaned against a tree trunk, her head throbbing, both from being tossed around by magic as well as the intangible war going on inside.

With all of the images passing through her mind, one thought still trumped the rest. Diomedes wanted to kill her himself. Kiegan had made that quite clear. She had to pause again. Her lungs ached as she began to hyperventilate. Her brother, a man who possessed more magic than the world had ever seen, wanted her dead. She clasped her hand over her mouth.

Sliding down the tree, Ellayne wrapped her arms around her knees. Dio wanted to kill her. Bile burned at the back of her throat, and she had to force her mind to focus on breathing. One breath in, one out. But with every breath she inhaled, she pictured her brother standing over her in Bolee with his dagger, ready to slit her throat like her mother's. With every breath out, she saw a dead body. Her mother's, bleeding out over the marble floor beneath the ceiling covered with purple flowers. In, Dio. Out, her father slumped over with a streak of blood trailing down the wall behind him. In, Dio. Out, the Dark King lying in his son's lap, looking smaller than he had ever looked before.

Ellayne shook, rocking back and forth. Her heart thudded in her chest. A ringing sound overtook her hearing, and she let go of her knees to cover ears. She couldn't shut her eyes, couldn't stop from seeing image after image of the people she'd seen die. They haunted her, peeking out from beneath the trees.

Who would be next?

Who would join them?

Would she?

"Ellayne? Over here, I think I found her." The call sounded muffled through Ellayne's hands. A figure brushed past the image of her father standing several trees away, and the person raced to her side. "E? Ellayne? Are you okay? What happened?" Dayla knelt down in front of Ellayne, pulling her hands down from her ears. "Talk to me, E. Matt, she's over here."

Another set of footsteps resounded nearby, and soon Matt knelt down in front of her next to Dayla.

"Your Majesty, are you all right? Where's the Dark Prince?" Matt asked, quickly scanning their surroundings.

"E, where's Kade?" Dayla's voice was soft, and her eyes widened. "Is he—"

Ellayne's breathing was still irregular, but after looking behind them and reassuring herself all of the dead people from her imagination had disappeared, she tried to compose herself. "K-Kade is fine. He's w-with the Dark Soldiers."

"Dark Soldiers?" Matt asked as he pushed himself to his feet. He offered a hand to help Ellayne, which she gladly took.

Her legs trembled, and she leaned back against the tree for support. "The Dark King came to Phildeterre to fight alongside us."

"That's good news, right?" Dayla asked, wrapping an arm around Ellayne as they started walking in the direction the two of them had come. "What happened that upset you?"

"I need to speak to Armannii," Ellayne said, her head spinning as they picked up the pace.

"But, E, what—"

"Of course, Your Majesty. We'll take you straight to him. We aren't far," Matt said, cutting Dayla off. Ellayne couldn't have been more thankful.

Armannii rubbed his temple, his face drawn. "Is the kid all right? That's a horrible thing to witness."

Ellayne shook her head. "No, he's not. It was awful, Armannii. Awful. A-and my heart hurts for him because I know what he's going through. I know what it is to lose both of my parents, and to my brother no less." She wrapped her arms tighter around herself as she remembered the tears spilling out of Kade's eyes. "But when he told me to leave, I did. He wanted to take care of it all. But was I wrong to leave? Was leaving him alone a mistake? He was so upset."

"It might have been." Armannii rolled one of the wooden group markers from the map between his pointer and thumb. "But you're here now, and we have things we need to work out. Details, I mean. We have to go soon, especially since the longer we wait, the more time we give Diomedes to strike first."

"And what if he does? Would that be so bad?"

"Yes." He turned back to her. "If the kid could set the Black Forest on fire, then Diomedes could do worse. His magic is not based on the power he was born with but the power he traded his humanity for. Diomedes's dark magic isn't bound like Kade's, the Dark King's, or even Kiegan's. Your brother's magic is closer to the limit of magic one person can have than I ever thought possible. He's the opposite of those without magic. In fact, I've been wondering how he's still in one piece."

"What do you mean?" Ellayne asked, her forehead wrinkling as she concentrated on his words. After the emotional whirlwind, her eyes were begging for her to let them close for a long time, possibly forever. Her body complained every time she had to move, and her mind had waves of mist rolling through, fogging up her thoughts.

"He's unbalanced. He should be volatile. Humanity makes magic in us stable. He traded it for ultimate power. It's an unnatural way of getting magic, but he should be regulated by the same need for balance, technically. He doesn't seem to have it, though. In theory"—he lowered his voice—"someone who is all magic and power with no humanity should cease to exist.

Humanity is the vessel. Take away the vessel, and the magic disperses."

"And Dio's magic doesn't conform to that."

"Right. Well, I mean, it might. But it doesn't seem like it."

"How so?" Ellayne covered her mouth, trying to hide a yawn.

Armannii didn't mention her exhausted state. Instead, he put the marker piece down and shrugged. "Well, the Curse of Infiniti is one example. The amount of power it took to create the Curse of Infiniti probably would've killed anyone with less power. Kind of a sacrifice-yourself-to-curse-your-greatest-enemy type of thing. But your brother was fine afterward, like it was no problem."

"What do I do then, Armannii? I feel like I'm out of options. And now, with him giving the signal to his men for battle, I'm out of time." Ellayne slouched under the weight of her situation. "I still have no idea how to face Dio and somehow make it out alive. I know that's negative, but it's true. I-I don't know what to do."

He remained silent for a moment, then put his hands on her shoulders. "I don't know, Ellayne. I wish I had the answers for you, but I don't."

Her eyes filled with moisture, and she couldn't stop them from overflowing again. "I'm scared," she said, her voice barely a whisper.

Armannii pulled her into a bear hug, and she squeezed her eyes shut. "I'd be concerned for your sanity if you weren't. But if anyone can do this, it's you."

"What makes you so sure?" she asked, her voice breaking halfway through. It came out muffled by his vest.

He pulled back, keeping his hands on her shoulders. "Because I've seen you overcome things that would kill anyone weaker. You were cursed by your own kin, forced month after month to restart at rock bottom, yet you still tried to break the curse every single time. And when you did break it, you didn't stop until you freed your father too. You've lost loved ones and escaped death yourself more than once. And when you found out your father had named you queen, you could've run away, disappeared, and lived without the weight of the crown. But you didn't. Your heart for your people, for *your* country, goes beyond any I've seen. Even the Dark King saw that in you, and you know how I felt about him."

Ellayne sniffled, wiping her hand across her cheek as she nodded.

"Look, I don't have any idea how to get rid of Diomedes, and I understand why you don't want to kill him—probably better than most—but I know he's the biggest threat to your people right now, and I know you're the only person who might be able to face him and come out on top."

"Why?" Ellayne asked, but there was no skepticism in her voice, just genuine curiosity. "Because the prophecy says so?"

"No. Because I've gotten to know you. And because of that, I know you're stubborn. If your brother is going to take the country, he's going to have to go through us first." He let go of Ellayne, stepping back and putting his hands in his pockets. "You're not alone in this. We are all fighting for a new Phildeterre. We will all be there with you."

His words left her speechless. They might not have helped ease the nerves moving up and down her body like snakes, but they did cause her to stop crying. And what was more, his eyes had remained silver through the whole thing. He wasn't lying, trying to boost her confidence. He truly believed in her, and that alone lifted some of the pressure she was feeling.

"Thank you, Armannii. I-I don't know how I would do this without you. Or Kade. Or any of the people outside this tent. You're right. Diomedes isn't going to win, not without putting an end to every single one of us. And I'm going to make sure that doesn't happen."

Armannii grinned at her, his eyes sparkling. "Then let's go get your people ready to fight. I hear there's a war about to start, and I, for one, don't want to miss it."

Chapter Thirty-Four

llayne looked out over the faces of her people—people who were about to follow her into a battle they might not walk away from. It had taken her longer than she thought it would to come up with what to say to them. In that moment, she ran through her planned speech, but all of it seemed stiff. Forced. Neither her father nor any of her tutors had prepared her for how to tell her subjects they might never see their loved ones again.

"Presenting Her Royal Majesty, Queen Ellayne," Armannii said, gesturing toward her.

It took effort to force her feet to move forward to where he stood. Though she could hide the uncertainty she felt about the battle from her subjects, the guilt of keeping significant truths from them left her squirming. She questioned what her father would do in her situation. Fighting the urge to rub her medallion, Ellayne squeezed her hands into fists.

Silence filled the forest as the people waited for her to address them. Chills ran up and down Ellayne's back. She shivered. Her father would've already started talking. Words stuck in her throat, and she couldn't get them out. Glancing back at Armannii, he gave her a reassuring nod. *I don't know what I'm doing,* she tried to tell him with her eyes, but he didn't react. *Breathe,* she reminded herself. *If only my magic could help me form the words my people need to hear.* She hoped there would be a flicker of warmth that followed the thought, that maybe her magic would take over the speech she was dreading. But that didn't happen. Instead, she found a pair of square-shaped glasses, and she focused on her smiling aunt as she began.

"W-we now find ourselves standing at a fork in the road." She spoke in crisp syllables. "Do we remain in the shadows, overpowered by voices that persecute us, or do we step into a battle to fight for our country and a vision of peace Phildeterre has not seen in nearly four generations?"

The crowd shifted, mumbling their hushed responses to the options laid before them. However, not a single person walked away. Instead, they all returned their focus to her, a look of determination on each of their faces.

"There are risks along both paths." She paused, taking a deep breath. "And you deserve to know that the road leading into battle does not promise an outcome of success. Our enemies are strong—stronger than we could ever imagine. Not only that, King Diomedes and his followers believe they are fighting for righteous reasons. But where their convictions have led to the persecution of innocent people, ours do not. And as misguided as their positions may be, neither he nor his people will give up on them without a fight.

"I will not make promises I cannot keep," she said, hesitating. "But I do promise to fight for our country and for a future in which we begin to repair the damage of our ancestors. Of *my* ancestors. Are you ready and willing to fight alongside me for a brighter future?"

After a moment of silence, a cheer echoed through the rebels, starting at the back of the crowd.

"Long live the queen! Long live the queen! Long live the queen!" they shouted.

Her heart swelled. Just like Armannii had said, they believed in her. She gave a determined smile, trying to make eye contact with as many of them as she could. Eventually, Ellayne stepped back, letting Armannii control the crowd. As he passed her, he whispered in her ear.

"I may not have known your parents that well, but they would be proud of you right now. I know I am." He squeezed her shoulder before raising his hands to silence the crowd.

It took a minute or so, but eventually the chaos subsided. Armannii divided the people into groups they had previously discussed so the troops could strike the castle from different directions. As he was explaining who would lead each group, a hand tapped Ellayne on the shoulder, making her jump.

"Your Majesty." Elowen bowed her head. "I have news."

Ellayne glanced at Armannii, then stepped behind the nearest tree. "What is it? What's happened?"

"The Dark Prince deserted the Dark Soldiers. Your friend is gone."

Her heart raced faster than her feet did as she followed Elowen through the trees to the Dark Soldiers. *Why did he leave? Where did he go?* Elowen hadn't known the answer to either of her questions, leaving Ellayne to try to form answers herself. But she knew them somewhere deep down. He had gone after Kiegan.

"Queen Ellayne." A Dark Soldier bowed as she and Elowen entered their ranks. "I apologize for interrupting you as you were preparing your people, but as you've heard, the Dark Prince is gone."

Ellayne nodded. "I heard. Thank you for sending Elowen to me." She crossed her arms over her chest, bobbing her head when Elowen said she was going to return to the camp. "Did the Dark Prince say anything before he left?"

"Not that I'm aware of. One of the soldiers saw him running off that way." He pointed off to the side. "He had speed runes on. The soldier tried to follow, but we cannot draw runes on—"

"Your armor. Right." Ellayne started pacing before she knew what she was doing. "He ran in the direction of Cyanthia. My guess is he is pursuing the man who killed his father." Her hands shook as she raised them to her temples. She rubbed the sides of her head. A headache was forming, and that was the last thing she needed to mix with the exhaustion.

"You." He pointed to a nearby soldier. "Grab someone else and scout ahead."

"It's no use." Ellayne shook her head. "He's long gone."

"What do you suggest then?"

"Who is in charge when the king and his heir are not present?" she asked, pausing in the middle of her pacing.

The Dark Soldier straightened his posture. "I am, Your Majesty."

"And your name?"

"Criss Pike."

Ellayne refrained from making any indication that she had heard his name before. She was sure it was the Criss that both Armannii and Kade had referred to. "Then I need you to prepare your men to go into battle."

"But the Dark Prince—"

"The best thing we can do for Kade is send in everything we've got and get him the backup he's going to need. I'm sure you know Armannii Ovair?"

He grunted. "I do."

"Good," she said. "I'm going to have him discuss a course of action with you. He and I have been planning where our forces are going to go, and I think it's wise for a collaboration of minds."

"Is that necessary?"

"Yes." The word came out clipped. "We need to make sure we conduct a coordinated attack. If you would come with me to the camp, we can figure all of this out." When he didn't say anything in response, she added, "And then we can get the Dark Prince back."

"All right. I'll make sure my men are prepared, then I'll join you."

"That's going to leave my soldiers open to be countered by the king's men. I will not put them in that spot," Criss said as he shook his head. He had taken off his helmet upon entering the soundproof tent with Armannii. He had red hair trimmed short to his scalp, and a scar ran from his jaw down his neck. With the cover his armor provided, it was impossible to know how long the scar was. Criss was shorter and bulkier than Armannii.

Armannii, unlike the soldier, grinned. "That *would* be the case if I were an imbecile, which I'm not. We have a group of sirens coming up the river to this point here." He pointed down at a map—one drawn by Kade.

The thought of Kade running off after Kiegan left Ellayne's heart heavy, and she desired to leave the tent, to be alone. But there was a chance that the civility between Armannii and Criss would run out as soon as she left, so she slouched on the ground.

"We're trusting that your men will cover for our sirens since they will be serving as a distraction for the group positioned here," Armannii continued, and Criss followed his finger as he moved it around the parchment.

"Why there? Why not here?" Criss pointed to a different location.

"Because we need them to cause a distraction outside of where the queen and I will be sneaking into the castle," Armannii responded, nodding toward Ellayne.

"Why do you need to get into the castle?" the Dark Soldier asked Ellayne instead of Armannii.

Ellayne straightened up, sighing as she cracked her neck. "We may not have to, but I assume Diomedes is going to control the battle from the inside. If that's the case, then Armannii and I will go inside to break that control."

"What do you mean by control? And how are you going to stop him?"

"It could be as simple as giving commands to his higher-ups, but I'm not naive enough to think he won't be using magic to control the battleground. He's already completely blackened the sky above Cyanthia. I'm not sure how he'll do it, but I'm confident he'll do what he can to give his royal guards an upper hand." *As for how I'm going to stop him, your guess is as good as mine.* She hoped he wouldn't notice that she hadn't answered the second question. He didn't.

"What's the plan to get the Dark Prince out safely?"

"That depends on where he went," Armannii said, answering for Ellayne. "If he did go to Cyanthia, which we all assume he did, then he could be at the castle already, especially with the speed runes."

"And if he is?"

"Then we'll do everything in our power to get him out safely," Ellayne said. "Kade is my best friend. He's just as much my priority as he is yours. You have my word that I will do what I can to get him out of there in one piece."

Criss watched her carefully and eventually nodded.

"All right." He held out his hand, and she shook it. "To the battlefield."

Chapter Thirty-Five

hen the first group of rebels left, Ellayne felt a sense of dread weigh her down. She watched them disappear in the darkness as they headed in the direction of the Cyanthian castle. How many of them would not return home to their families?

"Queenie," Armannii called, but she didn't move. Her feet felt like boulders, so she didn't turn when he said her name again. "Queenie? Hey, Ellayne?" He joined her where she stood. "He's going to be okay."

"What? Oh." She gripped her arms, shivering. "I hope you're right."

"Linetta talked to you, right?"

Ellayne furrowed her eyebrows as she looked up at him. "Yes. Why do you ask?"

"I just wanted to make sure she found you." He put his hands in his pockets. Neither of them spoke as the faint sound of people talking hummed in the background.

"I love him," she said, surprising even herself with her candor.

"I know." He hid the smile on his face but could not hide it in the sound of his words. "I've known since he helped break your curse."

"What?"

"It was obvious, especially the way you drooled over him when your memories were slipping away. Even then you loved him." Armannii shrugged. "Then there was the way he watched you when you weren't looking. Or the way he came to the Dark despite his previous encounters in it. He did that for you."

"I said I love him, not the other way around."

He chuckled. "You're brave like your mother and wise like your father, but you're still one of the densest people I know."

"Armannii, don't—"

"Kade loves you, and you can check my eyes to see if I'm lying."

"It doesn't matter if you're lying," she said, noting that his eyes were silver. "Because you're not the one whose truth it is. Kade . . ." She hesitated. Running her fingers over her bracelet, she organized her thoughts. "Kade is my best friend, and I want what's best for him. He's just been through so much. I was going to tell him, but it's the wrong time. With all of the times I've had to take him away from his own problems to focus on mine . . . My life is a mess."

Armannii rolled his eyes. "Well, I guess we can't all have as simple a relationship as Dayla and Matt." He raised an eyebrow while she processed what he had just said.

Ellayne's eyes widened. "Wait, what? But—"

"Matt's been pursuing Dayla since he first laid eyes on her. One of those love-at-first-sight things. Rare, I know. He was thrilled when you sent him on a mission with her, and they came back basically engaged."

"I ran into them outside the camp after the Dark King died, but—well, I was distracted."

"They've been sneaking around since they got back, trying to spend time together without making a big deal of it. So, Queenie, I say this as your friend. Whether it be right timing or a siren with a knack for baking, for the love of all that is good, stop trying to place obstacles in between you and the kid—for everyone's sanity, including your own."

Ellayne's mind spun, and she felt her magic flutter inside of her. "Matt and Dayla?" she asked again, still searching for the clues Armannii was so adamant about.

"Honestly, I thought you'd be bright enough to see it." He scrunched his nose, wrinkling his forehead. "But I was wrong, apparently."

"Hey!" She smacked him on the arm. "I am bright."

"Bright as an unlit candle." He grinned when she smacked him again. "Now, can we send the next round of rebels? I'd like to stop all this boy talk and shoot some arrows at Diomedes's men."

"Yes," Ellayne said. "And thanks, Armannii."

"Anything for you, Queenie."

"How is he doing that with the sky?" Ellayne asked as they stood on the edge of the Cylan River across from Cyanthia. The sight in front of them reminded her of a dream she had when she was cursed where the sky had been drained of its rich blue color, leaving it a lifeless dark gray. The darkest part of the sky swirled like a storm directly over the castle.

"I'm going to guess he's doing it with magic," Armannii responded from next to her. "But that's just a theory."

Ellayne rolled her eyes. "You're the worst."

"What did you want me to say? That it's a super powerful spell and we should all fear for our lives? No? I didn't think so. I'll stick with the more humorous response."

"Do you think the men up north are in place yet?" she asked, changing the subject. "We sent them out half an hour ago, and with speed runes—"

"Unless they ran into trouble, they should be in position, yes." Armannii rubbed his thumb along the wood of his bow. "But we should still be careful when we enter town."

"Does that mean you're ready?"

Armannii took out his rune pen. "If you are."

The rune that would change her appearance didn't cause the same reaction as the first time, which Ellayne was thankful for.

"I'm glad I don't have to try to sneak into battle while stopping to vomit in every alleyway," she said, scratching her wrist where the rune irritated her skin.

"Unfortunately, it still itches," Armannii said as he finished his.

It took a minute for their new appearances to fully develop, leaving one teenage boy with curly hair and a woman in her late forties or early fifties with graying chestnut hair in a pixie cut.

Ellayne ran her fingers through the short hair. "Maybe I should cut mine. This is nice."

"I've never understood how people deal with long hair. I once grew mine down to my shoulders but couldn't stand the way it stuck to everything when I trained. Chopped it off in frustration one day, and it's never gotten longer than a few inches since then. And with that being said, shall we?"

She inhaled deeply. "I guess it's now or never."

"I don't remember Cyanthia ever being this empty in the mid afternoon before," Ellayne whispered as they walked along the streets. Shutters were locked, and they hadn't seen a single person for the first half of their walk through the town, at least until they saw a flash of a cloak when someone ran into a building and slammed the door.

"Whatever the king is doing to the sky is probably what's causing people to stay inside. They're probably scared," Armannii said.

"It's eerie."

"Agreed."

"But hopefully it'll keep innocent lives from being lost," she added, gripping her cloak tighter. "Especially if the fighting stays at the castle." She whispered the last part to avoid being heard by anyone trying to eavesdrop. Not that anyone would be able to eavesdrop unless they had elf-like hearing.

Armannii wrapped his arm around hers, guiding her to the side and catching her off guard.

"What are you—"

"We're being followed," he whispered. "Don't turn. Try to use the reflection in the windows around us to see instead." Armannii nodded toward a shop window.

Ellayne used her peripheral vision so as not to be obvious and caught a flicker of a black cloak ducking into an alleyway behind them. Her heart began racing, and she clutched Armannii's arm tighter.

"What should we do?" she asked as he steered her down another street. "You're going to take us in a circle if you keep turning right."

"I want to make sure he's actually following."

"He is," Ellayne said, checking in another window. "And now there are two."

"Three," he corrected. "One on the roofs following us from above."

"Do you think they know?"

"I don't know how they'd know," he said. She felt him adjust his grip on her arm. "But what I do know is that I'm not going to be able to get my bow out quickly, so if need be, you may have to do what you can to give me a few extra seconds."

Ellayne moved her right hand inside her cloak, brushing her fingertips over the hilt of her sword. "I can do that, but how do you know they're going to attack?"

"I recognize the crest on their cloaks," he muttered, turning them down another street. "It's from a town in Byshan, what used to be the northern kingdom. I guess it was wishful thinking to hope we wouldn't run into any of the king's northern allies. They're deadly."

"That is a true statement," a voice said from Ellayne's right, and before she could pull out her sword, something hot struck her in the chest, breaking her grip on Armannii. She stumbled backward.

Ellayne grasped the edge of a building, leaning on it as she caught her breath. Whatever hit her stung but hadn't cut her. A grunt pulled her attention from her injuries, and she saw Armannii duck out of the way of a battle-ax.

"You were warned not to enter the streets," another voice said from behind her, and she whirled around in time to see another ax flying toward her face. She dropped to the ground, letting the ax split the wood above her head.

Warmth grew inside of her as magic spread through her hands. A grin slid across her lips, and she hurled a blast of magic into the stomach of her attacker, who was in the middle of trying to get his ax unstuck from the building. The force of the blow sent him flying several feet away. He did not get back up afterward.

Her chest still hurt, and somewhere in her mind she wondered what had caused the impact, but the question answered itself when she turned to see Armannii dodge a blast of light magic. And it wasn't hers.

Surprise filled Ellayne at the sight of another person with light magic, but it did not stop her from pulling her sword from its sheath. She raised it horizontally above her head when one of the northern attackers, the one who had been following them on the roofs, jumped down with an ax raised.

"Does everyone in the north use an ax in battle?" Ellayne asked as she fell back into her fighting stance. "Seems a little obnoxious to carry around."

"It's called a halberd," the mercenary spat, swinging the bladed end at Ellayne. She ducked but had to step back because of the length of the weapon. "And yes. We do."

Her new opponent's hood fell back, and a woman about the age of Ellayne's fake identity peered at her. They circled each other with weapons ready.

"You shouldn't have come outside," the woman said, revealing two pointed teeth.

Vampire. Great. Ellayne tightened her grip on the sword, but she knew it wouldn't do much to the vampire unless she managed to swing hard enough to cut her head off. *What I wouldn't give for a wooden spear right now,* she thought. *A wooden spear and a speed rune.*

"Believe me," Ellayne responded, trying not to flinch when another blast of magic struck a building nearby, "I'd prefer not to be here too."

The vampire charged her in a blur, and Ellayne only had time to block with her sword. However, her boots skidded backward as the vampire shoved her into the side of a building. Ellayne cried out when the woman twisted her wrist, forcing her to let go of the sword.

Not good, not good, not good, her mind screamed at her. The woman gripped her around the throat, pinning her to the wall with nonhuman strength.

The woman grinned, showing her fangs. "You know, I was feeling a bit peckish."

Chapter Thirty-Six

llayne tried to pull her arm away, but the woman was stronger as she brought Ellayne's wrist up to her mouth. The pinch of the bite left Ellayne sucking in air, but only a second later, she felt the world wash away, replaced by a sense of weightlessness. She felt like she was gliding, soaring above the surface of Phildeterre. Her heartbeat quickened. Ellayne enjoyed the elation as though it were a sweet to be devoured.

Every weight she'd been worried about before disappeared. Colors and shapes danced behind her eyelids, and she sucked in air faster. Each breath sent chills down her body, and she enjoyed the goose bumps that arose. It left her skin tingling.

She couldn't remember where she was or even who she was. For some reason, the emptiness in her mind felt familiar, but she couldn't remember why. The colors swirled, distracting her from any uneasiness or confusion.

But something wasn't quite right. A heat continued to build in her stomach, and it spread directly to her right wrist. The visions dancing behind her closed eyes couldn't erase the new sense of panic rising with the heat. A tiny voice in the back of her head told her to fight back, that she was in trouble. *What kind of trouble?* she wondered, her heartbeat speeding up even more than it already had. She focused on the heat, hoping it would tell her more; instead, it flared up.

Ellayne let out a scream when the peaceful sensation shattered, and she opened her eyes to see the vampire sprawled out on the ground a few feet from her.

Pushing herself to her feet—she must've slid down the wall at some point—she peered down at her wrist. Her own blood smeared her skin, and at the center of the blood were two puncture marks, which continued to bleed. The area around the injury glowed from her magic.

Ellayne's eyes widened when she saw the face of the vampire. The woman looked like she'd stuck her face in an open flame, and giant blisters formed where the skin wasn't already raw and red. The vampire was sprawled out on the cobblestone street, twitching every few seconds.

"Hey!" came a shout to her right, and it took her a second to recognize Armannii in his disguised state. "You okay?"

She bent down to pick up her sword, and with another glance at the vampire, she nodded. "I think so. But if I start craving blood, I'll let you know."

He held out his hand when she got to him and examined the bite wound. "You'll be fine. It's not as easy to turn vampire as people would have you believe. Everything in magic works only if there's intention behind it, or at least proof of action."

"Whatever that means," Ellayne muttered, using the hem of her tunic to press against her wrist. "What happened to the guy with light magic?"

Armannii pointed to a pair of boots sticking out from one of the alleyways. They weren't moving.

"Is he—"

"Dead?" Armannii exhaled, glancing down at his boots. "Yes. We're in war. I will do what I must to keep you safe."

Ellayne couldn't take her eyes off of the pair of boots. They belonged to someone's son. Maybe someone's brother or father. "And did you actually k—"

"Shoot him in the throat with an arrow?" Armannii put his bow in one hand and offered his arm to Ellayne again. "Yes, I did."

"Are you okay?" Ellayne said as her stomach heaved.

"Come on." He tugged her in the direction they'd originally come from, ignoring her question completely. "We've got some ground to cover." Armannii may not have responded verbally to her question, but his shoulders were tense. He kept his jaw clenched and his gaze forward, avoiding all eye contact. It was his only way of lying that everything was okay.

No other northern mercenaries, or anyone else for that matter, stepped foot on the street as they continued through the heart of Cyanthia. Each step added a drop of adrenaline to Ellayne's system until she felt like she was vibrating with the stuff.

"It's begun, hasn't it?" she asked. When Armannii raised an eyebrow at her, she said, "The fighting, I mean."

"If everyone got to where they're supposed to be, then yes."

"So you think it'll be clear for us to get in?"

"Is it ever that easy?"

Ellayne sighed. "I wish."

"And every single person who has tried to change history has probably wished for that too. But if change were easy, we'd all be living in a better world. What we're doing is difficult and trying, but it's necessary."

She grinned. "How is it you have some of the wittiest comments one second and then some sort of word of wisdom the next? You don't make sense."

"It's all part of my charm, Queenie." He winked at her. "But you've known that for a while."

She snorted, but the grin on her lips faded as she looked up at the sky. The darkness sucked Ellayne's attention toward the castle walls they were approaching. Somewhere in there, her brother was preparing to kill her. And while that was what most of her mind focused on, a small fragment sorted through memories of the past. She could still hear her own shrieks of laughter as she remembered chasing Diomedes down the long hallways or the overwhelming glee at a successful kitchen heist with him.

"What is it?"

Ellayne glanced at Armannii, her eyes not quite focused, still lost in memories. "I just wish it could be like it used to be."

"What do you mean?"

"I wish he could go back to being my older brother. Someone I looked up to."

Armannii paused. "Are you going to be able to go through with what we're about to do?"

She sighed, turning her face back to the dark sky above them. "Yes. I mean, maybe. It's just . . . I miss him."

"Diomedes?"

"Yes. And my father, and my mother, and Calder. There've already been so many lives lost. I don't want to lose my brother too."

"If we don't follow through, the only promised outcome is more unnecessary spilled blood. Can you do this or not?"

"That's the question, isn't it?" She touched her bracelet, trying to understand how the man who'd filled her head with stories of nymphs and dragons could be the same person who killed her parents and tried to curse her for all eternity. She choked on whatever words she was going to say.

"I understand." He exhaled. "He was like a brother to me. I trusted him and would've given my life for his. But he's not the person we used to know. I wish . . . I wish I could believe he's still in there somewhere. That we could somehow reach him. But Ellayne"—he gripped her by the shoulders—"I think the best thing for this country is to rid it of the threat before we lose other lives."

"I know," she said, dropping her sight to the ground. "I just— I want him back."

"I know. I do too."

Chapter Thirty-Seven

he sound of screams and metal clanking together had Ellayne's blood running cold the second she heard it. In just a minute or so, she was going to see the nightmare she had sent her people into. As she clutched the hilt of her sword in her hand, she only hoped to see something better than when she had walked into the destroyed remains of Pingbi.

"Careful, Queenie," Armannii said from in front of her. "We don't know what we're about to enter." He peered around the building they were standing behind. The rune they used to disguise themselves continued to keep them from drawing too much attention, and Ellayne wondered how much longer they had before it started to wear off.

"Can you see anything?" she asked, taking a step forward to look around the corner, but he held up his hand to stop her.

"Wait," he whispered. "Something isn't right." Armannii's ears perked up, and he frowned. "Where are they?" he muttered. "Why aren't they here yet?"

"What are you talking about?" She raised her eyebrows, panic rising like the first moon would soon. "Who's not here? Tell me what's going on, Armannii."

His eyes were wide when he faced her. "Ellayne, the Dark Soldiers didn't show."

Before he could stop her, Ellayne ran around the corner. He chased after her, though he didn't dare call her name.

Ellayne knew full well which of her friends were in the group assigned to the gates of the castle. Matt and Dayla were supposed to be leading a group of sirens from the river. They were supposed to get there after the Dark Soldiers to help cause enough of a commotion that Ellayne and Armannii could sneak by disguised and unnoticed.

But if the Dark Soldiers hadn't shown up, that left the sirens exposed to attack. The peaceful sirens. The men and woman who were fighting only because they had already seen firsthand what her brother's men were capable of. Ellayne couldn't—wouldn't— let anything happen to Dayla. Not after seeing Calder cut down before her eyes.

Buildings flashed by, and Ellayne drew her sword as she approached the gate. Royal guards had spilled outside onto the hill leading up to the castle. She was unsure how long the fighting had been going on, but there were at least five dozen bodies on the ground, and only a few of them wore royal guard clothes.

Ellayne lunged at the first guard she came to, intercepting a downward strike that would've ended the life of yet another siren. She spun her sword, sending the guard and the weapon backward and away from the intended target. The guard grunted. He stepped forward. Sideways swing. Tilting her sword down, she blocked him, and with a kick, she took the guard down to his knees, where she walloped him on the side of the head with the hilt of her sword.

With a spin, she offered her hand to the siren on the ground. The woman thanked her, scrambling to her feet with Ellayne's help.

"Where are the Dark Soldiers?" Ellayne asked her, scanning the area to make sure they were safe enough to talk.

"I don't know. We waited as long as we could, but—" The woman, who was probably in her thirties, breathed heavily, gripping her side. Ellayne's heartbeat quickened at the sight of a strip of red leaking through the siren's shirt.

"You're hurt," Ellayne said, helping the woman stand when her legs gave out.

"I-I'm fine. I have to help the queen."

Ellayne choked, her breathing speeding up. "I have to get you somewhere safe," she said, starting to pull the woman away from the battlefield.

But the woman shook her head. "No. I have to fight for Queen Ellayne."

A voice shouted from behind them, and Ellayne turned to see a royal guard charging. With one arm around the woman, Ellayne was unable to draw her weapon. But when the man came close enough that she could see the stain of blood on his sword, it fell out of view. The man made a gurgling noise and coughed up blood as he stumbled over to the side. It was as if he had been struck. And he had been—by an arrow.

Scanning the crowd, Ellayne saw Armannii—still disguised as a teenage boy—lower his bow, nodding to her. He watched the area, making sure none of the guards got near her by striking them in the throat with an arrow any time they approached. He felled three other guards before Ellayne was able to drag the woman to him.

By that time, the siren was delirious, rambling on about protecting her country.

"She was struck on the side," Ellayne said. "Heal her."

"What, no 'please?' " Armannii handed her his bow and whisked out his rune pen. "Watch my back."

"Can't I just use my magic?"

"Better to stay inconspicuous if we still want to get into the castle," he said as he ripped a bigger hole in the siren's tunic. The cut on her side oozed blood, and Armannii started to draw the healing rune above it.

Ellayne gripped the bow, hoping her aim hadn't gotten worse in the years she hadn't practiced. She got an arrow ready, noticing the way the green tip sparkled in the light.

"Not that arrow," Armannii said, glancing at her. "Use a different one."

"Why?"

"Shut up and switch arrows."

"Whatever," she said, obeying his order. After she put a new arrow in the bow, she spun in a full circle, scanning the field. Only one guard seemed to notice the three of them, and Ellayne met his eye as she raised her aim to point directly at his chest. She was ready to let the arrow fly as soon as the man charged her, but the moans from the siren beneath her caused enough of a distraction that Ellayne let the arrow go too soon. It went soaring above the guard's head.

Fumbling with the quiver, Ellayne couldn't get an arrow out fast enough. The man raised his sword, but he never struck her. Instead, she called for protection—a request she had made before. And like before, it created a barrier between her and the guard, shrouding her, Armannii, and the siren in a bubble of protection.

The man's sword bounced off the light shield, and he stumbled backward. Seeing an opportunity, Ellayne dropped the bow and switched to her sword. With a mental thank-you to her magic, she lowered the barrier and lunged at the guard. He sneered at her when their swords met with a clank.

"Magic scum," he growled, shoving away from Ellayne.

"You do realize"—Ellayne moved her cloak out of the way—"that the king you serve has magic, right?"

The guard's eyes glazed over, but he still swung at her, catching her off guard. She blocked him at the last minute, trying to comprehend what she'd seen.

"You lie," he said, sprinting toward her again; however, the fogginess behind his eyes cleared.

"I'm not lying," Ellayne said, moving to the side. "King Diomedes has magic."

Just as before, a haze covered his irises, and he lashed out at her. "Your words are treason against the king."

"Are you kidding me?" Ellayne asked. "Seriously, are you insane?"

The guard aimed low, going for her legs, but she leapt into the air. His swing missed, leaving him unbalanced. She took her chance, spinning her leg so it caught him directly in the rib cage. He dropped his sword, coughing as he staggered backward.

The man tried to run away, but Ellayne didn't let him get that far. Raising her hand, she focused her magic into a line that wrapped around him. With a jerk of her hand, she yanked him back, leaving him hovering a few inches above the ground.

"Evil witch. Magic beast," he hissed at her, spitting as he did so.

"Hey." Armannii stood up and walked up to her. "I thought I made it clear not to use magic."

"You weren't complaining about it when I saved our lives a minute ago," she responded. "Besides, look at his eyes."

Armannii squinted at the man and took a deep breath when he realized what she was talking about. "He's bewitched, just like most of them, I'd wager."

She swiveled her head, scanning the other guards. How many were fighting because they had no other choice? Ellayne's stomach twisted, and she found it difficult to swallow. Which ones knew exactly what they were doing as they sliced into the sirens, and which ones didn't understand what was really happening, their minds in a completely different place?

Ellayne's shoulders drooped. "Dio's using these people as living shields. That's—"

"Awful." He nodded. "Hold him still."

"Why?" she asked as Armannii approached the squirming man, who was still hurling insults at her.

"Loathsome bug-eating wretch. You disgusting—" The man slumped over the second Armannii swung his hand out and smacked his neck.

"Did you just—"

"No," Armannii said, motioning for her to drop him. "I just knocked him out. And you should be thankful. We don't need a rumor spreading around the country that the queen eats bugs."

"The queen?" The siren woman clutched her side as she stood up. Ellayne raced over to offer her some support.

"Easy now," Ellayne said, catching her under the arm. "You're still healing."

"You're the queen? Queen Ellayne?" the woman asked again, blinking her eyes at Ellayne. "But you don't look like her. I saw her give a speech in front of all those going to fight. And she—"

Ellayne pulled up her sleeve, revealing the appearance-changing rune. "I don't want to be recognized."

"And you're doing such a wonderful job of that," Armannii muttered as he picked up his bow from the ground.

"You're the one who called me queen," Ellayne pointed out, stepping back and letting the woman stand for herself when she seemed stable enough.

"That may be, but we need to keep moving."

A scream drew their attention, and the hair on the back of Ellayne's neck stood on end. The scream was familiar. The scream was Dayla's.

Chapter Thirty-Eight

rmannii caught Ellayne's wrist before she could run off again. "Don't. We have a job to do."

"Let go of me," Ellayne snapped, ripping her wrist away from his grip. "I am not leaving Dayla to be slaughtered. That is *not* going to happen." She glanced at the siren she had saved. "You know how to draw healing runes?"

The woman nodded. "I do, Your Majesty."

"Then your new job is to check the others who are down. See what you can do for them, and watch your back." Ellayne glanced at Armannii. "You're with me."

"Ellayne—"

She didn't let him argue. Turning on her heels, Ellayne sprinted in the direction of the scream. Armannii's footsteps fell in step behind her, and she focused on listening for Dayla.

"This is a risk. We don't have time to rescue everyone," Armannii said, and then he added, "but if you must know, I hear her. She's to the left more."

"I'm not going to argue." She let him take the lead, following him as he led her over the crest of a hill. Five figures stood at the bottom of the valley; three were dressed in the attire of royal guards, and the other two, a man and a woman, weren't. "Dayla," Ellayne breathed, pumping her arms faster.

"Wait," Armannii said, pulling her behind a tree. "They're about to execute them." He pointed to the man and Dayla, who were on their knees at the feet of one of the guards.

"No." Ellayne shook her head. "Not again."

"Ellayne," he snapped, but she freed herself from his hands and continued to run down the hill.

One guard stood behind each of them, and it was then that Ellayne recognized the man on his knees despite the blood trickling down his face. Matt held his chin up, facing the third guard with red along his collar. Everything became clear to Ellayne as the captain of the guard nodded to the two men behind Dayla and Matt.

Raising her hand as she ran, Ellayne screamed, hurling a blast of light magic that landed nearby, exploding the terrain into dust. The guard behind Dayla dove out of the way while the one behind Matt sprinted to meet Ellayne at the bottom of the hill. Matt collapsed to the side, crumpling on the ground as soon as the man holding him up moved. Dirt rained down, and Dayla lunged for the captain of the guard when he stumbled backward.

With a loud clank, Ellayne met the guard's sword with hers. She spun, waving her hand to the side, and used her magic to call a cloud of dust. It was enough to disable the guard. He coughed, clutching at his throat as the debris swirled around his head. Dropping to his knees, he was too distracted by the cloud of dirt surrounding him to notice Ellayne's boot as she kicked him square in the face.

She turned to meet the other guard—his sword inches from her. But just as before, an arrow soared through the air, striking him in the chest. She leapt out of the way as he collapsed right where she had been standing.

"You killed him. Admit it!" Dayla screamed. She had the captain of the guard pinned to the ground, and her sharpened fingernails came down on his face as she shouted at him to confess again.

"Do your worst, little girl." The captain spat in her face.

But before Dayla could hit him again, Ellayne called to her. "Dayla, stop." She held her hand out as if she could somehow reach across the ten feet between them to help her. Ellayne knew her appearance was distorted because of the rune, and when Dayla furrowed her eyebrows at her, she said, "It's me; it's Ellayne."

Armannii drew her focus for a second when he made it to the bottom of the hill, and he went straight to Matt. Ellayne turned her attention back to Dayla when she said her name.

"Ellayne, this is him." Dayla returned her focus to the captain and didn't look up as she continued speaking to Ellayne. "This is the man who gave the order to kill Cal. He deserves the same fate."

"Wait!" Ellayne shrieked as Dayla raised her hand again. "Cal wouldn't want you to do this. Dayla, this isn't going to bring your brother back."

Tears streamed down Dayla's cheeks when she finally turned to look at Ellayne. "But he killed him. He killed my brother."

"Day . . ." Matt coughed from where Armannii held him. He was in bad shape, and Armannii's pen skimmed over Matt's neck as he traced a healing rune. "Day, please. You don't want to do this."

"But I do," she snarled at the captain when he tried to shift underneath her. "I've wanted to since he took Cal away from me."

"This isn't the answer," Ellayne said, taking another step toward her. "Half of these guards are bewitched and have no idea what they're doing."

Dayla's eyes widened, and she glanced down at the captain. "But—"

"Dayla, love, don't do this." Matt moaned, and Ellayne assumed the healing rune was starting to feel like fire for him. But he fought through the pain. "Love, you can move on from this."

She shifted her glance from Ellayne to Matt, both of whom beckoned her away from the man. The captain of the guard grunted as Dayla stood up, shoving her boot into his side as she did so.

"You don't deserve to live," she said, venom behind her words. "But I'll give you the chance you stole from my brother."

She turned her back on him. Out of the corner of her eye, Ellayne tracked his movement. He grabbed something that glinted in the low light peaking through the dark sky. Ellayne started running before the captain of the guard could open his mouth

"That's your mistake," he said as he shot his loaded crossbow at Dayla.

Ellayne tackled Dayla, shoving her to the ground.

"What—" Dayla started to say, but she turned and saw the captain of the guard reloading it as fast as he could. "Big mistake." She pushed herself to her feet. "Sorry, Ellayne."

"Dayla, wait—"

Dayla cut her off by opening her mouth. With only a few screeches, Ellayne knew she was too late. The captain of the guard was completely under the control of Dayla's siren song.

"Do it," Dayla barked, and Ellayne turned away when the guard removed the arrow he had just loaded into the crossbow and dragged it across his own neck. A hollow bubbling sound erupted from his mouth. The thud of his body keeling over reverberated in the valley.

A second later, Dayla collapsed to her knees, sobbing. Ellayne knelt beside her, pulling her into her arms just as she had after her brother died.

"I'm so sorry, Ellayne," she said. "I know I shouldn't have, but—"

Armannii's touch on Dayla's shoulder cut her words off. "We are in the middle of a war. Deaths are to be expected."

Matt came around Armannii's side. One look at him and Dayla sprung to her feet, wrapping her arms around him. He stuck his face in her neck, rocking her back and forth.

"It's going to be okay." He kissed her forehead. "We'll get through this."

The sight of them reminded Ellayne of Kade, and her stomach turned. She wanted to find him, to tell him how she felt, to have him look at her the way Matt stared down at Dayla, like she was the only one who mattered in the world.

"You need to get back to the others," Ellayne said. "Things aren't going well back there. What happened to the Dark Soldiers?"

"We waited as long as we could for them to show," Dayla said as she looped an arm around Matt's waist, supporting him as much as she could. "But a dryad showed up and said the fighting had begun elsewhere and that you were coming. We knew we had to start."

Ellayne bit her lip, staring back at the hill she had run down. "The others are outnumbered ten to one. I-I'm not sure what to do."

"The Coves," Matt said, his voice raw. It appeared one of the guards must've tried to strangle him, and even with the healing rune, his vocal chords were straining. "Get them to fight like when we were attacked."

Dayla shook her head as Ellayne and Armannii gave questioning looks. "I can't ask them to do that again. It's against everything they know. It's against the rules. And after what I just did . . ." Dayla cast a glance over her shoulder. "I understand why."

"What happened at the Coves?" Ellayne asked, frowning.

"The king's men attacked after we had arrived, and my people didn't know what to do. When I saw one of them about to kill Millie, I started singing out of panic. The man turned on his friends when I told him to, and Millie caught on. But what we did, what I just did, it goes against what these people were taught. I don't think they'll do it."

"It may be our only shot. We have to try, otherwise every single siren up there is going to die." Armannii kept his eyes on Dayla when he pointed up the hill, using his bow as an extension of his arm.

Ellayne's headache was back, but she tried to push it away. "He's right. Please try."

"I—" Dayla glanced at Matt, who nodded at her with a weak smile. "I'll try."

"All right then," Armannii said, bobbing his head. "Let's go." He switched off with Dayla, helping Matt up the uneven terrain. Dayla and Ellayne ran ahead, and they found the sirens in even worse condition than before. Only a few remained, and they were surrounded by the guards.

"Oh no," Dayla whispered as they got to the top of the hill. "We're too late."

"No," Ellayne said, holding her hand. "Not yet. Start singing. Hopefully the others will catch on."

Dayla took a deep breath, hesitation written across her face in bold letters. But she did as Ellayne commanded. Opening her mouth, she began screeching out her siren song. A few of the guards surrounding the group went slack, and Ellayne grinned. *This is going to work,* she thought as she raised her sword. A nearby guard charged her but stopped in his tracks when Dayla turned her attention to him.

A few of the sirens had stopped what they were doing and were gawking at Dayla. The seconds dragged on, but nothing changed except the obedience of a few guards directly around Dayla and Ellayne. Then a new voice joined in. Ellayne tried to see who it was and couldn't help but smile at the woman she had saved earlier. One by one, other sirens joined in the song. Guards began to turn on one another, and those who were under control of the sirens began forcing the others back with their weapons ready.

"It's working," Ellayne whispered. "I can't believe it. It's actually working." She watched as the last of the guards ran into the gates, hunted by their comrades.

Dayla was panting as she hugged Ellayne, and there was a tired smile on her lips. The other sirens still left alive jogged over to them.

"Well done," Ellayne said, addressing all of the sirens at once. "Check for survivors and use as many healing runes as you can to save lives."

"Day," Matt said as he and Armannii finally reached the top of the hill. "Well done."

She beamed at him, then turned back to the other sirens. "You heard the queen. Let's get our injured out."

"Queen?" one of the sirens asked, raising an eyebrow at Ellayne. "She's not the queen."

Showing her wrist with the rune still inscribed on it, Ellayne explained the plan that had gone horribly wrong.

"I still don't know where the Dark Soldiers are," she said, glancing over her shoulder. She turned to Armannii. "But we need to go."

He didn't respond, his attention focused on the darkened sky. His jaw dropped, and she turned to see what he was looking at.

"Is that a—"

"Yeah." Armannii swallowed loudly. "It's a dragon."

Chapter Thirty-Nine

re you kidding me?" Ellayne asked, squinting up at the sky. "A dragon? I thought there were no more dragons left. Of course Dio found one." She remembered the painting of the dragon in her brother's office. They had been his favorite. And after hearing story after story of how they ripped their prey to shreds with their teeth, she quaked at the thought of facing one. "Could this day get any worse?"

"Better not ask that," Armannii said, placing an arrow in his bow. The disguise runes were wearing off, and he was slowly getting taller than her.

"How about I ask what you know about dragons instead?" Ellayne said as she scratched her wrist where her own rune was itching. She wrapped her growing hair back into a bun, missing the short hair already.

"Not much. They fly, breathe fire, and enjoy raw meat."

"I could've told you that much. Dio also loved pointing out that their scales make them difficult to attack, so I'm not sure what you think your bow is going to do." She tucked her sword away, knowing it wouldn't even scratch the dragon. And that was assuming she could get close without being burned, bitten, or bashed beneath its feet.

He continued to track the dragon, his bowstring taut. "I'm sure that's true, but I still feel better with this in my hands. And although we're clearly experts, I have a feeling we're about to learn a thing or two from this dragon."

"Hopefully how to take it down." Her mind raced over everything she had read in her father's office about dragons and any possible weaknesses they might have. She went back through all the conversations she could remember with her brother about the beasts too, but nothing seemed to stick in her mind. In fact, by the time the dragon made a nosedive in their direction, the only thing her brain was telling her was to run.

"Take cover!" she hollered, pointing to trees nearby. The sirens scattered, sprinting to the trees that Ellayne knew would not provide much cover. Not against fire.

The first time the dragon swooped down, the force from its wings stirred dust into the air, forcing Ellayne to shield her eyes. When it flew by, the air filled with the scent of smoke and burned flesh. *Think.* She scoured her brain for anything she had learned from the books, but as the dragon flew up into the sky again, she drew a blank.

The dragon's wingspan was at least thirty feet, and from nose to tail it was even longer. Light gray scales mixed with charcoal-gray scales, and they covered the head down to the tail. Every once in a while, a patch of metallic scales would reflect in the low light. The underside of the dragon's wings had blue-ash scales that sparkled purple from certain angles.

"E, what do we do?" Dayla asked from beside her. She and Armannii helped prop Matt up, but it was clear from his ashen face that the run to the trees had counteracted some of the good the healing rune had done.

"I'm thinking," Ellayne said, running her hand over her mouth.

The dragon nose-dived the valley again, and this time it didn't hold back its fiery breath. The grass in the field lit instantly, and Ellayne drew her cloak over her face to protect herself from some of the heat, not that it did much.

One of the trees nearby lit on fire, and the two sirens underneath it ran screaming to the next tree. But their shouts drew the attention of the dragon, and it turned around in the middle of its ascent to charge the new prey. One of the two sirens noticed the dragon and dropped to his stomach, but the other was not as lucky. The dragon's talons dug into the woman's shoulders, lifting her from the ground and carrying her into the sky.

"No," Ellayne breathed. "I have to do something." She took off from the tree before Dayla or Armannii could stop her. Sprinting with her hands at her sides, she reached the man who had fallen right as the dragon plunged straight for him. She threw her hand up, creating a magic barrier between herself and the dragon, but the force of the dragon hitting it knocked her to the ground. Her concentration broken, the barrier shattered into shimmering fragments of light magic.

The dragon recoiled after the shield broke, but it returned with a roar, aiming its talons for Ellayne this time. For a second, Ellayne wondered what had happened to the other woman, but the thought left as quickly as it had come when the dragon's talons gripped her underneath her arms, yanking her off the ground.

Ellayne screamed as the dragon lifted her into the sky; the trees became specks below her in a matter of seconds. The higher it went, the less air she could breathe. The dragon released her before she could prepare herself, and she plummeted toward the ground. Her stomach clenched, and it was hard to breathe as wind whipped her in the face. A shadow moved from behind her. The dragon. It swooped below and opened its mouth. Ellayne no longer wondered where the other siren had gone. She was most certainly dead, in the belly of the dragon. Just like Ellayne would be.

"Help!" she screamed, though she had meant it to be an inward plea to her magic. It listened to her nonetheless, creating a sphere of protection around her as she slammed into the dragon's mouth. The barrier did not protect her from the smells that came from the inside. The overwhelming scent of rotting corpses and burning flesh filled her nostrils, nearly causing her to vomit.

The inside and outside of her shook as the dragon's powerful jaw crunched on her barrier. Her magic fought to remain strong as the dragon shook her around. *Please,* she begged her magic, *find me a way out of this. I have to save my country; I have to save Kade.* She braced herself against the barrier, gritting her teeth as she tried to hold it together. A thought crossed her mind, and as the dragon sunk its teeth into the barrier, shattering it, she focused all of her energy on one word.

Burn.

Her body lit like a fuse, illuminating her in a fire she could not feel. The dragon made a screeching noise, and before the teeth came down on her, the beast spit Ellayne out.

Once again, she tumbled through the air, limbs flailing. The fire around her went out, and she focused on the ground fast approaching. She forced her mind away from the image it played of her body splattering over the field and instead bent it until she saw an image of herself floating a foot above the ground. *Please,* she thought, begging her magic to follow her commands.

Her stomach jolted when her momentum slowed down in a matter of a few seconds. With heart racing, she opened her eyes. Her feet hovered no more than a foot off the ground, and with a sigh of relief, she let herself down. Ellayne's boots crunched over the singed field as she crossed toward the trees.

A silhouette on the castle wall caught her attention, and she paused, staring at it.

"Ellayne!" Dayla met her in the field, tugging at her arm so she would move. "Come on. Are you okay? Are you hurt? Are you—"

"That's it!" Ellayne cried as she pulled her wrist from Dayla's grip.

"What? What are you—"

"Dayla, look," Ellayne said as she pointed to the person on the wall, whose hands were now raised.

"Who is that?"

"Ellayne!" Armannii shouted.

Ellayne turned in time to see the dragon swooping down. She shoved Dayla toward the trees, jumping behind one as another round of fire sent the field into a blaze again. Ellayne covered her nose and mouth, choking on the smoke.

"What is wrong with you?" Armannii asked, helping her to her feet. "Do you have a death wish or something?"

Ellayne pointed to the figure on the wall. "Armannii, shoot the dragon whisperer."

"The what? You could've been killed. Do you realize—"

"Shut up and do what I said." Ellayne smacked him on the arm, pointing again to the figure. "Shoot that person."

He grumbled as he lifted his bow, letting an arrow loose. Ellayne tracked it with her eyes, watching as it landed right in the cloaked person's chest. They clearly hadn't expected it because they tumbled backward off the wall. As soon as the person disappeared, Ellayne returned her attention to the dragon. It roared as it flew circles in the sky.

"Now would you please explain why—"

Ellayne reached up, gripped Armannii's chin, and turned it toward the silhouette above them.

"It's flying away," he said, shaking her grip off. "It's flying away! But why?"

"You killed the person who called it here. It didn't have control over what it was doing."

"How did you know?" Dayla asked.

"I remembered a line in one of the books I read as a child as soon as I saw the whisperer. Quick, Dayla, get the other sirens to regroup and check for survivors. Matt, go with her. Armannii, we have somewhere to be."

"Before we go," Armannii said, looking down at her, "can we please just take a moment to appreciate that you somehow didn't die a few minutes ago? I mean, seriously, Queenie."

"We can appreciate that later." She pushed on his back. "Good luck, you two," she said to Dayla and Matt as she and Armannii started running toward the gates.

"A dragon. A flying, fire-breathing dragon," Armannii said.

"Yes, yes it was."

"Awesome."

Chapter Forty

rmannii held out his arm to stop Ellayne from crossing when they made it to the gates. Although all of the royal guards had disappeared after the sirens had taken control of them, Armannii made her wait as he cleared the corner.

"Come on." He motioned for her to follow. "We need to be more careful now that our runes have worn off."

"Can't you just draw them again?"

"With transfiguration runes, it's in our best interest to give them a bit of a cooldown."

"For how long?" Ellayne asked, glancing back to make sure they weren't being followed as they approached the servants' entrance.

"A few days is best."

"And if we don't wait?"

Armannii snickered. "You could end up looking like a troll."

"That's not bad."

"Forever."

"Oh." Ellayne bit her cheek. "Let's not do that then."

He grinned at her. "I didn't think so. Let's just stay a bit more inconspicuous, okay?" He raised an eyebrow. "Which means let's limit the light magic."

"Okay, but he probably already knows we're here. He's got people everywhere."

"True, and there's a good chance Blanndynne has placed runes around the castle to alert them to our presence, but we may as well pretend they don't know and be careful nonetheless," he said as he raised his bow. He aimed it at the door, nodding at Ellayne to tell her to open it.

"Ready?" she asked as she drew her sword. "One, two, three," she said, yanking the door open.

They exchanged a look at the empty corridor.

"That's suspicious," Ellayne said. "It wasn't even locked."

"You'd think you'd remember to lock your doors when you know there's going to be a full-on siege happening at your castle," Armannii added as he entered the hallway.

"You'd think." Ellayne stepped in after him. "Is it just me, or is it freezing in here?" She shivered.

"It's probably from whatever spell Diomedes is casting that has caused the sky to go dark. He's pumping a lot of dark magic around these halls."

A freezing gush of air came from farther up the corridor, and it raised the hairs on Ellayne's arms. The bitter cold bit at any exposed skin, and she sniffled when her nose started to drip.

"I know you said no light magic, but wouldn't it be better if we made it to Diomedes without freezing to death?" Ellayne asked, her teeth chattering. "Maybe I could just do a little magic to warm up and then—"

"Sh." He held his finger up, and she nodded, pausing in the corridor when he did. His ears perked up, and he tilted his head, listening to something she couldn't hear.

Distracted by the silence of the hall, Ellayne's mind wandered to another time she had entered the castle through the same gate. The final reset of her curse. She remembered the weightlessness of freedom amidst the confusion that came with it. The events that had transpired felt like they had happened years ago when in reality it had only been a few months.

"Hey," Armannii said as he tapped her on the shoulder, nodding toward the ceiling. "I hear people above us."

She shook the memory out of her head, focusing on the task at hand. "Can you tell who they are?"

"Guards, I think."

"How many?" Ellayne asked, and when she focused hard, she could hear shuffling against the stone floors.

He took a deep breath before answering. "Hard to tell because the sound bounces around in the castle, but probably more than we can take on together."

"So what do we do then?"

"Need some help?" A male voice from around the corner left goose bumps crawling up Ellayne's arms as she pointed her sword in the voice's direction.

"Who's there?" Ellayne asked, clearing her throat when her voice came out weaker than she wanted it to.

A man in Dark Soldier garb stepped out of the shadows and nodded to her. "I'm surprised Ovair didn't hear us." Criss took his helmet off as Ellayne lowered her sword.

"I did hear you, but it sounded like you were—" Armannii stopped, his head turning as he listened again. "Tell your men to stand still," he said in a hoarse whisper.

Criss made a motion with his hands toward his soldiers, and they stopped moving. Armannii stayed silent for another minute before shaking his head.

"There are still guards above us. Maybe more now. I can't tell. Diomedes or Blanndynne must've done something to these corridors. It's hard to hear what direction anything is coming from."

"They probably assumed you'd be one of the ones coming in," Ellayne said, leaning around him to stare down the corridor. "He probably knows how much you rely on being able to hear what's happening through walls and ceilings."

"It'd be a smart move on his part, for sure." Criss straightened up, ignoring the peeved look on Armannii's face. "Well, what are we waiting for?" Criss asked, putting his helmet back on. "We came here for a fight."

"Late," Ellayne corrected. "You came here late." She took a deep breath, soothing her magic until it relaxed, knowing Armannii would not be happy at a light magic outburst. It did, however, warm her up, which she appreciated. "My people were slaughtered because of your tardiness."

"Your Majesty, my condolences for the death of your people. We ran into trouble crossing the river. It seems your brother was prepared for us, and he set up a brigade to counter my men. I lost soldiers as well." He cleared his throat. "But believe me when I say we were not intentional in our lateness."

Ellayne lifted her chin, thinking over the words she wanted to say next. "I'm sorry for your losses. I hope that we will not waste the opportunity our fallen have given us at the cost of their lives."

Criss nodded. "Well said, Your Majesty. Now, if I might make a suggestion, my men and I should go first to clear a way for you and Ovair to get through."

Armannii snorted. "That's very selfless of you, Criss. I didn't think you were capable of that."

"I'm capable of a lot more now than you'd know, Ovair."

The two men stared at each other until Ellayne stepped between them. "Whatever is between the two of you, leave it in the past and step forward. Together. We have a common enemy, and we aren't going to get very far if we don't recognize the commonalities between us. Understood?"

"Yes, Your Majesty."

"Of course," Armannii said, stepping back toward the wall. He swung his arm to the side, motioning for Criss and his men to go first.

They funneled by, marching in step with one another. It appeared to Ellayne that Criss had spoken the truth about being ambushed because there were fewer soldiers than she remembered, and some of them were limping. Though, she considered, he may have left a few outside to help the remaining sirens.

"I hear fighting," Armannii said after the final soldiers went up the stairs ahead of them. "We should give it a second before we go, just to make sure everyone who is engaged in combat is well distracted."

"What happened to make you and Criss hate each other so much?" Ellayne asked.

Armannii raised an eyebrow. "Seriously? We're about to head into battle, and that's what you're asking?"

"Yes."

He sighed. "Fine. He used to be a friend of mine in the Dark Castle. A good friend, actually. More like a brother. He's older than me. Showed me the ropes when I first started out, and I never let him hear the end of it when I outranked him." He lowered his head, scuffing a boot against the stone floor. "When I turned my back on the Dark King, he felt betrayed. Spent a lot of his time trying to hunt me down. He was one of the reasons I left the Dark for Phildeterre."

"You were scared of him?"

"No," he said as he shook his head. "I didn't have it in me to hurt him. His sentiments were not the same."

"Was he one of the soldiers who snuck into the dungeon and beat you up when we were there the first time?"

Armannii chuckled darkly. "Yeah. Yeah, he was. He and a few others I served with. They didn't understand why I chose a trespassing thief over the king and his laws. I guess Criss must've had a change in heart because the man I knew would never risk his life for someone he hates, especially not for me."

"Maybe he doesn't hate you anymore," Ellayne said, cocking her head to the side. She offered him a small smile, but he shrugged it away.

"Maybe. Either way, he's up there fighting, which means we should get ready to go. Out of the past and into the future, like you said, right?"

"Right."

Chapter Forty-One

he floor above the servants' quarters had completely descended into chaos when Armannii and Ellayne reached it. Weapons swung in the air, and cries of pain echoed against the brick walls. Armannii shoved Ellayne to the side when one of the guards lunged at her, stabbing the man in the neck with an arrow as he tumbled to the ground.

"Watch yourself, Queenie," he said, pulling the arrow from the man's body. "We've got a bit of fire and brimstone to get through before we can find your brother."

"Kade first. Dio after," she reminded him, drawing her sword. She and Armannii weaved in and out of the battle, avoiding the fights as much as possible.

Every once in a while, she would enter a fight to block the final blow of a guard against a Dark Soldier, which threw the guard off-balance in time for another Dark Soldier to come and aid their comrade.

Armannii stuck close to her, aiming his bow at anyone who dared to venture near them. However, the only arrows he loosed were toward three royal guards who had bows of their own. They stood on the second-floor balcony, sending arrows toward the tumult beneath them. The first sentry Armannii hit tumbled into the fray and was quickly trampled. The second one tried to locate who had shot the first one but found Armannii too late. The third had an arrow in the bow when Armannii sent him toppling over the banister.

"Come on," Ellayne said as the fights around her spread out. "We should head this way."

He nodded, keeping an eye on a guard who had spotted Ellayne. She noticed him too, and Ellayne countered his sword with her own. Her quick reaction caught him off guard. Ramming her shoulder into his rib cage, she slammed him against the wall. He slid down it, groaning.

"On second thought," Armannii said, "I shouldn't be surprised the dragon didn't make you dessert."

"What?" Ellayne asked.

"I'm proud of you."

She laughed—a contrasting sound to the atmosphere around her. "I'm sorry?"

"I'm serious," he said, pointing to his silver eyes, "and you can tell. See? I'm telling the truth. And here's another truth. I wish you were my little sister, not Diomedes's. He doesn't deserve to have a sister as—"

Ellayne cut him off, wrapping her arms around him. "Thank you, Armannii," she said into his vest. "Thank you." He hugged her back, reminding her of bear hugs she had received from her father and even from her brother at one point.

"When this is over," he said as he pulled back, "let me be the brother he wasn't. I'll teach you to write runes, and maybe I can teach you to shoot a bow and arrow."

"That would be—wait. What? I *can* shoot with a bow."

"If you're referring to what you did when I was healing that siren, then you are sadly mistaken. You're awful."

She smacked him in the arm, a grin on her face. "Rude." Ellayne's eyes softened when she looked up at him. "You promise you'll teach me?"

"I think it's my duty to the country."

"Promise?"

"I promise."

The castle shook, sending debris from the ceiling down on Armannii and Ellayne. Exchanging a glance, they raced down the empty corridor together without another word.

A large stained glass window in one of the main halls had shattered, sending fragments of glass in every direction on the floor. Ellayne pointed it out, and Armannii acknowledged it by stopping.

"In or out?" Ellayne asked, nodding toward the window.

"I think in. The glass would've exploded outward if someone had taken a swan dive. The glass is everywhere, so—"

"This was an entrance. Got it," she said, leaning her head out the window. They were still on the first floor, so the drop was only ten feet or so. The gardens outside seemed empty, but Ellayne didn't spend too long looking because another rumble sent some of the glass from the top of the window sprinkling down on her neck.

She shook the hood of her cloak out, and Armannii picked a piece of glass out of her mess of a bun.

"We'd better keep going," he said, examining the glass up close.

"What is it?" she asked when he handed her the glass fragment.

"Take a closer look."

Ellayne did as he said, peering at the orange shard in the palm of her hand. It felt cold, and it didn't take her long to see why. "It has dark magic remains on it." There were traces of black marks on the glass that trickled a chill into her skin when she touched it. It reminded her of the marks in the Dark Castle when Kade received his magic and in Bolee when Kiegan and Blanndynne had attacked.

Armannii nodded. "Could be Kade or Blanndynne's pet."

"Then we need to keep going," Ellayne said as she dropped the glass. "Because I'm pretty sure that's not red stained glass." She pointed to a few other fragments that had drops of blood on them.

Ellayne and Armannii stayed alert as they continued down the maze of hallways. The farther they went, the colder the air got.

"Is this all from Diomedes's dark magic?" she asked as they rounded another corner. Ellayne could see her breath as she spoke.

"I'm starting to doubt it," Armannii said, pulling the collar of his vest higher. "Unless he's intentionally trying to lower the temperature."

"You can do that?"

"You've got a lot to learn about magic, Queenie."

Apparently, she thought, stopping when Armannii paused in the middle of the hallway. He turned his head, angling his left ear toward the corridor ahead of them. She waited, knowing from experience that he would tell her what he heard when he was ready.

But before he did that, Ellayne took note of his change in stature. His hand clenched the bow tighter, and his eyes narrowed at the ground. Armannii pressed his lips together before shifting his gaze to Ellayne.

"What? What is it?"

"I hear the kid," he said, nodding toward the direction they had been going. He blocked her path with his bow to stop her from charging down the hallway. "He's not alone."

Ellayne cast a glance down the long corridor, then back to Armannii. "Who?"

"You're not gonna like it."

"Armannii—"

"Kiegan."

She stiffened, raising her free hand to her throat. It shouldn't have surprised her; she knew Kade had gone after Kiegan as soon as she found out he had disappeared from the camp. What made her hand shake as she lowered it was the way Armannii was staring at her, like Kade was already gone.

"Hey, wait!" He sprinted after her when she took off down the hallway.

Her ears were deaf to everything except the male voices getting louder the closer she got to the center of the castle. They were nearing the north wing, and each step was another degree lost in temperature.

A freezing wind blasted Ellayne in the face when she rounded the corner and stopped in her tracks at the sight that lay before her. Kade knelt in a circle of shadowy figures. She covered her mouth with her hand when all six of the figures turned around to face her. They all wore Kiegan's face. Somehow, he had multiplied himself.

"Hello, Ellayne," all six of them said in eerie synchronization. "Nice of you to join us. And you brought the elf."

Armannii stopped next to Ellayne, his bow drawn. "And I thought Diomedes had an ugly face when he did that spell. You take the cake, though. That's one ugly mug."

"Your petty insults don't bother me," the Kiegans said.

"They did back in Bolee," Armannii reminded him.

While Armannii hounded Kiegan, Ellayne fixed her attention on Kade. He was in a similar situation to when he had first fought his father, only he looked to be in worse shape. Dark magic encased him from his neck down, binding him. Ellayne's mind raced as she tried to understand how he had lost so badly. His parents were two of the strongest dark magic bearers of their generation, and even though Kiegan shared the same parentage, Kade's magic had always been so strong. But looking between him and the nearest copy of Kiegan, she understood why. He couldn't—wouldn't—fight his brother.

Kade's gaze found hers, but he couldn't speak; a thin strip of dark magic kept his mouth closed. His eyes were wide. Dark bloodstains covered his forehead, and from what she could see, his clothes were torn and bloodied in different places. Beneath one of the ringlets of dark magic, she could see the faint white spiderwebbing on his shoulder where Kiegan had nearly managed to kill him in Bolee.

"How did you find us?" One of the Kiegans stepped in front of Kade, blocking her view and forcing her to pay attention to the question they had asked.

"We just asked around to see where Blanndynne's mutt got to." Armannii smirked. "Everybody kindly pointed us in this direction."

Armannii's comment knocked the grin off of Kiegan's shadowy faces. They flickered for a second before whooshing back into a singular form. Kiegan stretched, rolling his shoulders as he turned his back on Kade.

"I'm going to make you regret saying that," Kiegan said, clutching his hands into fists. Dark magic pooled into them.

"You can try." Armannii stepped in front of Ellayne but froze when a new person entered the hallway.

"Actually, Kiegan darling, I'd like to give it a try."

Chapter Forty-Two

iegan's face flushed, but he bowed and gave Blanndynne a tight-lipped smile. "Of course, Your Majesty." He jerked his hand to the side, and Kade slid across the floor, slamming into the wall next to where Kiegan stepped. Kiegan placed a hand on his brother's shoulder, sneering at Ellayne as if to tempt her to try to help Kade.

"Armannii." Blanndynne opened her lips into a large smile, though her eyes were predatory. "It's been a long time since we've sparred. What do you say? Care for a little practice?"

Ellayne reached out to stop Armannii, but he stepped out of her reach toward the genie.

"I'm always up for a bit of combat." Armannii pulled out an arrow, setting it in his bow. He kept his voice level, but for a second his shoulders tensed.

"Perfect," Blanndynne said. "But let's make sure there's no outside interference." She raised her hands, and transparent walls shot up from the floor, encasing Armannii and Blanndynne in a box.

Slamming her fist on the wall in front of her, Ellayne flinched. It shimmered grayish, and from past conversations with Armannii, she knew it was from the mixture of light and dark magic that Blanndynne possessed. Even if it was weaker than light and dark magic combined from two different magic bearers, it was still stronger than Ellayne's magic alone.

The barrier did not prevent the sound within the box from reaching Ellayne's ears, and the only thing Ellayne could do was watch the battle unfold. Armannii was the best fighter she'd ever met; despite her concern for her friend, she had every confidence he would walk away the victor.

Armannii and Blanndynne circled each other, but neither had yet made the first move. Blanndynne reached into her vest, and her fingers came back gleaming with metal—throwing knives.

"You're just as handsome as the day you left, love," Blanndynne said, her red lips bearing yet another menacing smile.

"I'm well aware of that fact."

"And I'm sure it's been lonely for you without the king or me by your side."

The elf snorted. "Not as bad as you would think. Plenty of time to become a better man." Armannii ducked when Blanndynne threw the first knife, which ricocheted off the translucent wall in front of Ellayne's face. Ellayne flinched, taking a step back and covering her face. For a second, she was glad the barrier was up. But she was quickly drawn back in to the two people circling each other.

"You were already a good man until you turned your back on me. On *us*."

"He was wrong to do what he did. We were wrong to follow him." Armannii sent an arrow straight toward Blanndynne's chest, but she waved her hand and it flew around her, clattering against the barrier.

"Is that what you've decided during your extended time away?" She rose a few feet off the floor, hovering there as if it were normal.

It didn't faze Armannii, but Ellayne kept her eyes on the genie. How frustrating to have so much power yet be unable to use it as more than a distraction in a fight. Ellayne watched as Blanndynne threw another knife, but Armannii raised his bow in front of his face just as it soared toward him. The knife stuck into the wood of the bow, vibrating from the impact. Armannii yanked it out, tossing it to the side where it clattered.

"I didn't want to give up building a better future for the sake of gaining power, so I took my time and found others who shared my mindset. Only this time, there are no shortcuts. No trying to find the quick way out."

"You have to understand how ridiculous you sound saying that," Blanndynne said, letting out a shrill laugh that filled the hall. "That isn't you, Armannii. Or did you forget? You helped Diomedes and me get where we are. What happened to the elf who shoved an arrow through a man's hand just to get information? Or the one who stood next to me while our friend changed the course of the country?"

"Oh, he changed it all right. But not for the better."

"You're wrong."

"You truly believe that?" Armannii asked, shooting an arrow that got closer before Blanndynne waved it away. "You believe Diomedes has done something—anything—good? That man is incapable of goodness. When I look out these windows, all I see is a country in desperate need of a leader who will work with the people to fix past rifts. Someone who understands where both sides are coming from. Someone like her." He pointed his bow at Ellayne, though he kept his eyes on Blanndynne.

With another laugh, Blanndynne hurled three throwing knives at Armannii, which he deflected by spinning his bow in front of him.

"You really have gone soft, Armannii."

"I'll take that as a compliment." He stood tall, jumping to the side when she lunged at him, several knives held between her knuckles. He blocked her arm again, sending her spinning to the side.

Ellayne reached up and rubbed the back of her medallion, her eyes tracking them as they went into hand-to-hand combat. Blanndynne was quick, but Armannii was quicker. He caught her hand every time she tried to slice him with the weapons. Throwing her off-balance, Armannii kicked Blanndynne in the chest. She stumbled backward, some of the knives clanking against the stone floor when she dropped them.

"If I'm being honest, B, and you'll know if I'm not, I don't really want to fight you." Armannii lowered his bow, tilting his head to the side. His voice was lower when he spoke next, and Ellayne struggled to hear. "It's clear what your choice was back then, but you can make a different choice now. Make a better choice."

"I've already made the better choice." Blanndynne rubbed the palm of her hand across her chest, probably trying to soothe the ache of Armannii's boot. "You're the one who made the wrong choice. I'm happy with where I am."

"You're happy being his slave?"

"I am *not* his slave," she said, her eyes narrowing on Armannii. "Don't you say that to me. Not to me."

"You're as much Diomedes's slave as Kiegan and the guards are yours."

"I can make my own choices. They can't." She pointed at Kiegan without actually looking at him. He didn't flinch or react, simply watched her with a cloudy gaze. "There's a difference."

Armannii nodded as they began circling each other again. "I'm well aware of that."

Blanndynne continued to glare at Armannii until she tilted her head back and let out a shrill laugh. "I know what this is. This isn't even about me. You're still upset I didn't go with you—that I stayed here with him instead. You're still jealous."

It was Armannii's turn to chuckle, but his face grew solemn soon after. "B, you know I wanted you to come with me because I wanted what was best for you. This isn't what's best for you. Running his errands." Armannii jerked his bow toward Kade and Kiegan. "Doing his dirty work for him. You were meant for so much more."

"Diomedes freed me."

"The only reason you think that is because he was a prince, and his royal blood was what was required to free a genie. But, B, it was an accident. I don't know how many times I have to tell you this. He didn't intentionally free you. He and I were fighting over the vase. He had no idea you were in there. Diomedes didn't care about you, and he still doesn't. But that doesn't matter. Listen, I *know* you. I know what you're capable of. I'm the one who cared about what happened to you. I'm the one who still does." He stepped closer to her, and unlike before, she didn't counter him by taking a step back. Armannii kept his bow by his side, the next arrow ready in the same hand.

"But I'm the queen."

"Sure, fine. If that's what you want to call it. But there's no way you're happy here. Just take a second to look at who you married. Diomedes isn't the same, not since he got his magic. Even you admitted that, remember? On the cave ledge in the mountains? I don't think he meant to, but he's a monster now. And I know you see that." He took another step, leaving only a few feet between them.

"I can't."

"Yes, B. Yes, you can." He took one more step, closing the space between them. Armannii reached up, cupping the side of her downcast face. Blanndynne's shoulders slouched, and she kept her chin angled down.

Ellayne held her breath, risking a sidelong glance to see that Kiegan had changed position. He now leaned forward on the balls of his feet, his eyes glued to what was happening behind the see-through walls. Even Kade, as battered as he was, seemed absorbed.

"I can help you. B, please let me help you."

"I don't want your help," Blanndynne said, and before Ellayne could react, Blanndynne shoved one of her throwing knives through Armannii's heart. He gasped, a sharp cry tearing out of his lips.

Armannii stumbled backward, tripping on the floor and collapsing onto his back. His breathing was ragged, and he choked as Blanndynne strode over to his side. She knelt down next to him, cocking her head as he raised a shaking hand to the puddle of blood spilling over his chest.

Ellayne screamed, beating the barrier with her magic, but it did nothing. *Please open the barrier,* she asked her magic. But she couldn't. No matter how hard she tried, she couldn't get the walls down. Blanndynne's magic was too strong.

"I told you that you'd gone soft. And this is what you get." Blanndynne stroked Armannii's cheek.

Armannii raised his finger, motioning for Blanndynne to get closer. She obliged, leaning down so her black hair formed a curtain on one side. He struggled to lift his head.

"I forgive you." His voice was so weak, Ellayne barely heard it.

"Forgive me?" Blanndyne laughed, but her body jerked upward violently.

"But I c-can't let you hurt anyone e-else," he said, his head slamming backward when his strength gave out.

Ellayne wasn't sure what had happened as Blanndynne crumpled over top of Armannii. At the same time Kiegan collapsed to the ground, the barrier dissipated, and Ellayne couldn't scramble fast enough to Armannii's side. It was clear then what her friend had done. An arrow lined with jade halfway up the shaft stuck out of Blanndynne's chest when Ellayne shoved her off of Armannii. It was the same arrow he had told her to not use outside, an arrow he must've been saving for Blanndynne for some time.

"Armannii, please," Ellayne cried, wrapping her hands around the throwing knife and pressing down. Her hands turned crimson in seconds. "Tell me how to draw the healing rune. Armannii!" She shoved down on his chest, and his eyes fluttered for a second.

"Qu-Queenie." His voice was too soft, his skin too pale.

"Armannii, you have to teach me the rune. Quick. Please." Ellayne choked, wiping the tears away on her shoulder. She couldn't breathe in enough air; it kept escaping in rapid gasps.

"I'm s-sorry," he whispered.

"I forgive you, Armannii. I already told you that. I forgave you ages ago. But I need to know the healing rune. Please. Help!" she shouted. "Armannii, please." Her heart raced, and she couldn't see anything, her eyes having filled up with tears that flowed down her cheeks. "Please, you have to show me. Armannii, Armannii!" She shrieked his name, but he didn't react. His glossy eyes stared somewhere over her shoulder.

"No." Kade reached Ellayne and Armannii, and his hand shook as he placed it on Ellayne's arm. "Armannii, hey. Stay with us. Armannii?" His voice broke.

"Help, please, help," Ellayne said between sobs, turning to face Kade. "The healing rune. Kade, quick. Your rune pen. Quick, please. Please!"

Kade's eyes flickered from Ellayne to Armannii. "I-I don't know it."

"Please," she sobbed into his shoulder when he wrapped his arms around her. "Please, Kade. He can't die. He pr-promised to teach me. He promised."

"I'm so sorry, Ellayne." Kade's voice cracked again as he buried his face in her hair. "I'm so sorry."

"Armannii." She moaned her friend's name over and over, rocking back and forth. "Armannii, no. You promised." Ellayne pushed away from Kade, leaning over Armannii's body. "You pr-promised me." She shoved him, shaking his arm. "Please," she whimpered as she brought his hand up, clutching it to her chest. "Don't leave me. I n-need you here with me."

"Ellayne, he's gone." Kade placed a hand on her shoulder, but she jerked away.

"No, he can't. He can't."

"Ellayne, stop."

"I-I can't." Her lungs betrayed her, hyperventilating until she felt light-headed. "H-he promised me, Kade." She broke down again, falling into Kade's open arms. "He promised."

Chapter Forty-Three

ade ran his fingers over Ellayne's head, pressing her into his chest. Her breathing remained irregular for some time, and her mind was a mess of images. Armannii spilling wine all over her dress. Armannii saving her from her curse. Armannii apologizing for the pain he'd caused. Leading her to the Dark. Opening up about his past. Sharing in the memories of her brother. Joking about her and Kade. Calling her Princess. Standing by her when she spoke at her father's funeral. Helping her lead. Sticking by her side as she fought her way into the castle. Image after image, his silver eyes remained.

"I'm so sorry," she said, moaning into Kade's sleeve. "I'm sorry, Armannii." She choked on every word, her body heaving under her. She wished for nothing more than to be overcome by the darkness behind her eyelids. Her nose stayed wet no matter how many times she wiped it with the back of her hand. Every part of her body shook. Trembling. Shuddering.

"It's not your fault, Ellayne." Kade gripped her tighter. "None of this is your fault."

Kiegan, who had fallen to the ground when Blanndynne died, stirred near the wall, and Ellayne felt Kade shift as he turned to look at him. She felt his body tense against hers, his arms tightening. A barrier between her and Kiegan.

"I'll go talk to him," Kade said when Ellayne glanced up at him with puffy eyes. "Stay here."

Ellayne couldn't have moved if she wanted to. Not with grief weighing down on her like it never had before. She felt numb. It coursed through her until she was still, staring at Armannii's cloudy eyes.

She couldn't stay. The sight of his dead body broke through the unfeeling wall. It hurt. It hurt too much. Too much. She had to get away.

Her mind set, she wiped her eyes on the back of her sleeve, then smeared Armannii's blood off her hands and onto her trousers. With a quick glance up, she knew she needed to act while Kade was distracted with his brother. He knelt next to Kiegan with his back to Ellayne. Kiegan appeared distressed, rubbing his face with both hands. Neither one paid attention to Ellayne.

She rose to her feet as silently as she could. With one last look at Armannii, she set her jaw and ran toward a staircase typically used by servants.

"I'm sorry, Kade," she whispered, glancing over her shoulder. She let the door close before anyone noticed her absence.

With her brain too distracted by the storm within, her legs carried her to a familiar location—one that had always brought her solace. Ellayne had not been in her room since she had stayed at the castle before she broke her curse. Knowing she could not remember her identity, her brother must've found some form of entertainment in letting her stay in her own bedroom—sleep in her own bed—without knowing it was hers.

The upper floors, unlike the first floor, lacked the presence of fighting, and although Ellayne could still hear the muffled cries of fallen men and women from the hallway, the silence won out as soon as she closed her bedroom door behind her. However, when the latch clicked shut, all of the numbness protecting her shattered.

Ellayne could not stop the tears as they returned, spilling over her cheeks and down onto her tunic. Her whole body felt like lead. She barely made it to the bed before she collapsed with her shoulders heaving.

Each death she'd witnessed burdened her until she thought she might never move again. Her mother. Calder. Her father. Lenora. The Dark King. Armannii. The nameless people she'd seen die on her way into the castle. Every single one suffocated her until all she could do was pull her knees up to her chest and wrap her arms around them. Ducking her head down, she closed her eyes, but she couldn't stop the memories as they flashed beneath her eyelids. She saw their bodies after they had passed—bloody, cold, and lifeless.

Ghostlike images floated through her mind of people she had failed to protect—people who had died for her. And even as she sat there in the middle of her bed, countless others were doing the same.

Too quiet. It was too quiet. She wiped her nose on the back of her arm, rising to go to the window. The people below continued to fight. They were unaware of Armannii's death—how it had shaken Ellayne to the core. How much longer would they all have before they met the same fate?

Though she was too far away to make out any faces, one thing remained clear. Those were her subjects. Her people. And they were dying. They would continue to fight—to kill, to die—until someone put a stop to it.

Until she put a stop to it.

The prophecy. It was about her and her brother. Only she could put an end to his reign. Only she could change things. The longer she waited, the more people she would lose. The more of *her* people she would lose.

The Dark King, Dayla, and everyone else had been right. She hadn't wanted to face her brother—to face the monster he had become, to face the reality that he wasn't the big brother she remembered him to be. That choice—her choice—had drawn out the conflict, which led to the loss of more lives. And it would continue to do so until she faced him. Until she took her country back—or died trying.

Her heart still ached, but her mind cleared. She would never have control over Diomedes's redemption. That was something only he could choose. But she did have a choice, and as she walked to the door, straightening her tunic, she made it.

"I am the queen," she said, taking a deep breath. "This is my country, and I will protect it."

The moment the throne room doors slammed shut behind her and she crossed the threshold, a chilling wall of dark magic shot up from the floor, blocking the only way in or out. Even though she had gone in with the determination to put an end to the battle, panic trickled into her veins at the idea of being trapped.

"Welcome home, Ellayne." Diomedes stood in the center of the room with his arms clasped behind his back. Unlike the last time she had seen him in the castle, he did not wear a scarf to cover the black holes where his eyes should have been, nor did he wear gloves to cover his long blackened nails or the inky veins traveling up his arms. He was, however, wearing a shiny dark gray crown littered with jewels. He wore black from head to toe, though that was not out of character for him.

The room was below freezing, and she was sure it would've been cold enough to snow had they not been inside. She shivered. Whether it was from the temperature, exhaustion—mentally, emotionally, and physically—or fear at what would happen next, she was not sure. But she trembled as she stepped farther into the room.

She locked her attention on her brother, wrapping her arms around herself. Whatever he was doing to the room, it had created a gust of wind that rushed around, slicing through her until her teeth were chattering. Knowing her brother would use it against her in close combat, Ellayne had left her cloak in her room. She regretted that decision and begged her magic to keep her fingers and toes from freezing off.

Her voice wobbled when she spoke, breaking the silence. "Armannii's dead." Ellayne wasn't sure where the words came from as they tumbled out of her mouth. Part of her wanted him to react—to show some sort of emotion.

But he didn't.

"So I heard."

"And Blanndynne is dead."

Diomedes shrugged. "She served me well."

Ellayne's hands balled into fists. "They were your friends, Diomedes. She was your wife! How can you just stand there knowing that your two best friends killed each other because of you?"

"That is simple." He stepped forward and raised an arm out to the side. "I stopped troubling myself with feelings the moment I chose to give up the people I cared about for magic—for an end to the war. Besides, it's much simpler this way." Magic pooled into a sphere of dark mist around his outstretched hand, and when he pointed it at Ellayne, she collapsed to her knees.

"Caring is hurting. Love is vulnerability. They get in the way, and simply put, they are useless. When I became the most powerful person in the world, I quickly learned there's no need for such things."

She couldn't move. Dark magic swirled around her, and if she had control over her body, she would've responded—would've told him how wrong he was, how the only reason she was in front of him in that moment was because of the love and care she had received from so many others. She wished she could say it, and she squirmed as he kept her trapped in her head. Her mind raced, and she tried to remember what she'd done the previous times she had broken his binding spell.

Fight. Ellayne focused her mind on combatting the dark magic, on her light magic overwhelming it and breaking her free. It felt hopeless until she found her reason to fight. She focused on one person in particular, one man who had taught her how powerful love was. She thought of his curly hair, his dimple, the look of concentration when he was working. She imagined his laugh, his broken sobs, the sound of him saying her name. She thought of the spark. His touch. His smell. Images of Kade swelled in her mind, and she fought for him. Each push of magic came with a memory of Kade, reasons why she loved him. Sweat broke out on her forehead and the back of her neck, and as she stared up at Diomedes, she saw him clench his teeth.

With one last push against his magic, she sent a wave of heat into the room, rising to her feet, free from the spell.

"You're wrong," she said, rubbing the sweat off her forehead before it reached her eye. "I'm stronger *because* of my love and the people who love me. Not in spite of it."

"You are strong. Stronger than I gave you credit for," Diomedes said, rotating his wrist in a circle as if it ached.

"Stop the battle, Diomedes," Ellayne said, noticing her glowing hands out of the corner of her eye. "No one else has to die. Not you. Not me. No one. We can end this here and now."

"Now that"—he pointed a finger at her—"is not true. I'm very aware that you saw the prophecy about us. I know you broke into the castle a little while ago. In fact, I was bothered you didn't stop in here and say hello."

"Oh, I'm sure you were just heartbroken." Ellayne shook her head, her voice a low mumble. "Why do you care so much about what one person said?"

"Because." His voice boomed around the room, making her jump. "I will not be stopped by a sister who never should've existed in the first place."

With those words, Diomedes's magic snaked out and wrapped around her waist. It yanked her up into the air, turning her stomach as it flung her against a side wall. Ellayne felt her hand crunch against the stone when she tried to stop her momentum, and she screamed as her bones snapped. His magic released her, and she dropped several feet to the ground. The wind slammed out of her lungs, and she lay dazed for a second before the searing pain in her right hand elicited a moan from her lips.

"Dio, please," she said, clutching her hand to her chest. It was on fire. Any subtle movement had her sucking in air through her teeth. She wanted to cry out, to scream. She shifted to her knees before getting back to her feet. Ellayne stumbled to the right, her head spinning, but she caught herself. "That prophecy doesn't have to define us—doesn't have to define you."

Some part of her had hoped it wouldn't actually come to fighting, that somehow he would hear her—really hear her. That he would see how broken he was. But the agonizing pain in her hand snapped her back to reality. It also made it difficult to call on her magic, just like when the guard had nearly choked the life out of her in the clearing with the tiny house. There was too much pain. She couldn't concentrate.

He chuckled. "Don't you see? It already has." Diomedes lifted his hand into the air, and Ellayne went with it.

"Don't do this. Please, Dio," Ellayne begged, kicking her legs as his magic drew her closer to him. "We can both walk away from this."

"Not according to the prophecy." He brought his other hand out from behind his back, and Ellayne could do nothing as a thin line of dark magic snaked out and traveled toward her.

Ellayne tried to turn her head away, but it found her mouth and nose. The magic slithered into her, causing her to convulse. A faint memory crossed her mind of a story Kiegan had told her. A man with dark magic had killed a woman with light magic the same way—letting it creep in and destroy from the inside. Ellayne coughed, trying to force the magic out with her own. It wasn't working. She felt the magic squeezing her lungs, seeping in and slowing her heartbeat despite the growing panic fighting back. But even adrenaline couldn't stop the overwhelming strength of his magic strangling her.

"P-please." She choked. "I found . . . Lenora."

Diomedes dropped her. In less than a second, the dark magic left her quivering on the ground. She cradled her broken hand, knowing she had only bought herself a little extra time. The floor tiles sucked most of the remaining warmth out of her body, and with it some of her strength. Each second ticking by seemed to bring her closer to what was beginning to seem inevitable.

"My mother is dead." Diomedes stood over her, and he would've been glaring at her if he possessed the eyes to do so. His lip curled up in a sneer. "What do you mean you found her?"

How many times had they been in this position when he was training her? How many times had he offered her a hand to help her to her feet? How was this the same person? Ellayne used her good hand to push herself up to sitting position. "I found her in the Dark."

"You're lying."

"No! I found her. I was going to bring her back until—"

"Until what? Where is she?" Diomedes pulled out his black dagger, pointing it at Ellayne's face. "What did you do to her?"

She bit her lip, trying to think of a way to tell him what had happened in the Dark without him killing her right afterward.

"Speak!"

"I-I told her about you, and she said she wanted to come back to see you. She wanted to be with you. But—"

"But what?"

"But she tried to kill me."

He brought the dagger closer to her, and she could see her breath causing the dark metal to fog over. "So you killed her first."

"No!" Ellayne shook her head, but that made her pulsing headache worse. "No, I didn't kill her. S-she killed herself."

"You're lying!" He switched hands and gripped her neck, lifting her to her feet.

Ellayne rose onto her tiptoes to try to keep air going to her lungs, but she could only scratch at his hand with one of hers. "I-I'm not lying." Her voice came out weak. "Dio, please."

"Enough. I'm done with you."

"P-please. You're still my brother. I know you are," she said, tears forming in her eyes as a black haze crept around the edges of her vision. "I know you're s-still in there s-somewhere. Please, Dio." Her limbs tingled but felt heavy at the same time.

"I stopped being Dio a long time ago."

"No, he's still . . . you," she whispered. *Show me he's still Dio, please,* she begged her magic, and before she completely drifted away, she felt a burst of fire spread from her stomach and up her spine to her neck where her brother held her.

Everything went black.

Chapter Forty-Four

he first thing Ellayne noticed when she woke up was that her broken hand was all in one piece. No broken bones. In fact, she felt fine. No headache pounded inside her skull, and she could breathe with ease. With her eyes still closed, Ellayne recognized she was lying on her back.

A hallway came into view when Ellayne's eyes fluttered open, and she pushed herself to sit up. The corridor felt familiar. The ceiling was fifteen feet above, and two rows of windows let light spill down onto her. In between the windows were tapestries woven with strands of expensive fabrics and sometimes gold or silver. The hallway made up part of the royal floor where she and her family had lived while she was growing up.

She stood, using the wall for support. Her fingers brushed the edge of a nearby tapestry with a black panther in a tree, and she knew instantly which of the royal hallways she was in. She was near Diomedes's room. However, something still felt off, and she turned in a full circle twice before realizing what it was. The hallway leading back to the main part of the castle had no light coming in from the windows, leaving it cast in shadow.

Ellayne leaned her head to the side, trying to see what lurked in the darkness, but nothing moved. However, the baby hairs on the back of her neck stood on end, and she had the sense that someone was watching her.

"How did I get here?" Ellayne whispered, taking a step in the direction of the lit hallway. Her mind questioned whether she was dead or not, but a warmth inside her core told her she was still alive. "What happened?" She rubbed her temple with the hand that had been shattered a minute earlier.

Muffled voices down the hallway drew her attention, and she took a few steps in that direction. A door on the right materialized in front of her eyes, and she jumped back. Her memory of the castle did not have a door there, and she questioned once again where she was.

The voices sounded like they were on the other side of the door, and with a deep inhale, she turned the handle and walked in. Ellayne caught her breath when the door opened up to a view of the roof of the castle. The sun was setting on the horizon, setting the sky on fire with oranges and reds that mingled halfway up with the natural blues.

Ellayne knew of no door that led to the roof in such a direct manner, and she questioned who she had heard talking behind the door until she saw two silhouettes sitting farther down towards the edge of the roof. Lowering herself onto the stone shingles, she noticed that the door was hovering off the ground by a foot or two. Ellayne shuddered. Something strange was happening, and she had no idea what it was. She carefully made her way to the two people, pausing when she recognized not only the back of her own head, but the back of her brother's.

They sat next to each other, staring off at the sunset. Diomedes was speaking when she approached them.

"—not fair. Why should I stay behind when someday it'll be my job to rule the country? I'm nearly eighteen. Half of the other people going are bringing heirs who are younger than me." He picked at a piece of the roof. It came off in his hand, and he chucked it as far as it would go.

"I'm sorry, Dio," the little Ellayne next to him said. "I want to go too."

Her brother laughed. "Father should've let you. Let us."

Ellayne tried to remember what event they were talking about, but the only thing she vaguely remembered were a few conversations on the roof. Her brother had only taken her up there a few times when their father had left for conferences in other parts of the country. She had gone because her older brother had invited her, probably because it worried their father when they sat out there, and Diomedes consistently did things he knew would push his father's patience to its limits. But none of the conversations they had on the roof had stuck with Ellayne, even now as she eavesdropped.

"Maybe next time, Dio." Little Ellayne leaned her head against her brother's shoulder, and he didn't push her away.

The little version of Ellayne was right; the young man sitting beside her was Dio. *He* was her brother. Ellayne walked around, staring at his face. He had cut his hair recently, probably because one of the guards had teased him about it. It made him look older, but in a good way, like he was ready for the responsibility of accompanying their father on one of his trips. The orange glow cast over him, and his relaxed posture left Ellayne blinking back tears.

Despite all the times she'd recalled memories of her brother, she had forgotten what he had truly looked like, the youth and vitality that had once filled his face. His gaze traveled over the horizon. She had often seen him staring out the northern windows of the castle, and because of Lenora and the stories Armannii had told her, she knew why. That's where his mother had gone when she'd abandoned him and their father. Ellayne wondered how often had he thought of searching for her.

Glancing back at the door, Ellayne gave one last look to the siblings before climbing back up to the floating exit. The door opened for her without her even reaching for the handle, like the memory was asking her to leave.

Back in the hallway, Ellayne gasped when she glanced over her shoulder to find the darkness had moved, blacking out the two nearest windows. The castle around her rumbled out of nowhere, and she gripped the wall to stay standing.

With her focus on the dark part of the hallway, she nearly missed a blur ducking around a corner in her peripheral vision. She spun back to the lit part of the corridor, but whatever or whoever had moved wasn't there anymore.

Knowing the darkness was spreading, Ellayne stepped farther into the light part of the hallway, startling when another door appeared, but this time on the left. In reality, there was once again no door there; in fact, if a door were there, it would've led to a three-story drop into the gardens. But when Ellayne opened it, she entered the kitchen.

She had been in and out of the kitchen many times growing up, but she didn't recognize the man wearing the head chef uniform. All her memories of the kitchen had a woman named Trina as the head chef. However, she hadn't officially been allowed into the kitchen until she was five years old, so maybe this man was the head chef before Trina.

"Stay out here. Yes, I promise," a teenage boy whispered from the kitchen entrance, and though he was two or three years younger than the previous memory, Ellayne still recognized her brother. His hair was longer, and a mischievous smile stretched across his face. "Hello, Dale," Diomedes said, putting his elbows on the counter and plopping his chin in his hands.

"Your Highness." The head chef bowed his head, but his voice was anything but friendly. "What are you doing in here?"

"I want a snack, and so does my sister."

"Your Highness, dinner is in an hour, and—"

"Dale, Dale, Dale. Who's the crown prince of Phildeterre?" Diomedes grinned at the chef, who seemed to be biting back whatever scolding he wanted to give the prince. While Ellayne couldn't blame him, she also found her brother's manipulative behavior a bit entertaining. The chef was at least twice his size.

"You are, Your Highness."

"And shouldn't the prince get what he wants?"

Dale rose to his full height, towering over Diomedes. "What is it that you want?"

"My sister and I both want a raspberry biscuit." Diomedes stood up, watching the head chef lift a blanket that lay over a basket.

"Will that be all, Your Highness?" Dale did not hide the bitterness in his query, shoving two pastries into Diomedes's hands.

"Yes," Diomedes said. "Thank you for the biscuits, Dale." He put emphasis on the head chef's name, smirking as he left the kitchen.

Ellayne heard a squeal of delight from around the corner, but she didn't remember the pastry or her brother taking her down to the kitchen.

She felt a pull from the door that led back to the hallway, and instead of investigating further, she left the room. To her horror, the darkness had spread once again, swallowing more of the corridor. For the first time since she had woken up on the floor, she felt cold spreading through her body. It seemed to be coming from the darkness, and she stepped toward the light in hopes that the chills would subside.

The patter of footsteps echoed along the hallway, and Ellayne spun around to see who was running, but she only saw a flash of white.

"Hello? Is someone there?" Ellayne called. She cocked her head to the side, waiting for a response. None came. With a hesitant look back at the growing darkness, Ellayne followed the steps, hoping that whoever she was following wasn't worse than whatever she was running from.

Chapter Forty-Five

llayne turned down another hallway, catching a glimpse of something white ducking into a door she knew for a fact existed in reality. It was Dio's room, a room she hadn't been in for at least five years. The castle heaved, flinging her to her knees. Ellayne covered her head to protect her skull from the rubble breaking off from the ceiling.

"What's happening?" she asked, coughing as she inhaled dust. Though she knew she had put some distance between herself and the darkness, when she peered around the corner she had just passed, only a black hallway peered back at her.

Scrambling to her feet, Ellayne raced toward the door and jumped inside. With a bang, she slammed the door shut and leaned against the frame, catching her breath. Ellayne wiped her hands over her face, removing some of the powder from the ceiling.

"But I didn't ask for one," said a small voice from deeper in the room.

Ellayne looked up, surveying her surroundings. It wasn't Diomedes's room like she had expected. Instead, she stood in the living space outside the king and queen's quarters. Long white curtains fluttered in the wind of the open balcony, letting in light and fresh air through the giant windows on either side of the doors. The ceilings were taller than those in the hallway, and Ellayne stared up at the paintings above her. It was a forest scene, and she spotted a few deer, birds, and other woodland creatures before another voice—a familiar voice—drew her attention back to the room.

"Well, Son, oftentimes the best gifts are the ones you didn't ask to receive." King Butch paced the span of the room, younger than Ellayne had ever seen him in person. Though he had a few strands of gray, most of them were hidden in his sandy hair.

"Father," Ellayne said, her voice soft as she reached out her hand, inches from touching her father's face.

Butch continued to walk forward, pausing right in front of Ellayne. For just a second, she thought he could see her, but he turned on his heels and strode back the length of the room. Her heart sank. All she wanted was to hug him, to tell him she loved him one more time. He kept his hands clasped behind his back, but his posture slumped. When he walked up to her again, she noticed dark circles under his eyes.

"How much longer?"

Ellayne ambled farther into the room, looking for the source of the other voice. A young boy with jet-black hair sat sideways in one of the armchairs, his feet dangling above the floor.

"Dio," Ellayne said, stepping closer to her brother.

His skin was pale but tanner than it had been as an adult. The young prince rested his chin on his hand, his charcoal eyes following his father as he paced the floor. Unlike almost all of the memories she had of him, he was wearing a light beige tunic instead of a black one.

"I'm not sure, but hopefully not much," her father said in response to his son's question. "Patience is a virtue, Diomedes."

Ellayne had no idea what they were waiting for, and she held no memories of the moment she was experiencing behind this door, just like the previous two she had entered. Try as she might, she could find no trace of herself. It was like she had entered someone else's memory—her brother's memory.

Realization hit her at the same time someone new entered the room, making Ellayne jump. It was a nursemaid, and she was holding blankets in her arms. Butch stopped pacing in the middle of the room, and Diomedes scrambled to his knees in the chair.

"Is she—" Butch started to say.

"The queen is healthy, and so is your new daughter," the woman said, shifting the blankets in her arms to reveal a baby.

"A daughter," the king said, his voice breathy. A wide grin spread on his face. "I have a daughter." He crossed the room in only two steps, gently taking the bundle out of the woman's arms and cradling the baby to his chest. The nursemaid curtsied and left the room.

"Hello there, beautiful."

Ellayne strode up next to him, looking over his shoulder at her own face. The nursemaids had cleaned up the baby, but her skin was still red and a bit blotchy. Her eyes were closed, but she was frowning, adjusting to the new world she'd just entered.

"Would you like to meet your new sister, Dio?" King Butch asked, his voice softer than before. Moisture gathered in his eyes, but none of escaped.

"I guess." The prince straightened up in the chair, holding out his arms for his father to place the bundle in. Both Ellayne and her father watched as Diomedes examined his baby sister. It took a minute, but he smiled, his dark eyes lighting up. "She's so small."

"She's going to need you to take care of her—to be her big brother." King Butch went around to the other side of the chair, kneeling down next to it so he could get a better look at his children.

"How soon can I teach her how to fight?" Dio asked, his wide eyes glancing up to his father, who chuckled.

"It'll be a few years before that can happen."

"Oh," her brother said, his eyes lowering back to the baby. He lifted a hand and pushed the blanket back from the baby's face. "I love her," he said with a smile.

"I love you both." King Butch ruffled his son's hair, light reflecting in his eyes.

Ellayne wrapped her arms around herself, her eyebrows furrowed. Her heart yearned for them to hear her, to see her. Her hand trembled as she reached up for her mother's medallion, stroking it with her thumb. She wanted the room to be reality, to have another chance at changing things before they all went wrong, to try again with the things she knew. Ellayne shifted her concentration when a rustle behind the couch distracted her. She hesitated before peering behind it, jumping when she saw what was there.

"Please don't hurt me," a little boy said—the same little boy holding a baby a few feet away.

"Dio?" Ellayne held both hands out in front of her. "I'm not going to hurt you. What are you doing here? How are there two of you?"

"Who are you?" Diomedes asked, standing up. Just like his copy sitting in the chair, he wore a light shirt with dark pants. He was the mirror image of her brother sitting across the room. "Why are you here?"

"I-I don't know where here is." She gestured around.

"Who are you?"

"I'm your sister. I'm Ellayne."

"Ellayne?" He raised an eyebrow. "That sister?" He pointed to the baby.

Ellayne nodded, glancing over her shoulder to where he pointed. "Yes. I'm your sister. But where am I? Where are we?"

Diomedes walked around to sit down on the couch, and Ellayne joined him. He pulled his feet up, sitting cross-legged. "This is my last memory." His chin trembled and he stared down at his hands, which fiddled with the hem of his tunic.

"Last? What do you mean?" Ellayne frowned, confusion painting her face.

The boy hesitated, looking toward the door to the hallway. "The darkness has taken the rest of them. Destroyed them. I hid in here, and it hasn't found me. I don't want it to find me." His entire body began trembling.

"Dio, what is this darkness?" Ellayne said, pushing her hair behind her ears. She was struggling to swallow, sensing her brother's fear and taking it on as her own. "I saw it, but I couldn't tell what it was."

"I dunno, but it's powerful." His eyes got big, and he shook harder. He looked so small, all curled up. "I-I'm scared of it."

Ellayne bobbed her head, glancing at the door when something behind it creaked. Dio looked too and scooted closer to Ellayne. "I am too. But you said we're safe in here, right? So there's no need to worry. I'm here with you, and—" She lurched forward when the room shook. Ellayne's pulse picked up as she scanned the room for somewhere to run or hide. With as little furniture as there was, there weren't many options. And at that point, it seemed too late.

Diomedes looked frantically from Ellayne to the door. "It's here! It found us! What do we do?" He crawled toward her on the couch, and she wrapped her arms around him. He was warm, and all she wanted to do was protect him from whatever was coming for them. This was her brother. She had found him, and she wasn't going to let the darkness take him away. She clutched him tighter, pressing a kiss to the top of his head and pulling him away from the darkness.

"I'm sorry. It must've followed me here," Ellayne said, pressing his head into her chest. Her eyes widened when color began to drain out of the room, all of it being sucked toward the door to the hallway. She tried to keep him from watching what was happening. "Don't look, Dio. Just keep your eyes closed." A black hole appeared where the door was, and tendrils of darkness leaked through it, spreading around the room. Whatever it touched began to vanish.

"I'm scared, Ellayne." His voice was barely a squeak. She could feel his tears soaking her tunic while hers wet his head.

"I'm scared too." She held him as parts of the room closest to the black hole started to disintegrate. She couldn't pull him any closer.

King Butch, the other Diomedes, and the baby didn't react. They couldn't see the ominous darkness swirling around them. They didn't recognize their impending destruction.

"Don't let it get me," Diomedes said, squeezing his arms around her. He curled up even smaller. Before she could stop him, he pulled his head away only to see a black tendril slithering along the bottom of the couch. He screamed and began hyperventilating. "I d-don't wanna die."

"Just hold on. Just hold on, Dio. I'm so sorry. Dio, I'm so sorry." Her chest tightened. She couldn't breathe, couldn't think. There was no way out. They were trapped.

"Please, I'm scared."

Ellayne held him as long as she could, but when she looked down at him, she saw him start to fade along with everything around her.

"I'm scared." His sight latched on to her, and Ellayne's heart raced as his feet disappeared in the blackness.

"Just keep your eyes on me. Look at me, Dio. I'm here. I won't leave you. I love you." Her voice broke, and she couldn't stop sobbing. But she didn't take her eyes off him. She wouldn't look away, wouldn't leave him alone in this nightmare.

The bottom of the couch was completely gone, and where light had once entered the room through the window, now only darkness. It swirled around her, filling her with chills. It seeped into every part of her, both body and mind. She couldn't stop shivering. No more warmth remained.

"I love you, Dio," she said, hugging him until he was no longer there—until she was alone in darkness.

Chapter Forty-Six

he pain in Ellayne's hand when she woke up on the throne room floor left her gasping for air. Ellayne's eyes opened. Her mind felt foggy, yet she still had the clear image of her brother clinging to her as darkness ripped him away. Residual tears rolled down her face, and she let out a sob at the thought of her brother succumbing to the freezing darkness. She clutched her hand to her chest as she sat up, her head throbbing.

A groan next to her had her scrambling to her feet, her knees weak when she remembered the beating Diomedes had put her through before—*before what?* Her mind raced as she sniffled. What had happened? How had she entered Diomedes's memories? Had it been real? Had she really found her brother again, only to lose him? Questions attacked her along with fatigue, and she stumbled away from the king.

"W-what was that?" Ellayne stuttered, putting distance between them. She trembled as the room temperature began to drop again with Diomedes's return to consciousness. "What just happened? Dio? Are you—"

With a shout, he flew into the air, dark magic surrounding him in a thick cloud. He hovered a foot or so above the ground, his arms stretched wide. A low rumble like laughter erupted from him, sending a shiver down Ellayne's sore spine. It turned manic, and his voice boomed around the walls.

"It's complete," he said, lifting his arms higher. "You found it."

"Found what?"

Diomedes pointed his finger at her, and she shot into the air, paralyzed and unable to move. Her magic simmered in the background, waiting to be directed. But her mind focused on Diomedes. The confusion in her mind begged for answers, and he was the only one who was going to satisfy that.

"You found the last shred of humanity in this body. We've been looking for it for years, but it evaded us."

"Humanity? Us?" Ellayne repeated, surprised to find that she had the ability to talk despite the paralysis. "What do you mean?"

"When you entered our mind, you found the last memories that held back the complete domination of magic. It was those memories that held the last glimpse of humanity, preventing us from being all-powerful."

"I-I didn't know." She stumbled over the words. The memories had been Dio's. Her Dio. Memories of her, with her; they'd been his last stand against whatever had taken him over. And she had ruined it. She had given this monster exactly what *it* wanted. Ellayne wished she could shiver, but the paralysis held her still. She could barely get enough air to her lungs as she began hyperventilating.

The person in front of her was all-powerful. No more humanity to bring any manner of balance.

And it was her fault.

She had led the darkness to the last part of her brother, had let it swallow him whole. Those memories, they'd been her last chance at saving Dio, and she had failed. He was dead because of her. Dio was dead. Her heart shattered. The one thing she'd been trying to prevent she'd completed the moment she walked through those doors. She had killed Dio, and it tore her up inside. Her eyes ached from the tears she had cried in the last few days, and just when she thought she had no more left to cry, they began again.

She tried to focus on her broken hand, trying—and failing—to overwhelm the pain and anger in her mind with the pain and agony of her fractured bones.

"Your ignorance is appreciated, Sister."

"I'm not your sister, and you're not my brother. Not anymore," she said, her jaw clenching. Ellayne felt the phantom arms of her brother wrapped around her in his last moments, and she choked. That was her brother, and he'd died in her arms. Like her father. Like Armannii. He'd died in front of her. Like her mother. Like Cal. Because of her. Like Lenora, the Dark King, and countless others.

"You're probably right. Now that we've destroyed the last of the host's memories, we suppose we have become our own person, you might say."

Ellayne's stomach sank, knowing it spoke the truth. Her brother no longer existed, no matter the face she saw before her. Even that held almost no resemblance to the Dio she had seen in his last memories. There was no life. No passion. Just power, malice, and greed. The dark magic had killed Diomedes with her help, had destroyed the last part of him. The only thing left now was the monster who had taken everything from her. The monster who had murdered her parents, the monster who had destroyed her family and her country.

And with that realization came a resurgence of strength. Her brother was gone. The thing holding her paralyzed was not him. It was the thing that had killed him. It was the thing she'd entered the castle to destroy.

"We have you to thank for this newfound freedom. And for that, we'll give you the gift of a swift death." He released the magic holding her up, and she screamed as she fell.

Tumbling as she hit the ground, she spun multiple times before coming to a stop on her stomach. Her broken hand shrieked in agony, but she focused her attention on her magic. *Help me.* Ellayne was not going to let the monster win without a fight. She owed at least that to her brother. She tried to slow her breathing but had no time before the monster struck again.

The dark magic blast struck her side, sending her flying several feet away. Her torso burned where she had been hit, and she groaned as she flopped onto her back. Her lungs struggled for air. *Help. Please.* The heat inside her flickered, and she coughed as she sat up. Every muscle ached. Every breath hurt.

But I'm not dead. Not yet. She clenched her good hand into a fist, watching it fill with light from her wrist—the same wrist the monster had cut to curse her, a curse she had broken with the help of her friends. Kade's face crossed her mind. He was somewhere in the castle, probably searching for her. She hadn't told him she loved him. *I can't die without him knowing.* Then the images of her people crossed her mind—Linetta, Dayla, Matt, Lydia, and so many others. They were depending on her—on their queen.

She pushed to her feet, squinting at the opposite wall to keep from falling over. Even with her body battered and broken as it was, she drew energy from the sight of her loved ones flickering through her mind. With a deep breath, Ellayne recalled one of the things Armannii had taught her in her first day of training. *"Something to use on Diomedes when you get the chance,"* he had said. She raised a hand with the palm down and her fingers spread out. *Silence,* she ordered as she lowered her hand back down to her side.

All sound in the room vanished, leaving a void where the noise should've been. She could see the monster's mouth moving; it was shouting something. Then it conjured up a blast of magic, sending it where she had been standing, but she had already moved halfway around the room.

It had no idea where she was.

The magic had worked exactly as Armannii had thought it would. She had blinded it. Whatever ability had allowed it to see with no eyes was linked in some way to its other senses, especially its hearing.

The monster threw three more blasts blindly. But even as they shook the walls, raining rubble and stone down, not a sound could be heard. However, she could feel the sweat forming on the back of her neck as she moved out of the way of another blast. The spell drew too much energy, and she could feel it losing strength even as the king let out another muted yell.

Then it all came rushing back.

The first thing she heard was her own heartbeat thundering in her ears. She panted, leaning against the nearest wall. As much as the spell had worked, she had been unable to pull on her magic while holding it. She had lost her chance.

The monster faced her as soon as the sound returned. "Enough tricks." It raised a hand and flicked its wrist toward Ellayne. She wasn't sure what was happening until she felt something wrap around her neck, pulling her off her feet. Out of the corner of her eye, she caught a glimpse of maroon. The monster had pulled her up using one of the floor-to-ceiling curtains lining the back wall.

Unable to breathe, Ellayne let out a gurgling noise. She clawed at the fabric with her good hand, kicking her feet in midair. But as the edges around her vision blurred and darkened, she saw a dark purple stain fluttering near her shoulder. She recognized it; she had made it the time she and her brother had built forts in the throne room. Ellayne focused hard on the image of her brother. She had watched him with adoring eyes as he read her stories, filling her head with magic—magic she had.

Gritting her teeth, Ellayne pushed her hand toward the monster, palm out. It skidded backward, and the curtain around her neck loosened. Ellayne rolled when she hit the ground and scrambled to her feet as quickly as she could.

"You've already failed. You shouldn't have even lasted this long," the king growled. "You're weak."

"Yet here I am." Ellayne scrounged up the boldest voice she could muster, which ended up being scratchy as bark from a tree thanks to nearly being strangled . . . again. But she caught sight of the two thrones nearby, and her parents flashed through her mind. She lifted her chin, filled with a new sense of confidence knowing that even if she failed, she would've made them proud. "The bane of your existence."

Cringing, Ellayne lifted both hands, biting back a cry of pain from her broken bones grinding against each other. She concentrated on the air, moving it around faster until a whirlwind surrounded the monster. From somewhere within, she could hear its laughter. But it stopped short as she moved her hands together, tightening the cyclone. The air in the center where the monster stood emptied out, creating a different kind of void—one that lacked anything to breathe. *"Make sure you concentrate on pulling the air out, otherwise your enemy will only end up with a bad hair day."* Armannii's instructions came back to her, and she clenched her teeth. *Pull,* she ordered, and her magic sucked even more air out than it already had.

But before she could celebrate, an explosion of dark magic erupted from the center, knocking her back to the wall and breaking her focus.

"Enough!" The monster choked, gripping its throat for a second before righting itself. "I have better things to do." The monster gripped its hand into a fist, and a piece of debris the size of a young colt rose a few feet into the air.

Ellayne scrambled away from the chunk of rubble the monster hurled at her. As soon as she was safely out of the way, she took a second to evaluate her opponent—something her brother had taught her when he first started training her.

It appeared strong—more than strong. All-powerful. But Ellayne knew better. Despite the dark magic radiating off it, there had to be a weakness—something she could exploit to finish the fight. The king's hands moved again, sending tendrils of darkness toward her. Ellayne raised her good hand again, concentrating her split attention to focus on a protective barrier. A shield of light separated her from the tendrils, but it flickered out after a few seconds.

Her mind fragmented in too many directions to hold her magic together. The frigid wisps of dark magic snatched her arms and legs, and she shrieked when it yanked her broken hand away from her chest. Her eyes squeezed shut against the waves of pain coursing through her. Her stomach heaved, and she thought she might throw up from the agony. The magic held her arms and legs spread out, pulling until it felt like her limbs would be ripped away from her body.

"Get . . . off . . . me!" She could barely get the words out. But even with her eyes shut, she could see the flash of light through her eyelids. Heat wrapped around her, freeing her from the grasp of the monster's magic.

When she did open her eyes, she noticed two things about the king: a sneer spread across his face, and black cracks creeped across the left side of his pale neck. It reminded her of the way her wrist looked when she had been cursed. But this was different. Through the cracks came wisps of magic.

Armannii's words trickled back to her once more. *"Magic is balanced by humanity."*

No humanity, no solid form. She may not have been able to save her friend and the others who had died, but there were people left to save.

Ellayne kept an eye on the mist, an idea forming in her mind. She shuffled to the right, and it tracked her movement, turning to face her no matter where she went.

"How did you get your magic?" Ellayne asked.

"You're just prolonging the inevitable," it said, a sinister grin etching across thin lips.

"It's a gift of mine. But I want to know."

The monster raised its hand, but instead of attacking Ellayne, a cloud of magic formed between them. Light flashed inside the cloud, and Ellayne frowned when images appeared. The first image was of mountains—the Elemental Mountains up north. A cave appeared in the cloud, followed by a dark winding tunnel through a mountain. Ellayne watched the images appear and disappear: navigating in the darkness, a door with runes on it, a giant room with a deep pit in the center. Then she saw an image of something she recognized.

The black dagger her brother had used to murder her mother and their father.

A pale hand reached out to grab the dagger, which lay on the ground at the bottom of the pit. Then darkness.

"I don't understand," Ellayne said when the cloud dispersed. "The dagger gave you magic?"

The monster shrugged. "In a way, yes. But it was actually the person who possessed the dagger before who passed on her magic. We'll let you venture a guess as to who it was."

Only one name entered Ellayne's mind. "Emmalee."

"Correct. The sorceress found a way to preserve her magic using the dagger as a vessel. She deemed this host worthy, and she has been here ever since."

"What?"

"Her body is gone, but her magic lives on. She's here. We are her, and she is us. When your brother found the dagger, he allowed us to give him power. Now, with your help, only we remain."

Ellayne's head throbbed even more as she tried to understand what the monster was saying. "And you are?"

"In a sense, we are the essence of dark magic users who have died before, leaving behind only their magic when their bodies decay. We have never before been given complete control over a host."

"So you just used my brother. Killed him." Ellayne's good hand clenched into a fist and started to glow. "And for what? A crown?"

"He was a means to an end. The end of all nonmagic beings, that is. A goal we have had for centuries. And despite your magic, it will mean your end as well, Ellayne Maudit. We appreciate your aid in completing our task, but your distractions have gone on long enough. Farewell."

Ellayne leapt out of the way of the blast that collapsed part of the wall behind her. She knew that as battered as her body was, one or two more direct hits would kill her. However, she also noticed that with each act of magic, the cracks on the monster's skin spread.

Unfortunately, it had noticed too. The king raised a hand to his face, and she imagined that if it still had eyes, they would've widened. "What's this? What did you do?"

"Did you know"—she blocked a blast with a barrier that fragmented as soon as it was struck—"that magic needs balance?"

The monster shrieked, leaping back into the air and hovering. "We possess more knowledge on magic than you could ever wish to understand." It howled again as a crack formed on its arm, leaking black mist.

"Clearly, you didn't realize that humanity is necessary," she said, mustering up enough strength to send her own ball of light whooshing toward the monster. It waved its hand with a flick of the wrist, sending her attack off course. Ellayne didn't care because it was proving her point. The fragmentation on its skin continued spreading.

"What is this? What kind of magic are you using against me?"

"This has nothing to do with me." She took a deep breath, letting her magic and what was left of her strength trickle down to her good hand. "You did this to yourself, you idiotic cloud of mist." She sent a tidal wave of light toward the monster. It blocked itself in with a sphere of darkness, but she could see fractures in the shield. She sent another wave. "I will *not* let you destroy my country."

With a third wave, the barrier protecting the monster broke, and it fell to the ground.

"What's happening?" it roared, pushing up from its knees to its feet.

"You're just lucky you can't see how awful you look." Ellayne stood straighter, though it ached in her side to do so. "You murdered my mother." She sent a blast of magic as she stepped forward. The monster caught it but slid backward. "You murdered my father." She sent another blast of light, and the monster's reaction time was slower. Ellayne stepped forward again, and she wiped slow-forming tears from her eyes. "And you murdered my brother."

The cracks turned into gashes. Mist and magic poured out of them, and the monster screeched when Ellayne sent a stream of light magic straight for it.

"How is this possible?" it screamed. Dark magic leaked onto the floor, slithering as the monster stirred the air by stumbling backward. "We are all-powerful."

"You may be all-powerful, but it comes at a price." Ellayne's head spun from exerting as much magic as she had. But when she pictured her family's faces and the faces of those she had lost, she felt a second wind of energy warming her core.

The monster clasped its face, trying to hold the magic in as it emptied from the tattered shell of her brother. The dark magic spilled out faster and faster as Diomedes's body disappeared into thin air.

"You failed. *You*. Not me," she said, raising her chin as she pointed her hand at the enemy one last time. Light filled the room as she turned her thoughts to every memory she could recall of time spent with her parents and Diomedes. With images of their laughing faces filling her head, she was distracted, but from somewhere in front of her, the final gurgled cry of the monster rang out.

When the light faded, not a trace of her brother or the monster he had become remained. The dagger that had destroyed him from the inside out lay at her feet, and Ellayne held the cold metal in her shaking fingers, staring down at her lonely reflection.

"I'm sorry, Dio."

Chapter Forty-Seven

he moment Ellayne destroyed the monster, the dark magic walls blocking the entrance to the throne room disappeared. Grief and exhaustion prevented Ellayne from moving from the spot in the middle of the throne room. She dropped to her knees. For what felt like the hundredth time that day, she let tears fall down her cheeks. But with her nerves frayed as they were, she wasn't quite sure why. Maybe for those she had lost. Maybe because of the physical pain she was in. But mostly, she thought, with relief it was over.

Everything hurt.

Ellayne tucked the dagger into an empty sheath on her belt, knowing it was her last connection to her brother. She leaned over, cradling her broken hand against her chest. Rocking back and forth, she allowed the tears to fall without wiping them away. When her mind replayed an image of her brother's broken and damaged body disappearing as it disintegrated, she realized she was crying for him because he was dead. Ellayne had known for a long time she couldn't kill him. Not because she wasn't angry at him. Not because she didn't blame him for killing her parents. Not even because he was stronger than she was. She couldn't—wouldn't—kill him because she still loved him.

But he was dead.

It was my fault, she thought, her shoulders heaving as she cried. She'd led the dark magic to where the last remainder of her brother hid in fear of being found. He'd died in her arms. And there was nothing she could've done to save him in that moment. No magic or manner of wishing could've stopped what she started the instant she let the monster in.

Ellayne hiccupped, wiping her eyes just to have them fill back up again. She pictured her brother's eyes—the fear swallowing them whole as the darkness ripped him into nothingness. And she couldn't save him, couldn't even ease his fear during his last moments.

She knew she hadn't been the one to kill him, but the weight of his death still rested on her shoulders.

What felt like an hour of processing the death of her brother and the destruction of the monster who had killed him was only a minute or two, and Ellayne stiffened when the double doors slammed open with a whoosh of dark magic. But she didn't look up. She stayed doubled over on the ground facing the thrones—facing where the monster had stood only a few minutes earlier.

"Ellayne!" Kade raced over, sliding to a stop in front of her. He dropped to his knees, reaching a hand up to lift her chin. "Are you—"

"He's dead," she whispered before he could finish. "My brother's dead." Ellayne squeezed her eyes shut, unable to keep them open because of the wave of emotion that struck her when she spoke the words out loud. "The prophecy was right."

"Prophecy? What prophecy?" Kade brushed her cheek, his thumb tracing the wet line of tears. His touch was soft, saying more words than his lips. The spark trickled around, following wherever his skin touched hers.

"The one about my brother and me. It said only one would survive. It was me." Ellayne's tired mind couldn't offer any other explanation; however, Kade didn't seem to mind as he stroked her cheeks.

"You were gone when I turned around," he mumbled. "I was so worried." Kade shifted before she could respond, and she opened her eyes to see the blurry vision of someone standing behind him.

"Ellayne, I—" Kiegan paused when Ellayne tensed. "I'm not going to hurt you. I-I'm sorry I ever hurt you. I—"

"Kiegan," Ellayne said, her eyes flickering from one man to the other. Kade removed his hand from her cheek but stayed near her.

It felt like her whole body was shaking, both from adrenaline and the intense storm of emotions flooding through her head. She didn't know whether to shrink back in fear from the man who used to be her friend or to race forward and hug him. Something about him had changed; his shoulders slouched, and there were bags under his eyes she didn't remember from before. He looked like he hadn't been able to sleep for weeks. How had she not noticed it before?

Standing up, Kade offered his hand down to Ellayne, who grabbed it with her good hand. He caught her under the elbow when she began shaking, her knees trembling beneath her. Blood drained from her head, and the room spun. Kade reached for her other hand but moved away as soon as Ellayne screamed in pain.

"Broken," she said, moaning. "Very broken."

"I'm sorry. I didn't know." Kade gripped her around the waist, but she sucked in more air through her teeth. He let go.

"Hit in the side too," she managed to get out between raspy breaths. "I-I'm fine."

Kade resolved to support her using her elbow, and she concentrated on Kiegan instead of the new tremors of pain spreading throughout her entire body. Despite the tears from the burning fire from her injuries, her other tears had subsided.

"Kiegan, you're . . . you're . . ." Ellayne couldn't think of a word that suited what she wanted to say. But it didn't matter because he filled in the blank for her.

"Free from the spell Blanndynne had me under," he said, rubbing the back of his neck. "I-I'm sorry, Ellayne. I tried to fight it—"

Ellayne stepped away from Kade and lowered her broken hand to her side as she pulled Kiegan into a hug with her good hand. He stood still for a moment, but then he gently wrapped his arms around her shoulders. Kiegan leaned his head into her neck, and she could hear his uneven breaths. He was crying.

"I'm so sorry, Ellayne," he said, his voice loud in her ear.

She pulled away, looking up at his red face. His eyes were already puffy, but there was a clarity to them that left her heart lighter than a second earlier. Since he had first joined Blanndynne, his eyes had moments of being just as cloudy as the eyes of other guards who had been bewitched—an overt mark that his mind had not been his own.

"I was so upset at you and Kade. I didn't know I had dark magic, and I was scared when it revealed itself. Blanndynne found me after I turned my back on you. I'm so sorry. At the time I resented you, both of you. And she used that. She bent my mind to hate you. As the enchantment would fade, I-I would try to escape, but she could tell. She could tell when any of the enchantments were weakening. She'd put me under again and again, and I couldn't seem to—"

"Kiegan," Ellayne said, stepping back. "I believe you. I-I forgive you." She watched his chest expand as he let out a relieved breath. "And I'm sorry I hurt you, for what you had to go through because of me."

"Thank you, Ellayne." His voice cracked. "I don't deserve it. I don't. I'm sorry about your father and your elf friend. I didn't know him, but he freed me. I owe him everything."

The mention of Armannii had Ellayne glancing toward the doors. They had closed again when Kiegan and Kade had entered, but she knew Armannii's body was somewhere in the castle. She wondered how many bodies awaited her outside the throne room, how many people would be in mourning like her.

It took her a second to realize Kiegan was still talking.

"And then to find out that we're brothers, if anything, I fought harder. But she kept strengthening the spell." Kiegan's words caught her attention, and Ellayne looked up at him. His attention was on Kade, who stood behind her. "I couldn't believe it at first. How could either of us be royalty? How am I—how are we the sons of the Dark King and the sorceress? If I hadn't overheard that while waiting on Blanndynne, we would've been at the tiny house sooner. But she knew she had to take my mind captive again or I'd find a way to break out while we were going to find you."

Ellayne glanced at Kade, not turning away when she found him staring at her.

"I-I killed my father. Our father." Kiegan's voice was weak, and he dropped his head when she turned her gaze back to him. Kade stiffened next to her, and she shivered when he began radiating cold.

With a deep breath, Ellayne looked up at Kiegan. "Like you said, you weren't in control. Blanndynne used you as a weapon. Armannii said Blanndynne was talented at bewitching. Your body may have done it, but I know your mind was fighting tooth and nail against it during every second." Ellayne placed her hand on his arm, and he looked at her through his long eyelashes.

"Still," he said, his voice but a whisper. "I killed him. My hands. My sword. And he wasn't the only one."

Ellayne took a deep breath, stepping back next to Kade, who still remained a statue. "It's going to take a lot of time for *all* of us to heal from the last few months." She flicked her sight between both of them. "But we will. We have to. Eventually."

Kade's steady gaze remained on her, and he finally nodded. "It won't be easy. Not with the scars left behind. They take time to heal." He rubbed his shoulder, clenching it with white knuckles. "But they will fade." With a deep exhale, he took a step forward, placing his hands on Kiegan's shoulders. "And we will get through this," he said, glancing at Ellayne. "Together."

Something about the way he looked at her sent her stomach swirling, and she straightened up as much as her injuries would allow.

"Kiegan, I need you to do me a favor." She took a second of silence to organize her thoughts. "I need you to go spread the word that the battle is over. Diomedes fell. I will address everyone in an hour. Tell people to gather in the castle courtyard—if it's still standing, that is. Make sure it's cleared out as much as possible so we can have the maximum number of people there. I will have the castle healers sent to the courtyard for those who are injured. And . . ." She hesitated with the next order. "Please have Armannii's body taken to a room to be prepared for burial. We'll be burying many others as well, I'm sure."

"What about you?" Kade asked, nodding toward her hand.

Her injuries swelled in a rush of pain at the mention of them, but she pushed it down as best as she could. "I'll send for Dayla, if she's still—"

"I'm sure she's fine," he said, his lips tightening. "What would you like me to do?"

Ellayne's eyes bounced between the two men. Her stomach flipped again, but she had made up her mind. "I'd like a word with you, if you wouldn't mind."

"Of course." He nodded.

"I'll go then," Kiegan said. He offered her a small smile and gripped Kade on the shoulder before he left the throne room. He must not have noticed the way Kade became motionless at his touch, but Ellayne did.

She watched him go, as did Kade, neither of them daring to move before the door shut behind him, neither saying a word until it was just the two of them.

Alone.

Chapter Forty-Eight

ilence followed Kiegan's departure. For what seemed like ages, the only thing Kade and Ellayne did was stare at each other. His face was still bloody from his fight with Kiegan, and it stuck some of his curly black hair to his temple. The tunic he wore was tattered, torn in more places than she could count, and most of the torn sections had crimson lining the edges. He favored his left leg. There was no telling what other injuries he was hiding, but Kade didn't show the physical pain he was in.

Instead, he kept his gaze locked on Ellayne. His keen eyes scanned her, stopping at her broken hand, which had started swelling. He stepped closer, holding his hand out for her to place hers in. She kept the broken one where it was and placed her good one in it. Buzzing spread through her at his touch, and the closer he got, the more fog entered her mind. She welcomed it, reveling in the peace it brought to her deafening thoughts.

"How did you do it?" Kade finally asked, breaking his eye contact to glance down at her hand in his. "How did you beat him?"

Ellayne closed her eyes to focus so she could answer his question. However, as soon as she shut them, she saw images of her brother clinging to her, begging her to help him. It left her trembling, and she had to open her eyes to ground herself in Kade—to remember that it was over.

"It's complicated," she said with a deep sigh.

"You don't have to if—"

"It's fine. I just—I saw Dio. The real Dio. My magic led me inside of his head, and I got to see my brother. He was just like I remembered him. A-and he died because of me." Her hand shook in Kade's, and he squeezed it gently.

"You were in his mind?"

She nodded. "His magic consumed him. It killed the last part of Dio. It killed him." Ellayne bit her cheek, deciding to tell him how her brother had gotten his magic from Emmalee at another time. "It overwhelmed him. His last piece of humanity—his last memory—was a memory of the day I was born. And the magic destroyed it. It became all-powerful. My brother's body became a host for the magic, but it was unstable. Magic and humanity must have balance. When the monster used its powers, it began to crack and fade away. I wish I could've saved my brother, but—"

"He was already gone." Kade bowed his head. "I'm sorry, Ellayne. You've lost so many loved ones."

Ellayne lowered her head, her eyes focusing on their intertwined hands. The sparks still made her skin tingle, reminding her that she hadn't lost everyone.

"Kade, I—"

"Kiegan and I talked," he said at the same time. When she didn't keep going, he continued. "I-I think it's going to take a while for me to trust him again. And I guess it'll never go back to the way it was. How could it? Especially with all of the messed-up things Blanndynne had him do. He's so broken inside."

"I understand. And it's going to take time for him to trust us too. But this was the best possible outcome after we found out you're brothers. Most, if not all, of the things he said and did while he was under her control wasn't him. And though that's going to leave plenty of scars, I know he's going to be okay," Ellayne said, rubbing her thumb over the back of his hand. "He's got you."

"He's not the only one." Kade's voice dropped lower, and his eyes found hers. "I-I talked to him about what happened in the castle when he found us in the portrait hall. It feels like years ago. I told him that there wasn't anything between us."

Ellayne's stomach fell. Her shoulders slumped, and she closed her eyes. It had all been a lie. He didn't love her. Armannii had been wrong.

"Hey," he said, using his other hand to lift her chin. "Look at me. I'm not finished."

Her eyes fluttered open, and she tried to contain the sadness creeping behind them. She didn't want to hear any more. Losing Armannii and her brother had been difficult enough without having her heart broken.

"Kade, please—"

"Sh," he said, placing his finger to her lips. "It's my turn to talk. Okay? So listen. You have frustrated me more than any other person I've ever met. You're stubborn, and you rarely think things through before diving into situations that could get you killed, yet you balance that with your passion and courage. And you have no trouble thinking of others before yourself. I've never met someone as compassionate as you."

He slid his hand to her cheek and stepped closer. She could feel her heart pounding, making a racket she was surprised he couldn't hear inside her chest. Warmth spread from her core, meeting the cool air billowing off him. She wanted to be closer, hoped with all her heart he'd tug until there was no space for cold or warm air between them.

"I've been trying to find the right time to talk to you. It never works out. And maybe this isn't the right timing either. I mean, we just went through a lot, but I'm not going to wait anymore." As if he had read her mind, he pulled her into him, careful not to jostle her broken hand or squeeze her wounded side.

Kade's face was only inches away, and she stared at his lips as he formed the next words. "I love your heart, your mind, your magic, your stubbornness, and your humor. I love your ability to put me in my place." He brushed a strand of hair behind her ear, leaving his hand resting gently on the side of her neck. She leaned into it, relishing the heat spreading inside her. "I love you, Ellayne, and I have for longer than I care to admit. Sometimes I love you so much it annoys me. Most of the time you're all I can think about. It's infuriating. But you've brought out the best in me, and I am who I am because of you."

Tears spilled from her eyes, and a smile spread over her lips, which parted ever so slightly. Inside she was floating, reliving every word he had just said. He loved her.

"Finally." She hadn't meant to say the word out loud, but she didn't care. "Finally," she said again.

He laughed, but she cut it short. Reaching up, she gripped him from behind the neck. With a tug, she yanked him down, and his face met hers—a moment she had thought about for what felt like forever. The moment their lips touched, she felt the spark it created travel through her whole body, sending tingles to every inch. She dragged him closer, needing him to be nearer to her than was physically possible. His hand slipped to her back, needing the same thing, needing to be closer. Electricity sparked between them. Her mind buzzed. Her heart flew. She felt powerful—invincible. She kissed him harder. All the pain, both physical and mental, faded away. Her entire body hummed with energy.

The world continued spinning around them while they stood still. Ellayne felt weightless, like she could lift off the floor and fly.

As her magic warmed up inside her, she wondered for a second if they just might.

Then he touched her injured side, and she winced. The moment ended.

"It took you long enough to admit it," she said, easing his worry with a grin.

"Hey now. This better not be a one-sided thing." His dimple popped out.

She raised an eyebrow, smirking. "I was pretty sure I made that clear."

"Well," he said, his breath a whisper tucked into a grin. "I wouldn't mind a little more clarification."

"I guess in that case . . ." She ran her hand through his hair like she had always seen him do, leaving her hand resting on his shoulder. "I love you. It took me a long time to admit it too, but I love you more than you could know. I don't have a long speech planned out like you did though, so you're going to have to be satisfied with this: with every part of me, I love you, Kade."

He leaned forward and kissed her forehead. "I've wanted to hear that for a long time."

She stepped back an inch. "You could've heard it sooner if you hadn't run off." She started it as a joke, but her expression became serious when she saw him lower his face. "I was worried you were going to get yourself killed before I could tell you."

"I'm sorry, Ellayne. I really am. I wanted to see Kiegan. I wanted to try to break the spell Blanndynne had over him. I didn't know how strong the enchantment was, otherwise—"

"We both know you would've gone after him whether you knew or not," she said, resting her hand on his bicep. She took a moment to appreciate how he'd bulked up over the last few weeks now that she had ample opportunity to feel it. It distracted her for a second before Kade cleared his throat.

His dark eyes watched her. "You're right. I would've gone after him either way."

"Yeah," she said, drawn in by his gaze. Her focus drifted around his face, landing on his smile. A smile she wanted to kiss again. And again. She already missed the carefree feeling it had given her. The world outside the one they had created for themselves in the throne room was slowly slinking in, tainting the high she was soaring on.

"Let's find Dayla," Kade said, clearing his throat as he drew his gaze back to her eyes from her parted lips. "We need to get you fixed up before you address everyone."

"Mm-hmm." Her mind refused to focus what with the sparks distracting her. Standing in his arms, she was safe. Ellayne wanted to stay there, pressed against her best friend forever.

Until she bumped her broken hand and pain shattered the peaceful moment. Again. She hissed through her teeth. "Fine, let's find Dayla."

Chapter Forty-Nine

llayne gripped Kade's hand tighter when the quietness of the castle hallways hit her like a brick. The chill of dark magic no longer radiated through the corridors, yet she still shivered.

"Where do you want Dayla to meet us?" Kade asked, pausing in the middle of the hall.

Us. Ellayne enjoyed the way her stomach fluttered at the word.

"My old room." She squeezed his hand before unweaving her fingers from his.

Ellayne would've preferred not to move, but with the other hand out of service, she reluctantly let go. Thinking of Dayla, she called on her magic to send a message to the siren. A wisp of light slid from her fingers, disappearing down the hall.

"You'll have to teach me that one," Kade said, his gaze following the wisp until it was out of sight. "It seems handy."

She laced her fingers back in with his, tugging at his hand to keep walking. "It's easy. I just think of the person I want to send a message to and then ask my magic to relay it."

"You make it sound easier than it probably is."

"I just remember to say please and thank you," she said, grinning up at him. However, her smile faltered when she remembered who had taught her. "Armannii said to treat it with respect." Her shoulders dipped, and Kade rubbed the back of her hand with his thumb.

"He was a good teacher."

"He promised to teach me more. He was supposed to teach me runes." Ellayne squeezed her eyes shut, but after all the tears she had shed that day, she wasn't sure she could produce any more even if she wanted to.

Kade stopped, and she paused next to him. He reached into the pocket inside his vest and pulled out a rune pen—Armannii's. Kade released her hand only to flip it over, palm up. His eyes stayed locked on hers as he laid the pen in her open hand.

"I took it after . . . well, you know. I think he would've wanted you to have it."

Ellayne's fingers closed over the pen, grasping it like it was the last thread connected to her friend. "Thank you," she said, the words barely a whisper.

Opening his arms, he pulled her into a hug, careful to avoid her injuries. Ellayne pressed her face against Kade's chest, trying to do what she could to maintain her composure. She couldn't stop her mind from seeing the image of Armannii bleeding out on the floor. Ellayne cringed, and Kade sighed against her. But after a few minutes of standing in the middle of the hallway, Ellayne stepped back, sniffling as she slipped the rune pen into her boot.

"Come on," she said, exhaling louder than she intended. "There's one more place I want to go before we meet with Dayla."

She held out her hand. When Kade took it, he brought it up to his lips, brushing her knuckles with a soft kiss.

"I'd follow you to the end of the world."

Though she blushed, she couldn't help but laugh. "So you confess your love for me, and now you're some sort of romantic sap?" She shook her head, and he rolled his eyes.

"Way to ruin the moment." He squeezed her hand as he interlaced his fingers with hers. "And I'll be a sap if I want to be."

She responded with a smirk, pulling his hand up to her lips to kiss. "Then I will be too."

They didn't run into a single person as they took a servants' staircase up to the third floor. The portrait hall was empty as well, which was exactly what Ellayne hoped for. They stood in front of her family's portrait, and Ellayne took in the young faces of her father, mother, and brother.

"Is it strange to see yourself in the portrait this time?" Kade asked after a few minutes of silence.

Ellayne contemplated the question by staring at her younger self perched on her father's knee. She hadn't been able to see the little girl the last time she and Kade had snuck into the portrait hall because the curse prevented her and everyone else from seeing the other heir—everyone except for Kade and Kiegan.

"It feels like a lifetime ago we were here," she said, running her fingers along the bottom edge of the frame. They came away covered in dust, which she wiped on her trousers. "It's not strange, mainly because I have my memories back. It's strange to me that . . . that I'm the only one left from this portrait. They're all gone."

Her mind wandered through hallway after hallway of memories. Some were good, and others left her shaking. Kade stepped up behind her, placing his hand on her shoulder. He didn't say anything, just let her stand there, lost in her thoughts.

Staring up at her parents and brother, she wondered what they'd say to her now that it was over. She hoped her mother and father would be proud of her and that her brother would be glad it was over. A part of her wanted to know if Diomedes regretted the decision to go after magic he had no right possessing, if he was sorry for the family he destroyed and the country he nearly led back into war. Those weren't questions she had thought to ask the last remaining fragment of her brother, and she was glad she hadn't. He had been so young, just like in the portrait in front of her. When she gazed up at each of them—her mother, her father, her brother—she ached to see them one last time. But that wasn't possible, and she knew it. Her head drooped, and she closed her eyes.

Finally, she turned her back on the portraits, opened her eyes, and faced Kade. "What are you going to do?"

He raised an eyebrow, clearly caught off guard by the question. "What do you mean?"

"Are you going to go back to the Dark?" She knew the timing of the question wasn't ideal, but after staring at the painting of the family she had lost, her mind had turned to those she could still lose.

"I-I have to talk with Kiegan. With my father gone, one of us needs to take the throne. I'm not sure, Ellayne. He's the one who killed him. But outside the three of us, I don't think anyone else knows. I can't decide what the right thing to do would be. Do I make it known or keep it secret? And to add to that, he's never even been to the Dark." Kade rubbed his fingers back and forth over his right eyebrow.

"You're right. You need to talk with him, figure out a plan together. I just, I want you to know that while I want you to do what's best for your people, I also selfishly wish you wouldn't go." She tilted her head down, sighing.

He lifted her chin, brushing her hair out of her face. "If I go back, it's not forever. I refuse to spend more time away from you than necessary. Besides"—his dimple popped out as he grinned, taking a step closer to her—"you're going to need my help running the country."

"How so?"

"You're going to need someone to think your outrageous plans through," he said, wincing when she smacked him on the arm lightly.

After she hit him, she pulled him closer. "I know you have duties to the Dark, and I know your father was training you to take his place someday. But . . . but I want you to know that I *want* you here. Beside me. Always."

"Oh yeah?"

"Mm-hmm," she said, leaning closer. "It's the truth."

"I guess I'll stick around then. Who else would argue with you?" he whispered, an inch away. A breath away.

"I wouldn't choose anyone else."

Dayla was waiting with Matt in Ellayne's old room when Kade and Ellayne arrived.

"Oh, thank goodness!" Dayla said, rushing toward them as soon as they entered the room. "I was so worried and—"

Ellayne stopped her by holding her good hand out between them. "I'm a little too banged up for a hug, Dayla. I'm sorry."

"Of course," the siren said, nodding. "You should sit on the bed, and I'll do what I can."

"I'm glad to see you're all right, Matt," Kade said, shaking Matt's hand.

"Thanks to Her Majesty and Day, I'm alive and well. What about you?" Matt asked.

Kade glanced sideways at Ellayne, a smile on his face. "I'm better than expected."

Matt and Dayla exchanged a glance before Dayla squealed. "You told her?" When Kade nodded, Dayla squealed again. "Finally! It took you long enough."

"Funny," Kade said, snorting. "That's what she said."

Ellayne laughed as she let Dayla pull her by her good hand to the bed. From the pink tinge on his cheeks, Ellayne could tell Kade was blushing, and she was loving every second of it.

"I've been waiting for him to tell you for ages. I knew it from the moment you two showed up in Bolee. I tried to convince him to tell you *so* many times, but you know him. He's stubborn." Dayla beamed as she pulled out her rune pen.

"Yeah." Ellayne winked at Kade. "*He's* the stubborn one."

Kade sat down on the window seat, rolling his eyes twice just to make sure Ellayne saw.

"And what did you say?" Dayla asked, taking Ellayne's broken hand gently into hers.

"I told him I feel the same way," Ellayne said, trying to not focus on the searing fire starting up in her hand where Dayla was tracing the healing rune.

"Aw." Dayla kept her eyes focused on the rune, but Ellayne had no trouble seeing the wide smile on her face. "Armannii, Matt, and I have been waiting for you two to get together for so long. Where is Armannii?"

Ellayne felt all of the air leave her lungs the second Dayla said Armannii's name. Kade cleared his throat, and out of the corner of her eye, Ellayne watched him shake his head slowly. Matt caught on first.

"He always said he would go out fighting. What better than a battle that will redefine our worlds?"

With her throat feeling dry, the only thing Ellayne could do was nod. Dayla glanced up, and her face changed when she saw Ellayne's downcast expression.

"Oh, E, I didn't know. I-I'm so sorry."

"It's not your fault," Ellayne whispered. "A lot of people died today, but Matt's right. They didn't die in vain. I—we—will work to heal our lands."

Dayla nodded, and a new wave of heat traveled up Ellayne's arm when she started the rune again. Cringing, Ellayne closed her eyes. Only when Dayla had finished all of the healing runes around her injuries did Ellayne finally open them again.

"Cal would be proud of the woman you've become, Dayla," Ellayne said. Her voice was raspy as she tried not to show the fire spreading through her body from the healing runes.

The siren nodded as she stood up. "I know he would. And he would've been so excited to see this day come, to see you officially become the queen."

After Dayla had finished with Kade's injuries, the four of them made their way to the balcony where Ellayne was supposed to address the country. Kiegan and a few others, including Linetta, waited for her just inside the balcony doors.

"Ellayne," Linetta said, pushing past a few others to reach her. She pulled her into a hug, and Ellayne was thankful for the healing runes' quick work. "I'm so thankful you're okay."

"I'm glad you're okay too," Ellayne said, pulling back to look her aunt over.

When Linetta had demanded she be allowed to fight, Ellayne had put her in a group farthest away from where most of the fighting would take place. Her plan seemed to have worked, as her aunt appeared mostly unscathed from the battle, except for the broken left lens in her glasses.

"I did what you asked, and the people are waiting to hear from you," Kiegan said, stepping forward. He kept his hands clasped behind his back, and he wouldn't hold eye contact for any longer than a second.

Dayla's eyebrows furrowed, and she turned to Kade. "What's he doing here?"

Kade took a deep breath. "Kiegan was one of the people bewitched by Blanndynne. He, along with many of the royal guard, was not in control of himself or his actions. When Blanndynne died, the spell broke. He's—"

"Really sorry, Dayla," Kiegan said, cutting Kade off and stepping closer. "I know I destroyed the town you were staying in—"

"Among other things," Dayla said, leaning closer to Matt, who kept a protective arm around Dayla's waist. Ellayne wasn't sure if it was to protect Dayla or to protect Kiegan *from* Dayla. "Enchantment or not, how could you possibly show your face here after the things you did?"

"Dayla, it's not his—" Ellayne started, but Kiegan shook his head.

"She's right, Ellayne. I-I really shouldn't be here." He rubbed his hand over the back of his neck.

"Here is exactly where you should be." Ellayne shook her head. "Kiegan, we've already talked about this. It may take time for other people to forgive you, but I already have." She turned to the siren. "Dayla, I'm not telling you to forgive him, but I am asking you to accept that he is here. That I *want* him here. All right?"

Kiegan opened his mouth like he was about to argue, but Dayla spoke first.

"Fine. That's your decision, E. But I can't say I agree with it."

"And I'm okay with that," Ellayne said, clasping Dayla's hand.

"Your Highness." Criss stepped forward, his helmet in his hand, and saluted Kade, who nodded. "I'm relieved to see you're all right. Did you find your father's murderer?"

Kade lifted his chin, keeping his eyes on his soldier, not giving off any indication that the man standing next to Criss was the Dark King's killer. "I have resolved the issue. You, my brother, and I will speak after the queen addresses the crowd."

Criss's eyebrows rose. "Your Highness?"

"I have a brother." Kade bobbed his head once. "You heard that correctly," he said, nodding toward Kiegan. "It's a long story."

"Of course, Your Highness." Criss inclined his head, nodding toward the doors leading outside. "And I am eager to hear it. But first, the people of Phildeterre and my men are waiting to hear from you, Your Majesty."

"Right," Ellayne said, biting her lip. "I guess I should address them then."

Kade took her newly healed hand in his. "You've got this, Ellayne." He bent down and kissed her forehead. Leaning in, his breath tickled her neck when he added, "And I've got you."

She felt someone take her other hand, and when she turned, she saw Dayla beaming up at her. "Don't mess up, E. No pressure, though."

Ellayne snorted, squeezing their hands before nodding for Criss and another Dark Soldier to open the double doors to the courtyard balcony.

"Oh, before you go," Dayla said, letting go of Ellayne's hand. "I have a rune that will help you project your voice so you don't ruin your vocal chords. But after I draw it, don't talk until you're ready." Her rune pen tickled Ellayne's neck. "There."

Dayla fell back with Matt when Ellayne stepped through, but Kade stayed by her side the whole way up to the railing. Countless faces stared up at her, and for a second a hush fell over the crowd. The moment shattered when a roar of cheers arose from the people.

Torches lit the courtyard below as well as the balcony they stood on. How many speeches had she been present for when her father and mother stood in the exact spot she stood? Countless. Yet never once had she considered she would be addressing the country. Her country.

Kade released her hand, nudging her to the center of the balcony. However, he only took a step back—near enough to turn to if need be. Kiegan, Criss, Matt, Dayla, and Linetta stood back by the doors, out of sight from most of the crowd. Ellayne glanced back at them. Linetta grinned at her with pride in her eyes, Dayla gave her a thumbs-up, Matt and Criss bowed their heads to her, and Kiegan stood taller when her eyes landed on him. She turned her attention back to Kade, who winked, nodding toward the crowd.

Ellayne took a deep breath, letting the air fill her lungs. When she opened her mouth and spoke, her words were amplified across the courtyard for everyone to hear thanks to Dayla's rune.

"The Second Split of Phildeterre is over. King Diomedes is dead, as is his queen."

The crowd cheered even louder, only falling silent when Ellayne lifted her hand to quiet them.

"People of Phildeterre and our friends from the Dark, for generations we have been unbalanced." Ellayne glanced at Kade, finding his eyes resting on her. He nodded at her to continue, and she faced the crowd again. "I have learned firsthand what that means. Friends, our worlds demand balance: balance between magic and nonmagic, balance between light and dark magic, and balance within even ourselves. The Dark King once told me that for peace to exist, there must first be balance. I agree with that fully.

"Phildeterre has been hurting for years, and it is up to us to change that. We must come together in unity to help heal the wounds of the past—to heal the rift in our society. I know the title of queen falls on me, but I am not saying any of this as your queen. Instead, I say this as a fellow citizen of our beloved country. I am asking you to stand beside me to rebuild our nation.

"As for our friends from the Dark who came to our aid, I am determined to begin a new era of alliance with you. Many of your ancestors or you yourself came from Phildeterre, and as we begin to heal our country, I invite you to do the same. In this difficult time, we have proven the strength we have together.

"We must also remember those we've lost. Many died in this battle in hopes they would bring a bright future to those who remain. We mustn't fail them, and we should honor them in the decisions we make from here forward. What we do now will affect generations that follow. Remember this when you face those with whom you may not agree. Forgiveness is an essential part of healing, both for those who hurt and those who caused the hurt. It will take time, and it may not be easy, but we must show grace to those around us if we are going to succeed in healing both ourselves and our land.

"Let today go down in history as the day Phildeterre began to heal. Let us step into tomorrow knowing that we chose the world we want our children to live in. Let us grow in unity, balanced and at peace. Thank you."

A thunder of applause arose from the crowd, and someone started a chant that caught on like fire to dry grass.

"Long live the queen! Long live the queen!"

Ellayne stepped out of sight of the people, and Dayla rushed forward before Ellayne said anything else. With a few strokes of her rune pen, Dayla removed the rune from Ellayne's neck.

"That was wonderful, E!" Dayla said, hugging Ellayne around the waist.

"Your parents would be proud," Linetta added, embracing Ellayne as soon as Dayla stepped away. "You are going to be a marvelous queen."

Kade's hand brushed Ellayne's waist and stayed there as the others made comments about her speech. Out of all the compliments, his touch said the most. She had made it through her first official address as queen now that the war was over. She had survived.

Criss bowed his head at Ellayne, but his face was strained when he looked up. "I beg your pardon, Your Majesty, but I need a word with the Dark Princes."

Kade leaned down and whispered in Ellayne's ear. "I'll find you later." When she nodded, he gave her a kiss on the forehead. Kade let go of Ellayne and led Criss inside the castle, motioning for Kiegan to follow. Two Dark Soldiers by the doors fell in step behind them, and Ellayne watched them go.

"Now what?" Dayla asked, wrapping her arm around Matt.

Ellayne listened to the multitude of voices below in the courtyard as people left. She knew some were leaving to prepare their dead for burial, some were going to have to repair their homes, and others were going to seek out healers other than the castle healers, who were already overwhelmed with injuries. But most of them were returning home, maybe for a late supper, maybe just to collapse in bed with exhaustion. The sun was a blip on the horizon, and soon the moons would rise.

"Your Majesty?" Matt said, tilting his head when Ellayne didn't respond right away.

"Hmm? Oh, right. Um, well . . ." A deep ache started in her chest when she realized she was waiting for guidance from Armannii. She wished he and her parents were there to show her what to do.

Raising her eyes, Ellayne met Linetta's reassuring gaze. Her chest expanded as she took a deep breath, letting it out slowly.

"First things first. I need a council, one I can trust and look to for help. I can't do this alone, and I want the three of you to be on it."

"Absolutely, E!" Dayla squealed.

Matt dipped his head, a grin crossing his face. "I would be honored, Your Majesty."

"Linetta?" Ellayne asked when her aunt didn't respond. "Will you be on my council?"

"Of course, Ellayne." Linetta clasped Ellayne's hand in both of hers. "I wish your mother could see you now. You are absolutely radiant."

"That reminds me," Ellayne said with a smirk. "My next order of business is to take a long hot bath. Then we can begin discussing how we are going to help Phildeterre begin to heal."

Chapter Fifty

llayne sat at the window seat in her room, brushing her wet hair as she watched the third moon come up from behind the horizon. She had retired to her room where a young girl, no more than fifteen, drew a bath for her. Ellayne had tested her lungs' limits, holding herself beneath the warm water, and just like in the secret watering hole behind Cal's village, the world disappeared. She'd floated in the water, weightless until her chest burned and cried out for a fresh breath. Over and over again, she used the side of the bath to hold herself under. Over and over until the water ran cold and her lips turned blue.

Even now, watching the world from her window, Ellayne wished she could sink back beneath the surface. It would've been easier. Would've hurt less. But as she sighed, pulling more hair to her shoulder, she knew eventually reality would find her.

A knock on her door had her jumping to her feet. The castle was too quiet, and every noise made her flinch. It was a drastic change from the places she had been staying for the last few months.

"Come in," she said, clearing her throat. Ellayne straightened out the simple dress she had found at the back of her closet. Sooner rather than later, she was going to have to get back to dressing in gowns, but today was not that day, and she knew that in the deepest parts of her heart she'd always prefer showing up in court wearing a tunic and trousers. How the lords and ladies would stare.

Kade peeked his head in, grinning when he saw her. "You always have a certain glow when you aren't covered in dirt, sweat, and blood. Can Kieg and I come in?"

She nodded, setting the brush on her dressing table. While they came in, she pulled the bench away from the dressing table, setting it across from the window seat.

"Hello, Ellayne." Kiegan's voice was quiet, a mere mumble. His gaze remained on the floor as his brother shut the door. Kiegan kept his hands in his pockets, his shoulders stiff and his jaw clenched. He stood in the middle of the room while Ellayne returned to where she had been when Kade knocked.

"Come on," Kade said as he passed him. "Sit down." Kade sat next to Ellayne on the window seat while Kiegan took the bench.

"How was the meeting with Criss?" Ellayne asked, glancing sideways at Kade. "That's what you came to talk to me about, right?"

Kade leaned forward, resting his elbows on his knees. He ran his hands through his hair, nodding as he hung his head. "Yeah, we just finished. I told Kieg we better come straight here to tell you what we decided."

With the way he was sitting and the downcast look on Kiegan's face, Ellayne's stomach began to tighten. He was going to have to leave her; she was sure of it. Why else would they have come straight to her?

"Tomorrow afternoon, all of the Dark Soldiers, Kiegan, and I will go back to the Dark." Kade exhaled as he spoke, pinching the bridge of his nose with two fingers. He stared at the floor beneath his feet.

"Oh," Ellayne said, gripping the skirt of her dress in her hands. "That's soon."

They both nodded, but besides exchanging looks with each other, they didn't react.

"Criss knows what happened in the forest with our father," Kade said, turning his head to look at Ellayne. "I was hesitant to tell him, but Kieg—"

"I'm not going to hide it, as much as I want to. I-I killed him, and I deserve to be punished for it," Kiegan said, staring Kade straight in the eye when he did.

"But it wasn't you; it was Blanndynne," Ellayne argued, her forehead creasing as she frowned at him. "You can't blame yourself for what your body did when your mind was under the control of an insane woman."

"And Criss somehow understood that," Kade said, pushing on his thighs to sit up straight. "He responded well to Kieg's confession." He shook his head, sighing. "Better than I would have."

Kiegan's gaze returned to the floor, and he gripped the bench with white knuckles. For a second, he squeezed his eyes shut, a shiver rolling through him. Ellayne struggled to see the resemblance between the Kiegan she had first met and the man sitting in front of her.

Ellayne tore her gaze away from Kiegan, casting a look at Kade. His jaw clenched and unclenched as he stared at his brother. She couldn't begin to imagine the thoughts circling around his head.

"What did Criss say?" she finally asked when the silence had all but eaten her up.

"He asked us to do a spell to figure out which of us is older. We did it." He showed her a strip of cloth wrapped around his forearm, probably because the spell required blood. Kiegan had a matching one. "And I'm older. I'm the successor of our father." Kade looked down again, and he made a sound like a short laugh. "I always knew I was the more mature one," he said, but the half smile on his lips disappeared when he glanced back up at his brother. Kiegan had not smiled. In fact, Ellayne hadn't seen him smile since the enchantment broke. Though she knew that shouldn't be strange, it was because Kiegan had been the type of person to smile any chance he got when they had first met. His lack of smile unsettled her.

"Kiegan, what is it?"

"He's not finished," Kiegan said, jerking his chin toward Kade. "Tell her what you said next."

Kade bit his cheek, then nodded. "I'm going to abdicate," he said, turning to face Ellayne. Her mouth opened, but no words came out. "And before you say anything, let me explain why." He reached for her hand and covered it with his. "As much as I want to make my father proud by taking his throne and helping his people, I know he'd be just as proud if I solidified the bridge between our realms. He had so much respect for you, and I think some part of him knew that my allegiance will always fall with the woman I love."

Ellayne's stomach fluttered, but she tried to ignore it as she frowned again. "Then why are you going back to the Dark too?"

Kade tapped his thumb against her hand, his focus on their intertwined fingers. "Because I have to make the announcement. And"—he glanced at his brother—"I promised Kieg I'd train and prepare him. But from what he was telling me, he won't need as much training as you might think." His words made her raise an eyebrow, and she also turned her attention to Kiegan.

"Blanndynne had me ranked as high as she could. The only two people in charge of me were her and the king. I was in charge of the royal guard, among other things. But that doesn't mean I can rule an entire kingdom. Not alone. Especially not the Dark. Not after what I did to our father." He split his gaze, half the time meeting Ellayne's eyes and the other his brother's.

"I know what you mean," Ellayne said, her voice soft. "My brother was the one my father trained, not me. I get it, but you're wrong, Kieg."

His gaze latched on to her. "What?"

Ellayne tilted her head to the side, trying to find a glimpse of the man she knew before. "You wouldn't be alone." She leaned forward and placed a hand on his. She could feel the cold wisping off of both brothers, one in each hand. "Ruling is not a one-person job; that's why we have councils and trusted advisors. It's why we keep our closest friends nearby. It's unbelievable pressure, but it's not done alone."

"She's right," Kade said, squeezing her hand as she sat back and let go of Kiegan. "I'm going to train you, and I'll stay as long as you need me. Then, when you're settled, I'll come back here and advise you from Phildeterre." He offered a small smile to Ellayne. "Besides, I have a feeling this one will require more political advisement than you, Kieg."

Rolling her eyes, Ellayne snorted. "I hate that you might be right."

Kiegan looked between the two of them, but something lightened on his face. He didn't smile, but his eyebrows relaxed and the crease in his forehead eased. "You're sure?" he asked Kade. "You're sure you want to do this? There's no turning back once you announce it."

Kade kept his eyes on Ellayne, his dimple showing as his gaze covered every part of her face. "I've never been more sure about anything in my life." The spark between them left her head spinning.

"All right then," Kiegan said with a short nod. "I'll do it. I'll be the next Dark King."

Epilogue

llayne glared at herself in the mirror. "I'm just saying that it would've been nice to know beforehand."

"It wouldn't have changed your decision," her handmaid, Terra, said with pins in her mouth. Her nimble fingers pulled a pin out and stuck it back into the fabric swinging near the floor. She narrowed her eyes at the hem of Ellayne's dress, which refused to lie even along the floor.

"True, but at least I could've been prepared. The amount of times people have said—"

"E! You're glowing!" Dayla squealed as she threw Ellayne's door open and ran in. She wore a dark blue dress that looked like rippling waves in certain light. Her hair, which she'd kept its natural deep brown since she'd joined the rebels, was wrapped up in an intricate bun, and her almond-shaped eyes had a light brushing of cyan over the lids.

"That. The amount of times people have said *that* in the last few days is driving me insane," Ellayne said, pointing her finger at the siren. "Hi, Dayla."

"You look lovely," Dayla said as she walked to the front of the mirror to gaze at Ellayne. "You're going to blow our visitors away. I even heard some of the sirens from the Coves have traveled down here to see the Dark King's return."

Ellayne nodded, her mind focused on the uneven hem reflected in the mirror. "It's no use, Terra. Besides, who's going to notice? They're all going to be staring at the more obvious thing."

"You mean the fact that you're glowing?"

She spun around—much to Terra's chagrin—and stuck her tongue out at Kade, who leaned against the doorframe. His eyes traveled from her uneven hem up to the delicate braids Terra had woven into her hair. Ellayne also looked him over, appreciating the light blue satin tunic he'd paired with a black vest. It suited his fair skin tone.

"Don't you start with me." She shook her finger at him. "This is entirely your fault."

He tilted his head back and laughed as he entered the room. "My fault? How is this my fault? You're the one with light magic." Kade held out his hand, and she took it. He spun her, catching her around the waist after one revolution.

"And you are the one who got me pregnant."

"I'm your husband, Ellayne. It's kinda my job." He kissed her on the forehead when she frowned.

"Then whose job was it to tell me that when a woman with light magic gets pregnant, she glows? Because I want them thrown in the dungeon until I stop lighting up like a candle."

"Technically, Your Majesty," Terra said as she gathered up her sewing materials, "you didn't start glowing until the third trimester began last week."

Ellayne rolled her eyes at her handmaid but thanked her as she left.

"Kieg's going to get a kick out of this," Kade said, looking at their reflection in the mirror.

"What? That I'm a glowworm? Yeah, probably." Ellayne pushed Kade, but he pulled her tighter, kissing her neck.

"I don't see what's so bad about it," Dayla said from a chair in the corner. "I think you look beautiful."

"Thank you, Dayla," Kade said, fluttering his eyelashes.

"Not you, idiot. Your wife."

Kade chuckled behind Ellayne. "She is beautiful, isn't she?"

"Okay, okay. That's enough," Ellayne said, pushing away from Kade.

He let her go, distracted by the sparkle of silver lying on her dresser. "I think you're forgetting something." Kade waved her mother's tiara in front of Ellayne. When she tried to grab it, he lifted it out of her reach. "Want to fight for it?"

"How about no?" Ellayne said, crossing her arms over her chest.

"Fine," he said, lowering the tiara onto her head. "But it would've been fun."

"And I thought Matt and I were bad." Dayla rolled her eyes.

"Where is he?" Ellayne asked, fixing the crooked tiara. "And where's your crown, love?"

"Oh," Kade said, his dimple popping out. "I'll go get it."

Dayla waited for Kade to leave before answering the question. "Matt's helping with last-minute preparations for the Dark King's arrival."

"Didn't you want to help with that?"

"Yes, but . . ." Dayla drew out the word until Ellayne looked at her. "I've been having awful morning sickness. You know . . . because I'm pregnant."

Ellayne's eyes widened, and she stumbled over her words. "Y-you're pregnant too! Dayla, that's wonderful!" She crossed the room and hugged the siren.

A wide smile crossed Dayla's face. "I've been wanting to tell you, but Matt said we should wait at least six weeks."

"I'm so happy for you two," Ellayne said, her eyes watering.

"Happy about what?" Kade asked as he waltzed back into the room. He wore Butch's old crown, one the old king had used on a daily basis. Kade had told Ellayne he preferred it to the formal one because it was less ostentatious.

"I'm pregnant," Dayla said with a shrug.

"It's about time," Kade said as he hugged her. "You and Matt got married before we did. We both figured you two would be first."

"It's been . . . complicated. But we're excited." Dayla didn't stop smiling, but Ellayne noticed a bit of sadness behind her eyes.

"Excuse me, Your Majesties," a young servant boy said as he popped his head in the room. "I'm sorry to interrupt, but the Dark King has arrived, and we are prepared to welcome him and his men in the throne room."

"Thank you," Ellayne said, nodding toward the boy. "We'll be right down."

Kade offered her his arm, and she took it. Dayla followed behind them, and her husband met them at the bottom of the main staircase. Kade patted Matt on the shoulder, congratulating him in a quiet voice. Matt beamed at Dayla, taking her arm and falling into step behind Ellayne and Kade. Ellayne could hear their names being announced to the room behind the closed doors.

Two royal guards opened the doors for them, and they strode down an aisle toward the thrones at the end. Much of the throne room, as well as other parts of the Cyanthian castle, had been redone over the last two years, but Ellayne insisted the throne room be decorated the same as when her parents were in charge.

Subjects from all over Phildeterre filled the throne room, separated by the aisle down the middle. Dayla and Matt took a spot near the front with Linetta, all of them smiling up at Kade and Ellayne as they took their places in front of their respective thrones.

A herald at the back of the room amplified his voice, silencing the soft chatter of the crowd. "Now announcing His Royal Majesty, the Dark King."

The double doors swung open, and in marched Kiegan wearing the Dark King's crown. He wore a maroon tunic and a black collared vest with a matching cape. His hair seemed darker and a bit curlier, like his brother's. There were dark circles under his eyes, but then again, Ellayne was sure she had some as well.

He walked to the front of the room and bowed at the same time Ellayne curtsied and Kade bowed next to her.

"Welcome back to Phildeterre, Your Majesty," Ellayne said with a grin. While the formalities annoyed her, she knew it was important for the subjects to see, especially with the progress the Dark and Phildeterre had made in the two years since the Second Split of Phildeterre had ended. However, she knew they were all waiting until they could be alone—be themselves.

After what seemed like too long, the herald announced their departure, and they waved goodbye to their subjects as they left through the open doors. Ellayne waited until they were alone in the family room before slouching. The strain of the baby on her back was destroying her good posture.

"Kieg," Kade said as he pulled his brother into a hug. "It's been too long."

"That's for sure," Kiegan said, clapping Kade on the back. "And Ellayne, you're glowing!"

"So I've heard." Ellayne rolled her eyes as he hugged her. "It's apparently a thing. How my mother got away with it, I'll never know."

"At least you don't have to hide it," Kiegan said as he sat down in a chair. "That would make life more difficult."

Ellayne thought of her mother, wondering if that was how her father had found out about her magic or if it had been earlier. Either way, she knew her mother would've needed to hide it from nearly everyone in the castle.

"It certainly would." She sat down next to her husband. "We're so glad you're back, Kiegan. We've missed you."

While her husband had taken frequent trips and spent plenty of time in the Dark with his brother, Ellayne had not seen her friend since the first anniversary of the war, which had been a few weeks after their wedding. He looked better than he had then, more confident. He sat straighter and smiled more easily. It put her heart at ease to see him grinning at them.

Kade put his arm behind Ellayne. "I'm glad you're here. It's good to be in the same room as you again."

"It's good to be back. I missed you two, and I missed the sun more than I ever thought I would. You and I look more like twins now than we ever have because I'm as pale as you," Kiegan said, nodding toward Kade.

"It definitely suits me better," Kade said, a smirk on his face.

"You wish."

Ellayne leaned against Kade, listening to the twins bicker and loving every second of it. Her magic filled her with warmth stirred by her happiness as well as pregnancy hormones. She had expected the second anniversary of the battle, like the first, and the months leading up to it to bring back difficult emotions. And it had. But

Kade had been there for every nightmare and every wave of tears. Somehow, she had made it two years as queen, one as a wife, and soon a mother. And with Kade—among many others—by her side, she no longer feared what the future might look like. She welcomed it and all of the twists and turns it promised.

* * *

Turn the Page to get a sneak peek of

the cover for the first prequel in the

Fallen Heir Duology!

Coming Soon!

THE HEIR'S DESCENT

THE FALLEN HEIR
BOOK ONE

RACHEL HETRICK

SIGN UP FOR MY AUTHOR NEWSLETTER

Enjoy interactive maps, character art, short stories, and other exclusives from this series by subscribing to my newsletter and visiting my website at:

www.rachelhetrickwrites.com

Acknowledgments

I honestly can't believe I'm sitting here (well, laying on the couch in my office) writing the acknowledgments to the final book in the *Infiniti Trilogy*! It's only been a little over a year since God made it clear I was supposed to pursue my childhood dream of being a published author, and here I am with three ACTUAL books published! God is good. I owe everything to Him, and I am so thankful for every sprinkle of creativity He has given me. All glory and praise to Christ!

Through this whole process, my parents, Marc and Beth, have never once stopped filling my heart and mind with encouragement. They have been my support forever, and their positivity has been SO beneficial to me growing in confidence. I am beyond blessed to have them in my life. They have been helpful throughout the process of putting out this entire series, and I couldn't have done it without them. My sister Becca is also one of my biggest supporters, and I couldn't be more thankful for her. And of course, I can't forget to give some love to my sweet distraction, Syra, who thinks the exhaust on the back of my laptop is the best source of warmth ever created.

Natalia Leigh is a superhero. I'm telling you, my editor at Enchanted Ink Publishing, is A.M.A.Z.I.N.G! She has helped pull this trilogy together and tied it off with a shiny bow. Natalia has taught me so much, and I was blessed to work with someone I looked up to from the start of my publishing journey. I can't wait to work with her again in the future (because believe me, I've got PLENTY of WIPs rattling around in my brain). I can't recommend Enchanted Ink Publishing enough! They are absolutely wonderful to work with! Thank you Natalia!

Feedback is so incredibly important with this job, and I owe a HUGE thank you to my beta readers. They have helped me find so many issues and plot holes, not to mention giving me amazing and encouraging comments that remind how me excited I get when people talk about my books and know my characters. This book, and this whole trilogy, would not be the same without them. They've made it infinitely better (see what I did there?). Thank you to Marc H. Hetrick, Elizabeth Hetrick, Rebecca Gilliam, Cydney Knight-Pinneo, Sarah Orr, and Sydney Fowler. Thank you all so much! You are wonderful!

I also want to give an extra shout out to my mom for proofreading on top of beta reading (and helping with the nightmare that is formatting a book in Word). Thank you so much for reading this book more than once!

Another company I would recommend to any indie author looking for a professional cover is Miblart. They created the stunning covers for all three books, and I fully intend to continue working with them in the future. I so appreciate their creativity and their quick responses. Thank you so much for working with me and staying patient as I narrowed down my vision. The cover for Infinit is DEFINITELY my favorite. You all were a pleasure to work with!

Now we get to one of my favorite parts: Thanking YOU. I am thrilled you decided to take this journey with me. I hope you enjoyed Phildeterre and the incredible magic woven within it. I'm honored that you chose to read my book. It means so much to me that you took the time to travel through the worlds I created with the characters I've grown to love as much as real people (sometimes more than real people if I'm being honest). It's a blessing to get to share these crazy stories with you, and I love hearing your thoughts.

I hope you loved this book (and series) as much as I loved writing it! If you enjoyed it, **please consider sharing it, writing a review, or telling your neighbor**. One of the best things you can do for an author is leave a review and a rating! You are loved more than you could possibly know!

About the Author

Rachel Hetrick has now published three books (*Curse of Infiniti, Defying Infiniti,* and *Infinit*), and is excited to release many more. She was born in Colorado, and graduated from the University of Colorado Colorado Springs in 2017 with a Bachelor of Arts degree in English Literature and a Creative Writing minor. Soon after she graduated, she moved to the opposite side of the world and taught English in Asia for a year and a half. However, when the world went nuts at the beginning of 2020, God made it clear that the time had come to pursue her childhood dream of becoming a published author. With the inspiration of many incredible authors on Youtube, Rachel grew as a writer, editor, and now publisher. She has since moved back to Colorado and lives with her Siamese cat, Syra (who kicked Feline Infectious Peritonitis, FIP, in the rear end). She looks forward to hearing from her readers!

YOU CAN CONNECT WITH RACHEL THROUGH:

WEBSITE: www.rachelhetrickwrites.com
INSTAGRAM: @rachel_hetrick_writes